Cynthia & Susan

A LOVE STORY

GEORGE ELIOT

To my beloved spouse, Mike —
who helped me with research and got my book published.

Chapter One
A MEETING IN THE PARK

Susan Asta made her high-heel shoes click against the red-brick sidewalk of High Street in Portland, Maine. She had a clerical position, a nothing job, at a moderately-busy office called the Diocesan Human Relations Services on the corner of High and Pleasant Streets near the High-Street Resource Center. High is a low-traffic street off of Congress, which is Portland, Maine's most bustling thoroughfare. Every afternoon at 1:00p.m., Susan would take her lunch-break in a park at the corner of High and Congress Streets. They gave her a whole hour, unpaid of course, and she spent it eating her meager lunch, while seated on a bench in the Congress Square Park.

In the cool of the afternoon the park bench seemed an oasis and as she grew unconscious of the traffic, the world became distant. She chewed her sandwich slowly relishing very bite. It was her first nourishment of the day, except for the constant coffee that the office employed her to make and compelled her to drink, there being no other beverage available. She was a professional and so didn't complain. Susan was also not on a diet. The reason for Susan's Spartan lunch was that she was poor, desperately poor; but she concealed it from her wealthier co-workers with soldierly grace. That was because Susan had a child to feed, house and keep in daycare and because she knew that even though DHRS's stated mission was to help the poor, the employees at this benevolent organization actually looked down upon the poor with prideful contempt. Consequently, they wouldn't like it if they knew that they were mingling with one. Susan returned to the water fountain several times, and Cynthia Hickey watched her with the keen eye of a marksman, studying Susan as a hunter studies the game.

Cynthia had mastered the skill of discerning people's hearts, because her livelihood depended upon it; but her fortune consisted only of food, shelter and clothing. For in reality Cynthia was no more than a slave. She had an apartment right across the street from the park; but in truth Cynthia was virtually homeless. She had been living with a man, Binny, for three years: eight months in Bath, nearly two years in Lewiston- Auburn and now six months in Portland. He was a cocaine and heroin dealer and High Street was filled with them so he really had to hustle and so did Cynthia; that was what she did for a living, she hustled.

The Congress Square Park, once the site of a Dunkin' Donuts, was the location at which Cynthia made a lot of money on her knees in the alley next to the park and behind its adjacent shops. The Portland Beautification Society, a division of the Maine Historical Preservation Commission had that Dunkin' Donuts torn down, not so much because it was an eyesore; but because it was a hangout for illegal enterprises mostly prostitution. However, this didn't stop the prostitutes from soliciting business, because the girls that worked that corner just moved into the park that was constructed on its site.

Marcel's, a four-star restaurant in the Old Port, also owned a little rooftop bistro with a view of what went on behind the shops on Congress Street. Dinners would sit at tables overlooking the alley and food prepared at the main restaurant was kept hot in the downstairs kitchen and served to the customers seated on the rooftop at an inflated rate. The patrons came for the X-rated attraction and a reciprocal relationship caused the bistro to reward the prostitutes with an occasional free entrée offered under the guise of charity. The clientele, all of whom were men and many of whom brought binoculars, thunderously applauded when the girls were finished orally servicing their tricks and several girls as though they were actresses would take a long low bow in the direction of their viewing public, when their assignments were completed.

In the park, a collection of wooden benches is perched on different levels and turned in different directions, these being interspersed with red brick walkways. The good citizens of Portland, Maine breathed a sigh of relief. Now the prostitutes, pimps, and drug pushers would have a structured environment in which to congregate. Maybe this structure would encourage them to play chess with one another and drink soda pop from aluminum cans rather than cheap wine and beer from glass bottles concealed inside brown-paper bags. It was an absurdly naive plan with an even more remote goal; but the park did attract the business-lunch crowd. Not the wealthy professional set; but the low- level office workers like Susan, who took their sack lunches in the open air and weren't afraid to mix with the street people many of whom were known to them. Some surprisingly-talented street musicians formed a kind of diplomatic corps interceding between the gross lifestyle of the criminal element and the struggling, working poor, who in turn mingled with the working middle class and rich:

MY GOD HOW THE MONEY ROLLS IN
[This is sung to the melody "My Bonnie Lies Over the
Ocean".]

My father makes book on the corner.
My auntie makes bootlegger's gin.
My sister makes love for ten dollars.

My God, how the money rolls in!

Chorus:

Rolls in, rolls in,

My God, how the money rolls in, rolls in!

Rolls in, rolls in, my God, how the money rolls in!

My mother's a bawdy-house keeper.

Every night when the evening grows dim.

She hangs out a little red lantern.

My God, how the money rolls in!

Chorus:

My grandma makes cheap prophylactics.

She pierces the end with a pin.

My grandpa gets rich on abortions.

My God, how the money rolls in!

Chorus:

My brother's a medical student.

With instruments, long, sharp, and thin.

He only does one operation.

My God, how the money rolls in!

Chorus:

My uncle's a street-corner preacher.

He saves wayward women from sin.

He'll save you a blonde for ten dollars.

My God, how the money rolls in!

Nearly everyone in Portland, Maine works in one fashion or another. People of modest means dress their best in order to integrate themselves with the dressed-down wealthy. They blended, mingled and became a mixture of disheartened and struggling humanity. So, it was a natural thing for a young mother making her way in a world, where speaking one's mind is frowned upon; to strike up a harmless conversation with a beautiful, eager, young woman who sought the normality of a regular life and was living so far from it, that at any moment, she could actually be arrested for merely appearing in public.

Cynthia, who liked to go by the name "Cyn", was seeking real companionship, vulnerability and intimacy; but what she received from the world instead was physical closeness to strangers who compensated her financially. The only escape people like Cyn ever have from this desert of spiritual loneliness and longing is the comfort of alcohol and drugs. This was the thing with which Binny, her present boyfriend and pimp, sought to infect Cyn. Because even though he would have begrudged her his wares; he would have preferred her to become an addict, rather than to have her continue as a lonely woman seeking the intimacy that neither he nor her sexual customers could provide.

It was because of this soul hunger that Cyn fastened onto Susan, who was eating her modest lunch with quiet repose and self-composed confidence. Susan was impeccably dressed in business attire; while Cyn was wearing a low-cut blouse, tight Capri pants and tennis shoes, worn more for their speed in a get-away than for what they might add to her appearance. Cyn would have much preferred to have been wearing the plain black pumps of the office set into which Susan had become integrated. She may even have thought that Susan's black, high-heeled shoes would have been better for business and Susan would have preferred to have been allowed to change out of her toe- pinching office shoes, part of the uniform of the business jungle and into those comfortable sneakers that Cyn always wore without socks or laces.

"Wh-ah do-ah you-ah awe-wahz ate ehn thahs pahk?" "*Why do you always eat in this park?*" Cyn began the conversation.

"Oh, it's far enough away from my office for me to forget what I have to do every day and it's close enough for me to get back from lunch on time. The rest of the office goes the other way to the fancy restaurants; but I only went with them once and it's too expensive. I have to eat here, because I always have a sack lunch, besides I'm not really part of their crowd", Susan said forthrightly and with no regard for concealing her present financial situation.

Cyn's poor, battered heart groped toward the honesty and simple, joyful quietness that Susan exuded. Cyn looked on Susan's openness with the reverence of an ascetic monk fastening his eyes upon the monstrance. She was inexorably drawn to Susan as a dying bird struggles to get to water. The way that Susan instantly included her into the universe of possible friends, made Cyn gasp in amazement. Susan treated Cyn like she would have treated a coworker or one of the ubiquitous street musicians chancing to strike up a conversation. When Susan met Cyn's gaze, her kind eyes, looked lovingly into Cyn's soul. The prostitute almost blushed; it had been a long time since she had been treated with such respect.

"Whahd do-ah you-ah do-ah?" "*What do you do?*" Cyn inquired, genuinely interested.

"I'm a secretary of sorts, more like a clerical worker, for two Catholic charities: 'the Refugee Resettlement Project' and 'the Diocesan Camping Office'. I sort of get kids out of camp in the morning and then I get kids into camp in the afternoon. I really love what I'm doing, even if the typing and filing get a bit tedious at times, because I know that what I'm accomplishing is really helping a lot of people, especially poor, refugee children."

"Ayur", Cyn remarked, Eeyah coahd rahl-lay gau fahr ah jahb lahk thahd, zoundz zo ex-cit-tehn." "*Oh, I could really go for a job like that, sounds so exciting.*"

Susan didn't ask what her new friend did for employment; it was obvious from the clothes she wore and the way she greeted the men who passed by the two of them there on the bench. Cyn volunteered anyway, "Eeyah-'em ah hor". "*I'm a whore*" she said with no sense of shame or disgust like a meteorologist reporting the temperature at the airport. Susan smiled and then finished her sandwich, she had only four minutes to get back to the office; but she felt awkward getting up right away after Cyn disclosed her occupation.

Susan said: "We'll talk again; I have to get back to the office really fast or I'll get docked!" and with that she gathered up her wrappers and other trash slipped them into the litter basket on the corner and casting a backwards glance at the bench, scooped up her small, black, shoulder-bag purse. Then, she ran back up High Street toward St. Elizabeth's and the DHRS offices. If Cyn had inspected the contents of Susan's purse, she would have found forty-five cents and a bus ticket in Susan's wallet. Cynthia had much more money than this concealed inside a navy-blue bandana, which was tied discretely inside the jute bag that she always carried over one shoulder. Cyn never had less than three hundred dollars with her at any time; but by 2:30 the following morning, she would have dutifully surrendered it all to Binny, while Susan would keep her forty-five cents for the next two days.

[Which of them was actually the wealthier? You decide!]

Susan needed to keep her financial situation a state secret; the other women in her office, who always wore designer clothing and took Jamaican vacations were never to find out about Susan's welfare checks and food stamps because Susan needed these "gifts from the government" just to survive. Diocesan Human Relations Services had no idea that among their staff was a humbler individual than any of their "clients". Susan was a widow, by all reckoning the church, some part of the Body of Christ, ought to have been supporting her, or at least helping her in some way; but none were, no not even a little bit.

Susan worked for one church, went to a second and affiliated with a third; but none of these organizations had every done anything for her materially. In fact, they all wanted her tithes; which she actually paid dividing the money between two mission societies: World Vision and Wycliffe Bible Translators. However, she never felt inclined to give her precious tithe to one of the wealthy institutions in which she worshipped. They after all had never seen to either her or her son's physical needs, everything had come from the government.

Susan was without an office, a desk, even a place to sit down except, when she squeezed into someone else's office behind someone else's typewriter stand. She was considered an inconsequential employee, unrewarded with an expense account or any of the perks of success. Yet, the main source of income to the DHRS for the past several months was a book that she had produced.

Cynthia was immediately rewarded for what she did, while Susan had to wait two weeks for her pay and then it was only eighty-seven dollars which reduced her welfare check and her food stamps to a combined total less than what she had originally received and when she started classes at Casco Bay College, her student loan eliminated her food stamps altogether.

By the time, Susan realized her mistake, it was too late to apply for the Pell Grant for which she was eligible and crazily could have received without diminishing her food stamp allotment at all. Susan resolved to make this information the central feature of the next edition of her book: "The Women's Resource Directory", which was a compilation of information on every charitable and governmental resource in the Greater Portland area and provided precious information about how to apply for everything from WIC products to the Portland Housing Authority. This manual contained the names, addresses, telephone numbers and a contact-person at forty-two agencies and resources. It was a unique treasure-trove of information assembled from hard-won investigation. Susan considered herself the first smart person that had ever had to go on welfare and she studied it like a science. The Arch-Diocese had sold tens of thousands of copies of her book for three dollars and fifty cents apiece. Sometimes while Colette Espérance, the office manager at DHRS was carrying a box of them down to City Hall, people would just throw five-dollar bills into her box and grab one. No bookseller in Portland could keep them on their shelves. It didn't matter; Susan neither received literary credit for her research and writing nor did she get a penny from the Church in royalties, after all this was all for charity.

Chapter Two

PARENTHOOD MEANS SACRIFICE

Susan left her son, Paul, at a government-funded daycare home every morning and even though he was still breast-feeding; she provided them with formula. Susan longed for Paul with the longing described in **Isaiah 49:15:**

"Can a woman forget her sucking child, that she should not have compassion on the son of her womb? Yea, they may forget, yet will I not forget thee."

Yet, she knew that it would be three hours, before she could walk to the daycare home to pick him up. Susan had tried private babysitters. One had left her baby with a cigarette burn on his back. It was not Nancy, the fifteen-year-old babysitter that Susan entrusted with her child and her career, which had inflicted this injury upon Paul. It was Rita, an unauthorized visitor, whom Nancy had invited into Susan's home while Susan was at work.

Rita brought cigarettes into Susan's home and she claimed that she had not intentionally burned Paul; but had merely dropped the lit cigarette onto the baby's back and then hurriedly picked it up again. Susan doubted this because of the shape of the burn; it was round as though it had come from the end of the cigarette, rather than the side, which seemed to indicate that it had been done intentionally.

Susan fumed angrily: "Rita, you shouldn't even be in my apartment and Nancy, you should have been watching Paul, not sitting in another room with your boyfriend and as far as that goes, look how many times I've had to escort him out of here? Once he even brought his bicycle inside. Aren't you intelligent enough to realize that that bike could have fallen on Paul? Or maybe you just don't care?"

A safe daycare home would have taken Susan's entire paycheck, because the Maine Department of Human Services, MDHS had the market cornered on licensed homes and that meant anyone who wanted safe, reliable child-care had to either be rich or would have to acquiesce to an army of social workers.

Nancy said: "Eeyah wahn't led eht hah-pen agahin!" "I won't let it happen again!"

Susan replied: "You bet you won't; you're fired!"

When Nancy's mother called, Susan explained: "Mrs. MacDonald, Nancy let two guests, into my apartment. We both told her: 'No Boys'; 'No Drugs'; 'No Cigarettes'; but when I found a cigarette burn on my son's back and learned it was caused by the careless smoking of a teen who shouldn't even have been in my home; it was the last straw!"

Susan told Nancy's mother that her daughter would be dismissed and that her pay would be withheld. Audrey MacDonald fought tenaciously for her daughter's pay, threatening Susan with legal action and waving it in her face that Nancy's father was an attorney. She said that they would take Susan to small claims court, the entire routine.

Susan stood her ground. She told Mrs. MacDonald that she took the child to the emergency room and had the burn photographed, she even threatened to sue. Audrey countered with: "Eht wahz prah-bah-lay you-ah thahd bahnd thah bay-bay! *"It was probably you who burned the baby!"* Susan said that that was absurd; because she didn't smoke and Rita admitted to it.

The next morning Susan was on the telephone desperately trying to reach Madeline Cartwright. She knew that she would have to turn on the tears; but saved them for the right person. Madeline Cartwright was definitely the person to whom Susan wanted to cry. Maddy was one of those rare social workers, who actually worked for the poor and not the government.

"Can I speak to Madeline Cartwright please?"

"Mahs. Cahrt-wraht ehz ehn ah meet-tehn." *"Ms. Cartwright is in a meeting."*

"Well then when can I call her; I need daycare by this afternoon or I'm fired." "Eeyah-'ll led har nah thahd you-ah cahld, Mahs. Ah-stah, bahd rah-lay, you-

ah wahl prahb-bah- lay hahv tah waht 'tahl Mahn-day". *"I'll let her know that you called, Ms. Asta, but really, you will probably have to wait until Monday".*

"I can't do that! They'll fire me! I need daycare right now!" She tried to stifle the throaty scream, that was welling up in her voice. "The private, teenaged, babysitter I had, let friends into my apartment, while I was at work and one of them burned Paul with a cigarette."

"Paul ehz you-ahr sahn?" *"Paul is your son?"*

"Yes, Paul is my infant son. Madeline knows us and would never let anything happen to us. Please put me through to her." Her tone of voice indicated desperation.

"Eeyah-'ll say whahd Eeyah cauhn do-ah, Mahs. Ah-stah", *"I'll see what I can do, Ms. Asta"*, then Susan heard an abrupt click on the telephone.

Susan was all alone, alone with Paul. She dropped her cares at God's door and picked up her crying baby: **"Casting all your care upon Him; for He careth for you" (I Peter 5:7)** repeating the verse to herself, as she rubbed Neosporin into Paul's burn and then engulfed him in the maternal embrace. Despite the delays and the frequent lack of fluids, Susan's milk was copious and sweet because she had wisely concealed rehydrated powered milk, the only kind of milk Susan could afford, in a plastic bottle in the back of the office refrigerator and substituted hot water for the ever-present office coffee.

Susan also pumped her breasts in the office restroom, when she was on break and drank the liquid she produced. It was bluish and thin; but surprisingly sweet to the taste. Susan sat on an old center couch section she had found in the alley and rocked her crying baby. She took the couch section into her home along with three old couch cushions that she had sanitized and covered with pillow cases. The couch section was wobbly and had to be supported on one side by a brick. She sat and rocked Paul singing a hymn and brushing away her tears.

There was no crib for Paul and he had outgrown his bassinette. Susan was making do with a fold-up play pen, a bureau drawer and her own bed. They were just settling down when she heard a knock at the door. Amazingly, Madeline Cartwright, the woman to whom Susan was desperate to show Paul's burn, was standing right outside her door. Susan had been forced to conceal the fact that she was a breast-feeding mother from her employer, the Roman Catholic Church. Madeline knew that Susan was the author of a book that had made a lot of money for the church; but that she was still in poverty.

"Let's see the burn honey," she said.

"Can we prosecute this kid, Maddy", Susan sobbed. "I blame myself for leaving him with Nancy; but she came highly recommended and she had passed a Red Cross baby-sitting class. Her mother still demanded her pay, can you believe it? They own a house on Munjoy Hill and they think that their daughter should get paid anyway by a welfare mom whose kid is wearing a burn mark, complements of their daughter!" The tears came streaming down Susan's cheeks.

"Susan", Madeline said: "Can I interview you for a spot in a licensed home?"

"Oh, would you Maddy, those are usually reserved for people who are well- connected and have waited a long time. I have to have something by tomorrow or the Dioceses will fire me."

"Don't worry dear", Madeline's voice was soft and encouraging, "You are well-connected and I know where I can get you in by tomorrow." Madeline Cartwright took the admission papers from her soft, black-leather case and began asking questions, "Does Paul know any words in a foreign language?" The question seemed absurd, silly, but Susan dutifully complied, "Yes, he can say, 'Mama' and 'ca-ca', that's a French word, I think."

Madeline replied, "No it's actually Spanish; but the Maine French use it all the time. Are you of French extraction, Susan?"

"No", I'm of Italian extraction and so was my late-husband, Mike". Susan said, not wishing to begin another subject that would start her crying again.

"And now, do you have any family in the area?"

"No", Susan replied, "it's just me and the baby."

Susan thought about adding that she and her husband had originally come from Illinois, six years earlier; but that was impractical with Maine people as they would always wonder aloud when "oud-dah-stay-tahs" **"out-of-staters" [A term by which Mainers refer to people who were not born, brought up and still living in the state of Maine, the term "flaht-lahnd-dahs" "flatlanders" is sometimes also used.]** were going to leave the state of Maine and return to wherever it was from which they had come. So, Susan wisely withheld this information and remained on-task about getting the licensed home.

When Madeline Cartwright was done, the precious document had been filled- out. This was a document of a closely-guarded secret nature, the kind which was only shared with a chosen few. Maine has many such government programs, reserved only for select people, who know about them or who know someone who can refer them. This is why "The Women's Resource Directory" had been such a big hit in town and why Susan couldn't reveal that she was its author. There was still no section in Susan's book on day-care and she made a mental note to upgrade her next edition.

After the interview with Maddy, Susan was handed a piece of paper with a name and address on it. She put Paul into the Snugli and walked up Grant Street to a clapboard tenement where a woman named Kitty Thibault "Tea-Bow" lived. Kitty was in her thirties, had three small children and was the landlady in her building. Kitty and her brother, Carter, who was gay and who was living with her were from an old Portland family. The two of them were making their living renting out the other apartments in their building and providing day-care, mostly to welfare recipients.

"This is good", thought Susan, as she stretched out one of her arms above her head in an attitude of praise. Then she knocked upon the unfamiliar door and gained entrance to a very gracious home. Portland, Maine has many such places: tenements that had first-floor laundromats, first-floor delicatessens and upper-floor penthouse apartments that were spectacular for their surroundings. These places are owned by families who have lived in the city for generations and all of these elite people are well-connected with Portland's rampant social-welfare establishment. Susan knew that she had to be on her best behavior with this woman. "Society people", especially those that cater to the "welfare crowd" are notoriously snooty and look down upon their clients with haughty distain. In this way, they are much like the staff at Susan's office.

People would wait for months, sometimes years to get a spot like this and only people who knew someone, who knew someone ever gained admission. Susan beamed a friendly smile into the dour face of a woman who looked much older than she though Kitty was actually only a few years older. Ms. Thibault was only thirty-two, but looked like she was fifty. Susan on the other hand was already twenty-nine, but she looked nineteen. There was an immediate occasion for Kitty to be suspicious.

Graciously she welcomed Susan into her home and when Susan was seated on Kitty's expensive davenport in the front parlor, she had taken Paul out of the Snugli Kitty began cooing over the infant like an aunt and then inquired, "Hahw do-ah you-ah nay, Mahd-day Cahrt-raht?" *"How do you know Maddy Cartwright?"*

"Well, I work at Diocesan Human Relations Services and Madeline works at Human Services and we got introduced. She's really great, isn't she?" Susan replied, dodging both the question and its eventual companion, "Why are you on welfare?"

Cronyism is the name of the game in New England, well really anyplace that has had its private sector devoured by government. Every aspect of life in a near, command-economy like Portland, Maine's, has an air of guarded congeniality about it. You have to know the right people, you have to be of a certain ethnic extraction or you have to have money. Susan certainly didn't have any money and she tried to make up for it by exuding charm. The name, Madeline Cartwright, was a talisman that could unlock practically any door in Portland, Maine; but this was information that could never be published in her book.

Madeline Cartwright was old-money liberality personified. She knew everyone and everything in Portland, Maine that turned on government hand-outs. Such women came from colleges like Smith and Wellesley were authorities on all things having to do with the Social Welfare System and never needed to use this system themselves because they were rich. They were generous and compassionate to the poor; but always with tax-payers' money not their own. When Kitty found out that Susan was a friend of Madeline Cartwright's, both she and her brother nodded approvingly.

Carter made some disparaging remarks about Christians seeing the little cross suspended from a chain around her neck and hoping that Susan would take the bait. She however, demurred. "Eeyah nehv-vah gau tah chahch", he said, "beh-'cahz thar 'r' jehs' tah mehn-nay hyp-pah-critz thar, Eeyah haht ehd way-un en-nay-Juan ehz ah hyp-pah- crit, dohn-'nah you-ah Sue-zahn?", *"I never go to church, because there are just too many hypocrites there, he said. I hate it when anyone is a hypocrite, don't you Susan?"* He had begun his tactical assault on both her convictions and her sensibilities.

"Well, hypocrites are just people trying to put their best foot forward and get along with as many people as possible," she said. "I don't know that I'm not a hypocrite" and then tilting her head ever so slightly downward and closing her eyes in an attitude of prayer, she displayed that air of modest confidence that is called Biblically: **"shamefacedness". (1 Timothy 2:9) [Artios:** Koine Greek **fully outfitted for a long journey; perfect.]**

The arrangements had been made and before Susan left, Paul was assured of a place in this licensed home. Kitty had ordered a time after which Paul could no later be brought to the home, 6:45 a.m. "I'm breast-feeding, Susan said, do you want me to pump my breasts and give you a bottle of breast-milk when I come or can I just store that at home and give you a canister of powered formula to use here?" Kitty frowned at both ideas and acted as though Susan had just divulged a terrible secret. The only women who performed this silly activity were those Fundamentalists who stay at home with their children and who had domineering husbands.

"Eeyah lahk thah red-day-mahd prah-dect ehn cauhnz." *"I like the ready- made product in cans."* She said, "Eeyah fah-nd thahd thah stahf ehn cauhnz ehz e-zee- ahst tah uhz." *"I find that the liquid stuff in cans is the easiest to use."* Susan knew that it was; but it was also the most expensive, as were the Pampers disposable diapers that Susan was ordered to bring. But, this was a minor sacrifice to gain the help of this family. Susan would now begin a whole travel bag for Paul, which included all the things that the Portland child-care set insisted were of necessity.

Susan said, "Sure Kitty, I'll have all those things here by 6:45a.m., you can count on me and then, "Dear"; she looked into Kitty's eyes, "just call me at this number, anytime during the day, when you have Paul and I will come running." It was Susan's work number at DHRS, not Susan's actually; but the work number of Collette Espérance and a direct line to her top floor, corner office suite. Susan had no desk from which to write her next book; but she had already written a book standing up and squatting on the floor next to the filing cabinet so this number was just going to have to do.

If Collette complained about Susan giving out her number, that would be a problem for another day. She had passed the test, she really knew the rules and she seemed nonchalant about them as though she had always had Paul in Pampers and had always feed him out of a bottle and a can. All she needed to do now was find the money to make these resources happen and by tomorrow morning. **"But, My God shall supply all of your need, according to His riches in glory by Christ, Jesus" (Philippians 4:18)** she said to herself as she skipped down the stairway to the sidewalk and back toward the Old Port.

With an image of a medium-sized, navy-blue carrying case with a red-plaid lining such as is used for airplane luggage in her mind, Susan strode confidently out to assemble it. The bag would prove Susan to be "normal" and build Kitty's trust in her. **"My Father has cattle on a thousand hills." (Psalm 50:10)** she said to herself as she turned to "St. Joseph the Provider" not the saint the store.

This store was a favorite of hers, because it was frequently the source of things for which she had just prayed. There was also some kind of charity going on with Father Lauzon, who anticipated Susan's needs, even before she asked. Father would discover new items that seemed to just appear on his shelves and then surrender them to Susan, who would inspect them to see if they conformed to the picture which God had just placed in her mind.

Often the priest would ask her for the exact sum of money that she had in her purse. It was as though God was telegraphing the whole thing to both of them at the same time. Father's gleeful face shone with delight, as he presented Susan with the piece of luggage. Susan unzipped it and discovered that its lining was indeed a red-plaid.

The case would have to contain at least nine brand-name, disposable diapers, preferably Pampers, at least two full changes of clothing, and a plastic bag to hold all the "accidents" then the wipes, lotions and powders that were designed to deal with the inevitable skin problems that babies whose bottoms are closed up in a bacterial incubator usually found of necessity, Desitin was a staple.

If Susan skimped on these luxury items, which most parents accepted as "normal", her son would be unwelcome in the day-care home and she knew it. So, having the day-care bag, clean and well-stocked with the correct items was of tactical necessity in keeping Paul in this home.

Once Susan realized what the world-at-large considered normal and planned her life accordingly, it never really mattered if she actually used these things at home or not. She was just always going to have to have them in the "travel bag". The bag and the work number gave the day-care provider a confidence about Susan's "normalcy" and that she saw disposable everything as a necessary part of life. Bringing the canned formula along with Paul in the morning was acquiescence to the accepted opinion in the community that it was better for babies and easier for care-givers. None of this is true; but Susan already knew that WIC would not give them both food which they needed and formula which they had always gotten along without. Perhaps, Susan could obtain a few plastic bottles and the cans of Enfamil with her next pay-check; but it certainly wasn't worth reassigning her whole WIC products protocol for this daily encounter even if these supplies were necessary to satisfy Kitty's demands.

Susan didn't want to get hooked on this form of feeding her son. Because she knew that its end was always the same: It would result in her milk drying up, her weight going up and it would also decrease the necessary bonding between mother and child. After her trip to Father Lauzon's, Susan was broke. So, as she walked down Congress Street and passed Paul's Market, where she always bought her office supplies and coffee, Susan turned in and made a proposal to Paul Trusiani, who was a businessman and knew her.

"Mr. Trusiani, I have a Porteus, Mitchell and Braun credit card now", Susan began. Paul Trusiani straightened his tie. He knew Susan when she was homeless on the street, looking for a landlord who would rent to a single mother with a baby. "I could leave it with you until my next payday; but I need some things to get my child into day- care in the morning and I'm a little pinched for cash right now." Mr. Trusiani had once surreptitiously slipped twenty-five dollars into Susan's hand, when he found her waiting for a bus with no umbrella and in the rain. She immediately stuffed it into a pocket and thanked him with her eyes, as he sped off to his store and his daily, never-ending work.

Relying on her credit was something Susan was just trying out for the first time. "I've got an apartment, a job and a credit card; let's see what all these things could bring", Susan thought. She decided to approach Paul Trusiani, after all Paul wasn't opposed to giving reliable people credit and he knew Mr. Cross, Susan's landlord. Susan had never been late with the rent. Making sacrifices for luxuries didn't make sense in the practical world of financial recovery. Susan had gone from destitution to survival. She knew her next pay-check was already spent; but after that maybe there might be: electricity, and a weekly supply of Enfamil, Desitin, baby wipes and Pampers.

Chapter Three

"COME ON IN MY KITCHEN"

"I wish that I had some great purpose in my life, that gave it shape and meaning", Cyn confided. Cynthia had practiced this sentence several times, saying it over and over to herself, until she got it to come out without her Downeast or Upcountry Maine accent. Cyn wanted to eliminate her accent when speaking to Susan and Susan also strove to eliminate her Chicago accent. As she had always done since high school, while Cynthia was only trying elocution for the first time. Only after much practice did she attempt this; but she really couldn't keep it up in normal conversation.

Susan's eyes fastened on her friend with warmth and quiet repose: "Maybe it's that we have no television sets you and I, that we think of such things." She lifted Paul out of the new child-seat Cyn had given to her and with her left hand cradling his head, slipped it under her blouse and drew him to her breast. Cyn smiled at her friend with admiration. She had never had so intimate a friendship.

"Shahl Eeyah mahk ahs sumb tah, Sue-zahn?" *"Shall I make us some tea, Susan?"* Cyn said, as she fumbling through her boxes of Celestial Seasons teas. "Please, Cyn, have you got any Red Zinger?" Cynthia frowned. "Nay, bahd you-ah shahd-n'ah hahv thahd ehn-nay-wahy, Eeyah-'vah behn mean-nehn tah tahlk tah you-ah au-boughd cah-fay.

Eeyah dohn' wahnt you-ah drahnk-ehn ehd ehn-nay-moh." *"No, but you shouldn't have that anyway, I've been meaning to talk to you about coffee. I don't want you drinking it anymore."* Cynthia always strove to eliminate her Downeast accent whenever she spoke to Susan, who was originally from the Chicagoland area and who also endeavored to speak without her Chicago accent to everyone but Walter Malien, whom she observed actually enjoyed listening to it.

"Lax, Cyn, I'm having hot water with the Cremora and sugar that they have on the coffee console in the break room and no one in the office is the wiser. Most of them don't know about Paul and that's the way I like it. If they should find out that their "Welfare Mom" was still breastfeeding, there would be talk and then judgmental inquiries. Why risk it?"

Now that Susan had the licensed day-care home, she didn't have to worry that some teen-aged babysitter ruining her career by deciding at the last minute not to show up. "There might even be some time now for a social life", Susan said, "such as it is."

Susan knew that Cynthia counted her as her best friend; but didn't know if she felt the same. Certainly, bringing Paul to Cyn's place was a risk, that man might come in at any time. They sat in the sunny kitchen with the gay, yellow and white wallpaper that looked out onto Congress and High Streets wondering aloud how their lives were progressing. "Eeyah rahl-lay nehd tah gaht oud ahv thah lahf", *"I really need to get out of the life"*, Cyn groaned. "Mah-beh, gau bahk tah scahl lahk you-ah hahv. Eeyah-'em thahnk-kehn au-boughd gau-ehn ehn-tah thah hahs-pah-tahl-leht-tea behz- nahz", *"Maybe, go back to school like you have. I'm thinking about going into the hospitality business"*, Susan laughed uproariously. Cyn caught the irony as well and started to laugh. They were both laughing and smiling when Binny came into the apartment. He was the original Captain Bring-Down and could suck the light and harmony out of any room by his mere presence.

"'R' you-ah gurlz hyah?" *"Are you girls high?"* he queried.

"I really have to go, Cyn", Susan said. "I've got a big day over at Casco Bay College, tomorrow." Susan gathered up her belongings and headed home.

"No, Binny, we were just having a laugh about something." Cyn said, looking up at him adoringly.

Cyn had transformed her kitchen, this tiny portion of her sordid life, into a wonderland of feminine homeliness. It contained a sink, a kitchen table and chairs; a toaster and a very old, but very clean refrigerator. There were four yellow cabinet doors and two drawers that were the exact color of the dominant yellow of her beautiful wallpaper. Cyn had an eye for color. She found a fruit-basket print tablecloth, which went with the flower-basket design of her wallpaper. Then she found two ladder-back chairs and painted them yellow.

Finally, she added navy blue and white, peel-and-stick floor tiles to complete her domain. The great room of Cyn and Binny's apartment was a snarl of mattresses covered with filth. It was around that darkened room, where a drug dealer dispenses his wares and where his drug customers shoot-up with shared works that their lives revolved. Cyn kept trying to clean it: "cahm-mit-tehn ah neht-ness" *"committing a neatness"* as Binny called it; but it never got any cleaner and every time she would push back against the filth, Binny got mad.

It irritated him whenever she would: "cahm-mit-tehn ah neht-ness", because Binny actually preferred it dirty. But, to Cyn walking through that room on the way to the bathroom was always a coming back to reality. She had begun painting it blue once; but needed to pause, when Binny's temper flared. Cyn had learned to always stop whatever she was doing when he got angry and creep quietly into the kitchen. There, she would crouch down in front of the corner windows as she had learned to do in the alley. This squatting in the corner was Cyn's discovered method for not being beaten and it had always worked for her.

When Susan met Binny, she observed that he was a difficult person to get to know. She wasn't yet acquainted with his lifestyle as a merchant of hard drugs nor did she know that he beat Cyn. She only discerned that Binny was as insolated, self- contained, self-absorbed and sullen as a man could be and still be alive. If any such men were capable of having a relationship with a woman that might be called friendship, Cyn was Binny's only friend. Susan determined not to let Binny remain Cyn's only friend and when Susan went home and Binny left to sell his cocaine and heroin, Cyn bravely completed painting the great room a beautiful, calming shade of steel blue. Binny treated Cynthia more like a human pet, than like a person that he loved. He would fawn over her and then beat her. These two activities were mixed and he would abruptly change from one to the other without warning.

Cyn also washed the bank of windows that let light into the great room, beneath these corner windows was a strange well of wooden steps descending to more and more windows, which looked out onto Congress Street. Remarkably though, there was no door at the foot of these stairs and Binny insisted that Cyn make some draperies out of an old, scratchy, brown, woolen blanket. Binny wanted to keep it dark in there, because what he did was so sordid and dangerous that his paranoid mind imagined prying eyes continually cast up on their third-floor walk-up.

The sun hadn't fully set, when Cyn began prowling the park across the street looking for men who would pay for a trick. She never worked during the day, because of the police. Sometimes during daylight hours, she would sit on a bench in the park where she always met with Susan for lunch and then try to arrange encounters for that evening in the miserable great room of her apartment. Most guys just wanted to go into the adjacent alley for some quick oral sex. She had worked the Dunkin' Donuts, which was once where the park is now; but the Portland Beautification Society had had it torn down.

You couldn't blame Portland, Maine for wanting to hide its open secret, that its "Artists' District" was actually a hang-out for pimps, prostitutes and drug dealers, most of whom, did a little of each. The "Artists' Studios" were all the same, either a great room with a kitchen and half a bath in the studio; or a great room with no kitchen and a full bathroom down the hall. These were worse than Cyn and Binny's place, because you could never keep the street people out of the bathroom and the landlords begrudged you what they jokingly referred to as, "hot water". Cyn could only take sponge baths in the sink and she had no where to hang up the toothbrush Susan had purchased for her.

Susan came back to Cyn's apartment immediately after work and school. She would lug her pull behind shopping cart up the three flights of stairs and continuously Susan constrained Cynthia to come over to her place: Susan would invite Cyn over and Cyn would refuse, Susan would try again and Cyn would refuse again, finally Susan would ask the third time with a kind of begging tone to her voice and then Cyn's refusal would be final. Susan was trying to break down the wall of bondage around the prison in which Cyn lived. At the last, Cynthia would shyly look away and then change the subject. Then, Susan would make everything sunny and bright she would hold her sleeping at her breast and then rub her nipple across his cheek. He would turn and pounce onto it like a little lion pouncing on the prey. Cyn would laugh; she felt as though The Virgin Mary had come over to enjoy a cup of tea with her in her kitchen. "To think that I could get a friend like this", Cyn said to herself as she poured Susan's tea and mentally practiced her elocution. The tea Cyn served was a Twinning's Chamomile, called "Bedtime Blend".

Cyn bought this tea especially for Susan. Susan made an "uhmmm" sound while savoring her tea. Her baby son, Paul was resting easily against her breast, the **S**nugli made it easy to breast-feed without taking him out. She had acquired it just before becoming homeless. This blue, corduroy hammock became Paul's only home for nearly five weeks and Susan had to wear it to every interview with a landlord questing for one who would rent to a single mother with a baby.

"Could we go to 'The Hollow Reed' for lunch tomorrow, Cyn?" "Suhr-rah, mah trayt." *"Sure, my treat."*

"No, you paid last time, let me".

"We-'ahl crahz thahd brahj...Sue-zahn." *"We'll cross that bridge...Susan."*

"Just like 'The Million-Dollar Bridge'", they laughed.

There was a familiarity between Cynthia and Susan that was almost as though they were sisters. It was the kind of rare friendship that typified something that had gone on for a long time; but they both knew had just begun. There was something magical about the way Susan and Cynthia could finish one another's sentences and make plans that just naturally included each other.

Cyn's favorite activity in her Congress Street apartment was baking. She especially liked whole-wheat bread and she was also adept at producing oatmeal raisin cookies and other baked confections. They had both done the vegetarian thing for a while. But, after Susan accepted Christ; she got over all her stringent, natural foods beliefs and was now free to take one bite of anything, anytime.

Cyn however was still a natural woman and held with her strict vegan ways abhorring chocolate and processed sugar. Maybe it was the way in which she explained to Binny why she didn't consume his constantly proffered drugs. True, Cyn occasionally smoked some marijuana; but since

Binny's stash was of a harder variety; she demurred. Besides, the great room of their apartment was so depressingly dark and dank that she didn't want to get high anywhere near there.

Most of Binny's customers were impressed that Binny had a white "hippie" girlfriend, who didn't take drugs. Binny would say: "Thah fars' Juan ehz fry", *"The first one is free"* and then you would hear his creepy laughter. He thought that if his customers knew Cyn didn't take drugs, it might be bad for business. So, he never introduced her to any of his "friends" at least not here in Portland. And Cyn became just a quiet, beautiful, blonde shadow that drifted in and out of their shabby, filthy great room while going from her pristine kitchen to the park across the street, where she would display her body as merchandise and then return to bestow all her earnings upon Binny, who would ungratefully collect and count it.

Susan discerned that Cyn was definitely estranged from her family and that she didn't wish to talk about them to Susan; who discretely tiptoed around this subject as gently and politely as she could. Susan learned that Cyn was from some little town Upcountry named: "Belfast", which was right on the coast and also the place Walter Malien's called his hometown; but Cyn didn't seem to have that small-town attitude that Susan knew from growing up in Bensenville, a small town just outside of the big city of Chicago and right next to the O'Hare Airport.

They both loved going to "The People's Building" on Brackett Street, where they were members of the Good Day Market Association. They frequently made shopping expeditions to this market to pick up fresh vegetables; whole-grain flours; herbs; spices; bulgur; soy grits and buckwheat grouts. Even though Cyn was a vegan and mostly frowned upon "animal exploitation"; she still deigned to put honey in her tea. The two friends cooked together interchangeably, losing track of whose food ingredients were whose. Many times, Susan would carry home pans of bread and trays of oatmeal raisin cookies, which together they had prepared in Cyn's kitchen.

An officious police detective, who may have thought that Susan was some kind of drug courier coming from Cyn and Binny's apartment, stopped Susan and checked her shopping cart. He was disappointed to find that she had "Bulgur Cum Tarragon" in a ceramic dish and a plastic bag filled with granola rather than a bag of marijuana. Once he actually confiscated one of her oatmeal raisin cookies, flirting with her and saying he was going to confiscated more of her cookies in the future. A close friendship in which both women enjoyed cooking, baking, and someone with whom they could share the enjoyment of natural foods was of necessity in the terrible, Jimmy Carter recession. It was also a way of connecting with one another that cemented their friendship which would bind them together for several years to come.

Chapter Four
FRENCH ROAST COFFEE

Colette Espérance, the office manager at Diocesan Human Relations Services, gave Susan a twenty-dollar bill for her to purchase the Folgers French Roast Coffee they liked at the office. Colette always glowered at Susan when she found her enjoying a hot drink; it was to her as though Susan was stealing something reserved only for her and the other office workers, who were Colette's friends from church and before that her sorority sisters. She didn't realize that Susan was actually only drinking hot water, mixed with a solution of powdered milk consumed in order that she would have breast milk later when she got home. As Susan passed the twenty to Paul Trusiani, he asked about the return of her Porteus, Mitchell and Braun card.

Susan said: "This money isn't from me, it's from my office. They want me to buy coffee for them and they want their change with the receipt in the bag". She smiled up at him as she presented the twenty. Paul Trusiani had already asked Susan, if her son was named after him. They had become close enough for him to show her a photograph of his 1979 Cadillac Fleetwood Brougham Elegance all smashed-in above the window-line. He had been in the car when the top was cut off by a semi-tractor trailer and the truck driver had lost his load right in front of a viaduct. Susan beamed approval at his miraculous escape from death. Paul Trusiani had had several brushes with death over his lifetime. He was a WWII veteran and a former bomber-pilot who had flown missions over Germany. He told her that he was hoping to leave the business to his young son Paul one day and then they got back to business.

"God saved you Paul; it's a miracle."

"He-ah suhr-rah deed." *"He sure did."* Paul Trusiani said: "He-ahz behn thar fahr meh awel mah lahf." *"He's been there for me all my life."*

I'll have your money for the formula and daycare supplies in another four days, Mr. Trusiani. I don't get paid untill Friday." This elicited a broad smile from Paul Trusiani and Susan let him know that parting with this twenty-dollar bill was an excruciating experience, especially to buy designer coffee. Susan was sure Colette would count every penny as she always did. It isn't that Maine people are careful with their money; they're careful with people who don't have the right accent and to whom they haven't been acquainted since childhood. Mainers are careful also of people whose last names are unfamiliar not French nor early New England; but Susan's Italian last name was a plus with Mr. Trusiani, who was a gregarious and good-hearted person.

The Italian community in Maine is extremely welcoming, especially to a well- dressed, young woman with a tiny infant in tow. Susan was extremely good at mixing with all sorts of people and she tried to be all things to all men and women; only sharing the gospel after God had opened a door of utterance. Otherwise, she was your sister, your co-worker and your friend. Susan wore formal business attire to work every day: She had a brown tweed pants suit with a vest, a well-worn navy-blue pin-striped skirt suit and a grey flannel blazer and skirt ensemble that nearly spoke to you out loud they had been worn so frequently.

There were other people in Portland, Maine immaculately dressed in only one or two suits of clothing. One of them, however, was not Walter

Malien, a street-person living on High and Congress streets where Cynthia worked. Walter was mourning the death of his beloved wife, Josephine, who had thrown herself from the "Million-Dollar Bridge" the previous year and Walter was insane as a result. Before this tragedy, Walter had been a fisherman; but after he lost Josephine, he gave the family boat to his younger brother and lived a beggar. Having no permanent address, he stayed with whatever friends and relatives that would shelter him and made himself busy: panhandling, passing out tracks, doing odd jobs and making conversation with imaginaries.

Walter had quite a thick Down-east accent; but spoke infrequently to people who could be seen by others. However, he was neither a thief nor a drug addict nor a drunkard. He was merely a person keeping company with those whom he alone could see, specifically: Jesus Christ and his beloved wife, Josephine. And though Walter's mind had been damaged by grief, he soldiered on in his feeble attempt to follow Christ and spread the Gospel. Walter would pathetically tell people that, although he wept every day for his lost love, the Love of Christ strengthened him.

Cynthia thought: "Thahs frahn-shop wid Sue-zahn ehz zo unique. Sue-zahn dah-zahn't wahnt mah mon-nay 'r' mah bah-day; shay jes' lahkz meh fahr mah-sef?" *"This friendship with Susan is so unique. Susan doesn't want my money or my body; she just likes me for myself?"* Cyn wondered why she always felt an aching and a longing in her heart for something unnamed, unknown. Susan told her that everyone felt that way and that was God's way of never allowing us to be satisfied, except by the love of Christ. Whatever that could mean? **And when they had found Him, (Jesus) they said to Him, "Master, all men seek for thee." (Mark 1: 37)**

Susan smiled encouragingly at Walter as she walked past the Longfellow Statue and down Congress Street to pick up her son at the daycare home on the corner of Weymouth and Grant Streets.

She was praising God in her heart for providing a safe place for Paul to stay while she was at work. As twilight was descending upon Portland, Maine, Cynthia found herself sitting alone on the Congress Square Park bench where she and Susan always met. She was fulfilling one of the side-jobs of her profession: making herself visible to men, as she did this Cyn contemplated the path that her young life had taken.

Chapter Five

A NIGHT ON THE PORCH

Cynthia Hickey was only seven years old when her mother Charlene made her sleep all night on the back porch. She kept pleading and crying: "Mah-mah, pah-leez led meh ehn. Eeyah wahn-n't baht Dah-dee ah-gahn." *"Mama, please let me in. I won't bite Daddy again"*. Marlin Thompson had a deep gash on his arm and a bite mark on his tongue. It all began while he was tucking the little girl in for the night. He couldn't help his hand from dipping below the covers and finding her tiny "Mound of Venus". Then he began slowly massaging it as he kissed her passionately on the mouth. As soon as Cynthia felt his tongue enter her mouth, she bit down hard pushing his hand away and then biting him again on his forearm in a defiant gesture of contempt and horror.

Marlin Thompson screamed like a girl and Charlene came plodding down the hallway to see what all the fuss was about. She immediately took his side even though the ruse of him biting his own tongue while Cynthia bit him on the forearm didn't make any sense. Charlene Hickey pressed her hands against her daughter's fragile shoulders and lifted her out of bed, "Thahs cell tahch you-ah!" *"This will teach you!"* she bellowed as her beer breath wafted into the child's face. Dressed only in a summer night gown and wearing nothing on her feet, Cynthia was deposited on the back porch with the kitchen door slammed in her face. The warmth of her mother's kitchen was just beyond her reach; Cynthia cried bitter tears.

Maine is reputed to have cold nights even in summertime. It was autumn of 1971 in Belfast, Maine. Cynthia lay down on the wooden boards and tried to stop crying. She whined and begged a little longer; but it did no use her mother was snuggling under blankets with her boyfriend in a bedroom which was right off the kitchen near the gas and oil stove. There was a crock of navy beans baking in the continually hot oven and sometimes Charlene would sit in a chair by the stove waiting for her bread dough to rise. She would place her bread pans under a damp towel balanced on the gas side of the stove and wait until the dough had doubled in size. Then she would place the bread pans into the oven and lay down on the kitchen linoleum next to the stove where it was warm.

Charlene Hickey reasoned that putting her daughter out on the porch for the night was a kind of child-abuse that no one would suspect and Cynthia's coughs and colds were a normal part of life in Maine. Her mother thought that if she got out the belt, someone might see bruises or those long red welts and begin to ask questions. Now that Cynthia had started school, any bruises would be noticed by her teachers and they might complain to the authorities.

Charlene Hickey had to temper her anger in order to keep her daughter in school. Frequently truant though she was, Cynthia was less trouble after school started principally, because they feed her there. Charlene's life was hard; but became much easier when she had a live-in boyfriend. Cynthia's life was harder, when Charlene's life was easier; but she had never before had a "daddy" that had touched her this way. Sometimes the "daddies" slapped Cynthia's face or ordered her to wait on them, bringing cold beer from the refrigerator or heaping bowls of pretzels or roasted peanuts in the shell. The kitchen floor where Charlene frequently slept was covered with peanut shells and other food debris. The place was crawling with roaches and mice; but this didn't keep Cynthia from finding and eating an occasionally dropped peanut or bread crust. The child was frequently cold and continually hungry.

Marlin Thompson was not yet ready to move on. He stayed with Charlene Hickey until her daughter became eleven years old. By then, it was no longer possible for mom to ignore what was going on in her daughter's bedroom at night. So, night after night the tucking in ritual was repeated and Cynthia learned not to fight back anymore. Instead, she actually began to admire her tormentor and look forward to his visits. The child was frequently rewarded afterwards with a piece of candy; but her childish heart longed for a mother who would sooth and protect her. Marlin Thompson, unfortunately, would not be the last "daddy", who imposed on Cynthia in this way.

Cynthia went to the Penobscot Bay Warf after school or sometimes after the school lunch was over. School administrators notice kids sneaking off after recess and countered this with an after-school snack. This tactic was designed to solve the problem of truancy. The teachers and administrators found that when these kids were able to look forward to something to eat at school in the afternoon, they wouldn't go looking for it elsewhere. While other kids snuck home after recess for a snack, Cynthia knew that her refrigerator would be empty of everything but beer; so, she turned instead to the Penobscot Wharf, where restaurants and co-ops would throw out good food that Cynthia could retrieve from the dumpster. The only milk the child ever got was that small carton that she received with her school lunch. The craving of her growing bones caused her to wait at the back doors of various Belfast eateries to get some cheese and other discarded calcium-rich foods. She even chewed and sucked on fish bones to quiet the craving she felt in her bones. Her pleading eyes would sometimes win her a clam cake or some broiled haddock sent back to the kitchen. Nothing along the Maine waterfront ever goes to waste. The seagulls endlessly circle the wharf, looking for scraps and are in all respects just like our tragic, desperate, little girl.

Chapter Six
STEALING FROM A SOUP KITCHEN

When Susan reached the bottom of the hill, Portland had so many hilly streets, she found herself in front of her own place, the darkened hallway led to a bank of locked mailboxes and a staircase going to the upper floors of the tenement. Sabine Tourmentin, the woman who lived across Susan's hallway was sitting lazily on the bottom steps of the staircase beside the mailboxes. Susan checked her mail. It was broken into again and all of Susan's food stamps were stolen while she was at work. People would wait in the hallway for hours trying to take their food stamps and other valuables sent through the mail out of the hands of the letter carrier as soon as the mail was delivered.

Sabine Tourmentin who also went by Marie Dubois and Michelle Bonior and was receiving welfare under all three names, was lounging her rotund body on the stairway while eating a bowl of American Chop Suey from a plastic dish. Susan knew it was no good to call the police; she would just have to run the six blocks to the Wayside Evening Soup Kitchen at 252 Oxford Street. She was going to have to leave Paul home alone, if she was going to be able to acquire enough food to keep them both fed for several days.

Susan strapped Paul into the new child-seat Cynthia had given her and placed it in the corner behind the bed. She wedged him in between the wall and the three couch cushions that she had found in the alley, sanitized and was currently using for furniture. This cushion-bordered crèche was covered by a light blue receiving blanket. She hoped that if this rambunctious little guy could get out of his child seat, which she doubted, he would fall onto one of these cushions and avoid injury. The receiving blanket that had been Paul's "blankie" since birth was there to keep prying eyes off her son and protect him from sunlight that might disturb his sleep. Susan thought that if Paul cried loudly enough it might alarm someone who would come to investigate. Susan wanted Paul to drift quietly off to sleep and sleep so soundly in his little shelter that no one would disturb him until she returned.

It was already 4:30 p.m. and Susan had to leave for the Soup Kitchen before it closed. She tied on Paul's Snugli, fastened it in back and then inserted a one-gallon, plastic milk jug that was the size of her baby inside its pouch. This was a disguise for a vehicle for theft. After secreting Paul into his crèche behind the bed, she ran the six blocks to the soup kitchen and then gathering herself into a dignified posture; she began sweet-talking drunken men into letting her ahead of them in line.

Pastor Bonyer attempted to give Susan a Gospel Tract as she came through the front door. "Why does he keep giving me a tract," she thought to herself. "Can't he discern that I'm already a born-again Christian?" Susan found it difficult to believe that most pastors weren't students of the Bible and couldn't discern spirits, speak in tongues, interpret or prophesy. "Maybe it's the only scriptural message he knows", she mused as she steadied herself and beamed a beautiful smile into the face of Joe Scardulo, a bearded man with a four-inch scar below his left eye.

Susan was certainly the most beautiful woman who had ever smiled at Joe, maybe the most beautiful woman that he had ever seen. Joe had seen a lot of beautiful women in a state of undress; but only on the pages of pornographic magazines. Joe had never had a real sweetheart, but he loved Susan from afar. Joe loved the idea of Susan and that she had a son for whom she would do anything. Joe had often peeked through Susan's windows late at night. He was disappointed to find her sleeping in modest pajamas and sleeping alone. He would sometimes spend the night in the alley under Susan's bedroom window. He was a scary man; but he was also a needy, homeless, man who was more of a protector than a Peeping Tom.

Joe enjoyed the solitude of Susan's alley, which had a rural feel to it and which was the nesting place for a family of skunks. They had never bothered Joe and he was sure that their presence protected him from intruders, especially the police. Susan was twelve people behind Joe in line and next to the milk machine. There is a lot of natural wildlife right within the city limits of Portland, Maine. Seagulls circling the warf and the fishing boats, turtle climbing up onto the beach and rocky shore, the natural intruders that didn't seem to realize that this was a human domain and seemed to just be waiting for the race of men to die out and be replaced by the denizens of the air and of the deep.

Susan first filled a plastic vessel with milk, tightened its cap and placed it into the cut-down milk jug within her Snugli. It was the kind of milk that made her feel wealthy, reminded her of the liquid coming from Wisconsin, New York and Connecticut that Canada resisted so vehemently. Then, steeling herself she propelled herself out of line and into Joe's direction. He received her like a mother hen receives her chick.

As she made her way down the line, Susan slipped apples; bunches of grapes; muffins and small, meal-sized boxes of Total cereal into her Snugli. Inside where Paul usually lay, a plastic milk jug with its top cut down with scissors was vehicle for theft. Susan inserted everything she could into this secret stash while Joe watching her back. He was in awe of her and as Susan turned to leave, Joe caught her by the arm and said: "Gaht soup, gaht soup, 'r' they-ah wahn-n't led you-ah through-ah thah lah-hn." *"Get soup, get soup, or they won't let you through the line."*

He was right of course. Susan took a tray and approached the soup line. "Can I have the Minestrone please", she asked. "Sorry!" the woman ladling soup replied: "Joe gahd thah lahs' ahv ehd; bahd, we-ah hahv Ah-mare-ah-cahn chop-sue-ah fahr you-ah". *"Joe got the last of it; but we have American chop suey for you".* "Sounds great", Susan replied taking the heaping bowl of a greasy macaroni and tomato sauce concoction famous in the State of Maine for its rib-sticking, quasi-Italian charm.

Susan walked to the table where Joe was seated. He exchanged a bowl of his Minestrone for her American Chop Suey and slipped a glass of milk onto her tray. Then he adored her, undressing her with his eyes as she gobbled down the first hot food that she had eaten that day. "Drahnk you-ah mahlk, bay-bay. Eeyah wahn-n't led you-ah oud-dah hee-yah ehf you-ah dohn-'nah." *"Drink your milk, baby. I won't let you out of here if you don't."* She looked up at him and beamed a disarming smile directly into his scared and scary face. Susan thought: "This doesn't hurt me and it gives Joe pleasure; a gift from God." Which was exactly what she thought the first time that she saw Joe watching her through her bedroom window, after she realized Joe wasn't there to hurt her or her child. The night sounds of Maine lulling her to sleep. Maine combines the wilderness with the scent of the open ocean. The night birds calling to one another and the knowledge that one was only fifty miles from the nearest forest, wet, dense and dark.

Joe Scardulo, the homeless man who loved Susan from afar was dressed in an almost floor-length, dirty, brown, woolen coat. He hadn't washed his face or hair in weeks; but his hands were scrupulously clean. He must have scrubbed them for hours in some public bathroom that he could stay in for to long with someone banging on the door. All the time, thinking that perhaps, perhaps Susan might come into the soup kitchen and that he might, might, have an opportunity to sit with her at a table. Joe also thought that perhaps Susan, the immaculately-dressed woman in front of him, wouldn't eat with him, unless his hands were clean. As she gulped down her milk and rose to leave, Susan thought about what had caused her life and her son's life to be balanced so precariously.

Chapter Seven
BIG BRASS BED

Susan's little son was only ten weeks old, when they, "baby-makes-two", moved into a "furnished" apartment on Myrtle Street. This was how Susan had ended her sojourn for living space, in a "tear-down" owned by Mr. David Cross. Cross was not just a generous, good-hearted human being; he was also a really good businessman. Unlike Mr. Stanley Adams, who had been Susan's previous landlord, David Cross believed that the human species needed to reproduce and that children deserved shelter, especially when their parents were willing and able to pay for it.

The duplex on Myrtle Street was wholly inadequate to bring up a baby. It was drafty, with no real floors, just planks of wood that had gaping holes in them. Actually, the whole place, which Cross intended to eventually demolish, was filled with holes. There were rat holes, even varmint holes, holes in the walls and holes behind the kitchen cabinets. All this for only one hundred and forty dollars a month. It was home.

The first thing Susan did, after she and the baby moved in, was to get a bed. Mr. Cross had this figured out too. He had a mock-brass bed, which he had gotten from an estate auction. It was worth next to nothing but it had looked expensive, with its thin veneer of brass which he had inspected with the side of a penny: "Jehs' ah coat-tehn", *"Just a coating"*, he thought to himself and recalculated what he was willing to pay for it. Tehn dahl-lahs", "*Ten dollars*", he shouted out and the auctioneer banged his gavel in response.

With Cross there, no one would be foolish enough to outbid him. Cross was bad for business! But, he was also the auctioneer's best customer. Cross could be counted on to snap up the best deals at the lowest prices. Sometimes, he didn't even have to put anything down to buy real estate. This had been the case with the Myrtle Street duplex that he had just renting to Susan. Cross just pushed his way in and bid on a tax- lien property. The bank and City Hall had sold it to him on his good name and his impressive bank account. Cross was an everyday multi-millionaire in a work-shirt and a pair of paint-spattered jeans; just like Donald R. Trump; but as yet with only millions not billions of dollars in net worth.

When Susan saw the bed, she knew immediately what had to be done. She measured its length and width, with Paul secured to her abdomen in the Snugli. The bed had an old-fashioned, spring and railing support system, which acted as a box-spring. It was going to require a hand-made, antique, horsehair-stuffed mattress to make it into a functional bed. Such mattresses no longer exist, except of course in the mind of God.

Next Susan would have to go to the Portland City Hall and get a home-goods voucher from Madeline Cartwright. This would involve four hours of waiting in line; but it was indoors and there was plenty of water, so that Paul could nurse. She had nursed Paul in public numerous times, while they were homeless. Once she nursed him on a bench in front of a studio hair salon, where they had stopped to rest. And once she had nursed him at a bus stop.

Susan would have loved to have been able to retreat to the privacy of the ladies' room; but that would mean getting out of line and it had already taken her three hours to get this far. Susan knew that she had to complete her task within an hour or she would have to forget about sleeping in a bed that night. Finally, the receptionist called Susan's name and she was ushered into Madeline Cartwright's office.

"Oh, look how big Paul is Susan", Madeline friendly, caring voice projected her pleasure in seeing the child still healthy. She had been, "praying for this family". Madeline knew that this was not your average welfare family. This mother was educated, the child was legitimate and there was no live-in boyfriend present. Susan didn't watch too much TV; she didn't have a drug or drinking problem; but the baby was at risk, because they had no real home.

Madeline was thrilled to find out about the place on Myrtle Street. She told Susan that she had a check for Mr. Cross for the first month's rent and damage deposit. Susan said: "Gee, Madeline, I've already paid him!"

Madeline replied, "I didn't hear that Susan" and smiled broadly as she handed over the check made out to Cross. Nobody knew what folks were supposed to say to people like Madeline Cartwright. You had to have a college degree in receiving welfare in order to figure out what words were the correct ones for getting you seen and getting you helped. Ms. Cartwright also knew that most welfare recipients were a bunch of cheats and liars so according to protocol, she wrote the check to Mr. David Cross and then she wrote the home-goods voucher for "any suitable mattress".

The Salvation Army Store didn't just give things away, especially when they could get some money out of City Hall. So, people who had basic needs couldn't just go to the Salvation Army for help. The Salvation Army always made the needy go through this extra step, so that the charity could pick up some added financial support from a government hand-out program.

Susan mentally claimed the mattress that God had waiting for her and walked from City Hall to the Salvation Army Store. She thanked Madeline, then God while she just assumed that a mattress that would exactly fit the brass bed would be waiting for her there. She trusted God to provide this mattress and then further trusted Him to transport it to her home, all the while; her little one sleeping soundly in his Snugli. Susan looked into her baby's serene, innocent face. He was oblivious to any need, any plan. All he knew was that he was being carried and cared for by, someone who loved him, someone who would provide for him. Susan saw how God wanted her to view Him by concentrating her attention on the face of her sleeping child. This was one of the valuable principles of the Word of God in the seminar: "Diamonds in The Rough", taught by Rev. Dell Ducan's wife, Nancy and provided to Way Believers, by the Ministry free of charge.

Susan had the check for Mr. Cross secreted away in her brassiere when she set out for the Salvation Army Thrift Store with the home-goods voucher in her hand. It was a daunting task, so daunting in fact, that when Susan succeeded with it; a photojournalist from United Press International, UPI notice her on Preble Street and shot her picture. Under the picture of Susan in that night's Portland Press Herald was the caption: "Young Mother Brings Home Mattress".

The mattress she had envisioned was atop a pile of mattresses at the back of the store. It looked just like the one that God had shown her in her mind: blue pin stripes; big cloth-covered buttons and overly wide and long, a hand-made antique, just like the one in the Lincoln Bedroom in the Executive Mansion on Pennsylvania Avenue. Susan measured it anyway, just to be sure. It fit perfectly!

The clerk inquired, "Hahw wahl you-ah gaht eht hahmb, you-ah hahv nah cah?" *"How will you get it home, you have no car?"*

Susan asked, "Could you deliver?" The Salvation Army Store clerk frowned and replied gruffly, "Eht eh'z you-ahr rah-spons-sah-bal-lah-tea tah gaht eht hahmb; baht, ehf you-ah wahl rah-tan tah Ci-tah Hahll fahr ah-nah-thah, "trahns-pah-tah-shun vou-chah", we-'ahl de-liv-vah eht tah you-ahr au-paht-mehn' ehn 'r' stay-shun wag- gehn." *It is your responsibility to get it home; but if you will return to City Hall for another, 'Transportation Voucher', we'll deliver it to your apartment in our station wagon."*

Susan groaned, she envisioned herself sleeping on the rough wooden floorboards in the dark, maybe even having vermin crawling over her. She knew this wasn't "God's best", so she "pushed her believing forward" and inquired, "Don't you supply shopping carts to the homeless? We could fold it in half and put it in a shopping cart, which I give you my word as a Christian; I will return to you tomorrow."

"Eeyah dohn-'nah nah, we-ah nehv-vah led thah cahrtz oud-dah thah stor- rah." *"I don't know. We never let the carts out of the store."*

Susan replied hopefully, "I give you my word as a Christian"; she repeated. "I'll have the cart back to you in the morning; it's almost closing time and you won't need it till tomorrow." "Pleez?": she begged; she looked up into his staunch, dour face, imploringly.

"Ok", he said and they folded the mattress, which Susan found that she would have to drag behind her on a string of old ties. Several times praying that the cart would not tip over; it didn't! No wonder the UPI reporter shot her picture. That evening after this harrowing task was completed, Susan walked to Al and Wendy's apartment and gave her "Twig Fellowship" a "praise report".

Al didn't believe it, until he saw the picture in that night's paper. Under Al Theriault's façade of spirituality, he was still just a natural man at heart. Here was the visual proof of God's deliverance. Al was both Susan's Branch and Twig leader and though he was quite well-to-do and Susan was a frequent guest in his home; he never even thought to help her, even though he knew that she and the baby were homeless. This is the manner in which "Way People" operate; they encouraged you to believe in God's provision, while carefully avoiding what we have come to refer to as "Christian charity".

Al inquired, "how did you-ah do-ah thahs?" "how did you do this?"

Susan answered, "oh it was nothing Al. Just like walking on water." They both laughed; but Al could have made this whole arduous and unnecessary journey end for Susan and the baby; but it never even crossed his mind to help them. He knew this family's situation, or should have and he had a car and could have even borrowed a truck; but he never did anything materially for this poor family even though he knew or should have known that Susan was a widow and her son, an orphan. This is because, "Way People" are always expected to keep their needs, even the needs of their dependent children to themselves at Twig. Any kind of asking for help from the "leadership" or other believers is strictly "verboten".

Consequently, saints at fellowship don't find out about the physical needs of others and needy believers lead quiet, desperate lives surrounded by people who could help them with a modicum of inconvenience. Way Believers are expected to rely solely upon God's provision, which God must cause to come to them from outside the Ministry.

The Myrtle Street apartment had electricity and a working gas stove all furnished by the benevolent, Mr. Cross. Susan wedged the bassinette between the bed and a piece of drywall Cross had hurriedly nailed over the bare slates, making them a bedroom. Now, if the baby fell out of his bassinette; he would fall into her bed. You have to think of these things when you are a parent with no money. Positioning herself between any possible varmints that might crawl out of the numerous holes in her apartment's walls and floors and her precious baby, Susan lay down on the prayed-up mattress. Lying there was simply glorious. Susan covered her little family with her mother's nursing cape, an heirloom treasure handed down in her family and intended as a "joke present" for her late husband, Mike. And then they drifted off to sleep in their own home. A peregrination of slammed doors and dashed hopes was over.

Madeline Cartwright introduced Susan to Mr. Cross. She said of him in the language of pure liberal distain, "He makes his money; but I guess he's fair and somewhat honest." Madeline neither showed approval of Cross nor did she admire his entrepreneurial spirit. To people of this mind-set the tax-paying public, like Cross, are looked upon as the villainous causes of the poverty of persons like Susan. Cross was just supposed to help Susan simply by virtue of the fact that he was rich and she was poor; but in actuality Cross had helped Susan more than had her own church.

Susan began questing for an apartment, that would take children when Mr. Richard Adams, her landlord of two years, came banging on the door of her little, matchbox apartment shouting, "Hahv you-ah gauhd ah bay-bay ehn they-ahr?" **"Have you got a baby in there?"** as though a baby was some kind of contraband. She and Mike were renting two rooms and a bath on the third floor of a dilapidated tenement; which was on the corner of State and Pine Streets, between the Mercy Hospital where Mike went to nursing school and the Maine Medical Center where Mike worked part- time.

It was a dump; but everything that is not luxurious and historical in Portland, Maine is in a wretched state of collapse. Once, a window frame had disintegrated in Mike's hand, as he tried to open the only window in the apartment. Then he watched in amazement, while the pane of glass crashed to the bottom of the alley, the locking mechanism still in his outstretched hand. Mike made feeble oaths and began picking wooden splinters out of his hand with tweezers.

He poured hydrogen peroxide on his wounded hand while looking down at the rotten window frame and shards of glass lying below him in the alley. Mike and Susan fell onto the couch laughing. They were really in love and took every minor setback in stride. This two-room kitchenette was the best that Mike could do for them and it was so close to both hospitals.

They had just moved from Biddeford, where Mike worked in the Emergency Room at the Webber Hospital. Now, Mike would no long have to make the long trek from the Mercy Hospital to the Webber Hospital by car and by night. Webber was a dilapidated and outmoded place that Cheryl Folsom, Carmen Berthiaume and others on the nursing staff secretly referred to as, "The Farm".

Now that they had this strategic apartment, an over-long and dangerous commute had ended for Mike and he could finally indulge his sensibilities with the avid study of medical practice specific to nursing procedure. He enjoyed the quick walk to the Maine Medical Center MMC after school. It certainly was a refreshing change from the previous, long trip in the car.

Chapter Eight
MOVING ON UP

When Cynthia Hickey was about to turn eleven, Marlin Thompson finally left her mother. Charlene was so agoraphobic, that she couldn't leave the house. Therefore, Thompson wasn't able to take full advantage of his power over her prepubescent daughter. Not wishing to waste any more time on an aging alcoholic, Thompson moved on to another woman, Claudette Kittredge, who worked all the time and who appreciated the way he cleaned the house and had dinner ready for her when she got home. Claudette owned a tavern right on Front Street near the Penobscot Bay Wharf.

He had become smitten with Claudette, who was the owner of his favorite watering hole and eatery. Claudette was well-off and a widow. Charlene's drinking was eating into his small income, which was principally made at the fish-processing plant. After work Thompson would head for Claudette's and when he had finished a few beers, he would get a six-pack to go for Charlene making his tardy return home much more acceptable. Thompson became a good listener both to Claudette's troubles with her business and to Charlene's troubles with her wayward daughter; but when it became possible for him to trade his wretched existence with Charlene for a more comfortable life with Claudette. Marlin Thompson made his move! First, he took his fishing gear. This was easy, he just had to tell Charlene that he was going fishing, while including his tool box and other hand tools with his gear. He secreted these away in Claudette's attic and then returned to Charlene's to collect the rest in two large plastic bins, which he placed on the kitchen table. Quickly he began gathering up: cooking pots, pans, eating utensils, glassware and dinnerware. He didn't really need these things, because they were in abundant supply at Claudette's; but he thought, "Ehf Clawed-dot trowz meh oud, Eeyah 'leas' hahv thahs kitch-hehn gee-ah." *If Claudette throws me out, I will at least have this kitchen gear.* "Taking things that didn't belong to him was just the way in which Marlin Thompson's mind worked. He could rationalize any kind of theft and this theft was ok because; Charlene hadn't been employed for years and these things must have been bought with money that he had earned. Charlene became alarmed when she saw her pans and crockery disappearing into Thompson's bins.

She tried to restrain him, as he carried another bin into their bedroom and started taking his clothes, their scanty assortment of books, records and the alarm clock. While he was in there, Charlene was able to rescue her beloved boat-shaped crockery cookie jars and bread boxes along with her set of kitchen canisters, resembling sailing boats and one of them containing her beloved fire-proof, recipe-card file.

Marlin Thompson was moving out; but why? He had not been com-plaining of late about her drinking, about her disobedient daughter, about her cooking, her never leaving the house, or even her beer-breath and lack of personal hygiene. In fact, he had not complained about anything for months. Unfortunately, these were the months in which he had been bending his elbow at Claudette's. Thompson had placed everything of value, except the heavy furniture into these bins and was making off with it; one bin under each arm. He had also managed to secret away a picture he had taken of little Cynthia in a tank top and shorts, a picture he intended to show to his friend Roz. Charlene knew that she must either get Marlin Thompson to return home or find a replacement for him and as rapidly as possible. Thompson was the longest lasting "daddy" that Cynthia had ever known. Neither Charlene nor her daughter were able to recall life without him.

As the kitchen door slammed behind him, Thompson resolved never to see either of them again; but wait, Cynthia was an awfully sweet little piece and she was almost ready. "Whahd ehf Roz cahme ov-vah tah caun-soul Chary? She awe-red-day nose-zim," *"What, if Roz came over to console Chary, (Charlene)? She already knows him,"* Marvin Thompson thought, calculating how he could turn this unfortunate situation to his advantage. Ross (Roz) Zyfler was an old drinking buddy of Marlin Thompson's and had passed out a time or two on Charlene's living room floor, "sleep- pehn eht ahf", *sleeping it off,* between the couch and the lobster trap topped with Plexiglas that served as a coffee table. If he was to pass Charlene on to Roz, who had been both a fishing captain and a pretty good businessman, then the two of them might be able to ensnare the little girl into a life of prostitution. They could first sell her virginity to a gentleman of means. Perhaps some rich "oud-dah-staht-tah" **"out-of-stater"** might be willing to pay for the privilege of deflowering a beauty of almost twelve years old.

Zyfler had many contacts in Belfast, Bath and Brunswick. He had been a boat captain: hauling freight, taking tourists on off-shore fishing expeditions and arranging meetings between business people and those who were in need of their services. This latest proposal from his friend Marlin Thompson was unexpected; but not entirely outside of his area of expertise or out of his comfort zone. Zyfler knew Jamaican ocean- liner captains, who said that they had had sex with underage girls in Trinidad, Jamaica and in Bridgetown, Barbados. West Indies, Indian, and South American crewmen all told stories about the prostitution rings in their home countries that were willing to pay handsomely for a beautiful, blonde virgin.

Thompson thought it would be easiest to arrange something in Bath, where ocean-going vessels would lay over for a refit. Bath had a lot more foreigners and rich yachtsmen than Belfast did. "Thah "Flaht-lahn-dahs" ahr awe-waz luk-kehn fahr sum-thehn nuer". *The "Flatlanders", are always looking for something new."* When they discussed it over beers at Claudette's tavern, Zyfler said that they would have to be careful because, if a foreign customer gained possession of Cynthia, then Roz and Thompson might never receive their pay, nor would they ever see their little protégé again. The idea was to meet up with someone who already trusted Zyfler and then arrange a tryst between her and a gentleman of means. After all, they weren't doing all this to raise money for Cynthia's college fund.

Chapter Nine
THE MYSTIC EXPANSE

Every time Mike made a night-crossing of the Scarborough Marsh a sense of dread swept over him in the soundless, lightless abyss. There were no noises coming from the numerous rookeries of Snow Geese, Canada Geese, Cormorants, Great Blue Herons, Snowy Egrets, Northern Gannets and Great Northern Loons. Only the stars and Moon gave any light, and this was obscured by the misty fog rising up from the lacework streams that come out of the Great Salt Marsh and descend in a labyrinth network down to the Rachel Carson's Wildlife Refuge near the beach at the Laudholms' Family Farm.

There beach-nesting birds, such as Least Terns and Piping Plovers are protected from dogs, other pets and people on foot, all are considered unwelcomed strangers and resisted like Nazis invading the French countryside. Fredrick and Diane Lord, who were still operating the Laudholm Family Farm, Mike's former employers, had long ago given up part of their property to make this refuge, which is a church-like sanctuary of indescribable beauty. There in its most secret recesses is a little pulpit and a clutch of benches for congregants to perch themselves as they listen to a sermon befitting the surroundings. Mike had never heard anybody preach from that podium; but he had always wanted to bring his Quaker meeting to that spot. They would have of course resisted not having a minister, but only a clerk.

Mike had tended the Laudholm farmland and forked hay up into their barn. Being a hired hand on this farm, which was his first job in the State of Maine, had given Mike two very valuable contacts: Jeff Folsom, who was their farm manager, the Lords of the Laudholm farm being entirely too rich to turn the earth themselves, and Jeff's wife Cheryl ,who worked in Biddeford at the Webber Hospital Emergency Room, was a miracle worker who could paste broken bodies back together and start people's hearts again after they had died. Mike had once taken a pair of little, red, high-top tennis shoes down to the morgue for her, after they had worked for hours on a six-year-old suicide victim. Cheryl, Mike and Dr. Ratnakar Andelkar, a doctor who came from India, made an extraordinary life-saving team.

Dr. Andelkar said, "I think this kid was just playing in the tree, don't you Mike?"

"Yeah, I do", Mike replied fighting back the tears. Cheryl knew Mike took

everything he did to save lives very seriously. As he grasped the little red shoes, Mike thought about the perfect hang-man's noose that had been cut down from the tree. There was no explanation for this, it was a great, unsolved mystery. When the Biddeford Police cut little Freddy down, no other kids were anywhere around. The boy had actually scratched the bark right off the tree desperately trying to correct his error and save his life.

Unfortunately, the rope was too long for his little arms and he strangled. Freddy still had a pulse when they brought him into the emergency room; but they couldn't get his breathing to resume. They gave up the fight at 2:43 a.m. and pronounced him dead just before his parents came in. Then, as his sobbing mother gripped his father's arm, Dr. Andelkar tried to explain to them how Freddy had, "accidently strangled while playing in an apple tree". Mike carried the shoes downstairs to the morgue and got the body ready for viewing. It was the morgue crew's job; but they were all union, so they really never had to do any work at night, just sit there.

While announcing: "Allahu Akbar", the Moslem plunged his blade into the Quaker's back, Dr. Andelkar excised a tiny, black mole on Mike's back. This was a going-away present to his friend of almost two years. The doctor had recommended Mike for the hospital scholarship fund and had written one of the two qualifying letters to various Mercy Hospital School of Nursing officials that gained Mike a year's proficiency of his nursing school classes and had put him at the top of their list of applicants. "It was the least that I could do, Mike, you have really thrown yourself at saving people's lives around here", he said.

"We've always made a good team," Mike said: "I think I'd like to become a Nurse Practitioner and then follow you to Norway, Maine after your residency is over."

"I would like that too, Mike", Dr. Andelkar replied, "I know that Susan and Supria both would like to raise kids in a small town, Upcountry and Norway is just right for all four of us." Dr. Andelkar was a caring, diplomatic man who truly deserved the descriptive: "Mentor". He had a quiet, simplicity about him that caused the word: "healer" to immediately leap to mind.

Mike and Dr. Andelkar talked about Dr. Tom Dooley, who was Mike's role model and inspiration. When things were slow, they would talk about medicine in the Third World, India's civil war and Mike's favorite subject: the effort to stamp out clitorectomy in Africa and the Islamic world.

Chapter Ten
BELFAST TO BATH AND BEYOND

R oss (Roz) Zyfler thought of renting a camper and parking it near the Bath Iron Works on the Kennebec River. He reasoned that a workman might use a camper for living quarters near his employment and then pull up stakes when his temporary assignment was finished. People frequently camp and fish near the mouth of the Kennebec River where it releases its burden of rain and snow melt into the Casco Bay. So, with their fishing gear loaded into the back of Thompson's rusted-out, station wagon, a basket of sandwiches packed by Claudette and an Igloo insulated, beverage-cooler filled with sweet tea from Charlene; Zyfler and Thompson went off on a fishing expedition, which just happened to include their little "niece".

Marlin Thompson nervously hoped that this would only be a dry run and finding the wealthy gentleman would come later. They drove to the house of a fishing, hunting and drinking buddy, Tim Sample, who owned a beautiful 1966 Airstream Safari 22' Travel Trailer and arranged to rent it for the weekend. Charlene wanting to go too; however, when she found that Thompson was also coming along, she said, "Daow, thahd'z awe-ride, ah-nah-thah tahm." *"No, that's alright, another time."* Zyfler loaded Charlene's refrigerator with beer and promised to bring her a present from Bath.

Cynthia tuned the radio to a rock and roll channel against the protestations of Roz who wanted country. They drove the seventy miles to the Casco Bay, passing through picturesque, little Camden, Warren and Newcastle.

The fragrance of White Pine, Atlantic-White Cedar, Red Cedar, Mulberry bushes, Eastern Hemlock, Ash and Aspen combined their piney perfume with the fresh salt air. The scent of rural Maine came wafting through the open window, making Cynthia's heart long for the preferred seat rather than the one she now occupied in between her two fathers. When they arrived in Bath, they crossed over the Kennebec River and made the mandatory stop at Dot's Ice Cream Shop on Front Street. When she came out of the ladies' room, both of her "daddies" were at the counter ready to buy her a double-dip of any kind of ice cream she wanted. Dot's has a fresh, homemade blueberry ice cream with real Maine blueberries. There was also a ginger which Cynthia had to try. She sampled as many as she was allowed, before a final decision had to be made. When the "skoup lay-day" *"scoop lady"* wouldn't give Cynthia another sample, she settled on "Mahn Blu-bar-rah" *"Maine Blueberry"* and "Fahj Dah-laht" *"Fudge Delight"*. This would be the last time Cynthia would ever eat chocolate. While Cynthia savored this blueberry and fudge confection, Thompson asked Zyfler, "Way-ahr shahd we-ah pahk thah cahm-pah?" *"Where should we park the camper?"*

There were a number of places in town to park their camper; but a location near the river would attract the least attention. They went East on Broad Street off of Front and then headed north on Commercial Street up to the "Kennebec Tavern and Marina", where they were able to park and get out. While Cynthia inquired about where they intended to fish, Zyfler went on foot to the tavern.

Thompson said to Cynthia, "We-ah ride on thah riv-vah hee-ah. You-ah coahd gau ahnd luk-eht thah boahdz, why we-ah gaht 'r' fahsh-shan gee-yah red-day fahr tah- mahr-rah. We 'r' gau-ehn tah beh stay-ehn 'tahl Sahn-duh." "*We are right on the river here. You could go and look at the boats, while we get our fishing gear ready for tomorrow. We are going to be staying until Sunday.*" He explained casually and without any sign of the nervousness he was feeling inside.

The Airstream Travel Trailer was perfect for what they wanted to do. It had a side door that opened onto a living room-kitchen area and then in the back there was a private sleeping room.

Thompson only needed to stay with his little charge until Zyfler returned from the Marina after he scouted out an ocean-going vessel. They were hoping to find a good-sized pleasure-craft like the one he used during his years spent in escorting wealthy clients on deep-sea fishing expeditions.

He never got less than one thousand dollars for a guided tour and three thousand if he used his own boat. However, keeping a boat at the marina had become pricey, so he sold the vessel and tried to use the boats of casual sailors by representing himself to the tourists as an experienced, fishing guide. There are many beautiful yachts at anchor in the Kennebec Marina and Zyfler tried to see if he recognized them.

Wealthy people from London, New York and Hong Kong all vacation in The State of Maine. Some like the Bush Family of Kennebunkport owned a summer home and others rented coastal property more for convenience than for thrift. Some were looking for a thrill, that they couldn't find at home and others wanted what they were used to having in Dubai or Jeddah, the company of a young, malleable woman, who wouldn't give them a disease, because she had never been with a man before.

Zyfler sat down at the bar near the marina and contemplated his beer. It wasn't long before he was joined by a businessman and amateur deep-sea fisherman, who remembered that Roz owed him money.

"Gud-day! Cap'n Roz! You-ah owe meh fif-dah bucks, you-ah nah",

"Good day, Captain Roz, you owe me fifty dollars, you know", came the greeting from Lionel Prescott, an acquaintance who had helped Zyfler get a charter last spring by steering him a deep-sea fishing client.

Lionel Prescott knew people who wanted to go out to the Georges Bank also called the Gulf of Maine. But most of their vessels were inadequate for such a long trip and gearing up for such an expedition, which was sixty nautical miles East of Portland, was a tremendous expense. Most people just wanted to go to the Gulf, because they knew the name and had heard that it had great fishing.

Zyfler painfully handed over the cash and then wondered aloud if Prescott knew of any pleasure-craft owners, who were interested in a guide to take along for deep-sea fishing.

Zyfler parted with this money grimly. "Prahs-scott ehz rahch, wahl Eeyah rahl-lay nahd thahd mon-nah!" *"Prescott is rich, while I really need that money!"* he thought, while acting as nonchalantly as he could. Then he tried to make conversation about deep-sea fishing or inclement weather, any subject that he could think of until the topic came around to charters. He wanted to inquire about any foreign pleasure-craft, that might lay-over in Bath for a refit or need a fishing guide. Asking about a gentleman willing to pay for sex with a minor was a subject not to be leaped into; but Zyfler didn't want to let Prescott walk away with his fifty dollars without getting something in exchange. He hoped Prescott would provide a lead that would pan-out and Lionel Prescott had helped Roz in the past.

"Ayuh-m wurk-kehn oud-dah Bah-fes' nah-ah-daz. Hahd tah gahv-ahp mah boahd lahs' sum-mah, 'cahz ahv mah halth." *"I am working out of Belfast now-a-days. I had to give up my boat last summer, because of my health. (Drinking)"* Zyfler said, hoping to gain Prescott's sympathy. "Ayuh wahz Juan-dren ehf you-ah coahd stee-yah meh ah plea-jah-crahf luk-kehn fahr ah gahd." *"I was wondering if you could steer me a pleasure-craft looking for a guide."* (Roz is soliciting business.) "Ayuh, Cap'n Roz, ah rahl-lay fahn-say yaht cahme ehn lahs' naht, ah sev-ven-day-fibe-fut clahs-sick Kahch, ah cahst-tahm-rah-fit oud-dah Bahth Ion-wahkz Ship-yahdz. Ehd hahz thrah ahft staht-rahmz shar-rehn tah hahdz wid sah-prahd 'com-mah-day-shunz fahr thrah crew- mahn. *"Yes, Roz, a really-fancy yacht came in last night, a seventy-five-foot classic Ketch, a custom-refit out of Bath Ironworks Shipyards. It has three aft staterooms sharing two heads and with separate accommodations for three crewmen."*

"Ahnd eht hahz ah few-ahl cah-pahs-sah-tea ahv tah towel-zen gahl-lenz, ahnd wahz tah hun-dirt ahnd fif-day towel-zen pounz. Ehd ehz ah wud-den yaht bahlt ahv tahk ahnd mah-haug-gahn-knee ehn ahn ohk frahm ahnd ehz ah-quahpd wid ah dee- cell ehn-jehn ahnd tah mahs'z wid fahl sahul." *"And it has a fuel capacity of two thousand gallons and weighs two hundred and fifty thousand pounds.* It is a wooden yacht built of teak and mahogany on an oak frame and is equipped with a diesel engine and two masts with full sail."

"Rahl-lay, wh-ah ehz shay im-pahrt?" *"Really, why is she (this ship) in port?"*

"Shay'z naught ehn thah mah-reen-ner, ehn-nay-moh, shay'z ehn ah cove thrah myelz frumb hee-yah thah own-nah jehs' flew ehn tah thah Paut-lan' Air-paht lahs' Turs-day ahnd wahnz tah tes' har oud bah-far he-ah tahkz har dahwn tah thah Car-ah- bee-an. They-ah say he-ah ehz gau-ehn tah Bah-bay-dose. He-ah'z frumb Sau-der Ar- ray-bee-er ahnd sech ahnd haz ah thahrd homb ehn Bah-she-ber, Bah-bay-dose, you-ah nah, ahnd jehs' flew ehn uhn hahz priv-vaht jet, awel priv-lejd ahnd sech",---*She's not in the marina anymore, she's in a cove three miles from here and the owner just flew in to the Portland Airport last Thursday and wants to test her out before he takes her down to the Caribbean. They say he is going to Barbados. He's from Saudi Arabia and such and has a third* home in Bathsheba, Barbados, you know, and *just flew in on his private jet, all privileged and such"*, divulged Prescott jealously.

Zyfler could taste the sarcasm and envy in Prescott's voice. Lionel Prescott got this way whenever discussing the toys of wealthier men, because the Prescott money had fled from his side of the family. Now, Zyfler was salivating, he said, "Eeyah'dah lahk tah gahd huhm tah thah Geor-jez Bahnk, bah-far he-ah cruz-zez dahwn tah thah Car-ah-bee-an. You-ah nah hahw Eeyah'cauhn mead huhm?" *"I'd like to guide him to the Georges Bank, (The Gulf of Maine) before he cruises down to the Caribbean. Do you know how I can meet him?"*

Cap'n Roz Zy-flah *(Captain Ross Zyfler)* needed to think quickly now; Prescott was only drinking Moxie, while Zyfler was having his fourth beer. It was about half gone and he was willing to leave it if he had to in order to get Prescott back to the camper and let Thompson know that there was a deal in progress.

Zyfler got up from the bar stool very casually, threw back the last of his beer and put one of his huge fisherman's hands on Prescott's shoulder. Then he said in almost a whisper:

"Eeh-hav' cahm dahwn hee-yah ehn ah cahm-pah ahnd mah paht-nah ehz bahk bah-hien' thah tah-vahn ehn thah cahm-pah say-ehn tah 'r' lit-tahl ni'ce." *"I have come down here in a camper and my partner is back behind the Kennebec Tavern and Marina in the camper, seeing to our little niece."*

Lionel Prescott wasn't the least bit suspicious.

Chapter Eleven
CHEAP THRILLS

Within two weeks of receiving the letter of acceptance from the Mercy Hospital School of Nursing, Mike and Susan initiated a hectic move to Portland, Maine. They had to rely on their aging Volkswagen Van with the flower decals on it, to get their "treasurers" to the big city. There wasn't much to move, some books, a guitar, about two-hundred-and-fifty priceless vinyl albums: Bob Dylan, Blind Faith, all the Beatles albums, everything Joan Baez had done up till that point Janis Joplin with Big Brother and the Holding Company "Cheap Thrills" a favorite of Mike's, there was also Buffalo Springfield and of course the Cream.

Mike and Susan had made some shelves with boards and decorative cinder block. Music had become an integral part of their lives together, it got them in the mood to make love and it reminded them of their shared history. The only thing of value that they owned was this record collection, a pair of over-sized speakers and a turn-table with a diamond stylus.

They had met on an archeological expedition to Zempoala in the Mexican, east-coastal state of Veracruz. Mike proposed to Susan on one knee, when they were both squatting in a trench, where Toltec burial goods had been discovered. Susan even looked good with 1,000-year-old dirt on her face and her excitement over pre- Columbian children's toys was infectious.

There was a magical quality about the way she spoke of long-dead civilizations as though they were people with whom she had recently conversed. Their shared love for all things wild and free was also magical; a love that caused them to be quickly married in a thoroughly romantic ceremony in a small Catholic Church by a Mexican priest. Soon after their return to the United States, Susan and Mike went straight to the State of Maine, where Mike, a native of the flat land of Central Illinois, had always wanted to live.

Mike was lured to Maine by the wonderous stories he heard of the Maine wilderness, its ocean beaches, free to the public and Maine's independent fisher folk, whose character and tenacity are legend. Because he was raised a farm kid in the flat country of Central Illinois, Mike had wanted to see the rolling hills, piney-wood forests and rocky seascapes of New England for himself. He remembered also that his father, Paul Asta, originally came from the State of New Jersey. His dad told him stories about an extensive wilderness area in New Jersey called, "The Pine Barrens". Mike had concealed a treasure map in the sleeve of his bomber jacket. It would, he hoped, lead him and his bride to a secret compound in which Mike's dad had lived and worked. This compound was where his father's sister, Pearl still lived and was the "Donna" of a prominent Italian family.

Paul Asta, who had once been heir to the Apponi-Carbone Family's olive oil business, went out to Illinois farm country seeking a simpler, more-wholesome life. When Mike's maternal grandparents, who owned the farm passed away, the land had to be sold for taxes, debts and other heirs. Mike, who was a Pre-Med student at Southern Illinois University got so rattled by his grandparents' death, his father's grave illness and his mother's hysteria, that he had to reassess his life's goal of becoming a doctor and drop out for a quarter. By the time, he got back on track the farm had been sold, his father had passed away and his mom was in a nursing home.

Mike's GDP had slipped from 4.6 to a 3.9 on a 5-point scale and repeating Micro and accepting a C in Genetics pretty-much finished things for his medical career. Genetics and Microbiology were SIU's Premed "flunk-out courses". So, with solemn regret he pulled himself together, realized that all he really wanted was to do was care for the sick and the injured and set his sights on a degree in Nursing.

Susan's two degrees one in Archeology, the other in Anthropology weren't of any interest to people hiring in the State of Maine. So, she contented herself with stitching second collar at a shoe shop on Factory Island between Biddeford and Saco. Mike became an Emergency Medical Technician at the Webber Hospital, Biddeford because this was the only medical job for which his three years of Pre-med at SIU had qualified him. They had both made terrible academic mistakes. They relied on what their high-school guidance counselors had told them, that a college degree was the path to a life of riches. Susan had gotten two degrees that hadn't qualified her of a paying job and Mike had completed three years of premed, which didn't qualify him for any medical career at all. Those three years if spent in a nursing program would have given him a career in medicine, which would have been both lucrative and satisfying; but there was no use crying over bad vocational choices.

They both had to start over again; but because of Gerald Ford's wretched economy, with his stupid "WIN – Whip Inflation Now" idea, everything was in free fall. They had to take jobs for which they were overqualified, hide their educations and do jobs that nobody else wanted. Fortunately, these kinds of jobs were plentiful in the State of Maine and therefore, Susan could get work cleaning the homes of wealthy vacationers, doing stoop labor, picking blueberries, processing fish and opening clams and scallops, while Mike could get farm-laborer work and work as an orderly.

An Archeologist is by definition not afraid to get his or her hands dirty;

but unfortunately, there are few jobs in the State of Maine for a BA and going after her Masters or PhD didn't make much sense at this time in her young life. Susan was pushing thirty and her biological clock was ringing off the nightstand. She and Mike had tried four times to have a live birth and failed. Mike and Susan longed to start a family; but they had been defeated time and time again, by the Christoi genes, which predisposed her to miscarry. Susan thought that Mike's family farm on the Illinois prairie would be a perfect place to rear children. So, it was with solemn regret that she learned of the sale of his grandparent's farm and that he would be dropping out of Pre-med because of his abysmal GPA. Susan hadn't married Mike because he was going to become a Doctor she married him because she loved him; but it wouldn't have been bad to have been married to a doctor. Susan dreamt of accompanying Mike on a Tom Dooley-styled expedition to some ancient, third-world country, where she could get into a dig site. It didn't happen and though she was disappointed in her expectations, Susan took it all in stride.

Most Mainers work in the textile or shoe industries, fishing, lumbering and the tourist trade. Mike and Susan sank every penny they had into a tourist shop on Perkin's Cove, hoping that their entrepreneurial spirit would cause them to strike it rich by taking a risk in buying items at low cost in Mexico and trying to resell them again; but it had barely paid the rental on their room at the Wisteria House in Ogunquit and their place of business.

Mike made a strategic contact at the Laudholm's Farm in Wells, Maine, where he became a farm-hand. This job led Mike to Cheryl Folsom and Cheryl led Mike to the Webber Hospital Emergency Room in Biddeford, where she became his charge nurse.

Susan always knew that Archeology has never been a science that one could barter for pay, at least not on the postgraduate level. PhDs in Archeology and Anthropology only got funding for their next dig or sometimes only their next forage into the wilderness. Susan was forced to settle into the uncomplaining acceptance of blueberry picking, housekeeping and piece work in a sweat shop. So, even though there is a large welfare population in the State of Maine, all kinds of jobs are going begging. There was bagging groceries, yard work for the wealthy estates, sweeping out stores and working in one of the "Factory Island" shoe-shops or textile mills or at "Saco Tanning". All these jobs are plentiful and all put food on the table; but none of them necessitated a college B. A. degree. Mike and Susan actually had to hide their educations in order to be hired.

Fish-processing plants, poultry-processing plants and clam shacks abound throughout the coastal corridor of Maine, known as Downeast, and though these jobs aren't glamorous and are frequently smelly, they pay well and are tailored for hard- working people. These are the kind of jobs, where you take a shower after work not before. A lot of Mainers work only during the summer months, go on welfare during the winter and never leave their stove-side while the blustering gales of the North Atlantic bring with them tons of snow and sub-zero temperatures, snow up to the window sills, snow heaped on street corners and in alleyways until there is only passage for one car at a time and then only in the direction of the hospital.

Chapter Twelve
MAIDENHEAD TO MASTHEAD

I. "I'm Your Vehicle, Baby":

How could Prescott know that these two men, one of whom was known to him, were pursuing an objective so ulterior that it could not even be named? Their little "niece" was unbeknownst to her being taken along as bait to lure a foreign prince to let them onto his boat and once there, get them a guide job and then get His Majesty to buy an eventual evening of sex with an innocent, uninformed virgin.

Lionel Prescott, even though he was a full-grown man, was every bit the ingénue that Cynthia was and he like her thought that this was just going to be a fishing trip or perhaps a tour of a splendid yacht. Prescott said to Zyfler, "Wahn-tah mead huhm, Cap'n? We-ah'l hahv tah gau tah thah plahz he-ah'z ah-stain." "Wahn-tah *(Would you like to) meet him, Captain? We'll have to go to the place where he's staying."* Lionel Prescott owned a brand-new 1973 Cadillac El Dorado and after a brief trip back to the Camper, they were all seated in it, with Cynthia getting to sit in the back with both windows rolled down, in order that she might enjoy the sweet, piney, salt, air streaming through the windows.

"Sehz thahs you-ah cah, Mah-stah. Prahs-scott?" *"Is this your car, Mr.*

Prescott?" Cynthia inquired excitedly and in a high-pitched voice trying to hold back her enthusiasm. She had never before ridden in so luxurious a car. Prescott smiled at her in the rear-view mirror as he chauffeured her and her "daddies" to the Happy Nook, which overlooked the New Meadows Cove, three miles west of Bath in a secluded area of the Casco Bay. The Happy Nook has a private, deep-water dock, which is only a few minutes from the ocean. At anchor in the dock was a seventy-five-foot; double-masted, wooden yacht, its name newly painted on the stern, "'Fatima' out of Bathsheba, Barbados."

It seemed queer to Lionel Prescott that a Saudi Prince would name his boat after a town in Portugal where the Virgin Mary had appeared. But, he was determined not to ask this Prince any impertinent questions, let the little girl do that. Prescott was always nervous when meeting new people, especially people who weren't even from Maine and people who didn't acknowledge his superiority to them, simply by virtue of the fact that he was a Prescott. His name, though well-respected in the city of Bath, was not widely known outside it. Perhaps, this Prince wouldn't suspect that Prescott too was royalty, even if it was only the royalty of the simple, fisher folk of Downeast, Maine.

They drove up a winding, private road off of Route One and came to a provincial cottage that was rented by the season always to "oud-dah-staht-tahz", **out-of-staters**, who were required to lay out a hefty damage deposit, the cottage being lavishly furnished. Summer-people are not accepted by Maine-folk; but they certainly are appreciated and their money is certainly accepted. They ate appreciated for the income they provide to shopkeepers, innkeepers, restaurateurs and the people who lease these luxurious summer rentals. However, this "oud-dah-staht-tah", **out-of-staters** was not interested in souvenirs or pictures of light houses, *he was studying America with a view toward one day subduing it.* They rang the bell which gave the sound of chimes.

The intercom bellowed the voice of a servant who always traveled with His Highness and who answered with a strange, Middle-Eastern accent. Lionel Prescott stepped forward to explain their mission, and Abdullah bin-Nassif, the chief butler of an unnamed Saudi Prince admitted them into the estate. Zyfler felt confident that the Cadillac El Dorado in which they arrived would gain them admittance to one of these grand houses which Maine folk slyly refer to as "cottages". This is because none of them have running water except in the Summer months, when water pipes are hurriedly connected and strung across the lawns.

"Could you come around to the side door?" Abdullah graciously inquired. When he opened the door, the servant was dressed in a floor-length, pure-white smock, which was not gathered at the waist and his head, Cyn thought, was adorned with a red, gingham tablecloth banded around his head with a black double coil. He seemed gigantic as he peered down on them in the side portico. Swiftly and silently he ushered them into a study lined with leather-bound books.

A Donegal Carpet adorned the hard-wood floor; but other than a desk, and a corpulent easy chair with its over-sized ottoman, there was no seating for guests. It seemed to Prescott, an odd place to use as a waiting room. The carpet took up the majority of the floor space. There was no bench or chairs, not even folding chairs, for guests to be seated.

After standing for at least twenty minutes, Zyfler and Thompson crossed the room and joined Prescott seating themselves on the edges of the ottoman. One of them could have sat behind the desk, but none dared. Cynthia was the only person brave enough to sit down on the carpet.

She was wearing her only skirt, a plain-white blouse with short sleeves, white ankle socks and a pair of black, patent-leather, Mary Jane's bought for her by a kindly teacher, who noticed her coming to school in sweat pants and wearing a pair of rubber galoshes in September. She quickly seated herself on the gorgeous rug, which was adorned with a mirror pattern in muted tones of green and brown. It had two central flower petals of burnished orange and red. They had an uncomfortably long wait; but that was the point and it gave Cynthia the opportunity to sit on the floor and enjoy stroking this magnificent carpet.

II. "A Royal Appearance":

His Highness was a slight fellow, in his thirties, wearing a sideways baseball cap and a fine Italian silk suit. He was a mad-cap playboy, who spent every penny of his considerable allowance on trinkets, toys, gadgets, gizmos and the pursuit of a continuous, exotic vacation. On his wrist was a Patek Phillipe Watch, which was easily the price of the Cadillac outside. He immediate gravitated towards the child on the rug and squatting down to her level, looked deeply into her beautiful blue eyes. She impertinently returned his gaze and they both smiled broadly recognizing one another as childlike, kindred souls. He thought of her as a blonde, beautiful, innocent; because that was what she was. For the rest of Cynthia's life, there would always remain a remnant of the virginal soul, which was seated on that Donegal Carpet between the leaves of rust-red, green, brown and gray.

It was not customary in his home country to speak to a child, much less a female child; before greeting the men in the room so he slipped a pure-white glove onto his right hand and crossed the room, greeting the three men in the manner customary to the Western World the grasping and shaking of the right hand. The men arose when His Highness entered the room; but not the little girl, she continued to sit on the carpet, unconscious of the glimpses he took of the awkward display she made of the white panties she wore beneath her blue-and green-plaid skirt.

Cynthia recalled later how the words, which were exchanged between her fathers, Mr. Prescott and the Arab Prince blurred together; as they spoke about yachts, huge fish and the inclement weather typically found in the Gulf of Maine which is also known as the Georges Bank.

Roz Zyfler mentioned the availability of giant tuna ranging from seven hundred and fifty to nine hundred pounds. These huge fish could only be landed by a trained angler, who had the equipment and the expertise not to be pulled overboard. There were also Thresher Sharks, which really fought when you had them on your line, as did Great Whites, Blues, Swordfish and the smaller Silver Hake, Haddock and Cod. Mr. Prescott took the lead now and fought Marlin Thompson for the right to claim the privilege of spinning a yarn about the hundred-pounder that got away and sadly, he mentioned, the now commercially-extinct "yell'er-tails", the flounder and the tuna which had all but disappeared from The Gulf of Maine. The Prince pledged to let any yellow-tailed fish he caught go, if only these Maine fishing experts would be pleased to inform him when one was on his line.

Overhearing this talk about the several kinds of wonderful fish and the anticipated ocean adventure that they might encounter only seventy nautical miles south-east of where Cynthia sat, filled her young, innocent heart with uncontainable excitement. She looked up from her carpet at her Prince, her fathers and their friend Mr. Prescott, then back again at the carpet's green, gold and rust-red Irish pattern. Donegal Carpets are found in castles and palaces throughout Europe, Buckingham Palace, the Vatican and the Whitehouse.

III. "Fatima out of Bathsheba":

Prescott thought it comical, that this sailboat, which was capable of easily subduing a nine-hundred-pound giant tuna; because it weighed nearly two hundred and twenty thousand pounds and had a fuel capacity of two thousand gallons, being also equipped with a full-sail, mast assemblies; would have a moniker more like that of a race horse than a ship. It was built for comfort, being appointed with three private staterooms, sharing two heads. The galley, which was going to be run by the Prince's chief butler, chef and Imam, Abdullah bin-Nassif, was capable of turning out four-star gourmet meals on its propane burners; but to their disappointment there was no stock of alcoholic beverages. These men were going to have to wait until they got back onto dry land, before they could resume pickling their livers.

The night before, Lionel Prescott had insisted that they move their camper to the Prescott Estate on the banks of the Kennebec River. Cynthia had learned to be a morning person; but getting up at half-passed midnight was something new. A diligent Mr. Prescott was knocking on the camper door and generously inviting them to a New England breakfast of bacon, eggs, pancakes, Florida orange juice and coffee strained through a sock in the middle of the night. This was followed by an arrival at the Prince's Cove at 3:30 a.m. and the Georges Bank as the morning light was breaking and without any sustenance for His Highness, Abdullah and the two crewmen; but the Mainers had eaten enough for all eight of them and they were off to a day of fishing.

Cynthia smiled broadly, while boarding this beautiful yacht and while enthusiastically baiting her own hook, reminding herself not to puncture her thumb the way she did when she was six. It is legend Downeast and all along the craggy coastal region of Maine, New Hampshire and Massachu-setts that children raised in these environs learn to fish and cut bait before they are potty trained.

Cynthia caught three beautiful haddock, before Roz could stop her, saying, "We-ahr luk-kehn fahr bahg too-ner ahnd bahg sahd-fahsh ahnd naught theze lit-tahl brahk traht". *"We are looking for big tuna and big swordfish and not these little brook trout".* The Prince and Cynthia looked at one another in amazement. They were both proud of her acquisitions; but putting out a child's line in these waters could prove dangerous. The girl might chance to catch a bigger fish than she could handle and it would pull her overboard.

The Prince, Abdullah and the two deck hands were all Saudis and as a consequence were careful not to touch any of the guides with their bare hands. Arab custom disparages touching a male infidel except to kill him, causing Muslim physicians to smirk and chuckle with wry irony. This proscription does not extend to women and girls; however and the Prince made a display of hovering over Cynthia's pole as though she was a marine biology student and he her professor.

Zyfler said that cod would make the best baitfish for the Tuna and Swordfish he wanted to catch. His big fishing poles were so huge that Cynthia couldn't pick one of them up by herself. The reels were as big as her head and the hooks the size of a man's hand. Zyfler attached his fishing gear to a fisherman's chair off the stern and Abdullah made Zyfler don a pair of brand-new fisherman's gloves, before he was allowed to strap Cynthia's prince into his own stern-mounted fishing chair.

While Prescott, who had gear of his own began setting up fishing chairs along the deck; but until the prince had caught the first big fish, they knew that they had to restrain themselves; it was, after all, the prince's boat.

Cynthia wanted to sit in His Highness's lap; but she thought, "he-ah'll thahnk Eeyah-'em raude". *"He'll think I'm rude".* They slowed the boat to just above two knots and lowered the Prince's hook baited with haddock, the only bait fish they so far had caught, letting the line drift out for a hundred yards. They had also set the drag on the reel just strong enough to keep the line from playing out any further. Everyone, including the butler, waited breathlessly for a fish to catch the Prince's line and then fight for open water. It didn't take long before a Thresher Shark took the bait.

Suddenly the line grew taut and began to sing off the reel, now the two crewmen were lifting their voices in a strange, tongue-wagging shout of triumph, comradery and encouragement; as the Thresher acknowledged her mistake and began trying to save her life. The fish ran for open water just as they expected; but found that there was no escape. The Prince pumped the rod as fast as He could; as Zyfler shouted: "thahs ehz ah gudd-uhn!", *This is a good one!* and poured cold sea water onto the line, bellowing, "Ayuh, Eeyah cauhn say har lahng tahl." *"Yes, I can see her long tail."* *The thresher shark is reputed to have the longest tail of any shark in the world.*

The forty-pounder began leaping out of the water, fighting for her life, as His Highness pumped the rod back and forth reeling in a foot of line at a time. While Prescott counseled Cynthia's Prince, "Dohn' tahch thah drahg 'r' yule brahk thah lion, jehs' kehp ah-pump-pehn ahnd ah-reel-lehn." *"Don't touch the drag or you will break the line, just keep pumping and reeling."*

As His Highness continued to make slow progress, suddenly the fish appeared twenty yards off the stern and catching sight of the boat, she remembered that she was a thresher shark suddenly beginning to make her final attempt to escape. She dove straight down and took fifteen yards of line. That was it! The fishermen had mastered the sea creature and she was ready to be hauled up. Zyfler reached out with a gaff and hooked the shark behind her gill hauling her aboard, while Thompson made ready with a club.

Abdullah bin-Nassif had plenty of chipped ice loaded into the hold and was thinking about how to prepare Thresher Shark. He reasoned that since the two crewmen and His Highness had eaten shark before in their home country, the shark would make a desirable meal for his Highness, himself, the Saudi crew, the girl and the infidel guides. He determined to cut the shark into two-inch steaks and keep the haddock, hake and the shark's vital organs on ice as bait for later.

Assembled in the galley were nineteen, two-inch-thick, fresher-than-fresh, thresher shark steaks, enough to give everyone two steaks apiece, although he doubted the child could eat two all by herself. While Abdullah was musing over his culinary interests, he observed the Amir and Cynthia sneaking down below. His only concern was for his Master, because to him the girl was only just an inconsequential plaything.

IV. "Playtime":

Cynthia imagined herself at a palace ball with her Prince, who had come to take her away from her dreary life in Belfast. As they held hands and ran down the long hallway to His stateroom, she envisioned a horse-drawn carriage taking her to a faraway land. A land where there were carpets like the one in the Prince's study, carpets that flew. Her childish heart could not imagine this man hurting her or being like Marlin Thompson had been in the dead of night, while her drunken mother snored in the next room.

As His Highness lifted Cynthia onto His bed, she imagined trusting someone again. First, he probed her with His finger discovering that indeed her hymen was intact and then He came to the realization of how easy it would be for Him to deflower her. She wasn't even resisting Him and she hadn't gone all stiff like His cousin, Aamina Misha'al, to whom He had been wed in a brief ceremony at the Tuwaiq Palace, the previous Spring. He would have thought, after all, that Amira Aamina having been anointed with all those traditional oils and perfumes that She would have been more relaxed. Cynthia didn't smell like the perfuming oils of Arabia, she smelled like peaches and her beautiful blue eyes weren't tightly shut like Aamina's had been in Riyadh.

It had been an auspicious marriage, even by Saudi standards. Aamina was a member of the Shammar Tribe, which meant that She, like His Highness, was descended from one of the cadet branches of the family of al-Saud. Like the children of Israel, they were all the progeny of one patriarch, Muhammad ibn Saud and thus, they were eligible to be wed.

Though Cynthia was accustomed to inappropriate touching from the age of seven, she was still unaware of what always followed and so was acting composed and self-assured. Aamina had been instructed by older women about what always followed and She had also only been touched by older women; but only when they tweezed her pubic hairs. Cynthia still had all of hers; but since she was only a month away from her twelfth birthday, it was sparse and blonde. The Prince wanted to take Cynthia's panties off in order to see more of it; but there wasn't time.

He sat back on a chair near the bed contemplating His finger, sniffing it. "Yes, Peaches." This confirmed His Highness's view of Westerners, that they were wanton and to be disdained. The Amir thought to offer her father money for her. This is called in Arabic parlance, a "Mutah Marriage". While Aamina had been trying desperately not to move, Cynthia had, after He sat down in the chair, turned on her side and was leaning up on her elbow actually speaking to him. Americans certainly were brazen! Abdullah would definitely have to speak to her father, whichever man that was His Highness was uncertain.

"'R' we-ah gau-ehn tah cahtch mah fahsh?" *"Are we going to catch more fish?"* She queried batting her eyelashes and trying to make her voice seem lissome and beguiling rather than childish and squeaky. Amira Aamina had been veiled in translucent gauze made from threads of silver intermingled with threads of white silk. According to the strict protocols of Her people, She, had done everything She could to appear terrified. Aamina was no actress; Her fear was genuine, as was Her fainting and collapsing onto the bed. In spite of this, a little over nine months from the day They were wed, Her Highness presented the Amir with a son.

Cynthia could never become part of the royal family not even as a secondary wife or concubine; but He mused, perhaps He could hire her as a household servant; no! she was still too young. The Americans weren't yet civilized enough to allow for an outright purchase and she would be considered too young in the estimation of her infidel people to be allowed to "work" outside her homeland. He sniffed his finger again. "Yes, Peaches!" Then, He was startled from his reverie by a sharp knock at the door.

It was Abdullah: "Amir, Your presence is missed on deck." He said trying not to notice the little girl, who while adjusting one of the straps on her Mary Janes was making another unfortunate display of her panties.

The rest of the conversation between the Amir and Abdullah was in Arabic. His Highness inquired of Abdullah, who was both His butler and His Imam, if he would speak to Cynthia's father, whichever of the three men that was, the Amir was unsure. Abdullah asked His Highness whether the girl was still a virgin, and the Amir answered, "Yes" hiding His blushing face behind His right hand on which He wore the gold ring engraved with the first part of the Shahada, "There is no God except Allah..." These things had to be done precisely, delicately, very delicately and in keeping with the words of the Prophet.

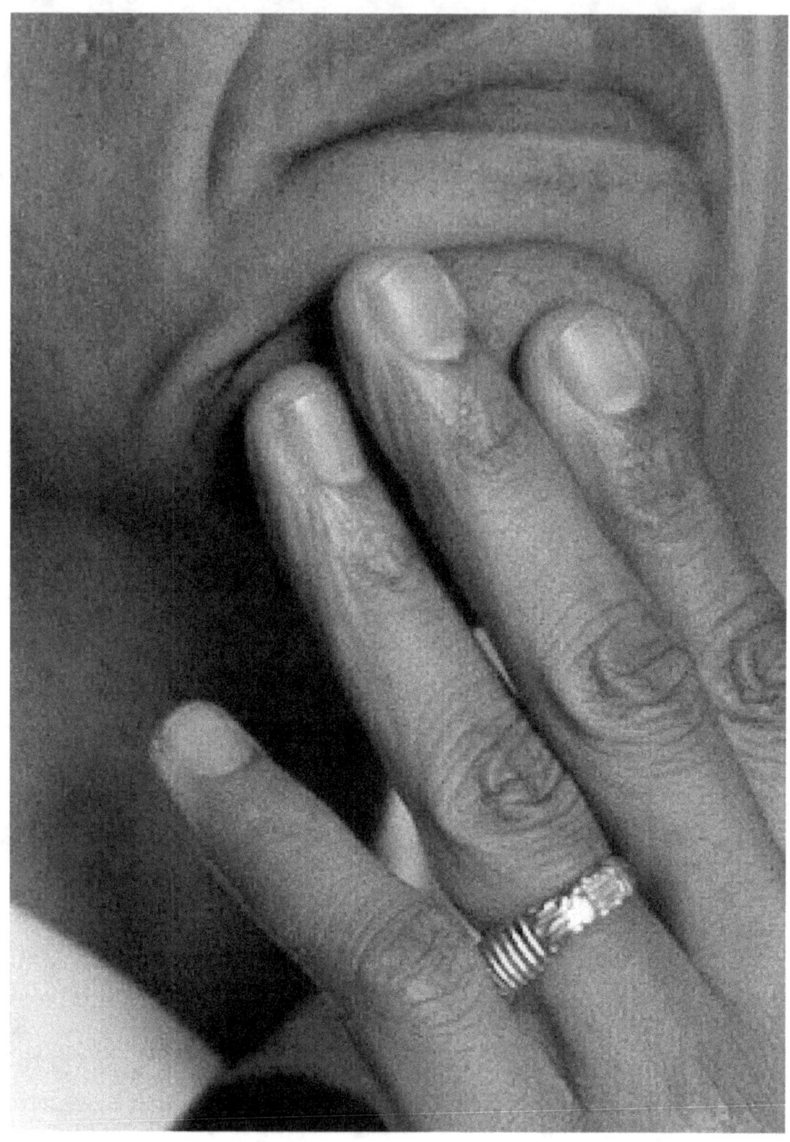

V. "Sumptuous Repast":

One of the crew cut open the shark and had begun washing its blood and entrails into the ocean. This bloody trail would bring other sharks; but it couldn't be avoided. Zyfler inquired aloud, "Do-ah you-ah A-rahbz lahk thah haht ahnd thah liv-vah?" *"Do you Arabs like the heart and the liver?"* He had barely noticed the Prince's and Cynthia's absence. They were both back on deck now; protective of their shoes and wary of slipping and falling into the blood, which was pooling and collecting in puddles on the deck.

The death of this large beast was an occasion of merriment to the Saudi crewmen and Abdullah already had the other parts of the banquet prepared, there was: hummus, tabouli, baba ghanoush, kibbie, falafel, samosas, pita bread and stuffed grape leaves. He started grilling nineteen, two-inch thick shark steaks on the propane stove in the galley and everything was fragrant with Mediterranean and Indian spices, limes, basil, coriander and turmeric. In the center of the eating area there was a tower of rice formed into little cakes with raisins and chick peas stuffed inside.

These people eat everything with their right hands; but their notorious hospitality caused them to remember to have forks for their guests. And everyone got a large soup spoon to scoop up the gravy made with clarified butter. This feast was spread out onto a white table cloth, which was placed directly on the floor of the dining room adjacent to the galley.

While at dinner Abdullah leaned over and asked Marlin Thompson, "Is she your daughter?" Before Roz could stop him, he replied, "Ayuh, sinz shay wahz siehx, Eeyah reck-kehn." *"Yes, since she was six, I recon."*

Mr. Prescott, being at the far end of the banquet and out of earshot of their talk, was unconcerned. He was also rather uncomfortable with this eating arrangement; but Cynthia thought it great fun like being at a picnic. Ross (Roz) Zyfler caught the inquiry about Cynthia; but it was already too late for him to interject himself and for the rest of the fishing expedition, Thompson would play the role of the father, even sleeping with his back to her state room door.

Abdullah made arrangements to meet Thompson in the wheelhouse, under the pretext of showing him the yacht's modern technology.

After a regal supper, the gigantic Arab whispered into Thompson's ear, "My master wishes to keep himself free from evils and corruptions by rewarding the father of the Mutah Bride and ensuring the preservation of her chastity by offering in payment: nineteen thousand dollars, which is a sacred number to my people, as a Bride Price. Abdullah cleared his throat and tried to remember the word Yankees used for sacred. Oh right: "Lucky". He said the English word "Lucky" to Marlin Thompson. This will preserve the honor of your house and your daughter's chastity. Do you understand? This will only be a temporary marriage and nothing will be taken from your daughter, except her virginity. So, you shouldn't worry that she will be harmed or become an adulteress."

Marlin Thompson definitely did not understand; but he did hear the words, "nineteen thousand dollars" put together with the unfamiliar words, "Bride Price". Feigning shock and horror, Thompson began calculating how to cheat Prescott and Zyfler out of as much money as possible. He would ask Abdullah to pay him two thousand up front and pay the remaining sixty-nine in one-hundred-dollar bills and two fifties to Zyfler. When the transaction was sealed and the yacht was at anchor, the three men left with Cynthia for Prescott's Cadillac where they divided the "Gahd Mon-nah" *Guide Money*.

Prescott watched while Zyfler counted out his own ten one hundred dollar bills and an additional ten one hundred dollar bills for his friend Thompson; but when Zyfler got to Prescott, he counted out only nine one hundred dollar bills with another fifty, "Eeyah-'ll pie you-ah thah ud-dah fif-tah nes' wahk", "*I'll pay you the other fifty next week*", Zyfler said; but when they got back to Thompson's rusty station wagon, they made arrangements to divide the six thousand dollars. In the traditional manner of Downeast business practice, at the end of the business transaction Zyfler continued to owe Prescott money; so, that Prescott would have a reason to seek Zyfler out once again, in order to get his fifty dollars back and thus another business transaction could commence.

When they got back to Belfast and had returned the Airstream to Tim Sample, Thompson and Zyfler divided the remainder of the "guide money". Zyfler paid out thirty, one-hundred-dollar bills to Thompson. They looked at one another and laughed the joke was played on Prescott; but it was also being played on Zyfler; who was unaware of the fraud which was being perpetrated upon him.

The arrangement as Zyfler understood it was to repeat the whole process again the following weekend; but on Monday afternoon, a truant Cynthia was traveling to Portland, Maine with her Uncle Marlin and Aunt Claudette. Claudette Kittredge took Cynthia to Jordan Marsh at the Maine Mall and bought her a Confirmation dress. There were racks of beautiful dresses and Aunt Claudette, who was always so business-like and practical; looked through all of them scowling and never even noticing the price tags. She held each satin and chiffon creation up under her "niece's" chin, frowned, shook her head and then put it back.

Remember this and always treasure this knowledge in your heart; Marlin Thompson was living with Claudette Kittredge. She knew what manner of man he was and she watched him like a hawk; because she had a daughter, Paulette, who was about twelve years old too. For the rest of Claudette Kittredge-Thompson's life, she would always say to herself as she viewed herself in her full-length, beveled-glass mirror, where she worshipped the only god she ever knew, "You-ah'r luk-kehn moe-ah ahnd moe-ah lahk Mah-lehn Thom-sun ev-ray day, Clawed-dot. You-ah'r eev-vahn wehr- rehn hahz lahs' naymb nah, 'r'-n't you-ah?" *"You're looking more and more like Marlin Thompson every day,* Claudette. You're even wearing his last name now, aren't you?" **This guilt always haunted Claudette, it never left her side, because guilt about past sin is the devil's favorite tool.**

One Sunday, Susan and Claudette chanced to meet at church. This was before Susan had ever laid eyes on Cynthia. It was the "Jesus Never Fails" Baptist church in Portland, Maine. This church was right next to City Hall and Susan passed by it several times while she was homeless. Susan was trying to pick out an alternative Sunday worship service to the Way Ministry and this church was very welcoming of young children. They actually had a room facing the service, which was sound-proofed and called "the Cry Room". So, when Susan said something that made them reject her right away; she was shocked. A wealthy attendee, named Claudette Kittredge-Thompson was at a Sunday "meet and greet" and struck up a conversation with Susan. Claudette said "Eeyah'em ah gudd pah-sahn, Sue-zahn; bahd, Eeyah sumb-tahmz do-ah bahd thengz." *"I'm a good person, Susan; but I sometimes do bad things."*

Susan replied, "I don't know Claudette, maybe you're a bad person that sometimes does good things." Claudette had disclosed to Susan Asta, all her guilt over this incident at Jordan Marsh, telling Susan how she got Cynthia ready for the Prince. Just then an older woman, who knew that Claudette was one of the "right kind of people to join the church", meaning that she put plenty of money in the collection plate. This older, sainted woman stepped in and rescued Claudette from an outspoken Susan, who was feeling the need to disclose even more truths to Claudette. This church unanimously decided never to have Susan back again, while making the decision that Claudette would be a very good candidate for membership. Neither Susan nor Walter Mailen were their type of Christians. She was a tactless, blunt-instrument of a person, while he was too insane to fit in. They were too busy "playing at church" to accept either of them. They realized his state of mental unbalance and so they pointedly told him to "stay ah-wahy" **"stay away".**

Cynthia wanted every dress on the rack. She thought, "Thahs sehz awel fahr meh; Eeyah caunt bah-leave ehd." *"This is all for me; I can't believe it."* Cynthia desperately hoped for the lavender organza; but she also loved a pleated, pink chiffon dress, which had only one shoulder strap made all of white-ribbon rosebuds entwining around one another and holding up the bodice. The little girl's heart beat faster and then seemed to float up into her mouth. Claudette finally acted the adult and chose an antique- white, long-sleeved, French-lace and polyester-satin dress that was marked down thirty percent. With the money, she saved she bought Cynthia a pair of open-toed crystal and gold shoes with one-inch heels.

Uncle Marlin wasn't sitting and holding Aunt Claudette's purse; he was racing out to the parking lot to drive his old, rust-bucket to the Cadillac dealer. When he got back he was driving a 1973 two-toned, melon and white, pumpkin carriage to take his Cinderella to the ball. Her "parents" drove "their little princess" directly from the Maine Mall to the Prince's rented palace, which overlooked the New Meadows Cove. When they pulled up to the Happy Nook, Abdullah came out to meet them in the circle driveway. Then he led them to the room with the Donegal carpet and Claudette Kittredge thought, "Wh-ah cauhn't Eeyah hahv ah cah-paht lahk thahs?" *"Why can't I have a carpet like this?"* Claudette's avarice over this carpet not withstanding, Abdullah brought in nineteen shrink-wrapped bundles of one hundred-dollar bills and a cup of tea for the "Mother of the Mutah Bride". Marlin Thompson took the money out to his car and locked it in the trunk and then fell asleep in the back seat, enjoying the new car smell while Claudette fell asleep in the Prince's comfy chair. He had wisely bought a plush, cotton towel at Jordan Marsh for Cynthia to sit on "afterwards". [**How could they fall asleep you ask? The way that all evil people sleep. Very well, thank you! There is nothing that Satan guards more carefully than the sleep of persons who have numbed their consciences and are doing his will.**] They waited for nine hours, until the Prince's appetite was satisfied. The Prince took Cynthia's panties off; but He never took off her dress, he wanted to enjoy this dress just as much as he enjoyed this child. When Abdullah returned "her daughter" to her, Claudette kissed the child on the forehead and Marlin Thompson came back into the house and emphatically and joyfully hugged Cynthia, lifting her up from the floor as he once did, when she was very young. Then "her parents" escorted her back to their new car.

The little girl's pristine and gossamer dress was now a white-lace ruin. Marvin Thompson spread the newly purchased towel over the back seat, after all he didn't want Cynthia to stain the new upholstery. As they drove the moaning, Mutah Bride back to their home above the tavern, Claudette thought about how she would explain this truancy to Charlene, the teachers at Cynthia's school and if she asked, her own daughter, Paulette. She vowed right there and then, not to let Paulette out of her sight and certainly not to let her go on any fishing expeditions with Marvin and Roz. But, most of all she wanted to cover up Thompson's terrible crime.

She took Cynthia to her bedroom upstairs, then took off the dress, laying a fresh towel down on the bed and made Cynthia lie down on it. Then, she hand-washed the dress in Woolite at the sink in her private bathroom. The words, "Out! Out! Damned Spot!" came to mind, Claudette knew it was from some Shakespearean play; but couldn't remember if it was Hamlet or Macbeth.

Then the object was to get the little girl back to Charlene's, without Chary noticing anything. When she had dressed the sleeping child in Paulette's own clothes. She carried her back to the car and made her lie down in the back seat again on a towel; then she and Thompson carried their little darling into the house and into Cynthia's own bed. Fortunately, Charlene was sleeping off quite a few of the beers that Roz and Thompson had put in her refrigerator before they ever went on their expedition to

Bath. When the dress had its stain thoroughly removed at the bathroom sink, Claudette hung it to dry in the forward compartment of the camper.

The words "Bride Price" got Thompson thinking, "Wh-ah naught prah-zent thahs fine-nahn-chall bown-tea tah Claw-dot; ah-lung wid thah ehn-gayj-men' rahng, thahd Eeyah baud har frumb Zales". *"Why not present this financial bounty to Claudette; along with the engagement ring that I bought her from Zales".* While the girls were shopping at the Maine Mall. Every penny of his Guide Money had gone into purchasing this dress, the ring and a down-payment on his new car. Marlin Thompson determined to have it also secure for him a half-interest in Claudette's Tavern. Zyfler was pretty irate when he discovered that he had been had and by his old friend. But, if fishing had taught Roz Zyfler anything it was that it didn't pay to cry over the one that got away.

Chapter Thirteen
NOR'EASTER

The icy chill of December winds come at gale-force and frost-biting capacity in a life-threatening blizzard known to Mainers as a "Nor'east-tah". Even Alaska isn't as cold as the coast of Maine, during a "Nor'easter". Mike wanted to avoid traversing the Great Salt Marsh in dead of winter. A car that hit a patch of black ice on that road could slide sideways right into the Marsh and be trapped there for hours. If this should happen, during the night and there were injuries; Mike knew from personal experience in the Webber Hospital Emergency Room, that the driver's body might not be found, until the next morning. Walking back from the deepest part of the Marsh at night and in winter was suicide.

If you could see a house light and had car trouble in the Marsh, you might have a chance; walking to it, if you were dressed warmly and you hadn't stepped into too many marshy pools of muck. If there was no house light; you were sunk. Then your only hope was to walk back to Biddeford, praying that you wouldn't lose a foot or both feet to frostbite. Young people had a chance; but anyone who was in anyway infirmed was lost. People in Biddeford would remind an intended traveler, "puhd ohn you-ah gau- lah-shayz". *"put on your galoshes"*. Before the hapless soul ventured forth to Portland or anywhere at night.

The Biddeford-Saco area provides a break in the roadway along Route

One, from Portland to the Rachel Carson's Wild Life Refuge; the Scarborough Marsh is only a small portion of the Great Salt Marsh between Saco and South Portland. This was a formidable commute that Mike wished to avoid and this is why he traded his secure position and his close friendships established in Biddeford, for a new part-time job at the Maine Medical Center, MMC. Finally, his over-long commute to the Mercy Hospital School of Nursing had come to an end.

With all of their attentions focused on Mike's nursing career, the young couple picked out a most-affordable, two-room, kitchenette on the corner of State and Pine Streets in Portland, Maine. Stanley Adams, the landlord inquired whether they would be having children. Mike and Susan replied giggling, "Well, of course we want to have children, but right now while Mike is in Nursing School, it's a bit impractical." Susan intended to get pregnant in time for Mike's graduation; but they didn't inform Stanley Adams of this, because they thought it quaint that he should have asked and it was none of his business.

Mike's final year in school and his auxiliary training in emergency medicine were going to take up all of their combined efforts and finances. Their tired VW van had to be traded in and being the practical couple that they were; they chose a small fuel- efficient little Toyota Corolla. It wasn't until the night of December 21st, 1978 during the worst blizzard in recent Maine history, that Mike and Susan's plans began to go awry.

It was during the "great blizzard of '78", when the snow in Downeast Maine was reaching to the windowsills and its roofs were collapsing under the weight of all that snow, that Mike Asta decided to sojourn to the Boston City Hospital to attend a required medical seminar on triage. Snow is a staple of the Maine lifestyle; complaining about it is an activity strictly frowned upon by long-time Maine folk.

Downeast Mainers view snow the way Upcountry Mainers view black flies. Snow is a necessary part of the Maine existence making life just difficult enough to chase away the out-a-staters at least during the times that they shouldn't be in Maine, namely the interval between Labor Day and Memorial Day. The summer months are the only time, when out-a-staters are tolerated by Mainers, unless we consider the skiers that enjoy the snows of Sugarloaf, Saddleback and Shawnee Peak. But when a real "Nor'east-tah" hits, people that have somewhere else to be, pack up and pack it in. It is the difficult winters that make the people of Maine so hardy and secure in the knowledge that the "Flaht-lahnd-dahz" *"Flat-landers"* will leave before things get too bad.

So, Mike and Susan's tenacity was unexpected as was their child-like exuberance, playing in the mountains of snow in the parking lot behind their Portland apartment. They threw snowballs at each other and brushed off both their tiny car and the cars on either side of them. Mike cheerfully swept Stanley Adams' roof as Susan brought out hot chocolate for both of them.

Mike never asked Mr. Adams for anything and Stanley Adams was happy to have someone help him with his snow for nothing. The sidewalks in front of the building and all the way to the Maine Medical Center were shoveled by Mike and Susan, who considered it their civic duty to help people get down the street in the direction of Maine's best medical facility. They also did the steps in front of their building, but Portland was running out of places to put the snow, and there were huge piles of snow on both sides of the walkway.

Susan turned over in the bed which was part of the cheap fold-out couch furnished with the studio apartment. Mike didn't see how this sort of sleeping arrangement was going to help his already bad back and Susan ran her fingers threw his hair and took off her nightgown pressing her breasts against the soft, reddish hairs on his muscular chest.

Mike hadn't actually worked out since he had been a farm hand two years ago; but he had really blossomed since their marriage, sprouting more chest hair and getting defined pectoral muscles. It turned Susan on and she kissed him passionately on the mouth. He was beyond arousal putting his arms around her lower body and drawing her to him in an embrace of dominance and passion. They knew that they wanted to have children and this was her most fertile time. So, they were breathless eager to merge with one another.

Mike got on top of Susan and sucked her breasts, making long stroking motions with his hands all up and down her thighs, then he fastened his mouth on her clitoris and began to stimulate her nether regions with his tongue. She opened her legs to him and when he entered her with a sudden thrust, she locked her legs behind his back drawing him into her further. The climax of their lovemaking was the beginning of a new life. Mike's sperm was released into Susan's vagina, purposely unencumbered by any contraceptive.

They really loved one another and wanted their lovemaking to culminate in a child. As his sperm cells fought each other for the privilege of making the trip through Susan's cervix and down her fallopian tube carrying them along to seek out the ovum which she had just released. The joy in what they were doing and how beautiful it was filled both of them with deep, unremitting passion. Their lovemaking served both as an act of procreation and also, cemented their hearts together in the matrimonial union.

To Mike and Susan making love was a little like making a batch of cookies, you always had more of it, when you were finished than when you began. When he awoke the next morning to start his day, Mike thought about the night of passion he had enjoyed with his beloved wife.

Susan was truly the person with whom he wanted to spend the rest of his life. He could hardly wait to find out if their lovemaking had resulted in a little son or daughter. If it hadn't, he was going to keep trying. Mike figured that it would take several months of this sort of thing to get Susan pregnant. Because she had already had four miscarriages, he was afraid to put her through it again if things weren't just right. As he got his uniform on for work and she prepared breakfast, he noted that a bond had developed between them was much stronger than the bond they had established when they were married. This was a covenant in which they cooperated with God, Himself to bring new life into the world.

He came up behind her while she was cooking the bacon and eggs and told her how much he loved her in the most physical way he could. Several times while getting ready for work, they had stopped to kiss one another and talk about what they were going to do when he returned to their love nest at the end of the day.

Over the next few months, Mike and Susan spent hours talking about their impending family. Whether they wanted a boy or a little girl and then agreeing that it didn't matter as long as the baby was healthy. Mike did his class homework at the kitchen table and Susan helped him by looking up the medications that his fictitious patients were taking in their PDR. She dutifully noted their interactions and possible contraindications, typing up a paper for his pharmacology class.

Susan was also doing some independent study of her own. Mike had encouraged her to begin reading the Bible and she spent the long hours while he was at work and she was at home without him, working at the kitchen table reading and contemplating the words of this ancient text. It seemed to Susan that she had read this whole thing before. Being brought up as a practicing Catholic, she had listened while the priest read from the Epistles and the Gospels every Sunday.

So, it was with a certain amount of consternation that she resisted Mike's implication that, "a person that hasn't read the Bible cover to cover, simply wasn't educated". She had read everything from the "Kazi Dawa-Samdup" translation of, "the Tibetan Book of the Dead" to Arnold Toynbee's twelve volume tome, "A Study of History". Susan had memorized a line from the Tibetan Book of the Dead. She thought about it now, "Such is the nature of truth, that all it asks and all it needs is the privledge of being heard. Truth stands out from all the world's lies; like light from a single candle stands out in the deepest, darkest cave."

She wondered if there would be any such truths in the Holy Bible. Mike had presented her with a copy of the New English Translation of the Bible; but it bothered her that he would call her uneducated? How could she be uneducated when she was so well-read? Well, he wasn't a judgmental or confrontational person, far from it, Mike was a Quaker. So, it was as dutifully as she had packed up her belongings and moved to the State of Maine, that Susan set about tackling the Bible.

After returning from class at the Mercy Hospital School of Nursing, Mike breathlessly and enthusiastically informed Susan that he had met some people who were just perfect for her. They seemed to know the answers to a number of questions that they had both been asking about Genesis, Leviticus and Job and they wanted to have Mike and Susan over for a meeting at their house that evening. The meeting was called a "Twig Fellowship" of the Way.

Could Susan come too? Mike was prepared to go without her, in case she wasn't feeling well. Susan had been throwing up in the morning and Mike ecstatically took it as a sign that she had caught. He hoped that Thanksgiving Day would be a day of thanks for more than just America's liberty, prosperity and peace; but also, an occasion to thank God for a little son or daughter. Susan said she would come to the meeting and even if she wasn't able to hold anything down, there might be an occasion for her to listen and ask some pertinent questions.

Mike wanted to know how a bunch of ignorant shepherds could possibly have known exactly what to do about quarantining contagion. And Susan wanted to know if Moses had had access to Pharaonic papyrus scrolls; because she knew that the legend of Gilgamesh had been disseminated throughout the ancient world and thought that there must have been something of this Sumerian myth in late-bronze-age Egyptian hands by the time of Moses.

These were questions that the Way Ministry was not ready to handle and they looked for more personal inquiries than the pursuit of pure knowledge for its own sake. How could they have known, that this happy young couple had neither vices nor spiritual problems and were only praying for two things: a healthy little boy or girl and an RN for Mike both coming next June?

Besides his class work, Mike had four hours of unpaid floor-time at Mercy Hospital every day and then there was his night job at MMC. Mike was a straight-A student and they both wanted to keep it that way. He would walk between the two hospitals and his home, which was midway between them every day. He was as fit as any young man of twenty-seven could be and he loved how the night air in Maine smelled. Sort of an ocean breeze, intermixed with pine and maybe cherry.

Susan typed Mike's class papers at the kitchen table and because they hoped that he would stay on the Dean's List until graduation, they applied themselves to the pursuit of his good grades. That's why it was such good news that Susan found a full-time job assembling toggle switches for Mr. Coffee Machines at the South Portland Switch Company Factory out on Route One. Unfortunately, this didn't leave them much time to be together. That's why they felt that every moment that they could be alone was a joyous occasion looked forward to with relish and jealously guarded.

Physical closeness to one another in their few hours together was something planned for and cherished. Their lives together, his nursing career and their impending family; all of their hopes and dreams were coming true. Mike wanted to make a difference in the world, he wanted what he did with his life to help others and Susan wanted their child to be a person whom she could shape into a leader of people. Someone who would really change the world.

Chapter Fourteen
A NEW BUSINESS IS BORN

When Marlin Thompson drove up to her house in a new Cadillac towing behind it a 1966 Airstream Safari Camper, Charlene Hickey thought how unfortunate she had been to have lost him just before he came into this windfall. Zyfler knew that if Thompson had a Cadillac Coup de Ville, the jewel that bought it for him was already gone; but Thompson was able to smooth Zyfler's ruffled feathers by offering him a partnership in this camper, which his drinking, fishing and hunting buddy: Tim Sample sold to him. After all, there were plenty of other men who would pay to be Cynthia's first and considering her narrow hips; Zyfler reasoned that a ball of cotton or a gauze compress soaked in Cynthia's own blood was all that was required to convince them that she had been deflowered again. Zyfler only needed to take a little blood from his very cooperative niece, then insert the blood-soaked compress into her vaginal canal. Exploiting this child came easily to Zyfler. Before the winter weather set in and made a camping excursion a ridiculous ruse, that wouldn't have even fooled her drunken mother, Roz Zyfler became a rich man.

Cynthia's two "daddies" would take her into the forward compartment of the camper and first bleed her a little with a lancet and then stuff the gauze compress into her vagina, then they would present her to the wealthy gentleman wearing the beautiful, white-lace dress. Knowing no difference, the man would take her for a virgin.

One thing Maine people could do in the wintertime was haul firewood. Next, Thompson showed up with a new 1973 Ford F-350 Super Camper Special Ranger; one-ton truck with an automatic transmission, heavy-duty suspension, and only nineteen miles on the odometer. It was a gift for his friend Roz. At least, his friend Roz would be parking it in his own driveway and not in the lot behind Claudette's, which was now paved with asphalt and packed with the cars of revealers every night. The gift of this truck, which was registered in Thompson's name made Marlin Thompson a full partner in Zyfler's firewood business, without obligating him to cut, haul or sell any firewood at all.

Claudette and Marlin invested in a big-screen television set to attract more customers to their tavern and there were three new draft-beer taps along the bar to keep the customers happy. Everyone benefitted from Cynthia's misery, except Cynthia herself. Charlene even got a part-time job at the tavern waiting tables and sweeping up. Cynthia however was still too young to work in a tavern and except for the alluring costumes they bought for her to wear in Bath, there was nothing in any of this for her personally; except that dress which she kept and used repeatedly to make herself appear more of an ingénue.

Eventually though, like an aging child star, Cynthia became too old to sell her virginity and the dress was becoming too tight on her now, anyway. Other girls in Cynthia's class at school, began to have beautiful dresses of their own. When Cynthia's dress no longer fit her, other girl's parents were buying them dresses to wear to the dances and balls that Maine people cherish as a vestige of their unique culture. Cynthia wasn't allowed to go to these dances, balls and chaperoned parties. She wasn't allowed to have young, unmarried men call on her. She was sheltered. Her parents were strict. But, every summer she would be taken to Bath on the weekends to have sexual relations with older men that she would never see again.

Marlin Thompson was now a successful tavern owner with a new wife; Roz Zyfler was the owner of a fifty-acre wood lot just outside of Belfast and was driving around in a new, 1973 Ford F350. On its side, it advertised the business: **"Zyfler's Firewood"**, **"BURN THE BEST WITH ZYFLER"**; but when spring came again this truck was used for another purpose, serving to haul a camper to Bath on the weekends.

That same year, a new store opened on Front Street selling wood stoves, fireplaces and kiln-dried firewood, it was named, "Zyfler's Stoves", using the same slogan: **"BURN THE BEST WITH ZYFLER"**. At last, Cynthia could participate in a "family business", that could actually legally employ her. Zyfler had become an established businessman in Belfast and had even joined the Chamber of Commerce, as did Thompson. They were beginning to joke that soon they would become richer than Lionel Prescott.

Cynthia started wearing her "whore clothes" even to school, where she was between quitting and being expelled. Then tragedy struck, Cynthia was pregnant, time to see the doctor. Planned Parenthood didn't yet have a satellite office near Belfast; so, they had to take her to Boston. It was 1976 and school nurses didn't as yet take high school students to Planned Parenthood for abortions without their parent's knowledge or consent.

Since she had financed two thriving businesses, which couldn't afford a scandal, Cynthia; she started calling herself: "Cyn"; left Boston with a six-month supply of Ortha Novum One and instructions not to have intercourse, until after her next period. Keeping track of Cyn's periods, was a daunting task for Zyfler, who had two businesses to run and a new, log home under construction. What to do? What to do?

Charlene was drunk all the time now and Claudette couldn't afford to keep her on at the tavern. Zyfler was sick of supporting her. She after all was not actually his wife; but he should have refrained from building the new house, before he decided to ditch Charlene. She went to an attorney and got half. Zyfler found a way to "buy Charlene's share" and a very clever scheme it was! There was a new man in Bath, a fellow named Binny who was "courting" Cyn.

It was 1977 Cyn was sixteen and able to drop out of high school, she was also too irresponsible to take her pill every day. What was Roz to do? Binny offered to take Cyn off his hands for eleven thousand dollars. The girl could make more than that in a month and Zyfler said that he just didn't know; so Binny upped his offer to eighteen thousand, if Roz and Thompson would throw in the camper.

They thought, why not it was getting old now anyway and they had really gotten their money's worth out of it. Behind his friend, Marlin's back, Roz pushed for a little more cash for himself. Binny said he would slip Roz an ounce of cocaine worth maybe one thousand dollars. So, in addition to his half: the nine thousand dollars, Zyfler would get an ounce of cocaine worth a thousand. That is, if he could just get Thompson to go along. They exchanged the money, the drugs and the camper with its pink slip made out to Cynthia. Now like a used car, Binny owned Cyn.

They had avoided getting caught with Cyn in the camper, which was both a product of knowing the right people in Bath, namely Lionel Prescott and paying off the right people in Bath, namely the city supervisor, the city mayor and the chief of police. True, Roz had to pay Planned Parenthood for one abortion; but they were a swell organization and never asked any questions about Cyn's being underage.

This had been a real money train for Roz, Thompson and Charlene Hickey; but now it was over. Marlin had sold Cyn once, now it was Roz's turn. After all, he reasoned, "Far-ehz-far" *"Fair Is Fair"*. Never did Charlene Hickey dream to question any of these trips to Bath in the camper; perhaps she didn't care? However, when it came time for a division of property with Zyfler, she happily agreed to return to her dilapidated, roach-infested rental becoming cash rich, but house poor. Charlene had been for many years, an alcoholic; but now she was also addicted to cocaine and she didn't care about anything anymore. Why not let Roz have his new log home in the Maine woods?

One last time, Roz Zyfler came over to Charlene's and they talked about the good times, their family traditions and all that they had been through together. She sighed deeply and smiled sweetly up at him saying, "Roz, you-ah cauhn awe-wahz cahm bahk!" *"Roz, you can always come back!"* and he smiled back at her as he spread the lines of white powder onto her Plexiglas-covered lobster-trap coffee table with a razor blade. Rolling up a hundred-dollar bill, he passed it to Charlene, who used it to snort the white powder passing the hundred back to Roz again. He sniffed the powder into his nostril, it wasn't cocaine. It was a mixture of milk powder and rat poison. He tried to get to the telephone to dial 911; white foam bubbling out of his nose and mouth. He looked back at Charlene; she was lying on the floor, choking. He put the receiver to his ear; the line was dead. "Thah lion wahz deed!" *"The line was dead!"* he thought. The phone had been disconnected. Charlene had neglected to pay the bill. Well after all, why would she pay; she didn't have anyone to call, never having cultivated any real friends.

Chapter Fifteen
DECEMBER 21, 1978

Mike was driving south on Route One toward the Scarborough Marsh on his way to a triage class at Boston Medical Center. The trauma unit at the BMC was the finest in New England and the nursing students that were going into emergency medicine wanted to learn triage from a hot trauma center where there might be gunshot wounds as well as multiple car accidents. So, it was with this in mind that Mike propelled his tiny car down the icy road. As he entered the area of the wetland, he saw the 1968 Chevy C10 Black Pickup truck swerving into his lane. The driver, an unemployed clam digger on his yearly welfare furlough, was drunk behind the wheel. Mike was frozen into inaction as the big black behemoth swerved and then wove back and forth between the lanes of the roadway.

Arthur Bickford was dazed and seeing double as he crossed the double yellow line and headed for Mike's Toyota. Mike lurked, when he saw the pick-up truck coming towards him and then wishing for a larger, sturdier vehicle he attempted to steer the little car onto the shoulder. Feeling the first jolt of pain as the front bumper of the truck rammed through his driver's side door, Mike realized his mistake. A peel of splintered glass and shredded steel showered the inside of the little car with projectiles, that preceded the truck's entrance into his front seat.

A torrent of curses rained down from Arthur Bickford's lips as the blowback from the collision cut his head and broke his arm. Afterward, he got on his CB radio and called for an ambulance, for himself of course. The man whose car had merged with his truck was not even an afterthought for Bickford. When the ambulance arrived at the Maine Medical Center, Mike was beyond help and Arthur Bickford was having his head bandaged and his broken arm set by the friends and coworkers of the fellow whom he had just killed.

Susan heard the phone ring and sat up in bed. It was Mrs. Parisian, the admissions nurse at the MMC Emergency Room. The nurse was crying and Susan was alarmed and tried to comfort her. Mrs. Parisian said, "Sue-zahn, cahm tah thah 'Mah- jhen-see Rahm; Mahk'z behn ehn ahn ahc-sid-den' ahnd we-ah coahd-'nah sahv huhm." *"Susan, come to the Emergency Room, Mike's been in an accident and we couldn't save him."*

"What?" Susan said, "I can't understand you!" "Mrs. Parisian, what are you saying?" Mrs. Parisian hung up the phone; but since it was a party line, all of the other members of Susan and Mike's party-line group began to chime in, "Sue-zahn, you-ah shahd gaht dahwn tah thah 'Mah-jehn-see Rahm ahnd say ehf Mahk'z ok!" *"Susan, you should get down to that Emergency Room and see if Mike's ok!"* Susan said, "Well, I don't know Irene, there's a blizzard going on outside and I'm three months pregnant." Irene, Susan's call-party member said, "Sue-zahn, you-ah nehd tah gau tah thah 'Mah- jehn-see Rahm ride nah, thahs maht beh thah own-lay 'r' lahs' tahm you-ah gaht tah say Mahk." *"Susan, you need to go to the Emergency Room right now, this might be the only or last time you get to see Mike."* She was right. Susan pulled her coat over her nightgown and put on her husband's long underwear bottoms, a wide-brim, floppy, fur hat, a muffler and a pair of red-velvet, rabbit-fur mittens and a pair of fur slipper-boots, that she had bought against the cruel Maine winters and headed towards the Maine

Medical Center, MMC on foot, bracing herself, because she didn't want to slip and fall while pregnant.

Rounding the corner of Pine and Brackett Streets, she walked in between two towering banks of packed snow, Susan tried to gain sure footing on the newly fallen snow, making looking at her feet a positive necessity. When she saw the distant lights of the MMC, she thought to herself, "There can't be anything wrong with Mike, besides he always says he inherited the luck of the Irish from his mom and God wouldn't let anything happen to him, ever."

When Susan entered the Emergency Room, there were Dr. Chambliss and Dr. Gordon both crying; Mrs. Parisian went over and hugged her. They had all wanted to save Mike. The horror of it was beginning to settle in on her with the density of smoke. There on the gurney facing the door, sat Arthur Bickford, his head wreathed in bandages and his left arm broken and in a sling.

Mrs. Parisian made arrangements to send him to the Ex-Ray Department. Mike's body had been covered with a sheet and was lying in a draped cubicle next to Bickford's. Susan approached with hesitation and repulsion. She didn't want it to be Mike lying there. She didn't want to have to face him. She and Mike had quarreled before he left in the car, "You don't have to do this in the middle of a snow-storm, Mike, you can go this spring when it's nicer out", she argued.

"But that's just going to prolong my graduation from nursing school and with a baby coming in June, we'll need that nurse's pay and we have so many bills, Susan", he pleaded and then stormed out the door. You couldn't reason with Mike when he was in one of these "plow-through this thing" snits. You just had to get out of his way and let him do whatever it was that he was going to do.

Susan breathed a sigh, which turned into a shudder and then into sobbing. Mrs. Parisian pointed at a man and said, "Hah'z thah Juan; ehd wahz huhm ehn thah ud- dah vee-ah-col, ah bahg blahck trahck" *"He's the one; it was him in the other vehicle, a big black truck"*. Susan focused her eyes on Arthur Bickford, who was leaning back on the gurney in a defensive posture. This had definitely been the worst night of his life, worse than the day that his wife left him taking the three kids, worse than the night they repossessed his truck and he had to go bail it out, for twelve hundred dollars. This was the absolutely worst evening of his life. He was really feeling sorry for himself, when he looked up into the eyes of this young woman. She was definitely not feeling sorry for Bickford. She was angry.

He became alarmed and said, "You-ah jehs'gaht ah-wahy frumb meh lay-dee." *"You just get away from me lady."*

"Are you the man who killed my Mikey?"

"You-ah cahm nee-nah meh lay-dee ahnd Eeyah-'ll sahck you-ah ride ehn thah fahus." *"You come near me lady and I'll sock you right in the face."*

Through God's mercy and grace, two orderlies came and rescued Bickford. Who was very relieved to be going to Ex-Ray, while Susan collapsed into Dr. Chambliss' arms. "I knew he shouldn't have gone tonight", she said to everyone in the room and to no one in particular. Then great heaving sighs of pain filled the room as she cried out her soul. The Emergency Room Staff cried too; Mike had been their crewmember and friend.

Chapter Sixteen
FIGHTING BACK

Susan awoke to an empty bed. It wasn't really a bed; it was a studio couch in an efficiency apartment, which was convenient to two places that Mike Asta would no longer visit. It was the morning of December 22, 1978. Three days before Christmas with tons of snow outside and no tree or presents inside. There would have been no place to put them anyway. This was the most cramped little apartment in which she had ever lived. At first, Susan wanted to believe that last night had just been a bad dream. But Mike wasn't there and that was testament to the reality that it had not been a dream. She struggled to get out of bed and then she went into the bathroom. Mike wasn't there either.

What to do now? Maybe just take the whole day off. She had started to read the Bible; maybe she should just immerse herself in that for the day? Then the phone rang. It was Irene, one of the ladies on Susan and Mike's party line, she wanted the skinny on what happened last night. Susan wasn't in the mood to share a juicy story with this busybody. So, she diplomatically told Irene that she had a lot of appointments that morning and hung up.

Then she called the MMC and then her sister, Elsie, in Illinois. Susan's parents were both deceased, and so was Mike's father, Paul. She would also have to call Mike's mom, Jean, who was now living in a nursing home.

How was Susan going to deal with all the expenses of burying her husband so far from family, home and money? She had to find out what kind of condition the car was in and then, she just didn't know.

Mike's body was probably in the morgue at the Maine Medical Center. What was Susan going to do to make funeral arrangements? She just didn't want to deal with it. Besides she was terrified that if she dwelt on this whole subject too intensely; she might miscarry again and then there would be nothing left of her Mikey.

Above all Susan needed to stay calm and stay off of her feet for a few days. She realized she was going to have to have prenatal care if this baby was going to have a good start in life. She tumbled back into their bed and began reading her Bible in the place where she had left off the night before. Susan was in The Book of Psalms and was intrigued by the word, Sheol, which appeared over and over again in the text. This was the New English Bible translation and for some reason, they had left this word in the familiar. Susan was determined to find out what the word meant; but by reading it in context.

She had read enough ancient books to know that they eventually told you what their words meant. She also called the hospital and found out that she had four days to claim Mike's body. Dr. Chambliss said that there might be some kind of fund to help her give Mike a decent burial. What about his student loans and his tuition payments to the Mercy Hospital? She made an appointment with the Dean of Students, A Sister of Mercy named Carmelia Marie, and then she got back to reading Psalm 139 and underlining parts of it. She thought about how "fearfully and wonderfully" her unborn child was being made inside her womb.

She decided right then and there, to name the child, Paul, after Mike's father if it was a boy. Susan hadn't as yet picked out a girl's name. A towing company called her and asked if she could come to the junk yard to see their car. A believer from the Way Ministry, named Ralph Magwood, drove her to the junkyard in his old Mercedes Benz sedan. When they arrived at the junk yard, Susan saw a flat-bed truck also arrived with her tiny Toyota automobile completely merged with a big, black, Chevy C10, pickup truck. The truck was only slightly damaged; but the car was totaled. Susan asked for the license plate number of the truck and then went through the phone book and found the number for an organization called, "MOTHERS AGAINST DRUNK DRIVING, CASCO BAY AREA"

She called them, and made an appointment. Then she wondered aloud what Bickford's blood alcohol level had been the night before. Susan called Mrs. Parisian and asked her if they had taken it, she said. "Eeyah" *"Yes"*. This would be good evidence for court. The reading was **0.49.** Mrs. Parisian said, "We-ah hahd tah sahnd huhm dah-reck-lay tah ah dah-tahx-ah-fah-kay-shun sen-tah. Hahz blahd al-cah-hall lah-vel wahz awe-mos' lee-thal. Eeyah baht ehf Eeyah hahd toad huhm, 'you-ah dahsahv tah dahy fahr whahd you-ah'v jehs' dahn'. Eeyah coahd hahv axe-ah-cute-dead huhm wid jehs' ah-nah-thah thrah fing-gahs ahv wahs-gay. He-ah prahb-bahb-blay wahd hahv drahnk ehd tah!" *"We had to send him directly to a detoxification center. His blood-alcohol level was almost lethal. I bet if I had told him, 'you deserve to die for what you've just done', I could have executed him with just another three-fingers of whiskey. He probably would have drunk it too!"* Mrs. Parisian was angry, and she shouldn't have revealed this information to a party to the case; but neither of them were thinking like that and Susan would keep her guilty secret.

Chapter Seventeen

"PARTING IS SUCH SWEET SORROW"

Cyn made the mandatory trip back to Belfast for the funeral. Uncle Marlin and Aunt Claudette were there, wearing black, Claudette was weeping. Cyn was obliged to cry as well; but couldn't quite fake it. They had hushed up the evidence that was left at the scene by bribing Charlene's landlord to burn the place down. He couldn't rent it anymore, anyway. It was in ill-repair, hadn't been painted in years, had two tiny bedrooms, a narrow living room, a leaky roof, an oil and gas stove which frequently went out and it also needed to be fumigated.

Marlin Thompson found Charlene's metal recipe boxes inside her boat-shaped breadbox with her other boat-shaped kitchen canisters. He relieved them of the money hidden inside them and bequeath the crockery to his niece the only real relative Charlene had ever had. The money in the metal card box which had been secreted inside the canister, he would keep for himself. This crockery set was greatly valued by both the Hickey women and was part of that custom crockery set that he had been unable to steal from her so long ago. He knew that Cynthia would cherish them and he wanted to be sure she got them. Behind each of Charlene's old bread recipes, she had secreted away several hundred-dollar bills. This crockery canister set and the metal recipe card boxes inside the canisters were the only things to survive the fire. When Marlin Thompson opened the boxes, he found nineteen thousand dollars in one-hundred-dollar bills. After all, as Abdullah said, it was a lucky number.

The hundred-dollar bill that Charlene and Roz had used to snort the "cocaine" was completely burned up as was any evidence that they had been killed with strychnine. The hundred-dollar bills which were secreted away in Charlene's boats were intact, spendable, and most important-ly investable. He and Claudette could move into the log home on the fifty-acre woodlot because, after all, he was Roz's business partner, and therefore the life insurance on Roz Zyfler paid out to the business firm of Thompson and Zyfler Holdings, Inc. which was the owner of Zyfler Stoves, Inc. a half-interest in Claudette's Tavern, Inc. Zyfler's Firewood, Inc. a fifty-acre woodlot with a kiln drier and a log home built on the property, a two-toned 1972 four-door Cadillac Calais and a 1973 Ford 350 Truck. These assets were now all transferred to Marlin Thompson, because they were all owned by the holding company set up by Weeks and Hutchins, LLC. Attorney Hutchins said, a holding company was the most tax-efficient way of owning property and he had been right.

Attorney Hutchins drew up a Guardian Ad Litem Agreement for little Cynthia; that he assured them would insure that Binny would never see a penny of this money. After all Uncle Marlin and Aunt Claudette were all the family that their little niece now had and they needed to protect her. With her tongue firmly planted in her cheek, Cynthia greeted her Uncle and Aunt at the funeral and thanked them for the flowers, "Thahz rethz wahr sar-than-lay thahd-fahl ahv you-ah, Uhn-cahl Mah-lehn." *Those wreaths were certainly thoughtful of you, Uncle Marlin.*

"Ehd wahz noth-tehn bay-bay, ehn-nay-tahme you-ahr ehn Beh-fes', cahm bah thah howz; bahd dohn-'nah brahng Bin-nah, 'k; 'cahz we-ah dohn-'nah wahn ehn-nay trahb-bahl." *"It was nothing baby, anytime you are in Belfast, come by the house, but don't bring Binny, ok; because we don't want any trouble."* He said, and she nodded agreeably. Binny wasn't welcome anywhere in town, because he had a reputation for trouble. They brought along the camper, Cynthia, who had begun referring to herself as "Cyn", considered it her "home" and Binny was hiding inside, while Cyn chauffeured him around town towing it behind the wheel of a 1961 Cadillac Coupe de Ville, Candy- Apple-Red Convertible, with a 390 V-8 engine, automatic tranny and power everything.

Cyn swung by the Weeks, Hutchin Law Firm on her way out of town and inquired of Attorney Hutchins as to whether there was any money, which was left to her by her "parents". He said that the court had appointed him her "guardian", whatever that was and that it was "important to his firm to guard her interests" and that she might be able to get some income from the various businesses in which she was an heir" then she drove out of town taking the same route to Bath she had traveled when she was just a little girl.

Chapter Eighteen
"IT IS WELL WITH MY SOUL"

Susan comforted herself by roaming the Western Promenade and while Mike's body lay in the morgue; this seemed the right place for her to contemplate burying his body. So, when the snow had stopped and the ice storms receded and those things were eventually going to happen; whether or not Mike took his fated trip toward Boston. Susan donned her warmest clothing and trudged through the snow on an expedition to the Western Promenade. Going down Brackett Street toward the MMC, Susan looked westward and saw the beautiful modern building of the Maine Medical Center. Then she continued south and came to the Western Cemetery a favorite haunt of both dog walkers and bird watcher. She decided at once that this would be a fitting place to bury her husband and with the funds that Drs. Chambliss and Gordon had spoken to her about; there would be a formal funeral and a lavish, closed-coffin wake.

A 27-year-old, new father, nursing student killed by a drunk driver would gain the compassion of the whole community and Mike's closed-coffin service had Dr. Gordon's help and sympathy. He told Susan that he would run interference for her if any of the snooty residents of The Western Promenade objected to the burial of someone outside their circle of the rich and the prominent. Actually, the Western Cemetery was the burial place for 19th Century Irish immigrants fleeing from the potato famine and none of the residence of the splendid homes surrounding this historic cemetery had anything legally to say about a son of Italy and Ireland being buried in their midst.

Susan called Mike's Quaker Meeting on Hill Street and asked if they would be coming and then she called the Mercy Hospital to see if Mike's thirty girlfriends could attend. Mike was the only man in a rather large class of women and when he told Susan that he was going out for a beer with the guys; he had always meant at least twelve women. Dr. Andelkar and Cheryl Folsom would have to be told and then there were the Way Believers.

They are a little like Puritans, always telling people how tragic circumstances came about through a lack of faith in God. Susan didn't believe it. She had already read the part in Genesis, where Joseph's misfortune of being sold into Egypt had been his brothers meaning something for evil but God turning it to the good of a whole people. Nevertheless, Mike had revisited their apartment several times in the weeks before his death acquainting himself with a banjo player who lived with them, who was named Mark Finks. Mark had come over to their apartment for a session of dueling guitar and banjo, which reminded Susan of the movie: "Deliverance".

Mark had asked Mike what Quakers believe and Mike smiled and said, "We believe in turning the other cheek; now don't do anything that will remind me of my Italian Mafia roots." The day of the funeral was also the day after Christmas. Susan was overcome with admiration as this compelling musician played: "Walking with the King", an old New Orleans Funeral March on his banjo.

Then Susan steadied herself and rose to sing:

IT IS WELL WITH MY SOUL

When peace, like a river, attendeth my way, When sorrows
like sea billows roll;
Whatever my lot, Thou hast taught me to say, It is well; it is
well, with my soul.

Refrain:

It is well, It-is-well, with my soul, with-my-soul, It is well, it
is well, with my soul.
Though Satan should buffet, though trials should come, Let
this blest assurance control,
That Christ hath regarded my helpless estate, And has shed
His own blood for my soul.

Refrain:

My sin, oh, the bliss of this glorious thought! My sin, not in
part but the whole,
Is nailed to His cross, and I bear it no more, Praise the Lord,
praise the Lord, O my soul!

Refrain:

For me, it is Christ, it is Christ yet to live:
If Jordan above me shall roll,
No pang shall be mine, for in death as in life Thou wilt
whisper Thy peace to my soul.

Refrain:

But, Lord, 'tis for Thee, for Thy coming we wait,
The sky, not the grave, is our goal;
Oh, trump of the angel! Oh, voice of the Lord! Blessed hope,

blessed peace to my soul!

Refrain:

And Lord, haste the day when my faith shall be sight, The
clouds be rolled back as a scroll;
The trump shall resound, and the Lord shall descend, Even
so, it is well with my soul.

Mark and Carole Finks helped Susan back to her apartment. She felt that this couple were like relatives to her, "Walking with the King" is such a happy song, Mark. Thank you for that." Susan said taking off her shoes and lying down on the couch. You know that I'm three months pregnant." Mark gasped at the realization that Susan was all alone in the world and that she was pregnant. He got a chair from the kitchen and bringing it to the side of the couch, he began reading to her from Psalms. As Susan cried and told him how she blamed herself for not restraining Mike from leaving the apartment on the night of his death.

"You-ah coah-d ah nahn", *"You couldn't have known."* He comforted, and then he went back to his reading.

Mark Finks was a man of few words, at least of his own, he would instead find the appropriate scripture in his mental repertoire and recited it by heart, but this occasion called for more than a scripture or two from memory; it called for words of comfort and exhortation and a reading of Psalms unencumbered by his own words, however pious. As he continued to read, a sense of calm spread over Susan and a peace filled her heart replacing sadness not with joy, but rather with a resolve and a strength she had never before known.

Mark was not a resident of Portland, Maine he was actually from Caribou, Maine and in accordance with Maine custom was staying with the Believers, while the winter would out. Carole, Mark's wife was also pregnant; but nearly due. Being "great with child", she had come with her husband to seek closeness to the Maine Medical Center and distance from the drifting snow and dangerously wintery surroundings Upcountry. Susan was glad for their company and when Carole sat in Susan's rocking chair she exclaimed, "Ayur Sue-zahn, thahs chah-yar cell mahk ah pah-fect plahs fahr you-ah tah nahs you-ah bay-bay!" *"Oh Susan, this chair will make a perfect place for you to nurse your baby!"*

Mark told Susan that a family of WOWs "Word Over the World Ambassadors" was going to be running "the class" and that Mike had put money down on it for both of them. Susan was thrilled to find out that she would be learning what the word, Sheol meant and anything that might distract her from the deep sorrow she was feeling was a benefit looked forward to with great anticipation. Because Susan was so young looking, numerous young Way Believers took her for a person of their own age and not being apprized that she was a widow assumed that she was pregnant out-of- wedlock. It wasn't any of their business, so Susan didn't disabuse them of their wrong believing but listened patiently while they chided her for having "forehead wrinkles". She meekly observed while Wendy, a girl of seventeen, found the verse in Job which said, **"Thou hast filled me up with wrinkles, which are a witness against me" (Job 16:8)** and then explain to Susan that the small, threadlike furrows on her brow were physical evidence that she lacked faith in God.

Susan opined that those lines might only be the evidence of a serious and thoughtful character and that she would try in the future to conceal them behind a few tendrils of her curly brown hair. "At least", she thought, "the girl knows her Bible and at that age I would never have known how to find such a verse or be so bold as to read it to an older woman."

Above all, Susan was determined to "stay off her feet" for the duration of her pregnancy; whatever the cost or whatever anyone said about her being lazy. Susan took walks certainly, sometimes long walks, but she knew she couldn't work an eight-hour shift if she wanted to continue her pregnancy. Way Ministry people have a penchant for confusing fault-finding with discerning-of-spirits and never noticing when brotherly love is supplanted by respect of persons. The children of Area Leaders, Limb Leaders and Branch Leaders had their crying overlooked at fellowship while humbler saints and their children were ejected from their meetings for the same offense.

Susan took all these trials in stride and when Al Theriault's teenaged bride- to-be told her, that she should have an abortion or give her unborn child up for adoption; Susan didn't lose her temper or even answer back. The suggestion came something like this, "Mah sis-tah hahd ah bay-bay lahs' ye-ah ahnd gahv har ahb fahr ah-dahp-shun". *"My sister had a baby last year and gave her up for adoption"*. Susan asked, "Well, Wendy, how old was your sister?" When Wendy replied that her sister was fifteen years old, Susan explained that she herself was twenty-eight years old and that this baby was the only memento she still had from her late husband. "Wendy, I have had four miscarriages now, this is my fifth pregnancy and I may never remarry. This may be the last opportunity for me to have a baby and this child may be the only hope for carrying on the Asta name."

Wendy thought that Susan was guilty of negative thinking and told her so to her face. The Way certainly had some interesting ideas. But Susan believed that following Christ wasn't about being right all the time, nor was it about defending oneself from false accusations. Wendy would after all outgrow these notions as she matured and she was a very sweet, young woman; if not just a little obsessed with worldly wealth. This willingness to overlook Wendy's few frivolous faults was all it took for this sincere, young woman to proffer her services as Susan's Lamaze partner. When Al

Theriault found out that Wendy was going to be Susan's labor coach he was insensed; apparently thinking that Susan wasn't a proper person for the fiancée of the Branch Leader to coach and it spurred him to try to "help Wendy get out of it".

Susan had completed both the "Foundational" and the "Intermediate" classes on "Power for Abundant Living"; but she still hadn't manifested holy spirit. In May of 1979 Susan was only a month and a half away from a normal delivery and she was experiencing false labor pains almost every day. It was becoming clear to some of the believers that her inability to Speak in Tongues, Interpret and Prophesy was an indication that perhaps; she wasn't really saved and they told her so to her face.

Chapter Nineteen

"WHEN WILL SUSAN MANIFEST?"

It was because of this tension over Susan's lack of the outward manifestation of the holy spirit; that she was visited by a young man named, John Mann. He was a WOW Ambassador and a friend of both Mark Finks and Al Theriault. He quietly suggested to Susan that she seek out a place where she would feel most comfortable and there she would manifest.

"Well John, I don't really feel more relaxed here at home than I do at Twig", she ventured.

"Where would you like to go Susan; I'll take you in Al's car. (a 1978 Steel-Blue Mercedes 450SL Roadster) I have it for the day! **[In 1978 this would have been a \$30,000 car, which if valued in 2018 dollars would be worth the equivalent of \$250,000!]**

"Well, I don't know, John, I can't really think of anyplace I'd rather be unless it's The Scarborough Marsh and the Rachel Carson Wildlife Refuge. I've never really visited the place where Mike died and I'd like to go to "the Church in the Wildwood" again. Perhaps I'm not manifesting, because I blame God for Mike's death in some way", she said pouting her lip and forgoing any desire to conceal a sin from a brother in Christ.

"Let's go!" He said with the genuine enthusiasm so reminiscent of Mike's sense of adventure. Susan saw qualities of her husband in John and told him so. They set out for the Great Salt Marsh of Down-East Maine.

Susan was wearing her dress paratrooper jump boots, which she always referred to as the **"Preparation of the Gospel of Peace" (Ephesians: 6:15)**; a denim maternity skirt that she had inherited from Carole Finks and an embroidered Mexican peasant blouse. She looked comical when she completed her ensemble by leaning her heavily pregnant body on the large walking staff that Walter Malien had fashioned for her.

John's heart was captivated and immediately proposed marriage. This would happen to Susan several more times over the next couple of years but she would always gently restrain the smitten suitor and pretend it hadn't happened. They set out for The Marsh first going downstairs passed Dr. Bonjour's office. They got into an almost new 1978 Mercedes Benz 450 convertible that was parked illegally on the corner.

John parked wherever he pleased and simply trusted God to see to it that he wasn't ticketed. Way People would make a convenience of observing neither parking- restrictions nor speed-limit signs and then glorify God for helping them not get caught. Susan told John that it somehow threw off the whole "Holiness of God" thing but that just made him laugh. The followers of the Way observe a principle that they call "Renewed-mind Recklessness", which is somewhat akin to the kind of belief that young men have in their own immortality, that makes them prone to feats of daring and causes them to become such good soldiers and athletes.

Susan realized that this was a quality that Mike Asta also possessed and it endeared John to her but not enough for her to disregard the observance of her period of mourning or their difference in age. Susan was almost eight years older than he was.

He cut the wrong way through the one-way alley behind the apartment house and then went west on Congress Street to St. John Street turning south out of town on Route One. Susan was enjoying the drive as she really hadn't been out of her apartment very much since her pregnancy began. They were driving through South Portland now and Susan tried to remember why Mike had been so determined to leave for Boston on that specific night. Perhaps he was responding to a call of destiny.

They were passing some affordable little homes on Main Street, South Portland and Susan thought that she and Mike would have soon been picking one out if he hadn't been killed. Susan surmised that this area would all go commercial one day and envisioned how they could have turned over some bargain property for a hefty profit.

While the scenery whizzed by, Susan reviewed her activities during the last few months. She had called her insurance agent after the "accident" and discovered that her "totaled" vehicle could be completely replaced with a new one; she being a practical person asked if the insurance company could simply liquidate their bank loan and then give her the balance in cash. He said that they could and a check appeared in the mail made out to Michael Asta. She took it to Sister Carmelia Marie and it seemed to satisfy her for Mike's debt to the school.

Since he was now deceased, Sister volunteered to give forgiveness for all his Student Loans as well. Then thinking she might be able to get Social Security for herself and her unborn child, Susan inquired at the SSN office. But, because they had been married in Mexico, the Social Security Administration informed Susan that she would have to seek AFDC instead. AFDC was a lot less money than SSN but, it did come with Medicaid which would cover Susan's prenatal care. The checks wouldn't start until after Susan's child was born which was the government's way of saying that Susan's unborn child wasn't really a person. Medicaid benefits however started immediately. This was compliments of Congressman Henry Hyde, who apparently considered the unborn baby a human being and was working hard to make the young one's entrance into the world as healthy and as unproblematic for his mother as possible.

At any rate, Susan was going to get her prenatal care and delivery for free and as long as she visited City Hall once a week, she would get a voucher for her rent. "This is good", Susan thought as she accepted the voucher from Madelyn Cartwright, a woman who would become a pivotal character in her life. All through her pregnancy, Susan would show up at Madelyn's office with another woman's baby in her arms. Ruth Burrell, a Way believer, was having Susan care for her daughter during the day, while she was at work. Wendy told Susan that she should work while she was pregnant and that the leadership, meaning Al, wanted it that way.

"Sue-zahn, Ruth Bur-rell ehz wahl-lehn tah pie fah-tah-fibe dahl-lahs ah wahk fahr sumb-Juan tah wahch Phil-lip-pah." *"Susan, Ruth Burrell is willing to pay forty-five dollars a week for someone to watch Phillipa."*

"Maybe she'll pay you that kind of money, Wendy", Susan said, "but I'm already taking care of Ruth's baby and she isn't paying me anything."

Susan would rise at 5:30 a.m.; walk thirteen city blocks to Ruth's apartment and take care of her baby until she came home from work. Ruth had replaced Susan at her job in South Portland and as John passed the factory, Susan thought about how difficult it had been to get that job, which was "piece work".

Susan introduced Ruth to Mr. Hatcher, her shift supervisor, Mr. Brice, the plant manager and Mr. Leviton, the owner of the South Portland Switch Company. She hoped that Ruth would acknowledge a "job sharing" arrangement, so that they could "trade off" working and child-care responsibilities but it seemed that this was also a way in which the Way Ministry was not quite a church.

"I should have requested that she sign an employment contract", Susan thought, and then turning to her companion and said, "You know, John, I like to give without keeping score, don't you?"

"Does this mean that you're not chipping in for gas, Susan?" John said.

"Yes", she smiled broadly, "yes, it does." Al Theriault owned an almost new, Baby-Blue, 1979 Mercedes-Benz sports car with a phone in it when car phones were still virtually unknown. Susan asked if the gas tank contained the seven gallons of gasoline required for this trip. She also wondered aloud if John had checked Al's water and oil before they left Portland and informed him that a car like this took premium- grade gasoline and that adding the cheap stuff would ruin Al's engine.

"Gee, Susan you certainly know a lot about fast cars for a car-less person", John remarked.

"Well, John I've had an MGB in the past, she was British-racing green, had an over-drive shift and wouldn't start if there was any dew on her engine. She was temperamental and a bit of a lemon, but I couldn't remember that anymore, when I got her up to 98 mph on the expressway. That was why I named her 'Floozy', because she was a fast-woman. Over-drive is a cruising-speed drive that lowers the engine RPMs and increases its fuel-efficiency while maintaining a higher speed", she said. This impressed John who was all in favor of going fast in a car. "Hold on John, there are speed traps along here and the police frown on, "Renewed-Mind Recklessness", they laughed.

Chapter Twenty
FILLED TO OVERFLOWING

They were a long way from **Rachel Carson's** and the little ponds and streams along the roadside were glimmering and shining in the sunlight. It was a bright, warm, spring morning and Susan started wondering again, "What if Mike had waited until May?" "What-if-ing" a sovereign God was part of Susan's problem and she knew it. She knew also that if you wanted to **"be endued with power from on high" (Luke 24:49)** you really had to stop questioning and let God be God. "Do you think that I'm still mad at Him, John?" Susan earnestly inquired.

John didn't ask, "Him Who?" he said, "I don't know, Susan, we'll find that out, before the day is through."

They turned left onto Route Nine, Pine Point Road and continued through the Scarborough Marsh until they came to the Audubon Nature Center, a converted clam shack from 1972. Susan being pregnant called for them to make a pit-stop and afterwards, they walked along the edge of the Marsh on a nature trail winding through the little streamlets and ponds. It wasn't long before Susan realized that this sort of an excursion could be downright dangerous in her condition and it was with some sadness that she hiked back to the car to complete her mission to Rachel Carson's.

John took the top down on Al's convertible roadster and they were flying along with the wind in their hair to where Route One joins the Piney Point

Road. It was only six miles to Biddeford, where Susan really wanted to drop in on Cheryl Fulsom and Dr. Andelkar but she thought that this wouldn't be very much fun for John. So, they continued on another fourteen miles to Kennebunk making a brief site-seeing stop on the Portland Road to see the spectacular "Wedding Cake House" on Summer Street. They would have gone down to Kennebunkport to see the Bush family summer home. But, the day was waning and so, they went back to Route One, then south toward the Laudholms Farm Road in Wells, Maine.

"There was a house on Wells Beach where Mike and I stayed in a commune for about six months", Susan said, smiling with anticipation.

"I didn't realize you were a hippie, Susan", John said with a grin.

"Oh, a real hippie, John, and a vegan to boot!" she smiled back. "You can make good money around here cleaning rich people's summer homes, John, and making natural foods in the restaurants. My recipe for granola is legend." She couldn't remember where Rachel Carson's was anymore, so they stopped at a gas station for directions.

"You-ah cauhn't gaht they-yah frumb hee-yah", came the reply, "You-ah hahv tah gau sumb-wair elz ahnd staht they-yah". "*You can't get there from here, came the reply, you have to go somewhere else and start there.*" They decided to look on a map, because maps are at least in English.

They turned off Route One and down the Laudholm Road going as far eastwardly as they could. Then, they parked Al's car in a sand lot adjacent to the beach. Their view of the ocean was blocked by three enormous houses that the Laudholms family referred to as cottages and right in front of a large red and black warning sign which announced, **"STOP, DANGER TO BEACH NESTING BIRDS"**. And another just as insistently proclaiming: **"NO JOGGING, NO SWIMMING, NO PETS,** and *NO ENTRANCE"*.

Before them lay a public beach and overlooking it on a rocky cliff, the

Lord family's mansion, barns and silos. Maine people have always congratulated themselves on their lack of observance of rich people's property rights. The Laudholm property which accepts public intrusion into its preserve with good humor, insists on keeping people and dogs away from the Piping Plovers and the Least Terns which nest on the eastern side of the Laudholm Beach.

This peculiarity had always elicited the same response from their beach guests, "Who are the Plovers?" The tenacity with which Fredrick and Diana Lord protected the beach-nesting birds was legend and many beach-goers considered them just snooty rich people and fought them for their "beach rights". All beaches in the State of Maine are public and people who own beach fronting property cannot keep the public off their property even if egress gives the intruder an opportunity to take a prolonged gaze through the homeowners' bedroom windows.

One could glimpse the Lords' cows coming down from the upper pasture; but behind the beachfront an insignificant path led up into a forested outcrop, which concealed a precipitous overhang facing the ocean. Down this winding path was a steep incline of pounded earth. It cut its way into the forest promontory. John took Susan's arm and she leaning on him went up sideways, balancing her pregnant body on the staff Walter Malien had made for her. When they reached the top of this stairway of stone and pounded earth, a pulpit appeared in the midst of the trees and behind it John pulled open his soft black leather-covered Bible and looked for the all the world like he had always been the senior pastor of this church.

"Susan, how did you find this place and how could you have known that this was here from the beach?"

"Mike worked here for about two years and we used to come here to pray when we lived in Ogunquit and then at Well's Beach", she said. Susan was breathless from both the scenery and the climb. As she took her seat on the first of several benches that all faced the podium, sitting quiet as a Quaker in the late morning light, she stared out of first one then another of this church's three "stained-glass windows". These windows were actually only opening in the thick undergrowth: the first, showed forth a pristine visage of the snaking streambeds of the Great Salt Marsh; the second, revealed a long vista to the Atlantic Ocean and the third, disclosed the hidden beauty of the forest with that secret, inner green both subdued and sparkling with dappled sunlight. This holy trinity of natural beauty was itself more spiritually moving than all the cathedrals of Europe.

John finally composed himself and found the first place in his Bible that dealt with the subject of worshipping God "in spirit and in truth" saying, "Turn in your Bibles to **John 4:23**."

"John, no one has a Bible here but you, why don't you just read it to me".

"But the hour cometh and now is, when the true worshippers shall worship the Father in spirit and in truth, for the Father seeketh such to worship Him. God is [π] Spirit and they that worship Him must worship Him in spirit and in truth [or truly via the spirit]." (John 4:24)

"Susan", John said, "do you want to worship God in Spirit and in Truth?" "With all my heart", she said.

"Let's review the other verses that deal with the holy spirit field", he implored.

I Corinthians 12:3, "Wherefore, I give you to understand, that no man speaking by the Spirit of God calleth Jesus accursed and no man can [really] say that Jesus is the Lord, except by [~~the~~] holy ghost [pneuma hagion]."

"Susan, if you want to say that **Jesus is Lord**", you have to do so by speaking in tongues.

Verse 7"...the manifestation of the Spirit is given to every man to

profit withal." "Now, that's every one of us, Susan, we who are born again of God's gift of holy spirit. All Christians have this gift from God and we can all manifest it; you just have to want to and believe to *lambano* it or (receive it into evidence)."

"I do want it John and I believe to receive it, **LORD, take away my unbelief**."

"Are you sure you understand that it's **perfect prayer, giving thanks well,** that you're **speaking not unto men but unto God (I. Corinthians 14:2)**, that you're **speaking the wonderful works of God (Acts 2:11)**, that you're **magnifying God (Acts 10:46)** in your spirit, **speaking mysteries (I Corinthians 14:2)** in your spirit? It's the only thing that the Word of God says will **edify (I Corinthians 14:4)** you, ah, spiritually."

"Let's look at **Jude 20**", he said, "**But ye, beloved, building yourselves up on your most holy faith, praying in the Holy Ghost.**" --- "When you speak in tongues, Susan, you're building yourself up in your most holy faith. You're praying in the Holy Ghost."

"I know that speaking in tongues builds up my faith and I need faith to speak in tongues, it all seems like circular reasoning to me", she said frowning.

"Maybe we should go right to **John 20:22**", John said, "**And when He (Jesus) had said this, He breathed, and saith unto them, *lambano* ye the Holy Ghost**". "Now, Susan, tilt your head back and take in a deep breath through your mouth." She did as instruct. She was still deeply inhaling though her mouth when he told her to stop, nothing had happened, "I don't want you to pass out from hyperventilating", he said. They hung around a little while longer, but still nothing happened."

A disheartened John didn't want to drive so Susan, who was quite familiar with a manual transmission, took over on the road back. When they got to the part of the Scarborough Marsh where Mike had been killed, John was fast asleep in the passenger seat clutching his Bible. Susan looked over at him, then she looked back across the road at the setting sun, its colors blending with the swirling clouds and then suddenly, she began speaking in tongues. "I guess God wanted to be in charge after all." Susan said to herself as she woke John with the good news, "He has fallen on me", she said.

Chapter Twenty-One
THE WEDDING CAKE

Ralph Magwood was a waiter at Marcel's in The Old Port. He could make $100 in tips every day. Ralph once said that he paid his bus boy twenty percent, why shouldn't he Abundantly Share twenty percent. He would watch as the Marcel's pastry chef made petites madeleines and studied the technique for whipping génoise cake batter. He was sure that if he had the equipment from the restaurant, a store of cake pans, and enough egg whites, he could create a masterpiece wedding cake for Al and Wendy. One of the cake layers would have to be thrown out, because the egg whites that were folded into the mix made it collapse under its own weight. Ralph believed so ardently in the Resurrection, that he saved this, soaking it in Napoleon Brandy and stuffing it with chocolate mousse to make the groom's cake, which he mounted on a cut-glass fluted pedestal.

Ralph hoped his creation would satisfy even Wendy's exorbitant tastes and beguile her from the "cake with a fountain in it" upon which she had insisted. With this goal in mind, Ralph ascended Susan's stairway with boxes and laundry baskets filled with baking implements, boxed cake mixes, powdered sugar, heavy cream and chocolate of several varieties.

If there was anything Ralph knew, it was how to cook, bake and throw a party. Susan was the person to whom everyone in the Limb turned for help with their various projects. Her hospitality if not her wealth was legend.

Staying home a lot did not mean staying inactive.

Susan already had a believer's plants in bathtub therapy: a solution of about two inches of warm water to which a small amount of a pregnant woman's urine has been added. Placing water permeable flower pots into this bath would restore the withered and neglected plants to robust health once again by the process of osmosis. This of course was a recipe that neither the kitchen crew nor anyone else in the Limb could be allowed to discover, and Susan posted a paper sign on the edge of the tub: **"DO NOT TOUCH WATER"**.

Back in the kitchen, Ralph, John and a blind saint named Richard Cook, who was washing the cake pans and implements, were whipping up a creation to rival the pastry chefs of Paris. "I can hardly believe all three of you guys fit into my teenie-weenie kitchen", she shouted above the hum of the power mixer on her Oster Kitchen Center. It was nearly five o'clock in the morning before all of their baking was done.

Ralph wanted the cakes to thoroughly cool before they were iced and to whip the icing just moments before rushing it to the festivities in Litchfield, which itself is a good hour's drive north of Portland. All the canned goods on Susan's pantry shelves had to be transferred to the fire escape as there was no room for them anywhere else in the apartment. One huge cake layer resting on a thin flexible plastic cutting board completely filled Susan's kitchen table, while a second layer was atop her refrigerator, a third layer lying on the same kind of cutting board with planks of wood for support was balanced over her sink. Besides this there were seven more layers of varying sizes perched on the shelves of her pantry.

Finally, there was a chocolate-mousse groom's cake atop a fluted, cut-glass cake-stand in the refrigerator. This cake had gotten the sole attention of Ralph and Susan, as it required them to remove all but one of the refrigerator's shelves. Dark chocolate icing, white chocolate puffs in the shape of roses and raspberry preserves completed the decoration of this chef-d'oeuvre. Ralph was afraid that the cake would collapse en route to the Limb Headquarters. You never divulged any kind of fear around these people; you couldn't even say, "I'm afraid I don't understand you." They always objected strenuously to any turn of phrase that implied the concept of fear. This is why everyone in their circle hid both their fears and their mistakes from view and why a person as meticulous as Ralph needed to be so guarded in his demeanor.

Ralph reasoned that the layers could be transported in the various boxes he had brought to the apartment and he used tissue paper as a deterrent against any hair or dust falling onto the cake as it was in transit. So, when John pulled up in a limousine wearing a very snappy chauffeur's uniform, the entire vehicle had to be used to transport the two cakes, the frosting and of course a trunk full of presents. Except for John and Ralph there was no more room in this stretch limousine for anyone else. "Call Al, Susan, and have him pick you up", was their suggestion as they sped off. Susan called Al and Wendy's number but got no answer. Eventually she gave up, took the canned goods off the fire escape and put the plants out there instead. Then she had to lie down again, because she was feeling another contraction.

Chapter Twenty-Two

LORD, PLEASE SEND ONE OF THE SAINTS IN HERE TO MINISTER TO ME

**"Call Now, If There Be Any That Will Answer Thee
And to Which of The Saints Wilt Thou Turn"**
Job 5:1 THE VERSE BESIDE THE TELEPHONE

Susan went for her next prenatal visit with Dr. Bonjour. It was so thoughtful and kind of God to have arrange for an Obstetrician/Neonatologist to have his office downstairs from her apartment. Dr. Bonjour told her that she was two centimeters dilated. "It's too soon", she said, "I can't lose this baby too!"

She called John and had him pick her up at her building. "I've just come from Dr. Bonjour's, John, it's not good". You could tell John, Ralph or Richard anything and they wouldn't give you an argument, nor would they tell you, "where you were believing wrongly" they would just listen.

Richard Cook and Zorro had come to fellowship to teach from the Bible that evening and Susan was eager to hear what the teaching would be about, she felt another pain and lay down on John's bed. Turning over on her side she prayed, "Father, send one of the saints in here to minister to me." She laughed out loud when Zorro came trotting in and licked her face. Zorro pranced around with joy whenever Richard removed his harness and allowed him be the pet he truly was. Zorro and Susan had a little conversation, she discovered a necklace that he always wore and read the inscription on its tag to him aloud, **"*Seeing Eye*"**.

"Oh Zorro, you're a Seeing-Eye dog!"

The German shepherd went nuts in response to her admiration. Richard was a dishwasher by trade but he knew more about the Bible than most ministers and as the dog's muzzle lay upon the bedspread, Susan stroked his head and felt the contractions subside.

She remembered how John Wesley, the circuit rider, prayed for his horse and the animal recovered. Zorro had done more for God than whole congregations of Methodists, this was just turn-about is fair play. Zorro was ministering healing to a believer as John Wesley had ministered healing to his horse.

Now that Al and Wendy were married, they could drop the pretense that she was sleeping in a tiny room down the hall. Jim Dopp insisted that all the believers: marry, quit living in sin, or quit the ministry and Al and Wendy's wedding was only the first of a parade of marriages that were long overdue. One Twig Leader actually had to divorce his wife in order to marry the gal he was living with and that with a church, a "Twig Fellowship", meeting in their home. Rev. Dopp had Al and Wendy take a covenant of salt, the blood covenant of matrimony having already been wasted. Susan tried to explain to Al and Wendy that sex before marriage ruined the marriage but it was reproof they couldn't accept from her and wouldn't accept until it came again from another source, the Limb leader, Rev. James Dopp.

It wasn't long before the voice of this strident, pedantic and doctrinaire Man of God was replaced by the dulcet tones of a man more in keeping with the modern zeitgeist, that lax homogeny of religiosity and popular custom so prevalent in the Church today. Rev. Jim Simmons, who had lived with his wife, Anne for a full year before they were married, had taken Rev. Dopp's place and for his first order of business, he initiated a telephone conversation with Susan while she was lying down in her apartment fighting another contraction.

"You get your butt out of bed and get back to work!"

"Isn't Anne pregnant too?" Susan inquired toying with this sanctimonious busybody.

"Yes!"

"Why don't you send her out to work as well?"

"She does work, in the garden, in the house and in the ministry."

"I have to stay off of my feet right now, Jim; because I've had four miscarriages and I don't want to lose this baby too!" she stated emphatically.

"Four miscarriages? How many times have you been married?"

"Just the one time, Jim. Mike Asta is dead now and I need to make sure that we carry on the Asta name."

He immediately changed the subject, "And those combat boots you always wear and that staff you lean on; not very feminine."

"They give me a lot of ankle support, Jim and when I walk over to Ruth Burrell's place, I need to lean on that staff."

"Ruth Burrell, she's a wonderful woman of God. Why do you go over there?"

"She needs child-care, Jim. She's got my old job at the South Portland Switch Company. I see her off to work every morning at 6:15. Would you feel more like I was a working person; if I charged her money?"

"No", he said and hung up. Susan reflected that Jim Simmons didn't seem to know a great deal about the "opportunities", that the members of his congregation were experiencing. (The euphemism, "Opportunities" means "opportunities to trust God" and is Way Ministry speak for "trou bles.") He never got it that Susan and Mike had been a married couple or that since Susan was a widow, her church should have been taking care of her. Maybe he didn't want to get it.

A WOW Ambassador named Iris came to Susan's door, there were more flower pots in Susan's bathtub and everyone wanted to know how she could revive dying plants, "It's a secret, Iris, but come in and we'll have some tea."

"One of those mysteries of God", Iris laughed, "Susan, your time is almost at hand, isn't it?"

"Almost, Iris, I've got three more weeks or so says Dr. Bonjour". "Would you like me to stay with you, till your time comes?"

Susan hugged her, now, she thought, here is real Christian Charity. "You know that Ruth Burrell is going to need someone to fill in for me when I get ready to give birth to Paul Victor or Celeste Hope." Susan had finally picked out the necessary girl's name for her baby. She took Dr. Wierwille's first name for her son's middle name, which was the only logical thing to do and then she chose Celeste Hope for the celestial hope of Our Lord's return.

"I'll be there for her, Susan, you can count on me but my WOW family is having some issues right now. And I think I need to be here for a while."

"Sure Iris, you're always welcome in my home."

Iris stayed the remaining three weeks of Susan's pregnancy and un complainingly arose at 5:30 a.m. just as Susan had done, walked to Ruth Burrell's and saw her off to work on the bus at 6:15a.m. Then one morning as Iris was getting ready to go, Susan's water broke, "Gee, I'm glad I wasn't in bed, Iris, can you call Wendy and tell her my water has broken and I'm ready."

Iris got on the phone calling Wendy and every other believer in Portland

and then when Susan felt another contraction she started timing her. Not one but two cars showed up at Susan's door and Susan told Iris to take the second one and go to Ruth's. Then she packed her suitcase with the swaddling clothes she had made by hand and departed with Wendy for the Mercy Hospital.

Chapter Twenty-Three
PAUL VICTOR

Wendy, Susan and a nurse got into the elevator at the hospital and went up to the Maternity Ward Susan said to the nurse, "That was a contraction" and when the door opened again she said, "That was another one". The nurse informed her that the contractions were coming about a minute and a half apart and that she should deliver within an hour. In the labor room both Wendy and Susan were speaking in tongues out loud and completely unconcerned about whoever might hear them.

The nursing staff had never seen this before but they noted that these two young women really "knew what they were doing" and Susan seemed to be having an easier time of it than most mothers. Her labor was definitely progressing faster than anticipated. Then the doctor called to say that he would be a little late and the nurses tried to cross Susan's legs, which was a procedure Wendy fought going into action and vehemently ordering them to back off. Wendy was becoming a little firebrand and Susan was proud of her. When the baby started crowning, Wendy tried to deliver him herself. The nurses realized that they were going to have to take over and deliver the baby themselves without the doctor. It wasn't Dr. Bonjour anyway; it was a physician that had promised to fill in for him. When this doctor finally did appear, everything was already accomplished and a beautiful little boy had been born into the world.

Wendy was ahead of her times, snapping picture of the baby coming out of his mother. But if Wendy was ahead of her times, Susan was behind them, before she would put her little boy to her breast, she had salted and swaddled him. This was something that the nursing staff at the Mercy Hospital Maternity Ward had never seen before and they were talking about it for weeks afterward.

Salting and swaddling a baby and yes you can do girls too consists of adding two tablespoons of table salt to the baby's first bath water. Then, you wrap him or her in hand-made and hand-hemmed strips of linen cloth that are about six inches long and about two inches wide. The baby is wrapped, starting at the sole of the foot and the legs are bound together with the arms bound down at the little one's sides.

They cry during this procedure, but it's good for their lungs. There is no need to diaper first as the swaddling clothes will absorb everything but the meconium and the infant probably won't pass his or her first stool for several hours. Swaddling clothes are only left on for the first hour or two. The salt symbolizes "The Truth" and the swaddling clothes symbolize "Straightness", when you swaddle your baby you are telling God right from the beginning, that you will try to raise him or her to be a "straight arrow" who is "true to the mark".

After swaddling you should begin breast feeding in order to dislodge the placenta and get the uterine fundus to descend. This helps prevent Post-Partum Depression also called "the baby blues". This is in no way a recommendation but there are women that cook and eat the placenta or afterbirth and this is also said to prevent post-partum depression. The placenta is actually a good source for the hormones estrogen and progesterone, which you can get in pill form from your OB/GYN. Although there is no hard-scientific evidence that eating the placenta reduces Post-Partum Depression, here are some recipes anyway:

Remember cook thoroughly, sautéing in butter at low temperature and this is not an endorsement or a recommendation. Herbs that can be added to your tea after childbirth and which are endorsed and highly recommended are: fenugreek and blessed thistle, of course you should always consult your physician.

According to Eastern custom, swaddling clothes are handed down in families for generations **Ezekiel 16:4, Luke 2:7, 12**. The ones that Christ wore portended the grave clothes that he would wear after death. Despite what you may have heard, swaddling clothes are not an affectation of poverty. Even Herod the Great was salted and swaddled at birth. Christ's swaddling clothes were an heirloom of his lineage going back to King David. Even Indian families that can afford exquisite layettes imported from London, salt and swaddle their newborns.

When Susan brought Paul home from the hospital, she found that Iris had gone home to Nebraska and her mother. The believer's plants were all dead, because Susan had over-stayed at the hospital and Iris had neglected to put them back into bathtub therapy before she left. There was also a note, "Quit the Ministry". When Susan called Ruth Burrell, she found that the telephone had been disconnected. She had also quit the ministry and had also gone home to her mother. To Way people, someone who has done this is dead to them and they seldom if ever spoke of these two young women again. Ruth had abandoned her apartment, leaving without cleaning it and thus forfeited her damage deposit. She had also neglected to pay the closing utility bills.

Rev. Simmons was furious and said, "People who can't keep their own word don't keep God's Word very well either and apparently, these girls were only playing at being grown-ups". Susan called Mr. Leviton and apologized to him for Ruth leaving her job without explanation or notice. She had assured him before she took over this job that Ruth was very dependable. Mr. Leviton was the foundering President of the Portland Switch Company and he was very pleased to hear that Susan had had a healthy little baby boy. He would have shown the same pleasure at the news that she had had a healthy little baby girl and asked if Susan would like to come back to work.

He said, "You-ahr sprahngz ahnd gahdz wahr fail-yah-pruf, Sue-zahn ahnd you-ah wahr awe-wahz uhn tahm ahnd au-bahv quot-tah. We-ah mahs you-ah, bahd tahk you-ahr tahme. Eht ehz zo nahs tah hee-yah thahd you-ah hahd ah beau-tah-fal, hell- thay, lit-tahl boyah." *"Your springs and guides were failure-proof, Susan and you were always on time and above quota. We miss you, but take your time. It is so nice to hear that you had a beautiful, healthy little boy."* Mr. Leviton was a beneficent yet humble man, who had just accepted a phone call from a former piece-work employee even though he had over eight hundred employees working in his factory. But, he really meant it when he said he wanted Susan to return to work. Unfortunately, the job was full-time and Susan didn't see how her maternal duties would allow her to work full-time for quite a while.

We should always look to God alone to meet our needs, but the apostle Paul described the church as a body for a reason. We all need to work together and "bear one another's burdens". What should have happened and didn't was that a Way Home accommodating young, single mothers, which the Way Ministry had in abundance, should have been established in Ruth Burrell's apartment. This would have facilitated sharing: quarters, expenses and child-care responsibilities. The leadership of both: The Branch, Al Theriault and the Limb, Jim Simmons, should have worked together to plant a Twig Fellowship in this home. This meeting could have greatly facilitated the outreach of The Word of God. But, unfortunately, this would have required a good deal more leadership than Al and Jim were willing to provide.

Rev. Simmons routinely opposed assisting needy saints, while constantly promoting believers who were "blessings" on the Ministry, meaning that they had money and connections. Al Theriault was more concerned about his commercial real estate and appraisal business than he was in his ministry to the saints. The only thing that recommended him for leadership was his wealth, at heart Al Theriault was just a natural man, who though he gloried in the accolations he received as Branch Leader, secretly looked down on Susan and the other saints who were less fortunate than himself with prideful contempt. In this way, he was much like the staff of the Diocesan Human Relations Services for which Susan would later work.

Chapter Twenty-Four
WOMANLY ARTS

You can revive a dying plant with love, water, fertilizer and prayer, but a dead plant is dead. When Anne Simmons came over to check on her plants, Susan had to give her the bad news, "There was resurrection for Jesus and there will be resurrection for us, Anne. But, dead plants stay dead! I guess Iris had too much to do while I was in the hospital. Ruth had too much to do, also. She couldn't even keep her job. She quit without notice."

"They are both home with their mother's now", Anne said.

"How's your tea?"

"It tastes like you put oregano in it."

"That's a mixture of Fenugreek and Blessed Thistle, Anne; they're both good for you after you've had a baby."

"How come you know so much about herbs, Susan?"

"I'm the herb lady at the Good Day Market. Did you see, I washed and ironed Paul's swaddling clothes? Would you like to pass them on to another mother in the Ministry?"

Anne had her little girl on Jordan Farms Goat's Milk, because she didn't think she produced enough breast milk. Susan sat and listened attentively and thought about asking Anne what had become of her copy of, "The Womanly Art of Breastfeeding". A request like this was problematic in the

Way Ministry, because when believers asked for things they were always told, "No!"

"My sister, Elsie is the president of her chapter of "La Leche League", perhaps I'll borrow their manual from her."

"Her name is Elsie?"

"That's right Anne, it's Elsie!"

At that moment, Gladys Harmon of the DHS Public Health Nurses called on Susan. Having a visiting nurse was part of the good treatment Medicaid recipients got from the government and was something that Congressman Henry Hyde had written into the bill that started Medicaid and Medicare. Madeline Cartwright was glad that Susan's baby was getting the best start in life and told her so by phone. Gladys Harmon gave Susan her weekly exam and checked Paul's weight. Anne wished for a visiting nurse to look in on her as well, but this weekly service, which was free for Susan, would have cost Jim and Anne a fortune. Anne asked the nurse if Post-Partum hair loss was normal. Gladys said it was but demurred to give Anne any-more free health-care advice. Before she left, Gladys said she detected a little jaundice in Paul and suggested Susan place his bassinette in the window to give him some sun.

Susan popped next door to tell her neighbor, Gregg Furlott that she had gotten home from the hospital and she asked him if he would like to come over and see her baby. Gregg was thrilled, but said his friend Ben wouldn't let him leave the apartment in the evening after work. Susan said, "no prob, Gregg, I'll bring Paul to you." And when she came back to show him her sleeping baby, Gregg asked, "'R' thah ahyez owe-pahn yeht?" *"Are the eyes open yet?"*

"No, Gregg", Susan said, "That's for kittens and puppies, the eyes of human

babies are open at birth."

When Ben got home and questioned his lover, he discovered that an unknown woman neighbor had come into the apartment to show Gregg her baby. He decided to call the landlord, Mr. Stanley Adams, and report that a neighbor had a child, a singularly unacceptable additional tenant and that he had heard it cry! Which, of course, was both a lie and impossible. This prompted a visit the following Monday morning to Susan's apartment.

Chapter Twenty-Five
"YOU-AH HAV TAH GAHT OUD"

When Paul was three days old and Susan was lying in bed nursing him, "Letting your milk down" is a studied art and a lot of women find the electric jolt of pain that comes with putting a sucking child to your breast for the first couple of times offensive. Anne Simmons confided to Susan that it, "got her out of fellowship". Mr. Stanley Adams came knocking and shouting, "Hahv you-ah gaht ah bay-bay ehn they- ah?" *"Have you got a baby in there?"*

When no one answered, he used his pass-key to gain entrance and strode into the room where Susan was lying in bed, her breast exposed, nursing her son. Mr. Stanley Adams said angrily to Susan, "You-ah wahr toad, Eeyah-'em tell-lehn you-ah ahnd Mahk, you-ah caunt hahv ah bay-bay. Nah, you-ah hahv tah gaht oud!" *"You were told, I'm telling you and Mike, you couldn't have a baby. Now, you have to get out!"* He stood over the bed where Susan was lying with her child to her breast. His face was beet red and the veins on his neck were protruding. "Eeyah toad you-ah, nah kidz, nah petz." *"I told you, no kids, no pets."* he said emphatically.

"No, Mr. Adams, it is you who will have to get out! Because, as you can see, I'm nursing my son right now and as you can also see. I'm in a state of undress."

When Stanley Adams left, the telephone rang, Susan answered it sobbing and said, "The landlord saw my baby."

"Thah lan-lahd'z sah hid you-ah bay-bay?" *"The landlord's saw hit your baby?"*

"The landlord saw my baby; he says I have to get out!" Susan sobbed. "Eeyah cauhn't uhnd-dah-stan' you-ah; Eeyah-'em try-ehn tah rahch Ah-rene." *"I can't understand you; I'm trying to reach Irene."*

"Sorry, Susan said, Irene is on my party line, if she isn't on the line she isn't at home."

Madeline Cartwright called Stanley Adams and asked, "Did you think she was smuggling a pumpkin, Stanley. I wish we had laws to keep people like you from doing this sort of thing to families."

"Thah bay-bay wahz cry-ehn ahnd des-turb-behn thah nay-bahs, Mahd-day; you-ah nay we-ah hahv tah prah-tec' they-ah quah-eht ehn-jah-mehn'." *"The baby was crying and disturbing the neighbors, Maddy; you know we have to protect their 'quiet enjoyment'."*

"It's a newborn, Stanley; their crying is a little peep."

"Eht-'ll gaht lahd-dah", *"It'll get louder"*, he hung up.

If Stanley Adams had done this when Mike was alive, Mike would have taken him on, Quaker or no. Mike would have said, "We were planning on getting a house in South Portland and now that I'm done with Nursing School, we can afford to move." That would have satisfied Adams who just wanted to know when Susan would be moving.

Susan didn't want to think about moving, didn't want this move to affect Paul and didn't want to leave the place where she had last seen Mike alive. She called Al Theriault and explained the whole problem. "Did-un't you-ah pie thah rahnt?" *"Didn't you pay the rent?"* was his question. "Didn't I what?" Susan said, "I think you must have me mixed up with someone else." He also asked her why she hadn't gone back and moved in with my parents. He had no concept that she was a widow and that both her parents were dead and that Mike's father was also dead and his mother was in a nursing home. Al didn't know, nor did he care to know that Susan was alone in the world and that she was in trouble. He was the closest thing to a pastor that the Way Ministry had in relation to Susan. Yet, he never sought to help her in any way, nor did he thank her for providing his wedding cake. He neither knew, nor cared to know which believers had given him his wedding presents. Thank you notes were all Wendy's department.

Mr. Stanley Adams picked up Paul's bassinette and carried it to the curb with the baby still inside. Susan, running beside him, rescued her tiny infant from the bassinette and flew back upstairs to call John. John, Ralph and Richard arrived like the Three Musketeers. Richard reached out into what for him was the dark and grasped the side of the bassinette. And, Zorro did something for God that he had never in his life done before. He growled and showed all his teeth. Ralph smiled diplomatically at Mr. Stanley Adams and asked, "Could there possibly be a way that you could please let her stay another month or so; she needs more time to look for another place. We'll all help her find someplace to move. We're her church!"

Adams relented when they gave their word that Susan would be out in a month and then Ralph mounted the stairway smiling and carrying the bassinette back into the apartment. John went out to get a newspaper, while Richard and Ralph tried to calm Susan down.

Susan was in near hysterics and talking about her milk drying up. Richard said to her, "Some things about negative believing do actually happen to you, Susan, now just push that idea out of your mind and confess three positive statements, right now. Your milk is not going to dry up! Say it after me."

"My milk is not going to dry up", she sobbed.

"I claim my milk, in the name of Jesus Christ.", he coached. "I claim my milk, in the name of Jesus Christ."

"My God shall supply all my need, according to His riches in glory, by Christ Jesus.", he coached again.

"My God shall supply all my need, according to his riches in glory, by Christ Jesus." (Philippians 4:18)": she continued.

"My milk is plentiful and will feed my child no matter what situation befalls us.", he coached once again.

"My milk is plentiful and will feed my child no matter what situation befalls us."

John came back in with the morning edition of the Portland Press Herald.

There were three apartments for rent that were furnished, "I can only budget Two Hundred Dollars for living expenses and these are all too much money". She went to see them anyway but few landlords in Portland would rent to a family with a young child. And if intact families with young children couldn't find affordable housing, a single mother with a tiny infant was really out of luck.

Jim Simmons found out that Ralph, Richard and John had promised to help Susan find housing and he had them over to the Limb Headquarter saying, "Susan isn't 'Way Home material'. And anyway, we're running another PFAL class at Al and Wendy's, so that has to take precedence over looking for an apartment for this gal."

"Why isn't she 'Way Home material', Jim? She comes to Twig; she Abundantly Shares; why isn't she 'Way Home material'?" Ralph was getting really frustrated and angry. "Do you even care that it isn't just her that's about to become homeless; it's her new-born son? I think she's a true Woman of God. I'll marry her myself, if that'll make her anymore 'Way Home material'." His voice was cracking and his eyes were welling up with tears.

"Ralph, the Area Leader, John Lynn is talking about ordering you into the Way Corp, he's pretty impressed with the dinner you put on for him, when he taught at Litchfield. All three of you guys are 'Way Corp material'."

"Ordered into the Way Corp, what?" Ralph was stupefied. If Rev. Simmons had said this to either Richard or John, they would have jumped at the chance, but not Ralph. "I don't want to go into the Way Corp., Jim. I want to marry Susan!" There was an audible gasp, nobody talked to Jim Simmons this way and apparently, this was just another indication that Susan was a bad influence on the believers. The three of them left but only one went directly back to Susan's apartment. Ralph had to tell Susan what transpired between himself and the Limb Leader.

"Ralph, it would have been nice if you had asked me first, before telling Jim Simmons you that were going to marry me. And anyway, I have yet to finish my period of mourning and in case you didn't know it Ralph, being 'order into the Way Corp' is a Way Ministry euphemism for, 'Congratulations, you've just been given a full scholarship'". Before he left, Ralph gave Susan the fifty dollars necessary to buy a "Snugli".

Susan felt that she was going to need this Snugli, if she didn't find housing soon. She had already begun storing her belongings on a granite ledge in Al and Wendy's basement. The food items from Susan's pantry could go to a family of WOWs with no strings attached but her pots and pans, the Oster Kitchen Center and her spice rack had to be left with them on the understanding that after she found housing, they would be returned. Everything else was placed on the ledge with her rocking chair and crib mattress covering the waist-high chest of drawers that Mike had bought for the baby so long ago. All these were covered with a blue plastic tarp to which was affixed a sign that said, "Property of Mike and Susan

Asta".

Mike's clothes were long overdue to be given away. Walter Malien was going to get the bulk of them. So, when Susan saw him walking around town wearing her husband's **Frye** brown-leather boots and his belt with the American flag belt buckle, she felt good about it, but she also cried. Since Walter was a homeless man and could only use what he could wear and carry in a knap-sack, most of Mike's things would have to be given to him later. Consequently, Susan secreted away her stereo system and record album collection, her jewelry box, her grandmother's china and her sterling silver at the bottom of a box of Mike's clothes to be given to Walter. Wendy kept reassuring Susan that everything was, "Sahf ahz how-zehz". *"Safe as houses"*.

Some of the Biblical principles that are taught in the class on Power for Abundant Living are: Believing is equal to receiving and that giving is also equal to receiving. Susan just expected to get a new apartment right away and have it be more spacious, and better furnished than her Pine Street place. Why shouldn't she have thought this way? After all, God would provide. The truth is: that when saints are in need around believers who have plenty; God waits in order to give those who have much the opportunity to get blessed helping those who have little. But, when this doesn't happen out of a selfish lack of concern for others. The whole body suffers: The outreach of The Word of God is stifled, married couples quarrel, believers get sick and as the Apostle Paul put it, **"Without were fightings, within were fears, nevertheless God, that comforteth those that are cast down, comforted us" (II Corinthians 7: 5-6).** When Susan went to see a really nice place with a porch, she was sure she would get it. But, instead the landlord took another family whose breadwinner was still alive.

Mike and Susan had stuffed quite a few treasures into their tiny apartment. Now, everything had to go. Then, four days before Susan was supposed to leave; she had her utilities turned off and the final bill sent to her in-care-of Al and Wendy Theriault. This was it! The bassinette, a few changes of clothing for Susan, Paul's baby clothes and diapers, a blanket, some dried foods and her Bible were all Susan would be taking with her to Jane Dyer's house on the outskirts of Portland.

Jane was still on AFDC, because she had four children and the money she earned from her civilian job typing and doing clerical work for the army, didn't go that far. And, because she needed the services of Human Services to make her ex-husband, Steve Dyer, come across with his child-support payments, she needed government. She had a good-paying, part-time job as a civilian, clerical worker for the Army and she was the ex-wife of A Way Believer and the mother of his child. Steve Dyer was making good money as an insurance agent and stockbroker. However, he still wouldn't pay his child support unless forced. Steve "Abundantly Shared", meaning he tithed fifteen percent of his income and in so doing he had become in the estimation of the Way Ministry, the benefactor of the work of God. Steve made an affectation of **"sounding a trumpet"** whenever he abundantly shared. Jesus would have said that **"he already had his reward". (Matthew 6: 1-4)**

Because Jane was not part of their "ministry", everyone but Susan rejected her. Jane's big heart and kind ways didn't seem to endear her to them. Maybe it was the way she exclaimed, "Mah-thah ahv Gahd" *"Mother of God"*, every time things went a little wrong for her or perhaps it was how she continued on with her dating and a social life even after four divorces. **[Remarriage after divorce is said to be, "the triumph of hope over experience"]** and Jane had an abundance of hope. Susan tried to stay out of her way and take as little from her as was humanly possible. Every morning Susan would go through the paper, trek out to seek after that elusive apartment and wish she could find a roommate with whom to share expenses. Jane had four kids and was living in a two-bedroom house, so this couldn't be Susan's final destination. Besides, Jane had boyfriends and some of them were eyeing Susan; something problematic for both of them.

Since there was a telephone at Jane's, Susan did all her phone calling from there before noon. The rest of the day until Susan fell down exhausted onto Jane's couch that evening was spent with Paul in the Snugli, trudging from one rental property to another looking for an apartment where the landlord would accept children. Without an apartment, everything else in life had to be put on hold. Susan couldn't go back to work or shop for food. She couldn't even catch up on her reading. But, thank God, Jane had an automatic washer and drier in her garage and with Paul in cloth diapers; it became necessary to wash clothes twice a day. Susan had acquired a Hoover washing machine and was just placing it into Wendy and Al's basement, when she noticed that her stereo and record collection were missing from Walter's box of clothes and some of the other boxes on the ledge were askew.

"Al, where is my turntable, my speakers, my albums? They were all in this box on the ledge?"

"Ayur thahd, weahl, Todd May-nahd gauhd oud ahnd tuk thahm tah hahz nuer ah-paht-mehn'." *"Oh that, well, Todd Maynard got out (moved) and took them to his new apartment."*

"What? He just took my things to his apartment, without asking? Al, I had labels taped up on all these boxes saying, 'Property of Mike and Susan Asta', what happened?"

"Eeyah dohn' nah, Sue-zahn, he-ah hahd sumd thengz stahrd dahwn they-yah tah ahnd zo deed ud-dah bah-leave-vahz. Eeyah caun't keep ahn ahye uhn ud-dah pea- ble'z thengz." *"I don't know, Susan, he had some things stored down there too and so did other believers. I can't keep an eye on other people's things."* Susan had another apartment to look at before returning to Jane Dyer's place. At least, she and the baby never had to stay out of doors at night. She quickly made two more paper signs claiming her belongings and taped them over her things before hurriedly calling another landlord named, David Cross and making arrangements to meet him at 46 Myrtle Street that afternoon. The City of Portland, Maine was tearing down the Dunkin' Donuts on the corner of High and Congress Streets and so everything was in a state of transition.

Susan thought that this would surely improve business for Paul Trusiani, where she bought some fruit, yogurt and cereal bars. The Portland Beautification Society had planted flowering fig trees all along Congress Street. Susan cash was bankable. But, not her food stamps. With Paul sleeping in the Snugli and nearly everything else in a knap-sack on her back; Susan cut a comical figure wearing combat boots, a knap-sack and leaning on a hand-made staff. There were storm clouds gathering on the horizon.

Mr. Cross, the landlord, she had arranged to meet was late. She decided to head back to Jane Dyer's place. But, along the way the sky opened up and Susan had to seek shelter in a telephone booth. A torrent of rain was pouring down and the baby was screaming. Susan called every believer she could think of who owned a car, trying to find someone to pick her up. Finally, she called Jim and Anne Simmons. When their phone rang, Jill Ireland, a woman who wanted to go into the Way Corp answered for the Limb.

"Thahs ehz thah Sim-mahnz rez-ah-denz, Jill Ahrh-lan' speak-kehn."
"This is the Simmons residence, Jill Ireland speaking."

"Oh, hello Jill, this is Susan Asta, I'm over here on Myrtle Street, where I was waiting for a landlord to show me an apartment. He didn't come and I'm now in a phone booth, it's cold, it's raining and the baby is crying. Would it be possible for you to come and get me and take me to Jane Dyer's?"

"Eeyah-'em rahl-lah sahr-ray, Sue-zahn, bahd we-'ah ehn thah mehd-dal ahv paint-tehn thah graht rahm, ahnd eht'z jehz' naught ah gudd tahm tah cahm gaht you- ah." *I'm really sorry, Susan, but we're in the middle of painting the great room, and it's just not a good time to come get you."*

"Jill, I'd go to Jane Dyer's on foot, if I could, but there's thunder and lightning outside and I'm a little afraid for the baby."

"Sahr-ray, Sue-zahn, yule jehz' hahv tah do-ah you-ah bes'." *"Sorry, Susan, you'll just have to do your best."* then Susan heard an abrupt click. Next, Susan called Jane Dyer, who said, "Way-ahr you-ah?" *"Where are you?"* and gave her directions to the nearest bus stop and then went one better, she met Susan in the rain at the bus stop nearest her home. When Susan got back to Jane's place Paul was shivering and Jane mixed up some pabulum that Susan had in her cabinet and exclaimed, "Ayur, he wahz hung-grey." *"Oh, he was hungry."* It was profound to see the difference between Jane Dyer's concern for Paul and Susan and Jill Ireland's lack thereof. Yet one woman was in the estimation of the Way Ministry, outside The Will of God while the other was at the heart of it.

Chapter Twenty-Six
ACTS 19 BURNING

When Ralph Magwood got to the soon to be former Limb Headquarters at Litchfield, Maine, he saw a large sign designating it, "FOR SALE". Besides the charity auction of the furniture and a lot of Jim and Anne's personal stuff, there was an "Acts 19 Burning" in the offing. Ralph had only one item to contribute, a pink, polyester dinner jacket. The Acts 19 Burning was a life-changing activity to which people were expected to bring their things that weren't "advancing their walk." This public disposal wasn't actually a bad idea. Way People are encouraged to yard-sale, give away or otherwise dispose of the things that make it harder to concentrate on The Call of God, but it's supposed to be something you pursue for your own spiritual furtherance, not something you inflicted on others. Ralph looked on in horror as he placed his jacket on the smoldering pile of people's "donated" items.

On the fiery pile, he could see Mike and Susan's albums already in flames with a sign attached to them that said, "PROPERTY OF MIKE AND SUSAN ASTA" clearly visible through the smoke. There was something that had always bothered Ralph Magwood about Todd Maynard. Maybe it was the way he angrily crushed his frog when it lost the frog-jumping contest or perhaps the way he always mentioned his sister Sarah's acceptance into The Way Corp as though it was his own achievement. Ralph was also repelled by Todd Maynard's overlong stay with Al and Wendy after they were married.

Ralph reasoned that Al was so glad to finally be alone with his bride, that he took no notice of the things gone from Susan's stuff in the basement and Ralph discovered that the vinyl album collection which he had found on the smoldering ACTS 19 pile was "donated" by Todd Maynard. Because of this, he determined to speak to Todd but wanted to wait for a more opportune time.

At the same time that Ralph was watching Mike and Susan Asta's record collection burning up, Susan was negotiating with David Cross to rent half of a duplex he planned to tear down next spring and writing him a check for the first month's rent and damage deposit. When Gladys Harmon arrived at the Myrtle Street apartment, she considered it completely unacceptable. Gladys brought things back to the twentieth century by pointing out the space under the front door and the series of holes in the floorboards.

"Gladys, you just have to see this from my point of view", Susan said, "This rent is well within my price range and the dilapidated condition of the home will spark my entrance into subsidized housing so much faster. I would say that I may even be able to get in there within a few months. If I play my cards right."

"Weahl, Eeyah-'em naught gao-ehn fahr eht, Sue-zahn!" *"Well, I'm not going for it, Susan!"* Gladys said as she slammed her blood pressure cuff down on the kitchen counter. Thahs plahz shahd beh tahrn dahwn!" *"This place should be torn down!"* she exclaimed, raising her voice to a shrill whine.

"Ahnd eht wahl beh tahrn dahwn, Mahs. Hah-man. Beh nes' Sprahng, Eeyah prahm-mahs, Eeyah-'em gau-ehn tah cohn-vaht thahs spahs ehn-tah ah pahk-kehn laht ahnd muv Sue-zahn ehn-tah ahn au-paht-mehn' bahld-dehn uhn Grahnt Straight, wahch Eeyah awe-zo own. Ehn thah mahn-tahm, shay cauhn sahv har mon-nay ahnd gaht sumb furn-nah-cha' way-un shay muvz ehn. ” *"And it will be torn down, Ms. Harmon. By next Spring, I promise, I'm going to convert this space into a parking lot and move Susan into an apartment building on Grant Street, which I also own. In the mean-time, she can save her money and get some furniture when she moves in."*

"Eeyah jes' dohn' nah", *"I just don't know"*, Gladys Harmon fussed. "Ehtz jes' naught ah prah-pah plahz tah brang homb ah bay-bay." *"It's just not a proper place to bring home a baby."*

"Eeyah ah-grey wid you-ah Mahs. Hah-man ahnd ehf Eeyah coahd gaht har ehn-tah mah Grahnt Straight bahld-dehn. Eeyah wahd, bahd Eeyah hahv sumb-Juah ehn they-ah ride nah ahnd Sue-zahn dah-zeh'n hahv ee-nuf ehn-cahm fahr thahd plahz, ehn- nay-wahy." *"I agree with you Ms. Harmon and if I could get her into my Grant Street building. I would, but I have someone else in there right now and Susan doesn't have enough income for that place, anyway."*

"Gladys, Paul and I haven't had a home for five weeks now. We'll just settle in here for the time being and be on our way before it snows, promise. But, I need a rest from walking and looking and I need to get a proper place to settle my belongings, get a closet together and get cleaned up enough to go out looking for work", Susan said assertively. "We'll be gone in just about two months or so, Gladys, just like Mr. Cross says, promise."

"Eeyah dohn' nah, Sue-zahn, this zoundz lahk thah kine ahv theng thahd Chid Prah-tect-tahv wahl hahv tah luk ehn-tah. ” *"I don't know, Susan, this sounds like the kind of thing that Child Protective will have to look into."*

A cold fear settled over the room when Gladys Harmon said this. Susan picked up her baby and held him to her breast. She sat down on the edge of her beautiful brass bed and began to pray. Then, God showed her how He wanted the room to look. The thought of one of those awful busy-bodies coming into her life made her shudder. David Cross was affixing dead bolt locks to all three doors and saw her feeding little Paul in the manner reminiscent of the Madonna and Child. He spoke to Susan as comfortingly as he could, "We-ah'll tahk cahr ahv thahs, Angel. Eeyah'll hahv ah dah-fin-nah-tav daht sart-tan, uhn wahch you-ah cauhn muv tah thah Grahnt Straight au- paht-men'. Nah, dohn' wahr-rah!" "We'll take care of this, Angel. I'll have a definitive date certain, on which you can move to the Grant Street apartment. *Now, don't worry!"* Susan put the check from Madeline Cartwright in David Cross's hand; it was after all made out to him. It was a small fortune to her, only a pittance to him.

Mr. Cross could have kept all the money if he wished. Maybe, say it would go for future rent. But, with the brass bed set up in her great room, a mattress that fit it acquired and several sheets of newspaper covering the windows; Cross could see that Susan had a handle on making this space into a real home. He hurriedly opened his wallet and handed her two hundred and ninety dollars in cash. Susan had turned a corner in her assent from poverty. She was no longer homeless, desperate and destitute.

She immediately gathered up the baby and went downtown to do some banking and buy some provisions. When she returned to her home, she was humming a hymn of praise to God and cleaning her "new" refrigerator; while placing one lone item in it, a box of instant milk. You can use a refrigerator even if you do not have electricity which Susan did, as a food safe. Place the items that you would normally put on your cabinet shelves, which will keep them from being devoured by animals. When the least comfort and security in life has to be gotten through prudence, self-denial and prayer; God becomes a real focal point in one's life. And this lesson in dependence upon Him alone is a valuable asset to any believer's package of survival skills.

Consulting God about the most trifling matters is a necessity when you are living on the edge. Susan hoped that she would never again allow her attention to be diverted from focusing on anything other than trusting God alone for His provision. God was providing for their needs, even if He had to go through City Hall and a man she barely knew; to do it. Susan looked around her in the growing gloom of her new home which though it had electricity was still only lit by whatever fading sunlight could filter through the newsprint coverings on the windows. Utilities came with the rent, but there were no lamps or pots and pans with which to make use of them. The beautiful brass bed was made up with a scratchy, woolen, Army blanket and her mother's nursing cape.

The various holes in her floor and walls were a constant source of concern to Susan and she spent the first night in her apartment in the dark, sleeping between her son and whatever might come out of those holes to harm him. She put her baby in his clean bassinet wedge between her bed and the wall and made a pillow of her purse and backpack. She lay down to sleep trusting God for His protection. The quiet, the appointments of poverty, the Bible on the bed with a little-league baseball bat beside it made Susan remember a Psalm. She shut her eyes and went off to sleep saying, **"I will both lay me down in peace and sleep: for Thou only, O LORD, my God maketh me to live unafraid." (Psalms 4:8)**

Chapter Twenty-Seven
BRAIDED RUG

Susan didn't expect to inhabit her den of two tiny rooms during the coming winter, but insulating your residence against the cold is a time-honored Maine activity, taken very seriously by the self-reliant folk around her and no single mom could ever convince a child-protective worker that she was "a proper parent"; unless her home was clean and the whistling wind, not to mention intruding vermin, were banished from every crack and hole.

When Susan returned from a shopping excursion she opened her door with a key. This was a real achievement and she went out again to return the Salvation Army Store's cart as promised. At the store, she happened to discover a bundle of winter coats in the back with a paper tag affixed to them saying: "Discard". She inquired about these and she discovered that they had been left over from the previous winter, had the smell of moth balls, and had become damp. There was also a stack of rusting, bake-ware that Susan got for nothing which consisted of several rusty jelly-roll pans, cookie sheets and baking pans.

Susan was gathering them up, when she noticed a pull-behind shopping cart, this would be her first purchase with her new-found wealth and she could pay cash. She negotiated with the clerk to allow her to remove the old coats and some sweaters and the rusty bake pans. She had plans for them.

An airing on the porch might get rid of the smell. There were also some children's toys, a Little League bat and a football helmet. Susan bought the bat, but demurred to buy the helmet. She went into the hardware store next door and purchased rat poison and a Stanley light-duty, staple gun. Susan returned to Al and Wendy's to collect her mop, broom and ringer bucket asking Wendy for the empty gallon milk jugs that she was just going to throw out anyway.

"Wendy, Dear, do you think you could wash out your used, plastic, gallon milk containers and fill them with water for me? I don't trust my pipes". Wendy said she didn't trust hers either and would be investing in a water purification system that hooked up to the faucet.

"Oh, good then, Wendy, if you could fill those up and place them next to my stuff in the basement that would help so much."

"You-ah gau-ehn tah hahv tah gaht you-ah thehnz oud ahv thah bahs-mend zoon, Sue-zahn; Al ehz talk-kehn au-boughd throw-ehn thahm oud." *"You're going to have to get your things out of the basement soon, Susan; Al is talking about throwing them out."*

"I know, but my place isn't really ready for them yet, Wendy, except the portable washing machine. I really need that to do a load of diapers." Wendy said she would get a believer with a car to help her and then put her arms around Susan and gave her a holy kiss. Susan was nervous about this, because she wondered if she smelled sweaty. And she was so glad that she had left the cart outside with the nasty-smelling woolens in it.

Susan reasoned that it was time to build a cleaning and repair kit, which she could later use to make money cleaning houses. She went back to the bank and got more cash to assemble these cleaning supplies and purchased a new, leather-covered Bible, a Nelson with super-wide margins. When she returned, she took **Pine Sol** and bleach and got to work.

She cut up the coats and sweaters into long strips and then pinned them to the porch clapboards with the staple gun. They would be protected from the rain and the wind by the overhang. Several layers of these woolen strips were now affixed to the porch making it look like it was wearing an overcoat. The lonely box of instant milk in the refrigerator had found the companionship of a clean gallon milk jug which Susan had gotten from Wendy. Susan mixed up and drank some milk and then lay down to take a nap, because a Godly breeze was coming through the window. Clutching her Little-League, baseball bat for protection and embracing her new leather-covered King James Version Bible, she closed her eyes in sleep.

Arising refreshed, she mopped the wooden floor boards and scraped away the patchy old linoleum in the kitchen with a butter knife. She made an inventory of all the animal holes and pushed rat poison down inside each one, placing a discarded, rusty metal baking pan on top of it. She was glad that her little one wasn't crawling yet and believed God to have a non-rat-infested home by the time he was. Discovering some mismatched wood paneling marked down at the hardware store, Susan got the idea to replace her cracked and speckled kitchen counters and cover more of the rat holes with it. So, she asked the clerk if she could get an additional discount for buying all the sheets of this paneling at one time; she could. Finally, her place was ready for Walter Malien to make his appearance.

Susan had salvaged a reading lamp from the trash bin around behind the Salvation Army Store and her collection of repair and cleaning supplies included a new extension cord and some light bulbs. She got the lamp to work, and perched it on a backless chair that she was using for a bedside table. She also plugged in an iron and used this backless chair as an ironing board. Mr. Cross contributed a pair of tin snips to her repair kit and asked her if she would be willing to clean for him. He said he had some other apartments to renovate. She said that she would be happy to and thanked God for this chance to earn some extra money.

The lamp was shining when Walter Malien arrived. He went around the small apartment, mumbling to himself and sniffing everything. Working with the tin snips, Walter cut down the sides of each metal pan and fitted them over the rat holes. He used an old tube sock filled with sand to cover the gap under the front door. He reasoned that this would keep out the whistling wind and it did. The following day Susan began making a braided rug. This was her first and she had to rely on a book she obtained from the Portland Public Library to tell her what to do.

First, she tied three strands of the coat material into a knot. Then, she folded each strip over on its edges ironing it down. Finally, she made tight braids, interspersing the more colorful materials from the sweaters with the tweeds and browns from the coats and jackets. She anchored the braid to the floor with her staple gun. This was where she envisioned a rug would appear. As the braid got longer, Susan wound it around in a circle; stitching it together with an upholstery needle.

She sat cross legged on the bare wood floor for hours as Walter came in and out, carrying sheets of paneling. He augmented the cabinet doors and covered the bare spaces. So, what, if Susan would only have one door that actually opened. Most of this was just for looks anyway. She was wisely preparing for an inspection by Children and Family Services and she wanted them to be impressed with what a good homemaker she was.

Walter took down her kitchen cabinets and nailed two cookie sheets over the holes made by the rats. There was a definite bulge which he fussed over; until he finally mounted the cabinet assembly again to the wall and realized that the bulge didn't show. He also overlaid the countertops and one cabinet door with paneling. The panels had deep groves in them, which made the countertop uneven and a difficult place to prepare food. Probably some wood putty pressed into the grooves would help, but this was an expense not included in the materials budget. When Walter was done for the day, Susan had kitchen cabinets in which she could safely store food. And by the time she turned in for the night, her circular, braided rug covered the entire floor of the great room. Consequently, the porch's "overcoat" was gone.

Susan couldn't believe how different it was to go to sleep that night unconcerned about intruders of both the human or animal variety. And best of all, inside her new pillow which was made from a burlap Basmati Rice bag that zipped up, were the remaining scrapes of the coats and sweaters. All of this was a subterfuge, concealing within it her savings book and checkbook on a new bank account containing three hundred and ten dollars.

The next morning John and Ralph brought over Susan's Hoover washing machine and they spent the better part of the afternoon adapting the faucet to accommodate it. Mr. Cross came back to turn the bathroom into a place where she could actually take a shower. And with these three men working on her plumbing, Susan took off for Jane Dyer's to retrieve her baby items. Jane's garage was the place where Susan had stored two plastic garbage bags filled with clean baby clothes. Jane had washed and folded these for her. What a wonderful Christian act!

Susan took one of the bags home in her pull-behind, piling it into the corner of her great room and returned to Jane's once more to retrieve the rest of her things. Then she asked John and Ralph if they could make one more trip to Al and Wendy's to get the rest of her stuff. She gave John a key and showed him where to hide it on the porch. When John and Ralph were done delivering her things, she gave both of them a holy kiss and said good bye.

With Paul in the Snugli, she pulled her shopping cart behind her, stopping along the way to nurse Paul at a bus stop. Susan stayed there until it stopped raining and then continued on to Jane's pulling her shopping cart behind her and singing Paul a lullaby.

The World got one good man,
That's enough
The World got one good man,
That's enough
The World got one good man,
That's enough
It won't get you.

I'm so glad that I can speak in tongues,
I'm so glad that I can speak in tongues,
I'm so glad that I can speak in tongues,
'Cause you sure can't.

Looking into her baby's sleeping face as she walked along, she saw his trust, his innocence. The Snugli was such a good investment and with the baby sound asleep in it, Susan began to count the things for which she was grateful to God: 1.) She was grateful that it was no longer raining, 2.) That Jane Dyer had a washer and dryer and 3.) That Jane had washed all those clothes without having to be asked. 4.) Susan was grateful for Ralph's car, "Fritz" and grateful that "Fritz" was not currently living up to his name. 5.) Susan was grateful that she had gotten her stuff out of Al's basement before he disposed of it and 6.) She was grateful also that the guys had hooked up her washing machine to the faucet of the kitchen sink and 7.) That her rocking chair would be waiting for her when she got home. 8.) She was especially grateful for Mr. Cross. 9.) That she had met him. 10.) That she could afford the rent and 11.) That he was dutifully installing a shower in her bathroom at that very moment. 12.) Susan was thankful for the waist- high dresser and crib-mattress, she was sure she was going to see when she got home. 13.) She was grateful as well for the rocking chair cushions that Mike had bought for the baby as soon as he found out that she was pregnant. 14.) She was thankful that Mike lived to discover that he was going to be a father. 15.) She was thankful that the crib mattress that Ruth Burrell had given her as a baby shower present was just the right size to fit on top of the dresser, so that she could change Paul when she got home. 16.) She was thankful for Walter and that Walter knew how to do so many things that you wouldn't think an insane, homeless man could do. 17.) She was thankful for her son, Paul. 18.) She was thankful for Paul's perfect health, sound mind and his unbroken sleep while traveling in the Snugli. 19.) Finally, she began with Ralph and brought to mind each person in her Twig and spoke in tongues for them. By the time she had arrived at Jane Dyer's house, she had prayed for everyone and everything that her imagination had brought to mind.

When Susan approached the house, she observed that the overhead garage door was open and she could see a man inside. He was loading Jane's meat into the trunk of his car which was open. Susan strolled over to the car and picked out two roasts putting them in her pull behind. The man was coming back to his car carrying more food. When he saw Susan and the baby standing behind his car, he dropping the bakery goods he was carrying, exploding a loaf of white bread. Then, he jumped into the car and drove away with the trunk still open. Susan had carefully observed the kind of car he was driving, its color, its make and model and then thought about his clothing and facial hair. She tried to remember how tall he was and what he was wearing. Then she went into Jane's house and called the police. By the time the police arrived, Jane was home and the "stolen" food was back in her freezer.

"Deed you-ah gaht thah lah-zens plaht numb-bah?" *"Did you get the license plate number?"* The police officer inquired.

"No, but I can describe the car to you it was a dark-colored Ford Escort with one missing hub cap on the right-rear wheel, I took two roasts, a chuck roast and a pork roast out of his trunk and suddenly he was standing in front of me. I didn't want to confront him, because I had the baby with me in this front carrier. But, when he dropped the bakery goods and ran to his car; I could see that the trunk was still open. I'll bet he's driving around with it still open now! He was wearing a pair of black corduroy pants and a baseball cap, which had some green on it. He had on a shirt that had writing on it and a picture of something maybe a sports team's logo or something. His hair was mid- length and brown and he had a goatee."

"Ayur! Eeyah nay who-ah thahd wahz!", *"Oh, I know who that was!",* Jane exclaimed in surprise. "Thahd wahz Greyg Mah-lan. Eeyah daht-tad huhm lahs' Mah- ah. Gahsh, he-ah nahz meh ahnd nahz Eeyah-'em ah sing-gal mahm wid fahr kidz. Wh- ah wahd he-ah tahk fah-ud frumb meh ahnd thah kidz, wahn he-ah nahz, hahw brahk we-ah 'r'?" *"That was Gregg Mylan. I dated him last May. Gosh, he knows me and knows I'm a single mom and that I have four kids. Why would he take food from me and the kids, when he knows how broke we are?"* she sobbed.

"Who-ah nahz wh-ah ehn-nay-bah-day dahz ehn-nay-thehn?" *"Who knows why anybody does anything?"* the police officer replied. "Cauhn you-ah vay-ah-fie thahd ehd wahz Greyg Mah-lan, Mahs. Ah-stah?" *"Can you verify that it was Greg Mylan, Ms. Asta?"*

"Whoa, I didn't say it was anybody. I just described the man that I saw; Jane said it was Greg Mylan. I don't even know him, but I bet I could identify him in a police lineup". Susan said, not wishing to get in over her head. When the officer heard the words, "police lineup", he thought about all the paperwork involved with something like that. And since it was "jehz' ah lit-tahl fah-ud", *"just a little food",* he said, "nah-hahm- dohn tahn".

"no harm done then". "Weahl thehn, they-yah'z nah ehv-vih-dance ahnd ehf you-ah gauhd thah mead bahk; Eeyah dohn' say whahd thah pah-lease cauhn do-ah au-boughd ehd." *"Well then, there's no evidence and if you got the meat back; I don't see what the police can do about it."*

"You-ah mehn you-ahr' naught eev-vahn gau-ehn ov-vah they-ah tah quahs- shun Greyg Mah-lan?", *"You mean you're not even going over there to question Greg Mylan?"* Jane asked.

"Eeyah-'em jehz' tahk-kehn ah rah-paht ride nah mahm." *"I'm just taking a report right now ma-am."*

He took Jane's name and address as well as Susan's information, which she actually had to look up on the lease in her purse. The officer found this "suspicious" and told her so to her face. He also told her she could be charged for taking the meat out of the man's trunk. After all, possession is nine tenths of the law. Then he told her that no crime had been committed and left. This was Susan's first experience with the Portland Police Department. But, it would not be her last. They filled out forms; they harassed victims; but they rarely followed up on anything and because of this, Portland, Maine was riddled with crime and corruption.

"Jane, I swear, I didn't leave the garage door open. And after I locked it; I put the key under the rock in the garden, just like you showed me. The least that cop could have done was give me a ride home with the rest of my stuff."

"Eeyah-'ll tahk you-ah hun-nay." *"I'll take you honey."* Jane said and went out to the garden to look for the extra key, which she wouldn't be hiding there anymore. Sure enough, it was right where Susan had left it. "Greg knew about the key under the rock, Susan, and he may have had one that I gave him once. I'll have to have the locks changed." They packed the last of Susan's things into Jane's tired old Chevy Impala which had 250,000 miles on it and burned oil like a hurricane lamp. Jane knew it would never pass Maine's strict air quality standards. But, she needed it to haul her kids and groceries.

They took off for a big-box store in a strip-mall on the outskirts of Portland. There was also a hardware store near there, where Susan bought Jane a new lock assembly and keys. Then, they went into the grocery store and spent most of Susan's food stamps.

Susan had always been generous with Jane. Jane was a good friend and someone who had stepped in when Susan's situation had become desperate. Acts of kindness, like Jane's, should never be unrequited. When you hear about food stamp fraud, people don't think about one desperate, destitute, single mom buying groceries for another desperate, destitute single mom. But, this is how most food stamps get used inappropriately. Jane was finally getting on her feet; she had a good-paying part-time job; but with four kids the money still didn't go that far; because her car always needed repair and it was her only transportation to work. Sometimes, Susan reasoned, Jane's family needed food more than hers did.

"Jane, could you save your empty cereal boxes for me; I need them to make my kitchen cabinets seem fuller. I have Child Protective Services coming over next week."

"Suhr-rah, Eeyah wahl, Sue-zahn, ahnd Eeyah'll fahll thahm wid sah-duhs' ahnd wud chibs; jehz' thah wahy Eeyah uhzd tah do-ah wahn Eeyah wahz uhn fah-ud stahmpz." *"Sure, I will, Susan, and I'll fill them with sawdust and wood chips; just the way I used to do with my own when I was on food stamps."* Surprise visits from social workers sometimes came with an inspection of the kitchen cabinets. If there weren't enough cereal boxes in the cabinets, the social workers would take away what little food stamp the family still had. Sometimes they would pick up the box and shake it to see if it was full, mothers learned to refill empty boxes with stuff that made the right sound, sawdust mixed with wood chips made the best decoy. When they returned to Susan's place, it felt like Christmas to her.

Walter was still there, putting the finishing touches on her kitchen and bathroom, Susan retrieved her key from under the rock outside and vowed never to leave it there again. Mr. Cross had installed a metal framed shower stall. And then he calked and waterproofed around it. There was even a new medicine cabinet above the bathroom sink, with a note on the glass cautioning Susan not to use the shower until the following evening. He also left spackling compound for use the next day and Walter said he needed a place to stay, hoping to stretch out on Susan's new carpet.

The two women started to whip up a wholesome meal for seven in Susan's new kitchen. This necessitated getting into the boxes Ralph and John had piled in the corner of Susan's great room. She became reacquainted with her Revere Ware, and her mismatched collection of plates, drinking vessels and eating utensils. The good china and silverware, however seemed to be gone. Cooking and sharing food is a human activity frowned upon by the government. But, hospitality is something visceral to the human spirit.

They couldn't help wanting to celebrate; Jane and Susan hadn't been killed. There was a kitchen to cook in. Walter was there and he was hungry from having worked hard all day. The kids were hungry because they were growing. That was enough for a celebration. Susan, Jane, Walter and Jane's four children sat down on the floor surrounding a table cloth made from the disposable, plastic bags in which the food had been carried home. And they ate a fried chicken dinner, joining hands to pray over their food.

They let Paul cry in his bassinette, while Walter prayed, "Fah-thah, You-ah nay thahd we-ah 'r' You-ahr chah-drehn ahnd thahd we-ah dah-pahnd uhn You-ah. Thahnk-You-ah fahr wah-chen ov-vah Jayne'z homb ride nah Fah-thah. Thahnk-You- ah fahr thahs fah-ud wahch we-ah 'r' au-boughd tah rah-seev, blahs eht tah thah strahg- than-nehn ahnd halth ahv 'r' bah-dayz ahnd rah-mine' ahs tah beh graht-fal tah You-ah fahr

You-ahr lahv ahnd prah-tec'-shun ehn thah naymb ahv Jahy-zuz Chrys', 'r' Lahd ahnd Sahv-ver. Ah-mahn." *"Father, You know that we are Your children and that we depend upon You. Thank You for watching over Jane's home right now, Father. Thank You for this food which we are about to receive, bless it to the strengthening and health of our bodies and remind us to be grateful to You for Your love and protection in the name of Jesus Christ, our Lord and Savior. Amen."*

Susan had never heard Walter pray before. It sounded like his sanity was returning; maybe that was the best thing that God had done for them that day. While cleaning up after dinner, she remarked to Jane, "my rocking chair isn't here Jane; I guess the guys must have left it in Al and Wendy's basement. Now, I'm going to have to go over there and get it tomorrow."

"Eeyah caun't tahk you-ah, Sue-zahn, yule' hahv tah mahk ud-dah 'range- mah'z, Eeyah hahv tah wurk ehn thah mahn-nehn." *"I can't take you, Susan, you'll have to make other arrangements, I have to work in the morning."*

"Oh, Ok Jane, I was just divulging something of concern to me, I'm missing my home entertainment center as well and all my albums, my speakers, my turntable and everything. They're not here! Walter should go home with you tonight; he doesn't have a place to stay and you'll need him tomorrow to install those locks."

They finished up the dishes and kissed goodbye. Susan had a home, a refrigerator full of food and almost all of her stuff. It hadn't been that bad a day. She worked into the night, rearranging her clothing, remaining books and other things, cleaning the kitchen, and putting away the food. She also inventoried her collection of glass jars and sealable tin boxes. Even though poor people display cereal boxes in their cabinets for the social workers' surprise inspections; they rarely stored their food in cardboard. Glass jars and metal tin can make wonderful storage devices that can be reused again and again. When Susan finally turned in for the night, she hugged her precious baby close to her and nursed him one last time.

Chapter Twenty-Eight
A STOLEN LIFE

The trip back to Bath wasn't the adventure Cyn remembered it being when she came that way in childhood; but now she was "an adult" and now she was "in charge". She had become sixteen-year-old and no longer obliged to go to school. She was in possession of a Maine driver's license. The camper was "hers", because its licenses and registrations were both in her name. As was the car she was driving. "Binny's Caddy" was a 1961 Candy-Apple Red Cadillac Coupe de Ville Convertible.

And the 1966 Airstream Safari were both in her name. This was because Binny had stolen two other people's identities over the years and therefore no longer had an identity of his own. Consequently, Binny couldn't legally own anything or make any real financial decisions. He had to do everything behind Cyn's identity. When they talk about people not having a State ID or a Driver's License in their own name, they're talking about people like Binny.

Like a demon that had forgotten his angelic name and only identified with the name of his ministry, Binny was wearing the name of a Jewish man whom he had met in New York City. This man was the first drug wholesaler Binny had ever known. Binny may as well have been calling himself "Pusher", because to him his name typified his occupation. Because of his "nameless condition", Binny was unable to get a driver's license or a vehicle registration in his own name and so had to do everything behind Cyn's identity. This however, was not something he minded doing at all.

Cyn had no police record, no real address except the camper and she was driving this beautiful, Candy-Apple Red Cadillac convertible. Switching back and forth between the rock and roll station she preferred and her eight-track which was playing, "Rocky Mountain High" by John Denver. Cyn drove the seventy miles back to Bath as fast as she dared.

Her boyfriend was sleeping off some cheap wine and reds in the bordel-lo- bedroom of her camper. This was, of course, illegal. But, everything Cyn and Binny did was a little Wild-Westy. She actually preferred him drunk, stoned, and sleeping rather than sitting next to her and playing his own eight tracks of "The Thrill Is Gone" by B. B. King and "Share" by Gürol Erkan.

She began singing along with her tape and when it ended she switched to the radio, which was belting out, Jefferson Starship's "Blows against the Empire" and "Baron von Tollbooth and the Chrome Nun" back to back. WTOS-FM, 57,000 watts out of Skowhegan, Maine was Cyn's favorite radio station.

"Coke", and "horse", cocaine and heroin injected together, also known as a "goofball" always made Binny jumpy. So, he took some wine and reds, which "settled him some". Cyn put a handful of sweet blueberries into her mouth. She couldn't wait to get back to Dot's Ice Cream. She loved their Ginger Ice Cream and, on the seat next to her was a plastic bag of all-natural granola. The Camper was decorated to reflect Cyn's personality and she worked on it tirelessly. The back room where Binny sold his "coke" and "horse" was bare, impersonal, and all-business. The front room where Cyn sold herself was one big bed covered with shag carpeting. The sleeping room's door had been removed and a curtain of beads was installed instead. Cyn had scrapped and scrubbed everything with Pine Sol removing from her bordello-sanctuary the last, lingering smell of beer. She tore up the rear room's beer-soaked carpeting and replaced it with linoleum tiles and she had the paneled walls of the forward compartment hung with Hippie-Indian tapestries and the ceiling decorated with mirror tiles. Binny complained that they'd come off and fall down on the customer's heads, but they didn't.

It might be that they could hazard a stop at Dot's before going on to the marina. Dot's Ice Cream had been a very lucky spot for Cyn and she figured that she could make "Three Large" there before the authorities sniffed her out and made them move on. Binny was still asleep when they arrived; he liked to creep into her brothel- compartment whenever the camper was in motion. Binny got car-sick easily and he had a bucket in there just in case. Cyn would spread a clean flat white sheet or sometimes just a pillowcase, before they got down to business and she used the storage underneath the bed to hold all her seamen-stained linens, until a laundromat could be found. This was the only real "work" either of them had ever done. Stopping at a laundromat and doing a load of linens. Binny knew where he could buy a kilo of "coke" and twelve decks of "horse" in Lewiston-Auburn and Cyn knew where the crews from the ocean- going cargo ships land and then disembark.

Chapter Twenty-Nine
CONFRONTING THIEVES

Susan inventoried her collection of things which had been in her apartment with Mike. Some of her jewelry was missing. Her mother's nursing pin with its seed pearls and rhinestones, gold and platinum. Her platinum, twenty-point diamond engagement ring was also missing from her jewelry box.

There was no sign of her six place settings of heavy, solid sterling silver flatware; the dresser that fit the crib mattress which Ruth Burrell gave her as a baby- shower present was also missing. Susan still had the mattress, however with its fitted bottom sheet. Her late father's glossy, oak rocking chair with its red-velvet cushions and the draperies that were on the windows of her Pine Street apartment were also missing. She had been looking forward to replacing the newspaper on the windows of this drafty duplex with these pretty, insulated drapes. Finally, her electric, Smith-Carona typewriter had vanished.

Her make-shift home entertainment center was only half there; its over-sized speakers, its turntable with its diamond stylus were gone as was her irreplaceable, 250 vinyl record album collection. Besides being cherished keepsakes from her former life, these items all had intrinsic value. Susan made three detailed lists of her missing items. She intended giving one of them to Al and Wendy as soon she got over to their place. She got dressed in clothes that she hadn't been able to wear since before her pregnancy. [**One thing about breastfeeding, it really helps you get your figure back quickly!**]

When Susan arrived at the Theriault home, Wendy Theriault let her in to their spacious foyer with its black and white checked tile floor and its full-length mirror with a mahogany table displaying a vase of fresh carnations. In the center of the ceiling the plaster molding framed an impressive crystal chandelier. A mahogany, spiral staircase led up to an attached brass lamp depicting a woman holding a torch. This fixture shed its light on the entire passage. The fixture looked more like the woman from Columbia Pictures than a replica of Bartholdi's mother.

Everything about Al and Wendy's home was calculated to impress visitors. Al was the Branch Leader after all; but this was a private home unsupported by church funds and a very imposing cite at which to hold A Twig Fellowship Meeting of the Way Ministry, or to run the class on "Power for Abundant Living". Alan Theriault was rich; but his home like most things that the Way used was rented. Upstairs from them lived a family that they didn't even know. These people used the same entrance and the same front porch; but they had a different doorbell. Al and Wendy's doorbell was labeled "The Way."

Their upstairs neighbors didn't need to maintain the entranceway. The Theriault's were happy to shoulder this responsibility themselves and the glass paneled doors leading into their private quarters were immaculately kept, being guarded from the slightest trace of a fingerprint through Wendy's expert homemaking skills. Wendy usually consulted people in the foyer and was reluctant to let anyone into the Theriault's private quarters without good reason Understandably, she trying to keep from having to polish this door all day long.

Al Theriault always maintained a certain cold aloofness around Susan and insisted that Wendy do the same. Susan told Wendy, in as kindly a way as possible, that the items which were delivered to her residence by John and Ralph the previous afternoon were not the complete store of her belongings left in the Theriault basement and which Wendy had assured Susan were "sahf ahz haz-zehz". *"safe as houses"*.

Susan thought she had a right to know where the rest of her belongings were. One of the things about "Renewed Mind Recklessness" was that it always let you skirt the line between "what is right" and "what is legal". People who want to be done with legalism, sometimes also want to be done with the laws of men as well. And man's law isn't always about parking restrictions and speed limits; sometimes it's about private property. She gave Wendy an itemized list of the things that she secured on the granite ledge which was carved from the "living rock" of their basement."

Wendy said, "Eeyah thahnk Eeyah sah you-ahr tahp-raht-tah dah-wn-stahz, Eeyah'll gau **a**hnd chahk". *"I think I saw your typewriter down-stairs, I'll go and check"*. She ascended the stairway, leaving Susan to wait in the foyer. While waiting, Susan bounced her baby boy and cooed at him first dancing and swaying around on the floor then sitting on the bottom stair. Wendy returned, skipping down the stairway, carrying a light blue, portable, manual typewriter. "This is awful Wendy. If I could just go into your basement, I'd be able to see for myself. Mine was a portable, electric Smith Corona. The one that you've got there, Wendy, is a manual, Brother typewriter."

"I think the Simmons got that in order to type up the Ministry Newsletter", Wendy said.

"Perhaps you could give this note to Al and tell him that it's a partial list of what I've found missing from my stuff." "My home entertainment center is gone, along with my record collection. I'm also missing my late father's rocking chair."

Later that afternoon, Susan stopped by the Way Home where Ralph Magwood was living. He came downstairs and met her in the parlor which was a well-furnished, sunny room with a Franklin stove and a piano. Ralph's sensitive, compassionate eyes looked lovingly into Susan's eyes and discerned the sense of pain and betrayal she was feeling. "Susan, are you alright"? He sat down by her side and took her hand.

"I'm just a little shaken Ralph, Wendy wouldn't let me into her basement when I came by to give her a note that listed my things that are missing from what you and John brought back to my apartment. That box of stuff was half empty and the home entertainment center has vanished". "The worst thing, Ralph, is that she tried to give me some other believer's typewriter and then admitted that mine was with the Simmons and that they were using it to type up the Ministry's newsletter. My stuff was only in Al and Wendy's basement for five weeks. How could it get picked through that quickly, unless they started taking things out right away as soon as I left them there! This is awful", she repeated.

"I know what happened to your albums, Susan, I saw them burning up at headquarters, when we had the 'Acts 19 Burning'. I didn't want to tell you. I hoped that it was some kind of mistake or that you said they could do that", he said looking sheepishly away.

"I've got to go over to the Simmons' place", she said, "and I've got to get my stuff back. I wonder how many other believers have my things and how many other believer's things are with other people! This is awful!"

"Why don't you just forget about it", he said. "It's not worth taking on the whole **Way** Leadership for, Susan."

"Maybe not worth it to you, Ralph, do you realize what this means, it means I can't trust God's people to do what's right, when my back is turned! It means that they're just as worldly as anybody else." Don't you realize that somebody went into my stuff and took my jewelry, my books and my other belongings that I had when I was married and reasonably prosperous. Now I'm penniless and they feel differently about me, don't they Ralph? They look down on me. They despise me." Jill Ireland came downstairs and took charge of the living room, "We-ah'r gau-ehn tah hahv Twahg hee- yah ehn ah lit-tahl wahl, Sue-zah, zo you-ah'r gau-ehn tah hahv tah leaf." *"We're going to have Twig here in a little while, Susan, so you're going to have to leave."* Jill couldn't look her in the eye; but she could get the words out of her mouth. Susan was no longer welcome at Twig.

The next day, Susan made herself as presentable as she possibly could and went to the Simmons' home to retrieve her belongings. Their home on Munjoy Hill was, like everything else the Way Ministry used; rented. The Way of Maine wasted no time in liquidating the Litchfield Limb Headquarters, which was given to them by a generous believer. This saint donated a mansion, which was attached to an auditorium big enough for an audience of three hundred worshippers. Believers who donate houses, lands and even businesses to the Way Ministry are deceived into thinking that they are leaving a legacy to the work of God. But, in reality, they are only giving away something that will be cashed in for money and as soon as possible.

None of the leadership of the Ministry never wanted to put down roots, so their headquarters were as transient as their membership. Few of them lived anywhere for more than a year and when a family owned their own home, or a business, or a farm, anything of value; they became the targets of considerable pressure to turn it over to the "work of God".

Susan rang the bell and after a long-time Anne Simmons came to the door and said, "Yes, can I help you?" Susan stood at the door with Paul in the Snugli and beamed a warm smile into the face of Anne Simmons, "I was just in the neighborhood and dropped by to pick up my electric typewriter; it's a Smith Corona. Wendy said you had it. May I come in?"

Anne frowned; but didn't want to seem rude. Susan was the object of much gossip in the Way Ministry and anyone about whom they gossiped was viewed with suspicion. Way People would say things like, "I get out of fellowship, when I think about her". Or, "He's not really walking the Word". Then that would be an occasion to gossip, make judgmental remarks and backbite.

The vehicle of shunning, which is done by most cults; but is only talked about in regards to the Amish, replaces Christian-Love with a kind of spiteful vengeance. This is sometimes referred to as "disfellowshipping" and is the Protestant equivalent of excommunication, which is a Catholic concept. It is also practiced by the Mormons, the Jehovah's Witnesses and the Plymouth Brethren to name a few.

In the Society of Friends (the Quakers) it is called, "Being Read Out of Your Meeting" and it happened to President Richard Nixon after he ordered the bombing of Haiphong Harbor near Hanoi, Vietnam. Way Believers, who are "not well-spoken-of" are less welcome at fellowship than strangers. Susan thought that maybe this would be the last time that she might ever see Anne Simmons again and she had to make the occasion work for her to reacquire as many of her things as she could.

Anne Simmons said to her, "You wait right here, I'll get your typewriter." Susan pushed the door open and stepped into Anne's immaculate home wearing her Army Dress Paratrooper Jump Boots. As Susan entered this opulent home, their parlor furniture was immediately evident. There in the corner of the room sat Susan's father's wooden rocking chair adorned with its red-velvet cushions. Susan walked over to it and leaning her hand on it turned and glared at Rev. and Mrs. Simmons saying, "You people didn't by any chance also acquire a sterling silver baby spoon, or six solid sterling silver place settings with a grape pattern on them, or know what has become of my diamond engagement and wedding ring set? Do you? You really take the cake, Anne! You saw this chair in my tiny living room, when you came over to visit me on Pine Street. Now, you've got it in your parlor and you don't know where it came from. My things that I stored in my Branch Leader's basement should have been safe, but they have been rifled through for anything of monetary value and stolen from by the very people that I trusted."

"I've been homeless on the street for over a month with a new-born and you have done nothing whatsoever to help me. Now, I find that you've participated in the theft of my belongings. You, who have so much have taken what little I had left from my former life. As I read my Bible; a widow with an orphaned child, crying against you to the LORD is a dangerous thing." As Jim Simmons strode confidently toward her, a heavy sense of dread swept over him. It made him dizzy, sick-to-his-stomach, confused, and disoriented then he remembered this verse from Exodus:

"Ye shall not afflict any widow, nor fatherless child. If thou afflict them in any wise and they cry at all unto me, I will surely hear their cry And my wrath shall wax hot and I will kill you with the sword; and your wives shall be widows and your children, fatherless."

Exodus: 22: 22 – 24

He kept telling himself that now; he wasn't under the law, but under grace. Then the words just came out of his mouth, almost without him meaning to say them, "I'll put anything that we might have of yours in the car, Susan". As cautiously and as softly as she could, Susan said, "You can start with my late father's rocking chair, Reverend, blinking her eyes coquettishly."

Jim Simmons picked up the chair and carried it outside and when he did, Susan crossed the room and sat down on their blood-red, velvet couch uninvited. It was then that it occurred to her why they had wanted the chair; it matched their décor. Anne went immediately to the kitchen and called Jill Ireland. She apparently felt that she would need reinforcements. When she came back from the kitchen, Susan was cooing to her son and waiting for Rev. Simmons to return. Anne came into the living room and sat down next to Susan on the couch.

"You really have to be going soon, Susan, we'll be having Twig here soon", Anne said assertively. It was of course a lie. Fellowship wasn't for several hours yet and Anne was expecting Jill to take care of transporting Susan and her recovered belongings back to her apartment on Mulberry Street.

"Why don't you go into the study, Anne, and get my typewriter and would you please look around for my Young's Analytical Concordance of the Bible, my Thompson Chain-Reference Bible and my copy of "Receiving the Holy Spirit Today". All of them have my name in them, the Bible has Larry Jaynes' name on the front cover in gold. He gave it to my late husband in lieu of fifty dollars which we lent him so long ago." Anne didn't budge, she answered, "How do I know these things are yours?"

"Because I told you they were mine, Anne; but you can just look on the inside jacket for 'Ex Libre, Mike and Susan Asta', our 'Receiving the Holy Spirit Today' was hard-bound. Why don't you just get up and look?" Anne rolled her eyes. Acting as though these pilfered items were insignificant and eventually came back into the living room with the typewriter. She looked guiltily away and Susan tried to appear nonchalant, as she picked up the typewriter and headed for the door saying, "so you didn't see the Concordance in there anywhere? Are you sure that you don't have two of them?"

"No, I didn't see it!" Anne emphatically stated, as she accompanied

Susan to the door. Then when Susan walked outside, Anne shut the door behind her with a thud and hoped that this would be the last she would see of this inconvenient woman. Outside Rev. Simmons sat on the porch and said, "You know there will be a believer coming by here any moment."

"Jill, I expect", Susan discerned. "Well I'll just wait here for her then. I have my typewriter and rocking chair back that's the main thing. But, I'm missing almost every good book I owned when I lived on Pine and State with my late husband. We had quite a bookshelf, Mike and I. I'm missing a Thompson Chain Reference Bible and a Young's Concordance of the Bible, all my collaterals, my Way Magazine collection, my copy of Flavius Josephus' "Antiquities of the Jews" and all my teaching tapes from International. They have our names in them on the back of the front cover", Susan said to him. And then she smiled sweetly and touched his arm saying, "You will look out for them won't you Reverend."

"Oh of course, Susan", he smiled back. "Losing stored valuables is always frustrating, but you need to concentrate on more spiritual matters and let your possessions go. Even if they have sentimental value for you, or they will take you over." Susan knew that this was very good advice, but she didn't want to hear it from a thief. They were standing in front of the grand house that Rev. James Simmons and his wife Anne had moved into after they sold the Litchfield Mansion and there was a brand-new Mercury Grand Marquis in their driveway.

Later when she was on better terms with Susan, Anne Simmons confided to her that she and Jim had had all their wedding presents, locked in a trunk and labeled with their names, stored at *International*. And somebody had broken open the lock, taken everything, rewrapped the gifts and subsequently gave them away to other believers also as wedding presents. She described it as a pivotal moment in her life. She decided to let go of those presents, like **"casting your crowns at Jesus' feet"**.

(Revelation 4:10, 11). She said she never looked back and that now she had **"exceedingly, abundantly above all she could ever hope for or dream of having". (Ephesians 3:20)**

It is one thing to have your private property rights violated. It's entirely another, to hear the people who stole from you waxing sanctimonious while discoursing with you about materialism. Once Susan had heard Jim Simmons preach that using someone else's deodorant spray, left on the shelf in front of the bathroom mirror, without his or her permission was stealing. Rev. James Simmons was right of course, but preaching what you don't observe is the definition of hypocrisy.

Jill Ireland arrived and drove Susan away from the tonier section of the Eastern Promenade and down Munjoy Hill to the humble abode that Susan shared with her tiny, young son. Jill began thinking about what she should say to her. Susan had to understand that everything that had happened to her was because of her wrong believing. It was because she had fear in her life. That was why all these calamities had befallen her: The death of her husband, the loss of certain of her possessions and the five weeks of homelessness that she endured, these all had resulted from Susan's negative believing. Jill Ireland explained that Susan's lack of forgiveness for Jim and Anne was drawing these misfortunes to her. Susan had to be made to realize this principle from the Word of God.

"Sue-zahn", Jill began, "Ehf you-ah wahn tah brahk thahs sigh-cahl ahv rah- graht ahnd ill-wahl, you-ah hahv tah staht giv-vehn ah-gahn." *"If you want to break this cycle of regret and ill-will, you have to start giving again."*

"Well, I don't know Jill. I really don't have much left to give. Most everything that I owned when I lived on State and Pine with my late-husband, Mike, is gone now and when you and I arrive at my new place you can come in and see the desperate poverty we are living in."

"Bahd, Sue-zahn, dohn' you-ah say, thahs ehz awel beh-cahz ahv you-ahr bah-leave-ehn." *"But, Susan, don't you see, this is all because of your believing."*

"Is it, Jill? I certainly didn't believe to have my stuff in the Branch Leader's basement rifled through and stolen from and by the people I trusted. But, you're right; we shouldn't trust in men but only in God. I never thought when my husband and I were 'abundantly sharing' to The Way Ministry, that I would become a widow or my son would become an orphan or that the church that I belonged to, tithed to and worked for would do so little to help me when I became homeless on the street with a new-born."

When they got to Myrtle Street, Jill wouldn't come in. She left the rocking chair and typewriter on Susan's porch and took off for fellowship. Susan let herself into her place with a key. She was exhausted and wanted to go immediately to bed; but the sounds coming from the alley-way outside her windows made her long for some company. There was none; save for her sleeping baby and God alone. She had no radio, no source of artificial light except for one small, shadeless lamp balancing on a backless chair. During the night, Paul fell out of his bassinet into Susan's bed.

She took a certain satisfaction in knowing that she had planned ahead. She had wedged the bassinet between her bed and the one clean piece of drywall Mr. Cross had nailed up. This was on his part, a stroke of genius and pressing the bed up against the bassinette and thereby pinning it to the wall was also genius. The baby went back to sleep in her arms and she vociferously thanked God for providing her this quiet, peaceful home.

Chapter Thirty
ARRESTED FOR THE FIRST TIME

Bath has no slummy section. It has its woodlands near the river and its wharfs with yachts and working boats for commercial fisherman. It has its docks with their ferries, which take tourists to the islands of the Casco Bay and it has its working people who ride the ferry daily journeying away from these scenic islands to the mainland and their employment.

Bath has nothing in the way of a sin district or an underclass of any kind. Consequently, people like Cyn and Binny lead nomadic, desperate lives in which they like Gypsy Moths, fly from one tree-lined refuge to another. Cyn's camper became her fortress, a kind of tourist shop with no Labor Day, no end of season.

While the snow collected and the Summer People fled from their coastal enchants, there was no respite for Cyn; nothing in the way of a vacation even in "Vacationland". Though she had no clock to punch, no commitments to keep and no rent to pay; she had desperation and she had anguish. In many ways, it was a free and easy life and in other ways it was a hard and demanding life. Always nearby her captor waited to collect her money; berate her just enough to make her submissive and sooth her just enough to sustain her through all this phony sexual "fun".

They parked by the marina, until they were chased away. They parked by the river, until the police came shining their flashlights into the camper windows and they had to leave. Cyn was more confident when Binny was with her. She needed him to satisfy her inner hunger for a family and for friends. At times, he became her whole world. These two intrepid ragamuffins straddled the line between moneyed flatlanders and the homegrown hunting, fishing and camping folk of Downeast Maine.

Binny said he was from New York City; but she couldn't discern his accent and they never really talked anyway. Binny mostly talked to his drug contacts. As long as Cyn gave him all her money, he let her manage her own "affairs". She walked a fine line between being allowed to spend money on her "whore costumes", as well as the continued cleaning and maintenance of the camper and being beaten for taking too much or what Binny called, "stealin'." The beatings would always begin with the same words: "You-ah bin stealin' ah-gahn". *"You've been stealing again."*

Cyn was nervous about returning to the Camper with less money than Binny hoped or more purchases than the magic number he would allow. The winters were always the worst for her because the Mainers would stay at home near their quiet fireplaces and warm stoves and the "Odd-ah-staters" would pack up and go back to warmer climes; stealing off to Bensonhurst or New Rochelle. Downeast Maine's seasonal businesses have their Memorial Day to Labor Day frenzy then oblivion. You have to make your money quickly, while it is warm outside; which meant Cyn really had to hustle.

Binny's business was constant; he had his "reg-gul-lahz". Like a dairyman, he had his "milk route" of poor addicts to use until they were consumed. Unlike Cyn, he was unable to bring customers to the camper; therefore, he was forced to go to them on foot carrying drugs on his person. This was a dangerous practice to say the least. So, he would stash drugs in secret places; so as to retrieve them for quick sale later, "ah holler' tray" *"a hollow tree"* as Binny called it.

Binny blamed the weather, the police, Cyn. His misfortunes were never of his own making, never a product of his own inadequacies or his own failures, everything was someone else's fault. Binny had paid nineteen thousand dollars for Cyn; close to everything he had. His "friends" said that he was "in love with a whore" and then they would hold their sides laughing at him. He complained that he had, "Trah-bahlz wid thah 'Luis-ton-Aubern crowd' wahd-ah'd gib meh cred-dat, ev-vahn doe Eeyah beh ah 'bes'-cust-tah-mah'. *Trouble with the 'Luiston-Aubern-Crowd' wouldn't give me credit, even though I be a 'best-customer'".*

Then, one of Binny's "bes'-cust-tah-mahz" O-Ded and he was inconsolable. It would attract the police, it would reduce his income and it would rattle most of his other customer. Binny viewed his clientele as though he was a Moses, leading them to the Promised Land. He thought of himself as their guide, their messiah. He was leading them on a journey alright; a journey to a new land, a small plot of land. He disliked having "his people" think about their own mortality; this got in the way of what he was trying to "chieve".

Sometimes he had to retrieve them, whenever they would go a little crazy and start going to church or to the Salvation Army, the missions, or those Narcotics Anonymous meetings. He would then be forced to take action: go to them, persuade them to come back, even give them some free "merch". (Mimicking Binny's manner of speech is difficult, because he was a native of New York City, perhaps the Bronx, Harlem, or Bedford Stuyvesant in Brooklyn. He may have also had a speech impediment; but he rarely spoke to anyone other than his drug contacts.)

On a cold winter's afternoon, Cyn was practicing her trade near the Stinson Cannery, a cod fish processing plant on the waterfront. Binny had taught her how to turn tricks while on her knees; which was great! It meant she no longer had to bring men back to the camper and Great! Now, she no longer needed to trouble herself about contraceptives and abortions. It was great! Now, she could even work during her period.

The fisherman and fish-processing plant workers stank; but they had money even in winter. Cyn was just finishing up and was walking to the Stinson Plant door shivering; hoping for new customers so she could make her quota, hoping also to get in out of the cold. When a man, the plant manager she thought, pointed at her and said, "They-yah shay ehz, ahf-fah-sah!" *"There she is, Officer!"* Cyn immediately began running the other way. She had nothing illegal on her person and she hadn't been caught in the act; but they arrested her anyway. Before Binny could come and bail her out; all her money had been stolen by the police. They said it was evidence; but she didn't go to court and she never saw it again.

Binny came to the jail and got her. He walked her back to the camper, his arm around her shoulder. All the time, she was crying so hard she didn't even know where she was walking and she kept telling him how awful it all had been. Then he held her, while she shivered and cried. This tenderness endeared Binny to Cyn in a way that nothing anyone else had ever done. She thought, "He-ah lahvz meh; he-ah rahl-lah, rahl- lah lahvz meh!" *"He loves me; he really, really loves me!"* He did love her; he loved her the way he loved his long, black leather coat with the hood and the fur lining. He loved her the way he loved his 1961 Candy-Apple Red Cadillac convertible and he loved her the way he loved his drugs.

They decided to move to Lewiston-Auburn, where they would be closer to his drug wholesaler, William "Bill" Lane. It was December 21st in the year 1968 and Mike Asta was driving his little Toyota Corolla toward the Scarborough Marsh on Route One. Neither Cyn nor Binny would ever meet Mike Asta. Nevertheless, Mike was going to play a pivotal role in both their lives.

It was impossible for Cyn to feel secure in Bath any longer. She didn't want to leave the trailer. She reverted to the agoraphobic lifestyle of her mother. If she didn't leave the camper, she couldn't make any money and if she didn't make any money; what good was she? And how could Binny afford his drugs. Even when Binny tried beating Cyn, she still wouldn't get up off the floor in front of the "kitchen" counter in the trailer. Cyn longed to have a real kitchen; but by the same token, she didn't want to live anywhere but in her beloved trailer. Cyn wanted a kitchen so that she could bake bread. She wanted to lie down on a clean kitchen floor near a hot oven and wait for her bread dough to rise. She wanted to wait for it to rise on the gas side of an oil and gas stove, just like her mother's stove in Belfast. Then Charlene would put her pans in the oven and smell her bread baking; this is what Cynthia had seen of her only female role model.

Both Charlene and Cynthia were bread bakers. They slathered their bread with butter or just margarine. They covered it with home-made jams, jellies and preserves. If they couldn't get anything else, they would cover it with pure, white cane sugar. It was a wonder, that the girl had any teeth. She, like her mother, loved the smell of bread baking in the oven. It gave the whole house a wholesome, inviting aroma. Sometimes, all they had was bread, that's because they were very poor. They were poor, because of all the beer Charlene "had" to buy and later on, they were poor, because of all the cocaine Charlene bought; because by that time, Charlene was one of Binny's "bes'-cust-tah-mahz".

No matter what Binny did, he couldn't make Cynthia get up off the floor and go out to "work". He beat her, he kicked her; but she was like a dead thing lying there on the floor. So, he accepted defeat, trying a different tack. He would rally her by begging for her to drive him to Lewiston-Auburn. She enjoyed being on the road and above all things; she really enjoyed breathing the fresh, piney, salt air of rural Maine.

Chapter Thirty-One

I'M FROM THE GOVERNMENT, AND I'M HERE TO HELP YOU.

There was a loud banging on the door. Susan sat up in bed and put the baby back in his bassinet. It was 9:00 a.m. and she had overslept; but she wasn't expecting anyone and today was a day on which she had intended to relax, read the Bible and reflect. A strange woman was at the door, dressed all in black with a cloth coat and a black, woolen cap. Except for her shoulder-length hair, Susan would have taken her for a man and as Susan opened her door to this visitor, Paul began to cry loudly.

"How do you do? I'm Kelly Zorn from Child Protective Services. May I come in?" Kelly Zorn didn't have a Down-east accent. Susan wanted to ask her why. Perhaps she speculated that Ms. Zorn had graduated from Wellesley College like Maddy Cartwright.

"Yes, of course, Ms. Zorn. What is it that you want?" Susan smiled and looked down sweetly into her upturned face. Kelly Zorn walked into Susan's seemingly immaculate kitchen. There was however; nowhere for her to sit down until they came into the great room. Susan invited Ms. Zorn to sit in the rocking chair and she, herself, sat on the edge of her own brass bed. Kelly Zorn was about four feet, seven inches tall and weighed eighty-seven pounds. She was also very drawn and unsmiling. And as she began to sort through the contents of her brief case, searching for the report from the Visiting Nurse, Gladys Harmon; she fidgeted nervously. "It seems we have an inhospitable home with a very, young child in it." Paul pulled himself up and tried to tumble out of the bassinet again. Susan reached over, picked him up and as she did so, Ms. Zorn's face took on a look less dour. Susan decided to put the baby down on the braided rug near the bed to crawl. His cloth diaper was clean and the stack of clean cloth diapers on the rug next to the bed, gave the place a look of austerity, mixed with an abundance of those things that were needful and the braided rag rug filled the entire room.

Ms. Zorn read the government report out loud, Susan began bouncing the baby on her lap. Then, eventually transferring him to the rug; she sat down beside him and began to help him learn to play. There was no lingering smell of mildew on the carpet now and the essence of Pine Sol gave the whole place a clean, cared-for aroma. Susan hoped that this Godly smell would indicate to her guest, that she was a good homemaker and mother. Over in the corner were the two cardboard boxes still holding many of Susan's possessions and next to them were the two newspaper-draped windows, which looked out onto the alley. The door-less closet had several items of clothing hanging in it; along with cleaning supplies and a repair kit of several tools. This gave an air of hopefulness and cheeriness to their surroundings. Mr. Cross had installed two shower curtains; one on the shower itself and the other over the bathroom doorway. While Zorn droned on about draftiness and a lack of cleanliness, Susan began laughing and playing with her son. When you accept welfare of any kind, you open your door to a host of people who manage to make a pretty, good living out of you and who have a legal right to tell you what to do. Susan wondered how much this visit was costing the taxpayers. It didn't matter; Zorn was to be tolerated and graciously or there would be repercussions.

As Susan and little Paul played on the braided rug, Ms. Zorn finished reading her "report" and then saw that the tiny family had begun to laugh. "Where did you get this bed and the beautiful braided rug? She asked, "They look like antiques!"

"Well, the bed was a present from Mr. Cross, my landlord. It was already in the apartment when we moved in and I have just acquired a mattress to fit it from the Salvation Army Store. But, the rug is of my own creation; I got some donated overcoats and sweaters from the Salvation Army and sat on the floor braiding it myself. There are books about this craft in the Portland Public Library; I still have mine. See, here it is!" Susan pushed her library book, across the empty space between them. Kelly Zorn leafed through it, amazed. None of her other clients had library books nor even visited the library.

"You made this yourself? Why, that's really quite remarkable" she said, pleasantly surprised.

"It's my first attempt too." Susan said proudly. "This kind of rug tends to curl up around the edges as you make it; so, you have to keep adding fabric as you go otherwise the rug will never lay down right and it will eventually take on the shape of a bowl. Then you have to rip out all your stitches and start over", she said with a note of achievement in her voice. "I had to rip my stitching out four times, until I discovered this trick".

They had finally gotten off the topic of Gladys Harmon's report and were conversing like normal people. Kelly smiled and in spite of herself, she was becoming fond of Susan and was eager to wrap up this interview so that she could find someone for whom her services were truly necessary. Susan often prayed for favor among men, which was her way of asking God to look out for her with the government set. Kelly knew that she had to inspect the home for "staples". Not the kind that were still embedded in the front porch, but the kind in Susan's cabinets. Asking to peek into a "client's" cabinets was a delicate matter. Some people became immediately hostile and social workers who just barged into the kitchen and "did it" were considered authoritarian busy-bodies in the extreme. Kelly knew that her status as a "child protective worker" held its own kind of intimidating clout, but, she was still new at this occupation and didn't want to antagonize Susan.

"When did you move in here?" she inquired.

"Nine days ago, Gladys was here that day. It really was a mess and rather badly in need of repairs; but I had a little help from Mr. Cross and from a friend who has some carpentry skills. I scrubbed, I patched and I've made this rug. I still have some more things to move in. I was homeless for almost two months and it was very hard on Paul. This is affordable, only one hundred and forty dollars a month and the utilities are included. It's better than I thought I could ever do."

"That is reasonable!" Kelly said, "How did you get it?"

"After my son, Paul, was born, we were thrown out of our studio-apartment, which I shared with my late husband. You know, Kelly, if you really wanted to do something to protect children; you could apply your efforts toward helping them not get evicted just because they're kids. What's happening to children in the State of Maine is just awful and not getting an apartment right away! Dreadful! How can somebody put, 'no children, no pets' on an ad in the newspaper and that's legal? Frequently while, I was homeless with this baby, Kelly, I was on the phone with my State Senator, my State Representative and the Governor telling them about my situation and begging them to introduce a bill into the legislature that would protect children from being thrown into the street, just for being kids. There should have been some other people making those phone calls for me, people like you, people who are paid to protect children." Kelly Zorn's mouth dropped open. She had never been spoken to so articulately.

Nor had she ever heard a more impassioned argument for children's rights. This was turning into a most surprising interview.

Once things get into the bureaucratic pipeline, they must turn out the way the government wants them to, or it isn't "progress". Government Workers are by and large Progressives and **Progressivism is a religion**. Unless one is a member of this "church", one is not hired by government. Government workers are hired to believe in something. That government is the solution to every problem. It didn't matter if the apartment was affordable, or if it was now clean; it still wasn't "appropriate" and therefore it wasn't going to be allowed. Kelly Zorn would have to rescind Gladys Harmon's report and stop the inevitable paperwork that accompanied such a visit. Then, the next time she came to the residence, there would have to be evidence that the occupant had "profited from the contact". Otherwise, there would have to be a supervisory meeting or even a formal inquest. Kelly was, after all, only a junior "Child and Family Worker" and therefore not allowed to just write "case closed" on this report and have done with it. Susan and Paul would have to be converted into that title that social workers loved so much; they would have to become "clients" of some government-funded program or agency.

"May I look in your cabinets before I leave," Ms. Zorn's face took on that eager, earnest expression so typical of young people, who were still unsure of themselves in a new career.

"Is it part of the inspection?" Susan inquired, feigning surprise; her heart in her mouth.

"Actually, yes, it'll just take us a minute, if you don't mind."

"Ok, I hardly have any food yet, seeing I just moved in." as they went into the kitchen and Susan dutifully opened the cabinet above the sink and prayed Kelly wouldn't take down one of the cereal boxes, shake it and discern it to be a fake. She didn't. Then they opened the refrigerator and

Ms. Zorn could see that there was: cheese, fruit, vegetables, left-over fried chicken and a gallon jug of milk. That was all Kelly needed. She would write on her report, that the house seemed clean and orderly and that there was food.

Chapter Thirty-Two
MEETING BINNY'S FRIENDS

It was an old, dark-gray house on a dreary street in Auburn, Maine. They drove up with their shiny chrome torpedo; Cyn was driving the beautiful, red, convertible caddy that she actually owned because, of course, nothing could be in Binny's name. Bill Lane was the owner and proprietor of this tenement-styled, older home that was cut up into individual apartments. Bill owned most of the neighborhood. His family had lived in Lewiston-Auburn for generations and the majority of his tenants were extended family. There were shrubs out in front of the house and there was a shed, still under construction, in the back of the building.

Along-side these two buildings was a gravel alley, where trash was frequently thrown out and where old refrigerators and other appliances that no longer worked were dumped off on the side of the road. The front of the building was obscured by large bushes, that had berries and long, large thorns on them. She parked her camper and the Cadillac in the alley, beside the house. Cyn got out and went around the front of the house and sat down on the porch. She was as depressed and sullen as the depressing structure in front of which she was sitting. This type of house typifies the ancient structures in this part of Maine. An old, rambling house which had been built for a single family of means, then cut up into individual apartments. Maine has many old families; where parents, brothers and sisters, distant cousin, uncles and aunts, all crowd into a single structure.

The shed behind this house was under construction, because Bill Lane needed a place outside his residence to store his drugs which were also his livelihood. His cousin, John had some carpentry skills which Bill wanted to use to his advantage. Besides, John was behind in his rent as were a lot of Bill's other tenants. And Bill reasoned that this would be a good way for him to "wurk ehd ahf." *"work it off."*

John Lane was out in the shed, working without an overcoat. He was a skinny, wizened man in late twenties or early thirties. He was constructing this outbuilding for his cousin, who was also his landlord and employer. He was constructing it without benefit of any contract, license, building permit or compensation. John happened to be a "speed-freak, meth-, reds-, and pot-head". Carpentry was his only skill, but what a skill he had. Everything was neat, precise and almost done. Only the interior of the building needed to be finished. Good thing too; it was just about time for more snow.

Roofs in Maine need constant maintenance. Enough snow can fall in one day to collapse a poorly constructed or decrepitly-old roof. John Lane shingled, hung the door and did all the exterior work, while it was still warm enough for him to work outside. He was putting the finishing touches on the interior; insulating it; dry-walling and painting it two beautiful shades of electric green and pink. But, this wasn't going to be living quarters for anyone, because it had no windows. There was just a double-bolt security door with a silent alarm which rang in the house. So, it was a perfect place to store drugs.

On the rear side of the shed that John Lane was constructing, there was an overhang or carport big enough for Cyn's little camper and the caddy to nestle securely against. But, its eventual purpose was to provide a shelter for stored firewood. The shed was equipped with a woodstove, which had a Metalbest 3VP-VC VP chimney-pipe venting-system. And on the side of the shed was a permanently attached ladder to facilitate easy sweeping of snow off the roof and ease in maintenance of the chimney pipe. People who don't watch their stove vents and roofs are anathema in the State of Maine, like "Frozen Charlotte". They have become the stuff of cautionary tales told around Mainers' warm stoves on snowy, wintery evenings, especially Upcountry.

The story of Frozen Charlotte is based on a poem by Seba Smith, first published in **"The Rover"**, a Maine newspaper, on December 28th 1843, under the title: "A Corpse Goes to a Ball".

This is a time-honored, Maine folk tale. Telling it makes one shiver on a long, cold, snowy, winter's night in Maine. It takes place out in the countryside of Northwestern Maine, which is also referred to as Upcountry. It was New Year's Eve, December 31, 1841 and back then people traveled by wagon in summer and by sleigh in winter. Upcountry people make their living farming and lumbering. Settlements and houses are far afield and during the gloomy winter months the natives never let an opportunity for merriment go to waste no matter how cold or snowy it may be.

A wealthy lumber baron had a beautiful daughter named Charlotte. He spoiled her. She was a very lovely, young woman and the apple of his eye. No dress was too expensive or delicate for Charlotte. She wore a whale-bone corset under her silken gown and she had lips of ruby red with blonde curls framing her beautiful face; but she was vain, completely taken with herself.

A ball was given on New Year's Eve and it would be the social event of the season. Charlotte's escort was the most debonair bachelor in Maine. Her ball gown was silk and gossamer blue, the bodice was low cut on her neck and shoulders and her skirt revealed her tiny waist. The night was clear and cold and there was a bitter wind blowing; but though her beau was wearing long underwear, a woolen scarf, a fur-lined cap and a heavy coat with a fur collar, Charlotte came out to meet him dressed only in a silken gown and a satin cape. She also wore a velvet muff on her left arm.

They traveled by open sleigh pulled by a team of white horses. The young man asked her,

"Chary, Chary, 'r' you-ah code?" *"Charlotte, Charlotte, are you cold?"*

"Ayuh, eht'z var-rah, var-rah code tahnahyt", *"Yes, it's very, very cold tonight"*, she shivered.

"Eeyah hahv ah blah-cat uhnd-dah thah sate, thahd Eeyah coahn rahp rahnd you-ah. Eht'z ah bit-tah nahyt ahnd ah lahng rahd." *"I have a blanket under the seat, that I could wrap around you. It's a bitter night and a long ride."*

"Ayur, daow!" *Oh, no!"* she cried, "Bah thah tahm, we-ah rahch thah pah-tea, Eeyah'll smahll ahz bahd ahz ah hahs' blah-cat ahnd they-ah cell lahf aht meh!" *"By the time, we reach the party, I'll smell as bad as a horse blanket and they will laugh at me!"*

A few miles from the ball, Charlotte's ruby lips were blue; there was frost in her hair and her escort was offering her a bearskin, which she also turned down saying, "Ehd wahd crah-sh mah drahs." *"It would crush my dress."*

"Chary! Chary! 'r' you-ah code?" *"Charlotte! Charlotte! Are you cold?"*, he asked, "Saht clahse tah meh ahnd we-ah cauhn shar mah bah-day hate." *"Sit close to me and we can share my body heat."*

But, she replied. "Thahd wud-de'n beh prah-pah; beh-sidez, Eeyah-'em gaht- tehn wahrm-mah nah." *"That wouldn't be proper; besides, I'm getting warmer now."*

When they arrived, the young man jumped down from the sleigh and cried, "Chary, Chary! We-ah 'r' hee-yah! Cahm ehn-sahd gaht wahrm!" *"Charlotte, Charlotte! We are here! Come inside get warm!"* Charlotte didn't say a word and when he took her hand to help her out of the sleigh; she was frozen solid! So, if you ever go for a sleigh ride on a long, cold, winter's night in UpCountry, Maine wear a fur coat, a woolen scarf, mittens and a hat or you may become like frozen Charlotte.

THE BALLAD OF FROZEN CHARLOTTE
By Kenneth Peacock (1844) and George Eliot (2018)

One New Year's Eve at setting sun,
Far looked Chary's wistful eye.
Out through the frosty window pane,
As merry sleighs went by.

In a village, fifteen miles away,
There was a ball that night.
And though the air was heavy and cold,
Her heart was warm and light.

How brightly and how happily,
Her suitor's sleigh appeared.
Upon the glistening snow it sped,
The cottage door it neared.

"O, daughter dear," her mother cried,
"This blanket 'round you fold.
It is a dreadful night out there,
You'll catch your death of cold."

"Oh nay! Oh nay!" young Charlotte cried,
My satin cloak's enough.

You know 'tis lined throughout,
Besides, I have my velvet muff.

She stepped into the sleigh that night,
Five miles at length were passed.
When her suitor shivering spoke,
His silence broke at last.

"Such a dreadful night nare' I saw,
The reins I scarce can hold."
Fair Charlotte shivering faintly said,
"I am exceedingly cold."

He cracked his whip, he urged his steeds,
Much faster than before.
And thus five other dreary miles,
In silence passed they o'er.

Said he: "How fast the wicked ice,
Is gathering on my brow".
And Charlotte still more faintly said,
"I'm growing warmer now".

So, on they rode through frosty air,
And glittering cold starlight.
Until at last in village lamps,
The ballroom came in sight.

They reached the door, then sprang he down,

Extending his hand to her.
She sat there like a monument,
He had no power to stir.

He called her once, he called her twice,
She answered not a word.
He asked her for her hand again,
And still she never stirred.

He took her hand in his - Oh God!
'Twas cold and hard as stone.
He tore the mantle from her face,
Cold stars upon it shone.

Then quickly to the glowing hall,
Her lifeless form he bore.
Fair Charlotte's eyes were closed in death,
Her voice was heard no more.

And there he sat right by her side,
While bitter tears did flow.
He cried: "My own, my charming one,
You never more will know".

He twined his arms around her neck,
He kissed her marble brow.
His thoughts flew back to where she said,
"I'm feeling warmer now".

He carried her back into his sleigh,

And with her rode he home.

And when he reached the cottage door,

How did her parents mourn.

Her parents mourned for many a year,

And he wept in his gloom.

Until at last, of grief he died,

And they lie in one tomb.

The construction of this new shed was undertaken, because William "Bill" D. Lane, who was Binny's wholesaler, needed a place outside his home to store his drugs. Bill Lane, who had a skill for manipulating people that Binny found enviable, owned the entire building. And, to Binny's astonishment, Bill Lane was actually able to collect the rent in one fashion or another from everyone in the household. The residents of "the Lane House" were all related to one another. The house was originally constructed in 1863 as the mansion of the owner of the lumber mill and later it was cut up into tenement housing for his mill workers, who were also Lane's. It was like one of those islands in the Casco Bay, like Diamond, where everyone has the same last name, but instead of Diamond it was Lane.

Bill Lane's tenants and relatives were all hard working, hard drinking and druggy people who used foul language, lived in sin with their girlfriends and always went to church on Sunday. They attended the Most Holy Trinity, United Church of Christ, UCC on a hilltop overlooking Auburn, Maine. While living with them, Cyn began to cultivate "reg-gul-lahz" of her own and like Binny, she began seeing only certain people and then only when scheduled. All of Cyn's "reg-gul-lahz" were members of the clergy and this may have been a consequence of her terrible experience in Bath, which she never wanted to repeat.

This house was a kind of Christianized commune, with the exception that the drugs were of a harder variety not the soft psychedelics passed around by the hippies and the "love" they shared wasn't free. All the Lane men fancied themselves ministers. They were actually more like those eastern holy men, who sit around meditating all day. In any case, if you knew what these holy men did for a living, you'd know what they did for Cynthia.

Bill Lane could see why Binny had paid so much money for gorgeous, voluptuous Cyn. She was a beautiful, blue-eyed blonde with a beguiling smile and a curvaceous figure. She was sweet, listened patiently to other people's problems and always had a word of encouragement for them. She greeted everyone in the morning, when they came into the kitchen and didn't mind making breakfast. She woke up smiling every day, even though she really didn't have anything to smile about. She was also a pretty good cook and bread baker.

Cyn was the only person who ever cleaned the oven, though another Cynthia: Cynthia Palmer was kept just to clean and really wasn't pulling her weight. Bill Lane was smitten with blonde Cynthia; he despised the other Cynthia with the dirty, stringy, thin, brown hair. Everything about "stringy Cynthia" was disgusting, from the way that she hung around his cousin John to the way she never bathed. She was "awe-fahl", "awful", he thought, "jehz' awe-fahl!" *just awful!* The only rational thing to do was to move Cynthia Palmer out of the basement and in with his cousin John. The basement became Binny and Cyn's domain and "Beautiful Cynthia" immediately installed mirror tiles on all the walls and the ceiling in one corner of the basement. This was going to become her new indoor bordello. One that wasn't affected by inclement weather. Bill wanted to be near beautiful Cyn; he wanted to invest in her. He didn't view this as coveting his neighbor's wife, because after all Cyn wasn't Binny's wife. She was just a whore.

When Cyn lit a scented candle to get her client into the mood to have sex, the light of that single candle would reflect off the mirror tiles on the walls and ceiling in her corner and sparkle throughout the whole basement. Because of these mirror tiles, that corner of Cyn's basement bordello shimmered with amazing light. She loved lying on that brand-new mattress and box spring, which she shoved into her corner as far as it would go. Above it the mirrored walls and ceiling sparkled and dazzled from the light of only that one single, scented candle.

Cyn put anti-freeze in the camper's pipes, she remembered this from her Uncle Marlin, who instructed her in how to maintain the camper. He showed her how to keep the camper's pipes from bursting during the wintertime when it was not in use. As just a girl of thirteen, Cyn watched her Uncle Marlin drain the old radiator water and pouring in a mixture of anti-freeze and fresh water. Since childhood, she had thought of the camper as her own. She considered it as her livelihood; her special home. So, it was with great shock and deep disappointment that she came back from a performance at a client's home to find it missing.

"Bin-nay, thah cahm-pah ehz mahn! Eht'z ehn mah naymb!", she cried. "Binny, the camper is mine! *It's in my name!*", she cried. "Eht'z naught meh, Cyn!", *"It's not me, Cyn!"* "Eht'z naught meh!" *It's not me!"* Binny answered, "Eht'z Bahll Lahne, he-ah wahnt-tad tah gahv thah cahm-pah tah hahz bah-shop fromb thah Uhn-I- dad Chahch ahv Chrys'!" *"It's Bill Lane, he wanted to give the camper to his bishop, from the United Church of Christ!"*

"Bahd, thahd bah-shop ehz Juan ahv mah reg-gul-lahz!" *"But, that bishop is one of my regulars!"* Cyn sobbed.

"Eeyah nehd-dad mah merch! Ehd-'ll beh awe-ride! Ehd ehz stehl teck-neck- lay you-ahrz, babe! We-'ahl gaht eht bahk, babe! Cahm nes' Sprahng prahm-mahs!" *I needed more merchandise! It'll be alright! It is still technically yours, babe! We'll get it back, babe! Come next Spring, promise!"*

She thought, "Eeyah-'ll nev-vah say thah cahm-pah ah-gahn!" *"I'll never see the camper again!"*

Cyn did some other things which did not ingratiate her to the people of the "Lane House". She suggested a yard sale, rather than throwing out all those surplus goods from the basement. When she washed a pile of laundry, which was well over her head and in "her part" of the basement. She considered it saleable and hers.

Bill Lane went around for days saying, "Mah pahl", "Mah pahl". *My pile, My pile.* Then, he carried it all to the dump in his pick-up truck. He wanted to get rid of it and in a way that wouldn't attract attention. Bill and John said, "We dohn'wahn ehn- nay stranj-jahz tah cahm sniff-fehn 'rahnd hee-yah bah thah shahd". *"We don't want any strangers to come sniffing around here by the shed."*

Cyn also gave the City of Auburn a telephone call concerning an old refrigerator, which she found when she was walking along the gravel drive behind the house. She didn't want some little boy or girl to climb into that refrigerator and smother. She turned out to be a very, inconvenient woman; who had no real concept that protecting their illicit way of life was paramount. And that the safety of children, especially other people's children, wasn't in any way significant. But, this would explain why nobody came when little Angela Palmer was burning up in her parent's oven.

On October 29th, 1984, Auburn-Maine AP reported that the police responded to a disturbance at an apartment in the "Lane House". Smelling the unmistakable odor of burning human flesh, someone called the police.

They arrested the mother and her live-in boyfriend, John Lane. Cynthia Palmer had two little girls Angela and Sara. And without the mother's knowledge or approval, John Lane placed little Angela in their electric oven. Then he jammed the oven door shut with a chair. According to him and Cynthia Palmer, who dutifully concurred, Lucifer had to be burned up in their oven. Angela's fitfully screams reverberated and echoed from the walls of their apartment. "Dah-dee led meh oud!", *"Daddy let me out!"*, "Dah-dee led meh oud!" ***"Daddy let me out!*** She screamed as she suffocated. Her death cries and her little feet pounding on the oven door were not audible over the loud, Christian music that her parents were playing as they sat on the couch reading the Bible. Their praise music was so loud, that the neighbors had to call the police. So, when the people in the building smelled the fumes; it was already too late to save little, four-year-old Angela Palmer.

Chapter Thirty-Three
AN INVITATION TO A MEETING

The rules for receiving welfare all begin with the word, "Don't": 1. Don't work, 2. Don't save, 3. Don't start a business, 4. Don't try to get out of poverty. A letter was waiting for Susan in the mailbox on the porch of her Myrtle Street apartment, when she returned from shopping for food and furnishings. The letter insisted that Paul and Susan attend a meeting at the Department of Health and Human Services on Marginal Way. The meeting was with a Case Worker named Mildred Harper and Mildred would be accompanied by two other Human Services workers, who were supposed to sign off on the case of Susan and Paul Asta.

These three-people wanted to see Susan and her baby at 1:30 p.m. on Wednesday of the following week. Susan wasn't working so this didn't interfere with her schedule, but she kept thinking that this mid-week, mid-day meeting was designed to keep her unemployed and available between the hours of 9:00 a.m. and 4.30 p.m. She was to be at their beck and call all day long during business hours. The notice was singularly uninformative about why the meeting was necessary, but it specified what documents she would have to bring with her.

The required documents where bank account statements going back three months, the lease for the apartment on Myrtle Street, any letters from DHS specifying the amount of her support check and food stamps and any other financial papers that might be relevant. Susan had a box under her bed to store any such documents. So, she would have everything she needed.

She wondered why people would send you a letter and then arrange a meeting at which time you were expected to show them that letter. The meeting was to occur in Mildred Harper's office on the second floor of the Human Services Building on Marginal Way and Susan came early. Mildred Harper turned out to be an alumna of Wesley College and a sorority sister of Maddy Cartwright. Susan was trying to get Mildred to tell her whether she had the right paperwork with her or not, when the phone rang. The woman on the other end of the phone was trying to get Mildred to help her procure after-school care for her nine-year-old son and Mildred did her best to explain to the caller that Human Services didn't actually serve anyone or act human. Susan overheard the conversation and realized that she had been given an opportunity to help both her friend, Jane Dyer and this unknown woman on the telephone.

"No ma'am, we don't know anybody that can help you." People that worked for the welfare department, always used the royal "We" in describing themselves.

"Jane Dyer will do it!" Susan blurted out.

"She's a mom on AFDC and could really use the money." To Susan's astonishment, Mildred Harper repeated what she had just said, verbatim. "Jane even lives in your neighborhood", Susan continued "your son can walk there from the bus stop", Susan said and Mildred repeated. Susan fumbled for her address book and triumphantly read Jane's address and phone number aloud. Mildred repeated the information and then hung up. It was time for their meeting. Susan hoped she had all of her paperwork together.

A short, paunchy man with glasses and a rumpled, brown suit named

André Françoise arrived and the meeting commenced. Mildred asked André why he looked so tired and he replied that he was paper-training a puppy and asked Susan if she had the necessary documents. She said she hoped so and handed them over. Then, she attended to the meeting, folding her hands on the table, the way the nuns had taught her to when she was in grade school.

Mr. Françoise looked at Susan over the tops of his bifocals and sorted through the paperwork, taking careful notice of an interest-bearing savings account passbook. His mouth fell open, he stared up at Susan, impressed. Other people in Susan's predicament were not savers, "Do-ah you-ah hahv sahb-sah-dized howz-zehn?" *"Do you have subsidized housing?"* he inquired, genuinely perplexed that she could make ends meet on such short funds.

"No sir, I don't, but the rent is less than my welfare check and I get food stamps and Medicaid." Susan replied, forthrightly and with no embarrassment about being on welfare, especially not here on Marginal Way. "Eeyah did-den't nah thahd they-ah wahr ehn-nay au-paht-mehnz ehn Paut-lan' thahd rahnt fahr lahs' thahn ah Mah- thah weahth own-lay Juan chahd gauhd frumb AFDC. Hahw 'r' you-ah do-ehn thahs?" *"I didn't know that there were any apartments in Portland that rent for less than the check a mother with only one child got from AFDC. How are you doing this?"* Susan thought about explaining to him that when you tithed, you actually get more money than if you didn't, but she decided that this would probably be impractical with this man and so demurred to volunteer any extraneous information, when he inquired how she could do this, his face beaming with admiration. She settled on talking about budgeting, which was also a Biblical principle that Susan was pursuing.

"It's a tear-down that my landlord, David Cross, is going to move me out of before it gets cold; he said so. He has an occupied unit that he promised me would be vacant, because the renter is scheduled to receive subsidized housing in a few months."

"Thah rah-pahrt sahz thahd thah prah-mah-sahz 'r' tah code ahnd drahf-tah tah prah-vahd ahd-dah-quat howz-zehn fahr ahn ehn-fahnt." *"The report says that the premises are too cold and drafty to provide adequate housing for an infant."* Mr. Françoise looked intently into Susan's eyes.

"'R'-ehn't you-ah ah-freyd fahr you-ah bay-bay?" *"Aren't you afraid for your baby?"* he asked, acknowledging the sleeping infant in Susan's arms.

"He's perfectly safe with me", Susan assured Mr. Françoise, "I've tightened up all the holes and made repairs to the kitchen cabinets. The landlord has repaired the shower and I have a decent bed. The baby is still in his bassinette and we've got food, gas, water and electricity. What more does a person need? I've started looking for a part-time job and that means more money in another month."

Mr. Françoise's face beamed with approval. He inquired, "Dohn' you-ah hahv en-nay fahm-lay 'r' sum-Juan thahd coahd gahv you-ah ah bah-tah plahz tah lib." *"Don't you have any family or someone that could give you a better place to live."*

Susan frowned, "It's just me and the baby, since my husband passed away and my parents are both dead. Mike's father is also dead now and his mother is in a nursing home. I've tried to get Mike's Social Security, but they denied my claim, because we were married in Mexico. So, AFDC is all that's available to us."

When Susan got home from the DHS, she was sure the compassionate Mildred Harper and André Françoise were going to allow her to stay in her newly- renovated home. She sat down on her bed and reflected. She missed Mike; she ached for him. There hadn't been time to mourn him properly with the hectic search for housing leaving her numb and unable to process her grief.

She sank into her bed holding her sleeping baby, rocking him and letting out deep sobs of grief and pain. This brief pause in her desperate situation gave Susan the respite necessary to assemble a good professional wardrobe and go out looking for employment. But, first she had to secure daycare. That evening she went to Twig at Ralph Magwood, Todd Maynard and Jill Ireland's Way Home. One nice thing about being disfellowshipped by an organization as loosely assembled as the Way Ministry, a lot of times people didn't know about it. She inquired if anybody knew of a stay-at-home mom in the Ministry, who would like to watch her son for forty dollars a week or an hourly fee of three dollars. This was good money back then.

She supplied these services for free to Ruth Burrell. But now that she needed child care, she discovered that reciprocity was another principle in which the Way Ministry did not believe. On the real Way Tree, everything flowed backwards from the leaves to the tree, not from the tree to the leaves as was the teaching in the "Way Tree" seminar Susan had taken.

Susan marveled that things were not in reality as they had been explained. The "leadership" lived much more comfortably than did average believers, which were considered the "Leaves". And, believers with children or handicaps were ignored, unless they were also wealthy or well-connected to the people at the top. So, Jim and Anne Simmons never wanted for someone to watch their daughter while single moms, like Susan, couldn't get desperately-need child care through the Way, even if they were willing and able to pay for it.

Susan found an ad in the paper, "Red-Cross, Babysitting-class graduate will sit for your child in your home; $60 a week plus overtime." She thought, "This might be the childcare I need. I wonder if I can talk her down to $40."

Chapter Thirty-Four

PENTHOUSE APARTMENT ON CONGRESS AND HIGH

When Binny and Cyn experienced a setback, his stuff managed to make it to the next stage in their lives while hers did not. Binny's Caddy was big enough to move all their things from Lewiston-Auburn to Portland, Maine. After all, Binny's only possession, besides his drugs was the 1961 Two-Door Cadillac Convertible Coupe de Ville, itself. All of Cyn's possessions could now fit into a small, paper bag and consisted mainly of thread-bare, sexy outfits. The camper was gone. When they got settled, Binny scouted out a "hol-lah-tray" *"hollow tree"* within the Portland City limits, in which to secret away his drugs. He settled on a rented garage for his Caddy, with his stash kept in its trunk. There had to be the mandatory, secondary drop location, because you just never knew.

Cyn looked for a place to solicit her sexual customers. She never needed to do anything but just stand or sit in public and work her sexy-child spirit. Men immediately gravitated to Cyn because of her beauty and the innocence she exuded, despite her occupation. Binny stood nearby hovering protectively warding off the fright that she had experienced in Bath.

What had just blown into Portland, Maine was a two-person, crime-wave, complete with an inventory of two keys of cocaine and twenty-four decks of pure heroin. (A deck is several glass tubules of liquid, injectable heroin, in rubber-banded quantities of ten.) Binny never bought marijuana in quantity, because the dogs could sniff it out too easily and then that would lead the police to the rest of his "merch".

He found several secondary drop locations and since Binny's "merch" was sealed in glassine bags; he hid it under large rocks in vacant lots all around the city. Like a squirrel with its nuts, he sometimes forgot where he had dropped his "merch", but he retained a secondary stash location on lower Chestnut Street, where he had a self-storage unit. This was one of those "you store it, you keep the key" units, which are so prevalent today. This was where Binny intended to eventually store guns when, in future, he branched out into other enterprises than the sale of drugs and his girlfriend. He kept the key for this very important stash attached to his belt.

Ever the optimist, Cyn thought, "Weahl aht lease', Eeyah fahn-lay hahv ah kit-chen ahv mah own!" *"Well at least, I finally have a kitchen of my own!"* The kitchen on the first floor of the Lane House in Auburn was never really hers. She could clean it and bake bread in its oven, but when her bread got distributed to "the family", she receiving no compensation for it whatsoever. "The joke" was that Cyn's bread was the only "free love" in the entire "Lane House" commune. Cyn finally had a warm place by the oven; where bread was baking. This was hers; "her place" a clean place, a safe place to lie down on the floor and feel and smell her bread baking. This was a place where there were no needles, no filth.

A strange well of stairs, leading down to nowhere, was right under the windows in the corner of the great room. These windows looked out onto the intersection of Congress and High Streets and this "well of stairs" held a metal footlocker, where Binny's paraphernalia and drug stash were located. Binny stored a few "emergency" glassine bags of cocaine and a few decks of heroin in this locker, which was completely covered with dirty rags and the sweepings from the great room floor. This was all the preventative necessary to keep the lazy narcotics officers on the PPD from going down those stairs, one narc actually looked down into the pit when the plywood was drawn back by, as always, Cynthia. He was posing as a stoner and was sitting on his haunches near the corner windows in the great room. It was enough for this undercover officer to look into the "merch pit" and see that all there was down there was a collection of dirty, bloody rags to lose interest in pursuing the matter. Ever so often, Binny would relieve it of its surplus "merch" or add to its supply. Whenever, Binny's "merch" became too plentiful for safety, or too low for commerce to proceed easily. The surplus or the lack of merchandise was solved after dark and after everyone other than Cynthia went home. Then Binny would process his merch and his money in secret and sometimes in the dark or by the light of a single candle or flashlight, because after all, he was pursuing an illegal enterprise. Binny always transferred his stash to a new "hol-lah-tray" whenever it became too plentiful, or he would fuss over his "merch pit" whenever they became too sparse. Binny had so many of these "hol-lah-trayz" scattered around town, that he lost track of their locations.

He thought that he didn't want to leave too much of his "merch" in this "merch pit" because it was located in his place of residence. If there was anything that Binny wanted to protect, it was his own habitation. Cyn wanted to protect it too, she swept everything into the stairwell, which they both began calling, "the merch pit". But, after one of Binny's stoners stepped over its side and fell down to the bottom breaking an ankle, Cyn carried in several sheets of plywood and covered it. Now on a daily basis, "the merch pit", became the pit into which all the accumulated filth of the great room was swept and under which a footlocker filled with drugs and "clean" needles were kept.

The great room became cluttered with several old mattresses, which Cyn covered with two fitted bed sheets, one on each side, stacking these against the wall. After mopping this wooden floor, which Cyn believed to be oak, she would leave it to dry in the sunlight and then replace the "merch pit's" plywood cover. Back when Cyn still had her beloved camper, she would sweep out Binny's rear compartment into the nearest ditch, but now Binny's "merch pit" served this purpose. Binny didn't want Cyn to sweep the great room at all. They argued incessantly, about this because Binny hated sunlight and cleanliness and Cyn wanted to keep from pricking a bare foot or a bottom on the inevitable dropped needle which could be lying on the floor or buried in a mattress. She wanted to be sure that when she lay down to sleep in that room at night, or when she entertained her sexual clientele there were no loose hypodermic syringes. This is why she cleaned its floor so judiciously before the sun set. She would use the sunlight streaming through the great room windows, to disclose the needles and act as disinfectant destroying contagion. This was the only way she could sleep in "peace". Cyn had made draperies for the corner windows from a scratchy, brown, army-surplus, blanket which darkened the room as much as Binny preferred, while leaving a way for Cyn to access sunlight for its daily cleaning. After sweeping, Cynthia would stack the dirty mattresses against the wall between the great room and the kitchen. This floor was filthier and more dangerous with sharp objects, than the pavement in the alley behind the shops on Congress Street. Once Cyn had swept it thoroughly, she would put the plywood back over the "merch pit" and get her rag mop and bucket out to make the great room smell like Pine-sol.

Binny was not a person that ever got cheated in a dope deal. He would always put his arm around the junky that cheated him or didn't pay him and generously bestow free drugs on that person, which they would of course accept. It would be their last "high". The potion he gave Roz and Charlene, a mixture of milk powder and strychnine; derived from commonly available rat poison was ever at hand. He would keep it hidden, just for this purpose; then, watch the luckless junky snort it, telling him or her that it was his special stash just for snorting and then when they were getting sick, walk them outside leaving them somewhere where someone could find them. In the city of Portland, this wasn't always a death sentence like it was in Lewiston-Auburn. There, he would take the junky he was sending to oblivion into the nearest wooded area and leave him or her for the bears. Maine has very few places that are so urban you are not within fifty miles of the wilderness. Binny would leave the stoner in the woods dying and calling out to him for help. There would be a wry smile on his face as he walked away, because before he left he would always smear the druggie with peanut butter to attract carnivores and scavengers. Once when Cyn was busy cleaning the great room, Binny came back with one of his clients to find her "cahm-mit-tehn ah neht-ness" *"committing a neatness"* and broke into a storm of angry swearing, saying, "you-ah 'nahsty-neht faht", *"you nasty-neat fart"*. Then she would have to clear out and let them pull the mattresses, that she had stacked against the wall back onto the newly mopped floor. However, as soon as he would leave again, she would come back and finish her sweeping, washing and moping.

Cyn was an avid reader and an avid follower of newspaper horoscopes and crossword puzzles and she pursued these activities in her kitchen after she had gotten her mandatory $300 dollars for the day. Binny was becoming a hard taskmaster; she couldn't rely on her old "reg-gul-lahz", like she had in Lewiston-Auburn. She had to go out onto a Portland street and find new customers until he made her quota. She really needed to hustle to find new customers without being caught by the police. Both Cyn and Binny feared the police, because now he no longer had a wholesale distributer like Bill Lane nearby. Cyn had to drive his Caddy up to Lewiston-Auburn which was a hassle and which was also the only outing they ever got. She would tool around town with Binny hanging out of the window looking for a "hol-lah-tray" *"hollow tree"*. Cyn loved driving the car. It was the only excursion he ever afforded her. He would thanklessly let her chauffer him from place to place in this luxurious, red car. All his "friends" envied him for his car and his girlfriend, because Cynthia would do anything for him. She worshipped him.

Chapter Thirty-Five
DESPERATE FOR DAYCARE

Susan went back to Jane Dyer's to use the telephone for the evening; she also thought she'd spend the night on Jane's couch, if Jane would have her. Susan had made a little crèche in the corner next to Jane's couch for Paul. She had made it several weeks ago, when she was homeless. Now she revisited it; because she was still phoneless. The crèche consisted of several pillows, rolled up blankets and the crib mattress from Ruth Burrell.

Since Susan was as earnest about searching for daycare and a job, as she had been about seeking after housing, she applied herself to answering these newspaper ads as aggressively as she did the rental ads. Jane had Mildred Harper's after-school-care referral sitting on her couch. She thanked Susan for this and encouraged her to use the telephone to get day-care. "Mah-thah ahv Gahd", *Mother of God*, she exclaimed as Susan set up her typewriter on Jane's kitchen table and banged out a resume. Then Susan got busy calling the ads featuring babysitting services, which were in the Portland Press Herald. What a joy it was to have this old machine back and what a help it was in making a resume of her education and experience.

"This is Susan Asta and I'm inquiring about your ad in the paper to provide babysitting services?"

"Oh yes", Audrey McDonald replied, "My daughter Nancy placed that ad. She is a graduate of an American Red Cross babysitting class."

"Ms. McDonald, would Nancy prefer to sit for my son at your home or at my place? I promise you it's far less comfortable than the home you enjoy."

"Your place will be fine, at least for the initial interview. How about two o'clock tomorrow afternoon. I'd like to accompany her at least the first time."

As Susan was walking back to the Portland Public Library from Jane's, she passed through the Deering Oaks Park and Deering Woods. These two parks combine into one park and are the site of "The Battle of Falmouth" also called, "The Battle of Fort Loyal" which was between early Portland settlers and the local Wabanaki Indians which lasted between May 16th and May 20th in 1690. The Indians who referred to themselves as the Wampanoag attacked Fort Loyal and its companion church, not yet called the First Parish Church of Portland, Maine in concert with their French allies. So, on the site of these two, present-day city parks a battle ensued in which the Wampanoag scalped Rev. George Burroughs. He survived without his hair and succeeded Rev. John Thorpe, the Calvinist minister, who founded the church. Thorpe was dismissed from his ministry by his congregation, who considered him a drunkard and profane. The First Parish Church is the oldest structure in Portland, Maine and is a true historical landmark. The Indians burned it and the fort down, but since it was made of stone it was easy to renovate. However, there remains quite a bit of char on the granite exterior to this day. The church is now equipped with a huge chandelier in the center of the ceiling and pews with doors on them preventing egress by less illustrious communicants. Pastor George Burroughs delivered a sermon disparaging hypocrisy and sin, a renowned witch hunter of the era name Cotton Mather was sitting in the church on that Sunday, took the sermon personally and the next Sunday, he and two other men waited for George Burroughs to be finished saying goodbye and enquiring about his congregant's personal needs and arrested him, gaging him and placing a bag over his head. Then with the help of these two other men Cotton Mather carried Burroughs back to Salem, Massachusetts, tried him for witchcraft and hung him himself all within the space of three days and without anyone in Portland becoming the wiser. The congregation when they heard of this, carried the body of Pastor Burroughs back to Portland with much lamentation and buried it behind the church under a huge tombstone, bearing the date August 19th, 1692.

Susan made a poster, which would proclaim her discipleship. She decided to position it on the wall opposite her bed in order to make it the focus of her spiritual attention from the time that she opened her eyes in the morning, until she closed them again at the end of the day. Using a ruler borrowed from the reference librarian, she divided the poster paper into eleven equal portions and made the lines as straight as she could. Using her best calligrapher's hand, she wrote out this edifying Scripture, returning to her Bible several more times to inspect the text and then crossed the room again to see her work from a distance. All the time speaking-in-tongues for the result,

    FINALLY, BRETHREN,
    WHATSOEVER THINGS ARE TRUE,
    WHATSOEVER THINGS ARE HONEST,
    WHATSOEVER THINGS ARE JUST,
    WHATSOEVER THINGS ARE PURE,
    WHATSOEVERTHINGS ARE LOVELY,
    WHATSOEVER THINGS ARE OF GOOD REPORT,
    IF THERE BE ANY VIRTUE,
    AND IF THERE BE ANY PRAISE,

THINK ON THESE THINGS.

Philippians 4:8

"This poster will really enhance the blank wall, in my great room", Susan thought. "It will also make a statement about my Faith to every visitor and help me focus my mind on my priorities." She set Paul in his bassinette and then mounted her work of art to the wall with tacks, going to the other side of the room to make sure both the poster and the lines of scripture were straight.

When Mr. Cross returned to put the finishing touches on the shower and pronounce it useable, he admired the poster and inquired if she thought she would have time to clean up the attached duplex and find another renter for him. Susan said she would and asked about a percentage of the rent on that unit for cleaning, showing and collecting its rent. They struck a bargain of forty dollars a month and Susan could see that her association with this shrewd businessman was going to prove beneficial for both of them. This is similar to the relationship that Diamond and Silk have with Donald Trump. When you do something for a honest businessman, it benefits you as well. These two sisters have gone from poverty to becoming millionaires, just by their association with Donald Trump. Susan typed up a newspaper advertisement to rent the unit, while balancing her typewriter on the kitchen counter.

Perhaps after it is cleaned and painted, she thought, "I can get more money for it than for my own place". Making future plans that take into account the hope of monetary gain was part of preparing to resume a normal life. The American Heritage Lifestyle has always featured, an independent spirit, strong family values and a firm dependence on the providence of God. Susan was intent upon limiting the ways in which government intruders might insinuate themselves into the place of provision, that God alone should hold.

She knew that the only way she was going to get out of poverty was by working and saving, but before she could go back to work, she had to have child care. This was something that she provided for Ruth Burrell for free, but now Ruth was gone and the followers of the Way had decidedly short memories. Reciprocity was unfortunately a principal that they didn't teach, so God was going to have to provide child care through another source.

The next morning, Paul climbed right over the side of his bassinette and landed in his mother's adjacent bed. It was time to give the bassinette away and find Paul another place to sleep. Susan wanted a crib. She kept trying to envisioning it and spoke in tongues for it, but she couldn't hold that image in her mind and she didn't know how to "need" a crib. Making do with what you have, had become a habit pattern for her. Susan looked over at her closet and realized that what she really needed was a good fitting business suit and a pair of high-heeled pumps, so necessary for landing a job in the business jungle. While getting ready, she experienced a vision about a fire and an empty drawer. This was odd indeed and she pushed it out of her mind.

She went to the Junior League's "Community Thrift Store" across from Paul's Market. Everything she wanted was on the mannequin in the window: a brown tweed pant-suit, a white silk blouse and a pair of black, high-heeled pumps. They were assembled all in one place and everything fit her, this was from God. She was glad to be thin again, so that she could fit into these becoming clothes. Some expensive, no skimping here, foundation garments from Porteous, Mitchell and Braun made it possible for her to fit into this business outfit making her presentable to the working world and disguising both her recent maternity and her poverty in one fell stroke.

[In order to get a believable pay-check, you must be wearing a believable ensemble when you interview for the job. This is as important as saying the right things during the interview. Your clothes and your resume must shout to a potential employer, "I am a thoroughly professional person, hire me!"] She also bought a pair of athletic shoes to walk back and forth to work. As she came out of the store, she saw Walter Malien, "Whad-da-yah think", she said to him, drawing attention to her new outfit and speaking in her best Chicago accent.

"Ayur, do-ah you-ah luk graht! You-ah gauhd you-ah fig-yahr bah-k af-tah hahv-vehn thah bay-bay"! He said, looking at her with masculine appreciation. *"Wow! Do you look great! You got your figure back after having the baby!"*

"Mr. Cross, my landlord wants to rent out the duplex next to mine" and there might be a chance for you to make some money repairing it! Could you come by this evening around 5:00p.m. and I'll show you the unit."

"Ayuh", *"Yes"* **[a term of acknowledgement like ayur]** he said. All-business Susan fought back the tears and smiled. Walter was wearing Mike's clothes: His Frye boots, his *Levi's* jeans and his God, Guns and Guts, Made America Free belt buckle! They fit him perfectly and he looked great in them. She was meeting with the McDonald women at her place, in twenty minutes and she didn't want to have puffy eyes when they arrived. Hurrying back up town she still took time to admire Federal Street and Monument Square which are paved with cobble stones, have granite curbs and are inlaid with red brick walkways. This pattern is truly Portland, Maine's signature architectural feature, giving its streets and buildings an aire of "old" New England charm though both these architectural treasures were brand new.

Throughout the nearly four centuries of its history, Portland Maine, has been called "the Phoenix" because of its fires which were as destructive as

Chicago's and "Forrest City" because of its numerous trees. The trees had been largely being destroyed by fires, blight and careless maintenance. The Portland Beautification Society was planting a new blight-resistant variety of flowering fig tree, which was a native of Pakistan, all around town. These were sparse and spindly now, but they would become full flowered and magnificent in about twenty years.

Chapter Thirty-Six
ALLEY WITH A VIEW

The alley behind the Dunkin' Donuts and Paul's was Cyn's place of commerce and the alley was cleaner than the great room of her apartment. She looked up one day from what she was doing to see that she had an audience. There were men cheering and gawking at her from atop one of the roofs overlooking the alley. A very lovely home facing High Street had a rooftop bistro. From its flat roof men were observing her, as she performed her service to society. Binny would point at that alley and say, "Thad'z you-ahr spahd!", *"That's your spot!"* and laughed his creepy laughter. Binny couldn't drive. So, Cyn drove around the several blocks, between the rented garage space and the Congress Square Park. Cyn chauffeured him all around Portland, Maine so that he could find another "hol-lah-tray", or travel down to his "merch" locker and either pick up or drop off some of his supply of drugs. It was through the window of Binny's Caddy, that he had first observed their present stronghold on Congress and High.

How many other people could say that they worked within walking distance of their place of employment? Binny's actual place of commerce was the great room of his apartment on the southeast corner of the intersection. But, he sold a lot of drugs right on the street, in the open, in broad daylight and seemingly right under the noses of the police. Once while Susan was waiting for a bus on that corner, she saw a drug deal go down on the adjacent sidewalk. A Portland Police Officer was standing less than five feet away from the transaction. She said to him, "Officer, aren't you supposed to be breaking up the dope deals on this corner or something? I mean isn't that your job?" He looked at her incredulously and claimed that he had never seen a thing. Apparently, willful blindness was a quality looked for in police recruits in Portland, Maine. It made Susan long to see Chicago's Finest, once again.

Binny would look out the car window and begin inventorying locations at which to establish another "hol-lah-tray" *"hollow tree"*. These were ex-cursions, which though pathetic, were the only real fun either Binny or Cyn ever had during the winter. Binny couldn't drive legally or otherwise. He came from New York City and had never been taught to drive; beside New York's government discourages driving. Binny had no identity with which to get a driver's license. Therefore, Cyn did all the driving. She never complained; because, after all, she was a very good friend.

Without mercy and without reason, Binny stole into every aspect of Cyn's life, until she had no personal life left at all, but then she never did. She was a wisp of a girl, eighteen years of age, no high school diploma, no plans for college or a career, no real friends and without much in the way of clothes. She didn't even have a winter coat and she lived in Maine! The winter was coming and she had no coat! What to do? Through-out the cold, snowy, winter months, Cyn stayed home in her kitchen and by her warm stove. It became, up to Binny, to support them while the winter would out. It never occurred to him to buy her a winter coat, like the other prostitutes had with them in the booths at Dunkin Donuts and Cyn didn't want to risk a beating using her $350 daily income to purchase a coat. What this meant was that there would be more people milling around in their great room and more filth to sweep down into the "merch" pit.

The customers called what they were doing "par-tah-ehn" *"partying"*; and though it seemed festive, it was deadly serious. Every time new people would show up in the great room Binny would become terrified that they were "Narcs". The only way to thwart this danger, he felt, was to proffer some free heroin. If the potential customer demurred or asked for marijuana; he or she would be shown the door.

Cyn usually stayed in the kitchen during one of these "pah-tahz" *"parties"*, sitting at the kitchen table, drinking tea and reading a good book or doing a crossword puzzle. Cyn was a constant borrower of books from whatever public library the camper was parked nearest. Cyn got a Bath Public Library card and later a Portland Public Library Card, because she was an avid reader of novels and poetry. She loved Carl Sandberg, Dostoyevsky, Jane Austin, Edna St. Vincent Millay and Lawrence Ferlinghetti. For a high school dropout from a school with no academic acclaim, she was extremely well read. Maybe it was all the hours of waiting for customers in her camper.

Customers who were men brought in to her by her two "dah-dees" and who afterwards, she would never see again. When she began living in Lewiston-Auburn, finding new Johns and then cultivating them as "reg-gul-las" became all her department. Before she met Binny she had a bleak life in Belfast and Bath, but he turned her boring life into a terrifying sojourn for drugs to Auburn and back again to Portland. Then in summer, when she wasn't in her alley, she made time for reading.

The Winter months caused Binny to cultivate new "reg-gul-lahz". And, while Cyn stayed indoors reading, seeing her "reg-gul-lahz" and baking bread, the crowd of people in the great room continued to grow and continued to track filth into the apartment. They dropped needles, bandaged collapsing and bleeding veins and left behind filthy bloody rags. The great room required constant maintenance, making Cyn both depressed and jumpy. Depressed because she had to stay indoors in Winter giving her "cabin fever" because the cleaning never ended and jumpy, because she lived in fear of the police. Narcs and vice cops were their nemesis.

The bistro across the alley from the park was closed during the Wintertime and the employees of Marcel's took up residence in this elegant home fronting High Street. Ralph Magwood could have lived in this home for free. But, he preferred to live in the Way Home with Todd Maynard and Jill Ireland. In Winter Marcel's would transport the restaurant tables to a storage locker and set up bunk beds in the downstairs dining room. But, in Spring the bunks were again replaced with the dining tables from storage and the employees were expected to find their own housing.

This was done so that Marcel's would have people on hand all winter long to maintain the roof. A flat roof, which was toward the back of the house and which provided the customers a place to observe the prostitutes, was ringed by a thirty-eight- inch wrought-iron railing and was only open during the Summer months. This railing, which matched the wrought-iron furniture was installed so that drunken patrons wouldn't fall to their deaths and fifty dollars was collected at the base of the stairway if customers wanted to dine al fresco.

This situation made the bistro a very lucrative seasonal business. The main restaurant was open all year long and Ralph was frequently offered free rent at this location, but he always declined because the Way Home after all needed him. Ralph would complain to Susan about the worldly and money-grubbing motives of his employer, but he never did anything about it personally. Christians have to be salt and light where they work as well as where they live and worship. Otherwise its just a blowing of the wind. Ralph also should have sat Jill and Todd down and explained to them the particulars of Christian love, especially in relation to respecting private property. He also should have gotten to the bottom of who rifled through

Susan's box of stuff in Al and Wendy's basement. Susan always suspected that it was Todd Maynard who stole her flatware and she knew he stole her albums and stereo. When the flatware appeared on Al and Wendy's diningroom table during a diner party at which Susan had volunteered to serve, she picked up two of her treasured sterling silver forks and carried them into the kitchen. Ralph had asked her to be his prep cook, because John Lyn was to be the guest of honor and he wanted the dinner to really impress him. What a terrible thing it was for them to serve dinner to that Man of God on a table set with stolen flatware.

Chapter Thirty-Seven
FOSTER GRANDPARENTS

Clement Gates of the Foster Grandparent's Program dialed-up one of his sponsors, Melissa Jordan and proposed, "Wahd you-ah beh wahl-lehn tah mead wid ah yahng wah-mahn, who-ah hahz jes' hahd ah bay-bay ahnd ehz rah-thah ehn knehd ahv sumb fost-tah-grahn-par-ehnt-tehn?" *"Would you be willing to meet with a young woman, who has just had a baby and is rather in need of some foster-grand-parenting?"* The Jordan family descended from the first settlers on the Maine coast and this made them Cape Elizabeth blue-bloods. Melissa used the Foster Grandparent's Program to scout out people, who were in need and "worthy" of her help, people she considered "of good character".

"Why yes, I would Clement, is she there now?"

The Foster Grandparent's Program was a quasi-private charity. Melissa Jordan both served on its board and helped some of the children. This office was frequently empty and Susan used it to conduct business of her own. When she was homeless with the baby, she called her State Representative from there and made contact with other government agencies, every single day.

Susan made certain that even Governor Joseph E. Brennan knew about her situation of being homeless with a new-born. The governor in turn championed a bill to stop "age discrimination" which is just a fancy way of saying, "kicking people out of their apartments, because they had a child". Joe Brennan had a private phone conversation with Susan, in which he disclosed his distain for landlords like Adams, who evicted long-time renters from their apartments because they had a baby. The Governor said to Susan, "whahd theze land-lahdz wahd lahk, Sue-zahn, ehz tah ehn- sest thahd rahnt-tahz beh star-ah-lyezd bah-far they-ah muv ehn." *"what these landlords would like, Susan, is to insist that renters be sterilized before they move in."* She laughed.

Clement Gates was a person, who really knew how to work the phones. He had become a great resource to Susan and a person of first resort, when tracking down needed supplies unavailable elsewhere. There are many creative methods of problem- solving, which Susan learned while homeless. She put them to use, now that she was looking for child care and employment. She frequently used both State and Federally- owned properties, that were just empty office space with desks and bathrooms and which were unoccupied. Susan and other people, who knew about them would dart in and change a diaper or nurse a crying infant.

Before long Melissa Jordan was engaged in a stimulating conversation with Susan about a range of topics that they had in common. Both of them knew the Lord's and through them had met Jeff Folsom, their farm manager and his wife, Cheryl. [**When you are cultivating someone, you must talk about what that person wants to talk about. Waiting for a door of utterance to open is a studied art and a skill which a person needs to acquire and use in a survival situation. This is also a skill that you will find useful while you are witnessing Christ to someone.**]

"Could we meet somewhere, Susan?" Melissa Jordan inquired, "I'd invite you up to Cape Elizabeth, but since you don't have a car it might be a difficult journey for you. Of course, I could just come down there, and pick you up." Maine people are so hospitable, even the very wealthy with those less fortunate than themselves.

As Susan began to tell her story to this kindly, older woman, a tear trickled down her cheek. Melissa exclaimed, "Susan, I had no idea that there was so much tragedy in your life. I wish that I had known Mike."

"You would have liked him, Melissa; he was, like you, a very caring person." "Doesn't the State of Maine fund child care?"

"It does, Melissa, but there are long waiting lists and I need daycare right away, because my financial situation is so dire. If I don't get employment soon, I may not be able to provide for my little son, Paul."

Susan discovered that Ms. Jordan and her sister Sara had inherited a working goat farm as one of their income sources. Sara tended the nanny goats on Jordan Farm Road while Melissa kept the he-goats in a barn, behind their mansion on Rocky Point Lane. "Oh", Susan remarked, "My friends, Jim and Anne Simmons have their little girl on your goat's milk, if Jordan Farm's Goat's Milk is your brand."

"It is", Melissa Jordan answered. The Jordan sisters, Diane Lord and Madeline Cartwright were all graduates of Smith College or Wesley College for women. These colleges do their diligence to relieve students of their accents; whether they are New Hampshire, Downeast, Upcountry Maine accents or Southern accents. All the students at these colleges get four years of elocution lessons. This is the opposite of the way things were when there was slaver. The men all have polished manners of speech and Southern girls spoke English like field hands. Susan tried to comply with Melissa's request. God whispering to her that this was an opportunity not to be missed, [**When you are without money, it doesn't hurt for you to cultivate a few wealthy friends.**"]

"They-ahr ehz ah bahs gau-ehn ride oud ahv Paut-lan' uhn Root 77, Sue-zahn. Thahd bahs cauhn drahp you-ah ahf aht Weh-lahrd Squahr, thehn you-ah cauhn wahk thah rahs' ahv thah wahy tah thah ah-staht uhn fut", *There is a bus going right out of Portland on Route 77, Susan. That bus can drop you off at Willard Square then you can walk the rest of the way to the estate on foot*", Clement Gates said.

Melissa's mansion faced the craggy bluffs of Staples Cove and granted the visitor a spectacular view of the ocean. The waves crashing against the shore and the sea wall of boulders fronting the Atlantic gave a picturesque view of the ocean and azure blue of the water gave Susan a thrill of new-found respect for the enchantment of Maine, "Vacationland" vistas. The exhilarating scenery, for which Maine is renowned took Susan's breath away. And, as she walked the country road to the Jordan Estate, she made a silent prayer for a camera with which to record this picture-postcard beauty on the next occasion that she visited. Susan had a photograph of Mike in her wallet. It was taken near an ocean promontory in Biddeford-Saco called, "Higgins Beach". The photograph, set Susan to thinking about Mike's strong, manly chin, his soulful, green eyes, his freckled face and his boyish grin. She kept looking for these qualities in Paul, who peaked out at her from the Snugli, but he was still too young.

Melissa answered her own door, "Did you come out here by bus? Oh Susan? You're really something!" She showed Susan her mansion with its two wings. The Eastern wing of the house had burned and it was still in ruins. The Western Wing connected to the barn, a fairly new structure and it gave the two he-goats almost complete access to the great room of the mansion. They poked their heads over the Dutch doors of the barn and looked into the great room where the two women and the baby were sitting. It looked strange to Susan that her friend would have such an arrangement with these goats, they seemed to be actually talking to Melissa. Their massive heads jutted out into the room; dominating the entire place. Susan jumped up and crossed the room to greet one of the billies, but, when he nibbled Paul's hair she thought better of it and withdrawing to the couch.

Susan asked why Melissa had two he-goats and she explained that they needed one another's moral support, because they were brothers and both for stud. They were simply, magnificent creatures with extraordinary bloodlines which went back hundreds of years like English gentry. They were magnificent, tame and intelligent animals. Melissa opined that the way you control a billy-goat was by grasping his beard with your hand this gave you power over him", She said. "So that you could direct him to do whatever you wanted". She said it worked for men too. "Melissa's boys" were so well trained, that they would actually politely waited their turns to mount the nanny goats without either he-goat pushing or crowding. Susan had to take her word for it as no servicing of nannies occurred while she was present.

Melissa explained that you have to keep the he-goats far enough away from the nannies because their scent would foul the nanny's milk. Melissa's sister Sara kept the dairy goats on their farm out on the Jordan Road. Melissa was loath to venture down that way and her sister, Sara, wore a surgical gown over her clothes and paper booties over her shoes while visiting. She wanted to keep from tracking the smell of he-goat back to the farm and risk tainting the nanny's milk with a musky favor. Actually, the sisters were quarreling and they used the goats as an excuse not to have to see each other. There was a goat shower in the barn for afterwards and Sara would pack the insemination with gauze. When Susan explained her predicament to "the sisters", they both immediately claimed Paul as their grandson.

Chapter Thirty-Eight

RICH OR POOR, THE GOVERNMENT OWNS US ALL

Susan was incensed; she couldn't believe the letter from Mildred Harper, which arrived in the mail. It was as though that horrible meeting, which she had been forced to endure had never taken place. Susan went down to Marginal Way again, uninvited this time and to her amazement all its Human Services employees were outside on the sidewalk in front of the building. Mr. André Françoise said that she was going to have to move and within thirty days. He was holding a picket sign and when he told her they were striking, she sang, **"UNION MAID"** by Woody Gutherie to him. She knew it by heart,

UNION MAID

There once was a union maid,

She never was afraid,

Of the goons and the ginks and company finks,

and the deputy sheriffs that made the raids.

She'd go to the union hall,

When a meeting it was called,
And when the company boys came around,
she always stood her guns.

Refrain:
Oh, you can't scare me,
I'm sticking to the union, I'm sticking to the union,
I'm sticking to the union. Oh, you can't scare me,
I'm sticking to the union, I'm sticking to the union 'til the
day I die.

This union maid was wise,
To the tricks of company spies.
She never be fooled by a company stool,
She'd always organize the guys,
And she'd always get her way,
When she'd ask for better pay.
She'd show her Union Card to the National Guard
and this is what she'd say:

Refrain:
Oh, you can't scare me, I'm sticking to the union,
I'm sticking to the union, I'm sticking to the union,
Oh, you can't scare me, I'm sticking to the union,
I'm sticking to the union, till the day I die.

It didn't mean anything to him though, he danced around while she
sang it; but he still evicted her anyway. It was incredible what Government
people had a right to do to you. She hoped that she might be able to present

this letter from Mildred Harper to the Portland Housing Authority and get into a subsidized unit a little more rapidly; but that didn't happen either. She found, she was on a very long waiting list and that the lady that worked at the PHA said, "Thrah yahz; ehf you-'ah luck-ah." *"Three years; if you're lucky."* Susan knew what lucky meant. It meant that you knew someone, who knew someone.

All these government programs, which are there to benefit the humblest among us, were actually designated for persons who were Portland's welfare elite. The Portland Housing Authority, Susan discovered, had a list within a list, on which certain households could be placed, if they became "homeless" due to a fire or other catastrophe. This, of course, was just a ruse for hiding the entrance of these elite families onto their list of "well-connected" family that had "gained the system". "Low-income people" would try to curry favor through volunteerism, which was designed to help certain politicians, "social-justice" groups and "environmental" groups. This meant that Leftists became entrenched in the bureaucracy and from there aided mostly the people who voted for them or who were willing to advance their political agendas in some way.

Maine's system is not much different from Chicago's. Susan was familiar with the Chicago system of "pay-to-play" reciprocal hiring of spouses, other family members and public-sector union representatives that negotiated for wage and pension increases with the administrators and politicians whom they had helped to elect.

Chicago's pay-to-play policy extends into every economic stratum of society. The big shots get their double-dip pensions and patronage jobs, while the little people get the crumbs of temporary work such as census taking and public housing maintenance. It is also why the Chicago Public Schools have janitorial work that is over- paid and never done and why the public sector in Chicago has bloated budgets, nepotism and an Illinois

Republican Party, whose candidates are often hand-selected by their Democrat opponents.

It's called "the Chicago Way" and it's the reason why so many Chicagoans never vote. They are discouraged about anything ever changing and complacent about corruption. It is also why they are lulled into taking hand-outs in exchange for their liberty. Susan could see that a similar situation existed here in Portland, Maine and is true in any Democrat-controlled, municipal government such as in Baltimore, St. Louis, Detroit and Los Angeles. Whenever Susan would receive a "service" from one of these agencies or government-funded programs, they would always solicit her vote or ask her to give her State Representative a phone call to make sure that their funding continued for another year. The workers at some of these agencies, didn't actually do anything at all. They would just come over and sit at the recipient's kitchen table daring the client to report them.

Now the "service" that Susan was receiving from government was eviction from her home. The letter from Mildred Harper that appeared in her mailbox, made it sound like something good that they were doing for her. Mr. Cross had an affordable rental property for Susan, but it was not going to be available until the following Spring. And though this "eviction" was putting Susan and the baby in jeopardy of becoming homeless once again it had to be done because these social workers had deemed her current apartment "inappropriate".

For the rest of Susan's life, she would always hate the sound of the word "inappropriate". It seemed that in an odd way, both Susan Asta and Melissa Jordan were being assaulted by the same kind of government regulations and by the same kind of government officials. The government had interfered with their personal lives and set "guidelines" for what they could and could not do in their own homes. Susan because she was destitute had to acquiesce to the dictates of an army of social workers. Who insisted that she leave her home regardless of how affordable it might have been. Melissa because she was wealthy and living in a historical mansion was going to have to remake the burned-out wing of her home in the exact style that the Historical Preservation people deemed "appropriate".

Melissa was even more determined than ever to help Susan move into the new apartment on Grant Street and Susan wanted to help Melissa and Sara reconcile and get their home remodeled. These women just naturally wanted to help each other and Susan wanted to see Melissa clean up the East Wing of the family estate, because this was her prayed-for desire. Susan gave the sisters a referral to an attorney, who had helped her when she was homeless. In this way they hoped that they would be able to reassert their private-property rights.

This contest with the Department of the Interior over whether Melissa and Sara were going to be allowed to put a working lavatory into the East Wing of their mansion brought the sisters closer together. By the time, Susan was moved into her new apartment, Sara and Melissa had become family once again.

[What right does government have to come into an individual's home and tell him or her how to live, whether they are rich or poor?] It took the Jordan family the better part of a decade to get the burned-out East Wing of their home restored to practical use. They fought in court to be allowed to put in a working kitchenette and two bathrooms. If those modifications had been completed in a timely fashion, there would have been a bedroom for Susan and the baby with a view of the sun rising over the Atlantic, instead of a tiny apartment furnished with things that she had found in an alley.

Chapter Thirty-Nine
STARING AT PASTRY

Cynthia sat in the Dunkin' Donuts on the corner of Congress and High Streets. She hated their donuts. She was actually eating an Italian from Paul's Market; sitting in a booth at Dunkin' Donuts sneaking tiny bites and pretending she was eating something else. She always had Paul's make her an Italian without meat, and then she would go to the Dunkin' Donuts next door, order a donut, and sit in a booth holding her Italian under the table between bites. Cyn said, "Eeyah-'em ah vay-ghen, Mah-stah. Trah-say-ahn- knee" *"I'm a vegan, Mr. Trusiani"* and he replied, "Eeyah thah-awet fahr ah min-nat, you-ah sahd vah-jhen, Cyn-tha-ah"; bahd, Eeyah-'em ahn It-tahl-yahn, wahch ehz moe- ah thahn jehz' ah san-wahch ahnd Eeyah-'em glahd tah nah you-ah". *"I thought for a minute, you said virgin, Cynthia"; but I'm an Italian, which is more than just a sandwich and I'm glad to know you".* He shook her hand.

It was embarrassing for an attractive, single woman to go into that Dunkin Donuts, because it was so sleazy. They would get propositioned just for sitting alone in a booth eating a donut. They shouldn't have been mistaken for prostitutes; the prostitutes never ate their donuts. They wore sexy outfits even in winter and had a fur coat next to them in the booth and just stared at their pastry. When a gentleman came by and stood next to their booth, they would look up at him and smile sensuously. Things were done a little more discretely back in the 1980's. The prostitutes were all watching their figures for professional reasons and so they, Cynthia included, would sit in the Dunkin' Donuts making themselves visible to men and not eating their pastries. After the prospective customer, the "John", would stop and talk to them and they would try to arrange an encounter.

Since Cyn had learned the technique for turning tricks while on her knees, she could get her three hundred dollars together without having to bring men across the street, but if she did and Binny wasn't home; it would be an occasion for her to stash some cash in the bread box. Cyn was feeling kind of depressed about the loss of her camper. This was because she had no girlfriend with which to talk or with which to go shopping and because her apartment was dark and filthy. But, one good thing in her life. At least, her kitchen was coming along. She wanted to go home, but where was home; certainly, not Belfast. She had never set foot in the log home that Uncle Marlin and Aunt Claudette now inhabited. Cyn didn't know that she could have gone into court and gotten that house for herself. If she had known how. Mr. Hutchins was her Guardian Ad Litem and would have explained the whole thing to her if she had asked him. Would her "Uncle and Aunt" really take her in? She doubted it and she didn't understand her property rights. She wasn't paying attention when Mr. Hutchins explained them to her, at the age of sixteen.

No one had any use for her but Binny. Cyn could revert to her sexy-child personae. It was something that she had learned to do with a flourish of her shoulder- length, naturally curly, blonde hair. It made her into another woman. A childlike, glamorous spirit would descend upon her. It attracted men to her like nothing else she had ever tried. It was a wave of feminine energy that gave her a cunning that couldn't be attributed to her make-up, her jewelry or her clothing.

Cyn had no girlfriends with which to bake. Since this was her favorite activity in the world. She had no real friends at all; except Binny. Her mom was dead now and she couldn't even cry about it. No not at the funeral either, where both Cyn and her Aunt Claudette had dug their fingernails into their palms as hard as they could just to wring out a few tears. Claudette secretly despised Charlene. Cyn couldn't feel sadness for her Mom dying either. She said to herself, "Whad ehf Mah-mah hahd cahm ehn tah sahv meh ehn thahd naht, ehn-stahd ahv pud-dehn meh oud on thah pahrch? Whad ehf shay hahd stahpd Dah-dee Mah-lehn ahnd Dah-dee Roz frumb tahk-kehn meh tah Bath?" *"What if Mama had come in to save me on that night, instead of putting me out on the porch? What if she had stopped Roz from taking me to Bath?"* Cyn still remember her night on the porch, nine years later. It was still fresh in her memory. The Dunkin' Donuts could actually be considered a war zone. So, she couldn't cry here, besides it was bad for business. She knew that she couldn't go back to the apartment, until she had made her obligatory three hundred dollars for the day. The "magic number" was still ephemeral. Binny had once beaten her when she brought home, four hundred dollars. She hadn't intended to give it all to him. She was going for the bread box to put away a hundred dollars of the money when he caught her "stahl-lehn" *"stealing"*.

When Cyn acquired more than the three hundred dollars that she "owed" Binny, she would always stash the "extra" money in one of her metal recipe card boxes which was secreted inside her kitchen canister set. She thought about getting a "hol-lah- tray" of her own, so that she wouldn't have to go back to the apartment to stash her extra money. We wish that she had known about banks and that her identification was all she needed to open a savings account. She had inherited these canisters from her mother and Uncle Marlin and he had given it to her at her parents' funeral. They were all beautiful, crockery boats which Charlene had cherished. Binny certainly didn't care about her baking. This was something that he had demonstrated in Lewiston-Auburn when Cyn was forced to give away all her home-baked bread and cookies to "the family". She loved baking in the oven of that old oil and gas stove on the third-floor of the Lane House. Cyn thought that she and Binny would get that place. When Bill Lane moved them down to the basement instead. He looked her up and down, and whispered sensuously, "Thahs ehz jehz' temp-pah-rare-ray. Eeyah nay you-ah wahn tah beh ahb- stars." *"This is just temporary. I know you want to be upstairs."* All of Bill's tenant- relatives wanted to live in the Penthouse apartment with its electric stove, but instead they were living in tiny little apartments all over the big, three-story house. John Lane wanted that apartment for himself and Cynthia Palmer and no one was surprised when he got it.

After all, he was Bill's cousin, but so was almost every other person in the house. Cyn remembered that joke about Ray who was from a little New England town, where he couldn't date any of the women, because they were all related to him "raisin bread". It was the only apartment, where there was an oil and gas stove. This was the kind of stove that her mother had. This was a stove, that she could use to let your bread dough rise, a stove in front of which the floor was always warm in the Winter. She wondered how those two sweet, little girls were going to fair in that "Christian" household where nobody actually cared about children. They didn't care if a kid climbed into an abandoned refrigerator. Like the one that was left outside and which Cyn had reported to the city of Auburn in order to get it hauled away. Bill and his tenant-cousins were really mad about that. Well, too bad it was the right thing to do!

She and Binny had moved down to the basement. John had offered to "fix up the Penthouse" if only Bill Lane would give the top-floor apartment to him and his girlfriend, Cynthia Palmer. Its stove was probably pretty greasy by now, since no one else ever cleaned it but Cyn. She and Binny had moved out taking her bread recipe- boxes with them, but all the crockery boat cannisters were gone with the camper. Just the bread box with the metal recipe box inside it accompanied them to Portland. Cyn needed a place where she could allow herself to lay down on a kitchen floor again and just hold herself and cry. Fashioning a safe place in which she could rest and bake bread was Cyn's life's goal. She thought about going back to her kitchen in her penthouse apartment. But, she couldn't until she had earned her required three hundred dollars. She started wallpapering her kitchen and the backs of her cabinet doors. She wanted it to look feminine and pretty in there. She wanted to make this portion of her sordid life, clean and normal.

When Cyn was in high school, she had a girlfriend. A girl named Sara Marie. A girl who was like other people. A girl who actually went to the Prom, dated, had boys call on the telephone and went to dances. Sarah was boy-crazy, talked about boys all the time and had guys calling on her. Cyn didn't talk about her excursions to Bath, maybe if she had, Sarah might have done something. Sarah treated Cyn like a real person. She overlooked Cyn's whore clothing, which her mother noticed and forbid Sarah from seeing Cyn anymore. Cyn loved Sara Marie; loved the idea that Sara had loving parents and good grades. In a lot of ways, Cyn grew up "sheltered". It meant without a normal social life, without a boyfriend or just guys calling on her to take her out. She was not allowed to date or go to school dances; but during the Summer months she was taken to Bath every weekend, where she would have sex with strange, older men, who later she would never see again. She loved the dress that Aunt Claudette and Uncle Marlin bought for her at Jordan Marsh. She loved the way she looked when she went to the Prince's house. What happened to her there stood out from the blur of men in the camper; but she didn't like to think about it. It turned out so differently from the fantasy that she had while riding in the back of Uncle Marlin's and Aunt Claudette's Cadillac. She loved the antique white lace and chiffon creation she wore; it made her look and feel like an eleven-year-old Cinderella.

She wished Roz and Charlene would have allowed her to wear it to school dances; but unfortunately, by the time her school had dances the dress was too small. It didn't matter, Roz and Charlene were so "strict", they wouldn't let her date or go to dances anyway. Cyn wanted to be like Sara Marie and have a normal life. She wanted be allowed to wear pretty, feminine clothing, not these low-cut sexy things that Cyn always had to wear for work.

Chapter Forty

"EUROPE HAS RUINS WHY NOT THE STATE OF MAINE?"

When Melissa Jordan came over to Susan's apartment, she was appalled at how dilapidated and Spartan it was. The shabby exterior of the building hadn't been painted in years and the floors were bare boards with spaces in between large enough for vermin to force their way into the home. Susan's draperies were newspaper and her walls were naked of everything but some ripped and soiled wallpaper and a beautiful poster of **Philippians 4:8** gracing one wall and giving the whole place a hopeful appearance. Covering the floor was a well-made, braided, rag rug that Melissa greatly admired. She was even more impressed, when she discovered that Susan had made it herself. They sat down on the edge of Susan's bed and talked, "Susan, I didn't know your place was this bad", Melissa began.

"Well, it's better than it was, Melissa, Paul and I are no longer homeless and we have a bed to sleep in." Paul has outgrown his bassinette and was sleeping with his mother temporarily. "I must admit it makes me nervous, when I consider what happened in **1 Kings 3**" which was the account of two mothers that fought over a baby after the other child had been overlaid by his mother in her sleep. "I certainly don't want that to happen to Paul. That's why I'd like to get him a crib, but I just can't afford to make that expenditure right now."

"Well, have you thought of putting Paul in a drawer? Lots of people have done that over the years."

"Have you looked around the room, Melissa? There aren't any drawers here, I used to have a chest of drawers when Mike and I lived on Pine Street; but I stored it in a friend's basement and it's gone missing."

"I have a drawer you can use, Susan. It's from a bureau that was in the east wing of the house before the fire. We were able to pull some of the drawers out of it; but the bureau itself was too heavy to lift and the fire consumed it. I'll bring it to you next time I come." Sara and Melissa Jordan and Susan Asta had an appointment with Leonard Nelson of Bernstein, Shur and Sawyer, to discuss the sister's property rights in opposition to the Maine Historical Preservation Commission legal maneuverings to keep them from rebuilding the part of their home that had burned. The sisters took Susan along, so she could show him the letters and reports that she had received from Mildred Harper, the social welfare administrator. Gladys Harmon, the visiting nurse and Kelly Zorn, the child-protective worker could have fixed this problem by giving Susan another home visit, noting that her home was clean and that her refrigerator was well stocked with food. When you think about it, Charlene Hickey had never had a home visit from anyone and she was a welfare mother too. The documents generated by these two women put Susan into a situation that was perilous for her and her baby. Even though Susan was not able to move for at least six months and that they were forcing her out of the only home that she and the baby had known since Paul was five weeks old. These government busy-bodies had barged into Susan's apartment, insisting that she move out having nowhere else to go.

Mr. Nelson was used to dealing with preliminary hearings about governmental regulations, which affected wealthy people and their historical estates, their businesses and their huge tracts of land. A paper affecting a poor widow, who was being forced out of her home by a bunch of pesky social workers was something new to him. "Ms. Asta these documents are of a grievous and alarming nature, these people actually have the power to do you great harm, they could even separate you from your child." Susan was stunned by his words, but she answered him in as cogent a manner as she could.

"Mr. Nelson, I'm aware of how self-important and predatory social workers can be, but could they really take Paul away just because I stayed overlong in an affordable apartment for which I searched through five weeks of homelessness? My son and I went from one rental unit to another all-over Portland never applying for one that was listed, "no children, no pets" and even so, every landlord that saw us said that the house or apartment was "taken" and "so sorry". Only Mr. Cross was willing to rent to us. If it wasn't for him, we'd probably still be out on the street."

Astonished, he inquired, "What about subsidized housing?" Wealthy people don't understand how things work for the poor. And the poor are just as lacking in understand of the concerns of the rich. They are like people living in two different countries. "We're on the Portland Housing Authority's waiting list, Mr. Nelson, but that's about three years long and the list within a list that we've heard about is only for people who have become homeless due to a fire or some natural disaster. We became homeless when my husband died and I subsequently gave birth to a child. Our landlord, Mr. Stanley Adams saw nothing wrong with throwing a new-born and his mother into the street." She was beginning to cry again and it was such a pathetic story that Sara and Melissa also started crying.

Mr. Nelson promised to call Marginal Way on her behalf. "Sometimes an attorney speaking up for you can frighten government people out of taking advantage, but most of the time they are unconcerned because there is nothing that you can do to them personally. They have unlimited legal resources and they cannot be personally sued", he said.

As the autumn leaves turned from red and orange to gold and brown, Susan clung to what she considered an already answered prayer of living in a warm, secure home with a comfortable cushion of cash in the bank. Mr. Cross assured Susan that an apartment in his property on Grant Street was going to be ready by Spring. He said that the occupant was approved for Section Eight Housing and would be moving out by then.

Melissa and Sara were growing much more like sisters as Susan became a trusted friend and her prayers for a healing of their familial breach was being answered. On December third, a preliminary hearing on the Jordan's Land Use Case #4818 went to a Board of Inquiry and Mr. Nelson's lawyerly abilities became evident as he argued the merits of the case.

He explained to the Board that the Jordans were a "working" family, that they had continually occupied this sea-side estate for more than two hundred years and that they were dairy farmers howbeit of goats not cows. The main house had been built over one hundred and fifty years ago and it had an attached "East Wing" constructed in the early 1920's which was the closest point to the ocean promontory. This was where the sisters wanted to put their bedrooms, a guest room, a full bath and a kitchenette. They only wanted to restore the structure to its previous outward appearance with some interior modern improvements and after all, it was their home.

They explained that the new guest room and kitchenette would afford Susan and the baby, someplace to stay when they visited. Mr. Nelson argued persuasively, that if the court would not allow the sisters to remodel their home making the "East Wing" a usable, living area once again; it would become a ruin. The Maine Historical Preservation Commission, a division of the Federal Department of the Interior, brought in some "expert witnesses", at taxpayer's expense, to testify that, "There are many homes in Europe, that have whole wings which have fallen into disuse and become 'ruins', many standing structures such as 'the Forum' in Rome are a complete ruin and the state of Maine will eventually have some kind of ruins. Why shouldn't this property become a ruin?"

People, who think that your property should be allowed to fall into ruins rather than you being allowed to rehab and remodel it have no respect for the Fifth Amendment to the Constitution of The United States of America and should never be called "experts". While saying such things in court, these people were actually being paid with public funds. The American Heritage Lifestyle embraces the value of "your home is your castle" and many people couldn't believe that this was happening until they saw it in the newspapers. Nevertheless, most ordinary people make a distinction between the rich and themselves and turn a blind eye whenever the rich are vexed by paid government workers. They sometimes see people with money as not being like themselves and not worthy of the same protections as the rest of us.

To set this matter in perspective, Susan took the stand and told the Board how the government was "evicting" her from an apartment that they weren't even renting to her and all because she had a baby. This was precisely the reason that Stanley Adams had evicted her from the Pine Street tenement and the primary reason that she and her baby had become homeless in the first place.

The inquest was determined in favor of Sara and Melissa Jordan with Susan's testimony about Property Rights and the rights of the citizen just to be left alone deciding the outcome. The sisters would be allowed to add to their domicile and put in a bathroom, two bedrooms and a kitchenette. However, they were ordered to "retain the historic appearance of the estate from the exterior". "We can't thank you enough, Susan, now our home will not remain in ruins.

"Well if you want to thank me, Mellissa, you'll take Paul for the weekend. Because, I think that there's going to be trouble this Friday. Kelly Zorn warned me in person, that I shouldn't be at home. She's really a sweet kid. She said that Child Protective was going to come over, but I can't avoid them forever." The three of them called Mr. Cross and explained the problem. He said he never thought that the government would go this far. Susan wasn't at home, when these busy-bodies came to call. Melissa was hosting her on the couch opposite the goat doors and Attorney Nelson was working on her case, pro-bono.

Suddenly, as if by a miracle, a tenant in the basement apartment of a building that Mr. Cross owned on Deering Avenue and Grant Street moved out due to a flood coming from the upper apartment. This water damage made the ceiling in the kitchen unsightly, yet it was structurally competent and Mr. Cross found this an occasion to give the apartment to Susan for nothing and for one month's time. It was a real mess, but rent-free couldn't be passed up. And, Susan labored long at improving and cleaning it. After moving in Susan attempted to get the utilities connected and discovered that Mr. Stanley Adams had made it impossible for her to get electricity in her new place.

Susan was furious when she went over to Al and Wendy's to pick up her mail and discovered a Central Maine Power bill waiting for her. Mr. Adams had reconnected the power in her old apartment and the bill was charged in the name of Mike Asta. Adams had completely remodeled the kitchen and bath using power tools and had run up a huge electric bill. He furthermore had augmented the rental agreement on the apartment by including "free" electricity to the amenities supplied to the next tenant. The bill was for two hundred and ninety dollars, plus fifty dollars for a deposit. Central Maine Power insisted she pay this before they would turn on the electricity in her new unit. She had to pay this staggering amount in full before they were going to turn the juice back on in her new Grant Street apartment. Susan thought of turning to the Jordan sisters and Mr. Nelson, but first she wanted to go over to Pine Street and call on the new tenant in her former home.

Susan called CMP and complained to them that there must have been a mistake, but the customer service representative was adamant. "Eht'z you-ahr rah-spons-sah-bal-lah-tea tah tahk car ahv thah bahl wahn eht cahmz do-ah." *"It's your responsibility to take care of the bill when it comes due."* He said, as though she hadn't paid her bill for the past two years. She asked him to check her basic bill for as many months back as he could go. Then they both agreed that $290 was an unheard-of amount. When her bill had only been $10 or $12 dollars at most. "Then, it must be a mistake, right?" Susan said, "Can't you fix this?"

The representative said: "nah" *"no"*, which was untrue and hung up. She went back to Bernstein, Shur and Sawyer asking for Mr. Nelson. "This is terrible; I don't understand what has happened. Susan didn't suspect foul play, until she returned to the tenement on Pine and State and called on the new tenant of her former unit. That was when she discovered that the place had been transformed into a modern, well-appointed apartment. The new tenant was paying almost twice what she and Mike had payed.

Just then, she heard Stanley Adams shouting at someone down the hall. She followed the sound of his voice and confronted him at the door of another tenant's apartment. This was also a mother with a young child that she had smuggled into her unit, thinking that if once her child was living there Adam couldn't or wouldn't evict her. Wrong! This baby was a toddler, so Adams didn't have to haul another bassinette to the street, but he was just as willing to evict a toddler as an infant. "Mr. Adams, the day you evicted me your face was as beet red as it is now and the veins on your neck were standing out! Now I return to see you in the same condition.

You know you have high blood pressure, don't you? If you don't sell this building soon, you're going to have a stroke." Most people wouldn't have cared what happened to someone who had first evicted, then robbed her. But, Susan wasn't most people. She was intent on heaping coals of fire on Adams head. **(Proverbs 25:22)**

Melissa and Sara Jordan, Madeline Cartwright and Leonard Nelson all knew that Mr. Stanley Adams was a dour, old curmudgeon, who was quick to take advantage of others and convinced that everyone was always trying to take advantage of him. Susan explained the situation to Melissa Jordan. "This electric bill, plus the deposit is three hundred and forty dollars and even though my electric bill has never exceeded $12.00 a month, CMP wouldn't believe that this was a mistake." The evidence that Stanley Adams had committed a fraud was that the extra kilowatt hours were all ascribed to her bill in the weeks after she moved out. Melissa's bureau drawer was actually safer for Paul than one of the drop-side cribs of that era. These cribs sometimes allowed babies to get their heads wedged in such a way that they strangled. By not answering Susan's prayers for a crib, God was actually looking out for Paul. Melissa asked Leonard Nelson to inquire of Central Maine Power, about the exorbitant previous electric bill and he took it upon himself to threaten to sue Adams; if Adams didn't return Susan's money. **[A place with no power and little in the way of furniture can still be a pleasant home when God is present.]** When Susan tried to remove her poster from the Myrtle Street apartment wall, but it ripped slightly. So, she bequeathed it to the next tenant, along with the beautiful brass bed, which Mr. Cross said wouldn't fit through the door in the new apartment anyway. The only furniture she took from her old place was the hard-won rocking chair, her washing machine, her rag rug and her typewriter.

The new tenant, who she found was a Jehovah's Witness, reciprocated by buying Susan a new single bed; a bedside table and a lamp; all from the Salvation Army Store. Stanley Adams, finally wrote, Susan the check for the electricity he stole from her. So, Susan gave up her place to another believer, however distantly related and praised God for His provision. Then she set about to clean and arranged her things in her new apartment. Meanwhile, David Cross came over and made repairs to Susan's new apartment. The kitchen ceiling still showed signs of water damage, but there was a double-bolt lock on the front door and he supplied a kitchen table, chairs and a center couch section which were all found in the alley. David Cross hooked up Susan's gas stove, but there was still no electricity. If HHS had discovered her lack of electricity, they would have added to her troubles by cutting off her food stamps.

Chapter Forty-One
"COME AND SEE"

"They said unto him, Rabbi, where dwellest thou? He saith
to them, Come and see."

John 1:38–39

"Cyn, why don't you ever come over to my home, I've been to your
place lots of times?"

Though Susan constrained Cynthia to come over to her apartment and
though she was a frequent guest in her friend's kitchen; Cyn wouldn't
reciprocate. Binny wanted Cyn to sit in the park all day long and most
of the evening attracting customers and then arranging meetings for that
evening in the great room of their High and Congress Street apartment; or
go with them to a motel on the outskirts of Portland. In this way, she could
make her mandatory three hundred dollars and he wouldn't need to beat
her. When Cyn returned from an unprofitable day, she would receive her
customary beating and then go into the kitchen and begin baking bread in
her oven. Cyn lived from day to day displaying her body as merchandise
and longing to see Susan, which was her only hiatus.

"Eeyah hahv ah prahb-blehm wid Binny naught wahnt-tehn meh tah
gau ehn- nay-wahr", *I have a problem with Binny not wanting me to go*

anywhere", Cyn said.

"That's awful Cyn. I wish I could get you away from him", Susan began to cry. [**You know, crying works on other women as well as it works on men; maybe even better.**] Cynthia bit her lip. They were sitting together on the park bench, where they always met for lunch. Susan divided her attentions between her sadness over Cyn's predicament and checking her watch to see when she would have to return to the office. They were sharing an orange and making plans to see each other in the evening.

"Hah'z thah own-lay boyah-frahnd thahd Eeyah-'ve ev-vah hahd!" *"He's the only boyfriend I've ever had!"* Cynthia exclaimed, feeling a little bit sheepish for expressing her feelings so forthrightly. She had never had so close a friendship, as she had with Susan. Susan pressed her hand into Cyn's hand. During their meetings in the park, they had shared with one another many intimate details of their lives. Susan told Cyn how painful it had been when Mike was killed leaving her all alone expecting a baby with no family around that could comfort and help her. Susan told Cynthia the truth about God's love for her and the way God felt about bondage. A verse from the Bible came to mind, **"Stand fast therefore in the liberty wherein Christ hath made us free and be not entangled again with the yoke of bondage." (Galatians 5:1)** and she recited it to Cyn from memory. Cynthia began to tell Susan about her "parents" dying in a fire. Cynthia was already living with Binny in the trailer, when they died. She never suspected Binny of poisoning them. She was actually sadder about "losing" her trailer than she was about losing her "parents".

She knew this confession wouldn't sit well with Susan, who seemed to care more about people than things. Cyn wanted very much to go over to Susan's place. She imagined the two of them baking cookies and pies together in Susan's immaculate kitchen. Susan had begun a regiment of secret prayer for Cynthia's deliverance and salvation. For nineteen days, she prayed on her knees that something would break. That Satan's hold on her friend, a hold that was personified in Binny would be broken. This man who tried and failed to get Cyn hooked on drugs and then stole into Cyn's daily life until Cynthia had to account to him for her every waking hour. She prayed that a rescuer would come and take Cyn away from this life of shame and misery. A rescuer that was in league with Jesus Christ, Himself, someone who would save Cynthia from this nightmare.

Chapter Forty-Two

WALTER MALIEN, MENDACANT EVANGELIST

On the corner of Congress and High a bedraggled, homeless man stood all alone waiting for people to drop coins into his jar. He then thanked them for their small act of charity, gave them a tract, along with an expression of faith in Jesus Christ. Walter had been homeless ever since his beloved wife, Josephine flung herself from the "Million-Dollar Bridge". They had a silly quarrel in which she threatened suicide; but Walter shrugged it off and just went out to get on his fishing boat and go to work. Up until that time, Walter had made a living from fishing; going often to the Georges Bank and returning again to Portland with his catch, which he would immediately sell on the wharf. Bringing with him all his fishy-smelling earnings, he raced home to find that Josephine was on the news. He was devastated. Instead of them having the opportunity to mend their rift, Josephine who had been battling depression, was dead.

His hopes of a warm reception, a good meal and the customary clean house were gone. Instead, Josephine, the love of his life, was nowhere to be found. The nightly newscast was reporting the tragic news that, "a woman named Josephine Malien had jumped off the Million-Dollar Bridge had broken her neck and was drowned." Their tiny, two-bedroom home in South Portland seemed to Walter, a prison of desperate despair. A perplexed Walter had presumed that they were reasonably happy that their argument was just something all couples have to deal with and that everything would be alright.

Josephine was just a little high-strung, maybe it had something to do with her hormones, he thought. They after all had a nice little house and were trying for a baby. Walter couldn't believe that this had happened to him. It was surreal. Walter was oblivious to the turn his life and the life his beloved wife had taken. He was like a dead man walking the Earth in the shadow of another distant life. He couldn't make sense of what had happened to Josephine. Why would she do that? What was her thinking at the end? Why would she do something like that? Every time he mulled this question in his mind, Satan came with accusations, it was all Walter's fault Satan would tell him. Only Jesus stood in the way of this spiritual assault. Only Jesus could defend him to the adversary. Kicking a man when he is down being the devil's chief delight. He would just kind of know when Walter was berating himself, and then pile on. Like a prosecuting attorney who had found another piece of evidence against Walter then he would race into court with it and there would be Jesus standing between him and Walter. Jesus playing the advocate.

Josephine, a life-long Portland native met Walter, who was originally from Belfast, through her long, extended family of fish mongers and tavern-keepers. Walter, unlike most fishermen, didn't drink much. So, it was unusual for her to meet a man in a Portland-area bar, who didn't actually have this vice. This was the attractive quality that Walter had for her. Her family thought that she had made "a pretty-good catch". They are a people who make their living trading with the local fishermen. Her family also used their capitalistic skills to try to get the most money that they could from trading in fish and clams on the Portland city wharf.

The "Old Port", which is still the center of commerce for the fishing industry and also for the tourist trade, became a magnet for idle fishermen that accumulated around its copious bars and pool halls. Maine people work at cleaning fish and purifying clams. Fish mongers, like Josephine's family, bought a fisherman's catch, cleaned it and made it available to retail purchasers both restaurateurs and housewives.

After Josephine's death, Walter could no longer concentrate on the things of the real world. He became so low. So, suicidal that his entire world was about to fly apart at any moment. This was why the intervention of Jesus Christ, who apparently has an affinity for fishermen, was so crucial. After a while, Jesus became Walter's only friend. Other people shied away from Walter, recognizing his state of mental unbalance. Therefore, he clung the more to Jesus, like a drowning man clings to a piece of flotsam from his wrecked vessel. When his insanity made it absolutely impossible for him to follow the fishing trade, he bestowed the family boat on a younger brother and concentrated on the only occupation he was still able to pursue, panhandling.

However, Walter continued obsessively telling passers-by about Christ. He never considered that perhaps he was no longer a very good witness for Jesus. It was almost a unanimous decision among local Christians, of all denominations, and all walks of life that Walter was actually "saved". They all knew that Walter's fervor for spreading the Gospel was sincere, genuine. But, they didn't care. They wanted Walter to be out of the public eye and they didn't want to fellowship with him, in one of their opulent churches. They didn't want Walter representing Jesus Christ. He was a disgrace to the church, a constant and very public reminder, that people living on the edge of the spiritual world were different, strange, and abnormal.

Cynthia had begun plying her trade in the park and in the adjacent alley behind Paul's Market and thereby met Walter, who exploited this same location to panhandle and pass out tracts. When they met in the iconic park, where Cynthia and Susan had met, they struck up a conversation discussing the park itself, "Ehd'z ah graht pahk, sehz-n't ehd?" *"It's a great park, isn't it?"* Walter tried to keep his conversation superficial, focused on the real world and politely centering on trivial matters. He was waiting for "a door of utterance."

Walter would chase men down who were dressed in impeccable three-piece suits. He would give them a tract and try to explain to them, how they could give their lives to Jesus Christ and be freed from the snares of a worldly life. They would laugh, take a tract, stuff it into a pocket and put a few coins in Walter's jar. If Walter Malien a clinically-insane, homeless person, dealing with unspeakable personal grief, could be a witness for Christ, why can't we with all our resources and business acumen witness Christ, where we work and live? There was no weather for this guy and he spent the surplus of his way of life purchasing tracts in bulk. He wasn't just out there on nice days, he was there in the rain and in the cold. Walter purchased his tracts from a little place called, **"Sword of the Lord Publishers, P.O. Box 1099, Murfreesboro, TN 37133.** He liked the tract, **"Salvation Plain and Simple"** and the tract, **"What must I Do to Be Saved?"** was also a favorite of his. Walter surprised Cyn and Binny by being someone who wanted to "help them". He went over to their place and volunteered to complete the wallpapering job that Cyn had begun in her kitchen. Walter and Cynthia got into a deep discussion about Jesus and what He accomplished for us on the Cross.

Walter said, "You-ah dohn' hahv tah thahnk ahv yah-sef ahz ah hor ehn-nay- moh, Cyn, you-ah cauhn thahnk ahv yah-sef ahz ah chid ahv Gahd. Jahy-zuz pied fahr ev-ray sign. Awhl ahv ahs hahv dahn bahd stahf ehn 'r' lahvz, Cyn. Bahd, Jahy-zuz wahshd ehd why-dah thahn snah." *"You don't have to think of yourself as a whore anymore, Cyn, you can think of yourself as a child of God. Jesus paid for every sin. All of us have done bad stuff in our lives, Cyn. But, Jesus washed it whiter than snow.*"

Cyn said, "Bahd Eeyah sign fahr ah lib-behn. Hahw cell Eeyah mahk ah lib- behn ehf Eeyah-'em naught ah hor?" *"But, I sin for a living. How will I make a living if I'm not a whore?"* Walter said, "Gahd cell tahk car ahv you-ah Cyn, thah wahy He- ah dahz meh. Luk, Eeyah dohn' cahtch fahsh ehn-nay-moh." *"God will take care of you Cyn, the way He does me. Look, I don't catch fish anymore."*

Walter continued, "They-ah ehz nah-bahd-dee ride-jus' nay naught Juan. (Romans 3:10) We-ah hahv awel signd ahnd cahm shaht ahv thah glah-ray ahv Gahd beh-ehn jehs'-stah-fried fry-lay bah hahz greyz threw thah rah-dehm-shun thahd sehz ehn Chrys' Jahy-zuz." **"There is nobody righteous, no not one. (Romans 3:10) We have all sinned and come short of the glory of God being justified freely by His grace through the redemption that is in Christ Jesus." (Romans 3:24)**

Cyn found his words compelling. The availability of eternal life, freely through the grace of God and the forgiveness that God has granted to those who merely repent of their sins and trust in Christ's shed blood. This appealed to her natural tendency to get a bargain. She decided not to allow this freebie to pass her by. Walter was so far the only man that she had ever met in her life who wanted nothing from her; but to help her. He smoothed the piece of wallpaper onto the wall behind them and then he encouraged Cyn to kneel down on the floor near the kitchen windows where the sunlight was flooding into the room.

Magnificently, it filled up the empty space beneath this corner nook with dazzling light. This is the place where Cynthia received Christ.

Chapter Forty-Three
JESUS IN MY KITCHEN

Cyn said aloud, "Jahy-zuz, Eeyah nah thahd Eeyah-'v dahn' rahng ehn mah lahf ahnd thahd Eeyah-'em naught wah-tha fahr you-ah tah cahme ehn-tah mah haht; bahd, ehf you-ah'll ov-vah-luk whad Eeyah-'ve dohn' ahnd beh-cahm Lahd ehn mah lahf, Eeyah-'ll sahrv own-lay you-ah. Eeyah bah-leave ehn mah haht thahd Gahd rahzd you-ah frumb thah dahd." **"Jesus, I know that I've done wrong in my life and that I'm not worthy for you to come into my heart; but if you'll overlook what I've done and become LORD in my life, I'll serve only you. I believe with all my heart that God raised you from the dead."** **(Romans 10: 9, 10).** At first it seemed like nothing had happened, then the wallpaper and the yellow paint began to crowd in on her. She had never felt like this before; it was as though the weight of many years of being used and using others had been lifted from her shoulders.

The dirty great room seemed to sparkle with light; the windows that looked out onto Congress Street and the blue and white squares of linoleum tiles she knelt upon seemed to dazzle with a brilliance that they had never known before. She struggled to her feet; looked around her and the whole place seemed transformed by the simple act of surrender that had just occurred. In one moment, both she and Walter Malien had metamorphically become new. He was no longer a lunatic that lived on the street; he was Billy Graham. She was no longer a prostitute; she was the daughter of the most- high God. Walter had saved one solitary life from hell and the grave. He had done more for God in this woman's kitchen than any minister or priest in Portland, Maine had ever done with all their cathedrals, pews and stained-glass windows. Cyn no longer wanted to earn a living through prostitution; but she didn't know what else she was qualified to do. She had no high school diploma and no skills of any kind. She wondered what she was going to do with her life, now. Then, Binny came back from peddling his drugs and collecting the drug money that was owed him. She didn't know how to explain the change in her life. She knew that Binny wouldn't be happy about it.

"Ayur Bin-nah, Eeyah-'em hahv-vehn meh pah-eeh-add, Eeyah-'em hahv- vehn crahmpz. Eeyah nehd tah lie dahwn". *"Oh Binny, I'm having my period, I'm having cramps. I need to lie down".* she said. This was at once a lie; but Cyn didn't know any other way to get out of having to go to work. Binny was not beguiled. He wanted her out on the street and he wanted the money, the nearly three hundred and fifty dollars that she could earn every day. Cyn lay down on the floor next to the stove and hugging the still warm oven. She didn't know what she could do to exit this life of shame. Then she remembered Walter's words, "Gahd cell tahk cahr ahv you-ah, Cyn; thah wahy He-ah dahz meh. Luk, Eeyah dohn' cahtch fahsh ehn-nay moh." *"God will take care of you, Cyn; the way He does me. Look, I don't catch fish anymore."*

Cyn was lying on the floor near the oven, where she had been baking bread. She kept repeating the words, "Eeyah-'em thah braud ahv lahf." *"I am the Bread of Life".* *"Eeyah-'em thah braud ahv lahf."* *"I am the Bread of Life."* This was something she had heard, when she was little and a school friend, Sara Marie, took her to church.

Something about these words and this bread was going to save her from having to go back across the street. She clung to her oven as though it was a male protector. Binny began kicking Cyn in her thighs and her buttock; kicking her as though she was a dog that had done something dirty on the rug. He was still kicking Cyn when Walter came back from the bathroom. Back to see the whole sordid story of their lives together as an illustration of what it meant to be a captive; a slave to sin.

Walter grabbed the back of Binny's shirt and pulled him away from Cyn. He said in a commanding voice, "Leaf har ah-lone". *"Leave her alone".* Binny, being the coward that he was, propelled himself in the direction of the door. He suddenly remembered, that he had cocaine and heroin to sell. Then he flew down the stairway and out onto Congress Street. And Susan made a fortunate appearance at Cyn and Binny's place. She was neither carrying the baby in the Snugli nor dragging the shopping cart behind her. She only had on a simple backpack laden with books from Casco Bay College. She had intended to bake bread with her friend that afternoon and bring the bread home and put it in her bread keeper. Susan was instead confronted with this scene of Cyn lying on the floor, holding her stomach and crying.

With the smell of fresh-baked bread, cooling on the stovetop, Walter took a deep breath and said, "We-ah'v gauhd tah gaht you-ah oud-dah hee-yah, Cyn. Eht sehz- n't sahf; eht sehz-n't wahr you-ah knehd tah beh." *"We've got to get you out of here, Cyn. It isn't safe; it isn't where you need to be."* Walter and Susan gathered Cynthia up and led her down the stairway to the sidewalk below. "You're cahm-mehn homb weahth meh!" Susan said emphatically breaking into her Chicago accent. She was going to keep Cynthia protected from Binny. However, she could and for however long as she could. She was going to save her from this detestable life of shame and pain. They marched three-abreast down the street. Cynthia in the center leaned upon both of them. She was resolute to seek a new life. They walked down the red-brick sidewalk, passing the Longfellow statue and turning onto Grant Street.

All the while, Satan was berating Cynthia, telling her, "Yule nev-vah ah-maht tah ehn-nay-thehn!" *"You'll never amount to anything!"* He was telling Susan, "This will all be for nothing, because, Cyn isn't going to go for it." He was telling Walter, "You-ah sahd beh bahk ehn thah pahk pas-sehn oud trahkz". *"You should be back in the park passing out tracts".* Susan thought about Jill Ireland leaving her in the phonebooth to fend for herself and the baby. She gave herself every reason in the book to abandon Cyn. She had a baby to take care of. She was broke. She couldn't take care of another person. The whole nine yards. The whispering in her ears became deafening. Walter and Cynthia heard it too. For each of them, it was different; but for each of them it was the same message and from the same entity. It was a message of discouragement. A message exhorting them to selfishness; to self-doubt; to think of themselves as failures.

Paul was waiting in the daycare home at the bottom of Grant and Weymouth. Susan had to drop Walter and Cynthia off at her place and then go collect her little, young son. When they got to her apartment, Susan put the kettle on; showed Walter where the tea and tea cups were kept. And, then as rapidly as she could, she made the foot journey to the daycare home to retrieve her baby son.

Chapter Forty-Four
"NEW LIVES FOR OLD"

Walter and Cyn were left alone in Susan's apartment and with Cynthia seeing everything differently now that Christ had come into her heart; this was the beginning of a whole new life for her. She was now in an entirely different place, with an entirely different kind of man. She actually felt safe with Walter. It was a curious sensation. They tried to make themselves at home in the unfamiliar surroundings of Susan's kitchen. There on the refrigerator door, they could see a piece of heart-burn medication taped up, with a sign next to it that said, "Get heartburn and have a mountaintop experience." A flyer with a picture of the Colorado Mountains from a Way Family Camp was mounted beside it. There on the wall next to the refrigerator was the iconic picture of the two disciples talking with Christ on the road to Emmaus. Under this picture, it said, **"Did not our hearts burn within us as He talked to us and opened to us the scriptures." (Luke 24:13-35)**

Walter and Cynthia didn't know what to make of this. Other people didn't put displays like this up in their kitchens. They sat opposite one another at Susan's kitchen table and talked. The time that it took Susan to collect her son passed quickly for them. Cynthia was amazed at how comfortable she felt in Walter's presence. Walter got up and got Susan's Bible; opening it to the passage in **Luke 24**. Explaining to Cynthia how the resurrected Christ appeared to the two disciples on the road to Emmaus and how later he also appeared to Saul on the road to Damascus. They were talking, laughing and reading when Susan returned. She put her little, young son down for a nap in his playpen and turned her attention to her stove. Before long the kettle was whistling and she was making tea for her two guests. She offered them some bread and home- made jam to go with their tea.

"Eeyah wahsh we-ah coahd hahv tahk-kehn thah braud ahf thah stauv-tahp". *"I wish we could have taken the bread off the stovetop."* Cynthia said eating her bread and jam.

"You-ah'r nev-vah gau-ehn bahk tah thahd plahz ah-gahn." *"You're never going back to that place again!"* Walter answered angrily and emphatically. As Walter and Cynthia enjoyed their tea, jam and bread, Susan went in to check on Paul, who was napping in the bedroom. God was talking to Susan and He was saying, **"Don't say anything to her right now; let Walter do all the talking."** But, she spoke back to God, "Father, Walter is insane and his Biblical thinking isn't right." God said, **"No, don't say anything to her, now! There will be time for you to talk to her later. I want my son in charge here!"** So, she set herself to doing what the **Book of Acts** called, **Serving Tables (Acts 6:2)**. She poured their tea. She offered more bread and jam, but she purposely didn't say anything. This was what God told her to do, by revelation, and she did it. Exactly the way He wanted her to, whether she agreed or

not, whether she saw God's plan or not. So, until Walter left on his own, Susan remained controlled and silently spoke in tongues.

After Walter left, Cynthia and Susan were alone together. This was going to be Cynthia's new home. Cynthia said, "Eeyah toad Bin-nah ah lye, Sue-zahn, ahnd eht'z bah-thah-ehn meh. Eeyah-'ve nehv-vah behn bah-thahd bah tel-lehn ah lye bah-fahr." *"I told Binny a lie, Susan, and it's bothering me. I've never been bothered by telling a lie before."*

"What is it Cyn?" She asked. "You can tell me."

Cynthia said, "Eeyah wahnd-did tah gaht oud ahv hahv-vehn tah gau au-crahs thah straight ahnd prah-stah-toot mah-sef. Bahd, Eeyah coahd-'dent fig-gahr oud ehn-nay ud-dah wahy ahv doh-ehn ehd. Zo, Eeyah toad Bin-nay thahd Eeyah wahz hahv-vehn mah pah-eeh-add ahnd thahd Eeyah (Cyn was getting nervous now, saying this.) wahz hahv-vehn crahmpz. Thahd wahz-en't trahoo beh-cahz, Eeyah've mahsd mah pah-eeh-add. Eeyah thahnk Eeyah've mahsd mah pah-eeh-add. (Cyn swallowed hard, now.) Eeyah thahnk Eeyah-ve mahsd eht fahr au-boughd tah wahkz nah." *"I wanted to get out of having to go across the street and prostitute myself. But, I couldn't figure out any other way of doing it. So, I told Binny that I was having my period, and that I (Cyn was getting nervous now, saying this.) was having cramps. That wasn't true because, I've missed my period. (Cyn swallowed hard, now.) I think that I've missed it for about two weeks now."*

Susan was floored. But, she waited until Cyn spoke further. "Thah lahs' tahme thahd thahs hah-pend tah meh; mah stahp-fah-thah tahk meh fahr ahn au-bahr-shun." *"The last time that this happened to me; my step-father took me for an abortion."*

"Well Cyn, the last time, I wanted to know if I was pregnant; I wound up at Planned Parenthood. The first step here would be getting you a pregnancy test. But, I'd rather you went to my doctor, than have you go to Planned Parenthood, even if they say that it's free, because they really don't like choice or babies over there."

"Rahl-lay?" *"Really?"* Cyn said, "Eeyah thah-awet thahd they-ah wahr awel au-boughd chauz ov-vah they-ahr." *"I thought that they were all about choice over there."*

"No Cyn!" Susan said emphatically, "They're only about the choices that enrich them. Margaret Sanger started Planned Parenthood and she was all about making money and oh yeah; exterminating black people and Mexicans. She would probably be all in favor of you having a baby, when she saw your blonde hair and blue eyes. But, when she learned what you do for a living or did do for a living, she would want to abort your kid."

"See, a human baby is human from the moment of conception. Anyone who tells you differently is just lying to you. Your little son or daughter is precious in the sight of God, made in His Image. God hates the shedding of innocent blood; hates it! It's just about the worst thing on God's list, **'There are six things that the LORD hates, seven which are an abomination unto Him: Haughty eyes; a lying tongue; hands that shed innocent blood; a heart that devises wicked plans; feet that run rapidly to evil; a false witness that utters lies and one who spreads strife among brethren." (Proverbs 16:19)**

"Ayuh Sue-zahn, you-ah mahm-mar-ahzed thahd, Eeyah-'em ehm-prahsd." **"Wow Susan, you memorized that, I'm impressed."**

"Well, if you want to avoid doing things that God hates and I do; then, you have to know what it is that He hates. It doesn't mean that you can't love people, who do these things; even people that do them to you. But, you just have to avoid doing them yourself. So far, I'm just concentrating on the **'spreading strife among brethren'** part of the verse, because I tend to be a little tactless at times. That's why I memorized this verse from the Bible." Susan said forthrightly and with no desire to hide a fleshly struggle from a sister in Christ. "See, living a holy life, no matter how difficult it may be, is something that we should all strive after. I mean; if you want to be a disciple."

This was the first-time Cynthia had considered the concept of discipleship. She had just gone through the transformative experience of salvation. Some Christians never go beyond that. But, this was a different kind of house. Susan knew that even though Walter was not believing the Word in a rightly-divide manner, that he walked and talked with Jesus Christ every day. This knowledge had great and sacred power for her. Walter had the same problem that Susan had experienced with the organized building. (That was how Susan referred to Churchy Christians, you know, people who played at church in a special building and on a special day of the week.) These people had no use for Susan or Walter. They didn't want them around, because they contributed nothing to their churches. See, no matter what your personal faith statement is, there is a connection between people who put their relationship with Jesus Christ ahead of what they may personally believe or their denominational affiliation.

The Christians that threw Susan and Walter out of their churches would have thrown the Apostle Paul out too. These people had **the form of Godliness,** but both Walter and Susan knew that they **denied the power**. The Bible says, **"From such turn away."** (II Timothy 3:5.) Susan and Walter weren't trying to recruit Cynthia into their personal religious denomination. They were trying to lift her up, like they had done supporting her on both sides, while she ventured down the street to seek a new life.

Cynthia went to bed that night; a real bed, not a mattress on the floor covered with filth and perhaps sporting the needle from a hypodermic syringe, but a real bed. It

was a single bed in a little boy's room and it was covered with clean linens and a clean comforter from the Salvation Army Store. Little Paul was fast asleep in a dresser drawer and Susan was lying on the floor beside her on three sanitized couch cushions, covering herself with a nurse's cape. Susan had given up the only bed in the house to her guest.

The next day was Saturday; Susan didn't have to go to work and so she took her friend to Dr. Bonjour's on Pine Street. Sure enough, Cynthia was pregnant! But, she wasn't two weeks pregnant, as she supposed, she was actually seven weeks along. The unborn baby was now fully-formed and modal, he or she had an assigned sex, brainwaves and a heartbeat or so Dr. Bonjour said. Susan was the only person there who was overjoyed. Dr. Bonjour was acting very professionally and Cynthia was acting apprehensive and a little bit dejected. Cyn asked Susan, "Whahd do-ah Eeyah do-ah nah?" *"What do I do now?"* Susan replied, "Well Cyn, what do you want to do? Dr. Bonjour told you what his professional opinion was. Didn't he?"

Susan asked Dr. Bonjour if he would give Cynthia some other tests, specifically for sexually transmitted diseases. This was a first for Cynthia. Planned Parenthood hadn't done this for her; even though they keep saying that they do "cancer screenings and STD tests"; they don't. At least, they hadn't for Cynthia; who was at that time, age sixteen, a working prostitute. Planned Parenthood had just given her the abortion and then contraceptives. Susan explained, "even oral sex can be an occasion for the transmission of a sexual disease, Cyn. We have to protect you and your unborn child from getting sick." Dr. Bonjour said that he would send her blood to a lab for testing and that the tests wouldn't come back for several days. Susan asked him to call them at home and then gave him her home phone number, now that she actually had one.

If Cyn was going to continue this pregnancy, God would have to shower her with the resources she needed and she would have to fend off people who wanted to "help her" by killing her baby. Of course, she would also have to trust God in the way that Susan trusted Him. She had never done this before; this was going to be another milestone in her life. Mostly though, she was going to have to stay away from the intersection of Congress and High Streets and maybe, Susan thought, Cyn would even have to stay indoors for the duration of her pregnancy. This would have to be in order to avoid Binny, who didn't know where Cyn was and Susan wanted to keep it that way.

This was a daunting task, Cynthia and Susan didn't immediately get an infusion of cash, nor did they have a bountiful, male protector or some charity waiting in the wings. Crisis Pregnancy Centers were still unknown at this time. If God was going to rectify Cynthia's situation, everything would have to come from His Beneficent Hand. Susan called Ralph Magwood at the Way Home and told her that she and Cynthia needed transportation and protection so that Cyn could open a savings and checking account to stash the precious three hundred dollars that she presently had on her person and in cash. Cyn had never had a bank account of her own before. She had never had someone who cared for her enough to make sure she kept her own money. Ralph picked Susan and Cynthia up the next Monday morning and brought both of them to the bank.

Mr. Cross came over to the apartment and found that Susan had acquired a "roommate". "Thahs ehz graht!" *"This is great!"* he thought, "Shay'll hahv sumb-Juan wid huhm, shay cauhn shahr thah rahnt." *"She'll have someone with whom she can share the rent."* Then, he began laying the rag rug in the forward bedroom of the new apartment. He also hooked up Susan's washing machine to the sink and presented Susan with a diaper pail, which he thought would be of use to her. Melissa Jordan came over with a check for $340.00 so that Susan could get the electricity turned on in her apartment. Susan told her, "Mr. Adams wrote me that check already Melissa and I have the light back on again. I also have a phone and you're the person I most want to have my phone number."

"Well, keep it anyway Susan; I'm sure you can use it." This would double Susan's balance in her savings account and the next Monday Cynthia and Susan went to the bank and Susan helped Cynthia open her very first checking and savings accounts. Cyn had about three hundred and fifty dollars in her jute bag, which she never went anywhere without. And now that it was in the bank Binny wouldn't ever get his hands on it.

Melissa Jordan got acquainted with Cynthia and discovered that she had a Cadillac convertible, parked in a rented garage. They arrange to go pick it up the next day. This became an occasion for Cynthia to confide in Susan that there were drugs in the trunk of the Caddy and that she was in a quandary about what to do now. Susan said: "Don't Worry Cyn!" and began writing the names for God on a blank sheet of paper. This is a technique that the Advanced Class on Power for Abundant Living teaches. This class explains that writing out the various names for God aids the believer in receiving revelation from God, also known as **Word of Knowledge, Word of Wisdom, and Discerning of Spirits**.

Susan asked Cynthia, "Besides the trunk of the Caddy, are there drugs in any other locations that you know of?"

"Weahl", **Well,** Cynthia said, "Awel ov-vah towhn; bahd mahs'-lay ehn thah stow-edge lah-cahr uhn Che'z-naht Straight". *"All over town; but mostly in the storage locker on Chestnut Street"*. Susan asked for the locker number and whether it was locked with a key or with a combination lock?

Cyn said, "Thah lah-cahr numb-bah sehz **281** ahnd ehd owe-pahnz wid ah kay, wahch Bin-nah awe-wahz kehpz wid huhm uhn ah rahng uhn hahz bahlt." *"The locker number is **281** and it opens with a key, which Binny always keeps with him on a ring on his belt."*

Susan said, "Great Cyn! Now I have to go make some phone calls." It wasn't yet 4:30pm and Susan thought that the office of the Federal Bureau of Investigation would still be open. She found them in the phone book and when a young lady with a pleasant voice answered the telephone. Susan asked if she could speak to an agent. She told the receptionist, that she preferred to talk to one who was in the Portland, Maine area or could get to the Portland, Maine area within a reasonable length of time. After being placed on hold for what seemed an interminable length of time; Susan got up and paced the room with the phone lying on the floor and off the hook. Pacing while waiting for revelation from God, is another technique she had learned in the Advanced Class on Power for Abundant Living. This was Susan's first opportunity to try these techniques out and she was excited about it. Finally, the phone call was transferred to a man with a deep baritone voice, "This is Agent Scott Rodgers; may I help you?" the man asked.

"Yes", Susan said. "I want to report the location of a whole lot of heroin and cocaine. Can I get an agent to meet me in front of the Boys' Club, it's at the intersection of Chestnut Street and Cumberland Avenue in Portland, Maine? You can select the time." Susan knew the locations of this Portland landmark; along with most of the other landmarks throughout the city. She discovered this information from her weeks of homelessness and this location was the one nearest to Binny's "Merch" locker.

"Yes Ma-am, how would 9:45 this evening be for you?" Susan quietly consulted God and then uttered the words, "Perfect, I'll meet you then." Agent Rodgers continued, "I will have to bring a DEA agent along with me; is that alright?"

"Great!" Susan replied, "Two men to protect me. The more the better! And you will need to bring along some bolt cutters, Agent Rodgers. Then after the meeting, we will have to travel together for about two blocks is that alright?"

"I understand", Agent Rodgers said and hung up the phone.

Melissa came over to their apartment about an hour later and said, "I have garage space for that car, Cyn. But, you probably should sell it as rapidly as you can." Then the two friends piled into Melissa's 1980 Buick Electra Park Avenue Station Wagon and went to see the landlord of the sheltered parking space where Binny had "his" Cadillac parked. The landlord was profoundly sad that he would be losing a tenant. But, Cyn's paperwork was in order and it was definitely her car. Susan brought along the extra key which Cynthia had wisely retained in the pocket of her Capri pants. Susan's new diaper pail concealed a disposable black plastic garbage bag.

While Cynthia and Melissa were negotiating with the landlord, Susan crept behind the car and opening the trunk, she relieved it of Binny's "Merch". Then, on the way back to Grant Street, she sat all alone in Melissa's back seat, clutching her diaper pail. Melissa's was a very good place to hide the Caddy from Binny. As he would never have imagined that "his" car was located in a garage behind a mansion in Cape

Elizabeth. Melissa drove back to her home with Cynthia following in the Caddy. Cynthia spent the night in Melissa's new guest room and Susan took care of the meeting with the two agents.

Susan knew that she would have to leave Paul alone again, unless Walter suddenly dropped in on them. Surprisingly, he did. Susan left Walter in charge of her home and baby, and even told him, "You should go into the refrigerator and freezer, Walter, and fix yourself something to eat and something for Paul too." Susan trusted Walter to scrounge up whatever food there was, cook it for himself and little Paul; who was teething and just trying out table food for the first time. Then she set out for her meeting with the agents carrying her diaper pail with the plastic bag of drugs in it.

When the men met Susan in front of the Boys' Club, they were wearing matching cheap, black suits and Susan was dressed in business attire. They politely greeted her and then got down to business by all getting in the car and driving the two blocks to the "Merch Locker". Susan was once again seated in the back seat, clutching her diaper pail. The two agents hunted for the locker marked, **"281"**. When they found it, it turned out to be just a normal storage locker with several metal utility shelves, lined with bins containing clear plastic bags filled with cocaine and about a hundred decks of pure heroin. They relieved the locker of its contents. But, while they were locking Binny's "Merch" in their trunk; Susan handed over the plastic bag that was conceal inside her diaper pail and thanked the officers for their service.

"What do you want for this contraband, Ma-am?" agent Rodgers queried. "Oh, nothing sir, I'm just a good citizen that wants to get this sort of thing off the street."

The agents dropped Susan off a block from her apartment and she returned home in the dark, clutching her now empty diaper pail and Speaking in Tongues out loud the whole time. She did this with no weapon of any kind, save the name of Jesus Christ alone.

Chapter Forty-Five

"THEY ALSO SERVE THAT ONLY STAND AND WAIT"

Agent Scott Rodgers had many harrowing experiences in his professional life; but mostly, he waited by the telephone to receive the kind of call that came from an anonymous source. Then, Agent Rodgers would spring into action, confronting something that threatens civil peace; the accumulated product of a chemist's labor which resembles innocent milk powder or powdered sugar. Sometimes he would even find the lab in which they produced this poison, called in the parlance of the criminal element a "Meth Lab". This "Merch" locker was an unthreatening repository of this powder. This is how the engine of the assault on our society is stored and concealed.

"Meth labs", "Merch lockers", crappy apartments and houses in poor neighborhoods or sometimes in relatively-affluent suburbs. These secret locations sometimes conceal brick-shaped, plastic-wrapped stores of cocaine and heroin. These are either a pristine white substance, like snow or a brownish product fresh from the jungles of Columbia and Peru. This product could also be from the poppy fields of Afghanistan and the Golden Triangle of Burma, Laos and Thailand.

This stuff is processed and stored in glassine bags or tiny glass vials called decks. These lockers and homes, some of them with young children living in them, are the holding and distribution centers for the poison leaving America in ruins. Sometimes they are guarded by vicious dogs and men with guns. But most of the time, they are locked with a single key and hiding in plain sight all over our communities around the country and are concealed by nothing more than anonymity and plainness.

This one, Binny's "Merch" treasury was an unguarded storage locker at an innocuous location, which was intended for the private storage of surplus household goods. Binny's "Merch" locker had an altar to Satan in it. It was made of cocaine bricks and was in one corner of the repository. The rest of the locker was lined with utility shelves. These shelves held bins storing the finished product ready for distribution. The desperate men and women of our communities, the ones who commit most of the crimes need what Binny processed, stored and sold in order to quiet the ever-present call of their addictions. Sometimes, he would go down to his locker and process his "Merch" for hours, standing in the cold and always looking over his shoulder to make sure that no one was coming. So, whenever a rash of robberies and break-ins plague our communities, a stash of this vile accumulation is somewhere present.

Agent Scott Rodger was also an avid supporter of the private ownership of firearms and a stocker of ammunition. Wise Survival Foods and rinsed out plastic milk containers which he filled with tap water and stored in the basement of his home in New Jersey. He relished the opportunity to save America from its enemies, by clearing out the stocks of these drug merchants' larders, while filling his own with survival gear. He also took his patriotism to the next level by training with his firearm on a firing range or in the wilderness. He was also determined to kill ever enemy of America with his firearm. Even if that person surrendered and made himself a willing prisoner. He sometimes apprehended a culprit unobserved by others.

When this happened, the pusher was a dead man.

He wanted to stop the distribution of drugs in our country and he was resolved to kill every drug dealers he could, wherever he found them and destroy their inventory of drugs and drug paraphernalia wherever it accumulated. Agent Scott Rodgers didn't kill Binny, because he hadn't confronted Binny at his "Merch" locker. If he had, he would have killed him. That's the way Agent Rodgers' mind worked and the way he acted. It's the way; all of us should think and act. If we did, this plague on America would have long ago been resolved.

"ON HIS BLINDNESS"
by John Milton

When I consider how my light is spent
Ere half my days in this dark world and wide,
And that one talent which is death to hide
Lodged with me useless, though my soul more bent

To serve there with my Savior, and present
My true account, lest he returning chide,
"Doth God exact day-labor, light denied?"
I fondly ask. But Patience, to prevent

That murmur, soon replies: "God doth not need
Either man's works or His own gifts: they who best
Bear his mild yoke, they serve him best.
His state is kingly; thousands at his bidding speed

And post over land and ocean without rest:

They also serve who only stand and wait."

Chapter Forty-Six
"THEREFORE CHOOSE LIFE."
(Deuteronomy 30:19)

When Cynthia answered the telephone the next Monday morning, Dr. Bonjour was on the phone. He related the happy news to her that she had no STDs (Sexually Transmitted Diseases) and then answered some of her questions about her unborn child. She also asked him how people, who seemed so smart about pregnancy, namely Planned Parenthood with which she had previously dealt, could have the idea that the baby forming in her womb was just a blob of tissue. "Ehf eht'z gauhd ah haht- beht ahnd awel thahd Dahk-tah hahw coahd they-ah sahy thahd eht'z naught ah-lyev yaht?" *"If it's got a heartbeat and all that Doctor how could they say that it's not alive yet?"*

"Because, when they want to kill somebody, Cynthia it's much easier if they can first depersonalize him or her. See, if you say 'it's just a fetus' or 'it's just a blob of tissue', killing him or her is so much easier. It seems so much less like taking an innocent, human life. The Nazis, for example, when they wanted to get rid of the Jews, made them 'a lower form of life' than the Aryans. That's why they shaved their heads and had them go into the gas chamber naked. They did it to dehumanize and depersonalize them. It's like what the Ku Klux Klan, KKK do to black people when they get ready to lynch them. Racist, Slave Merchants made it alright to enslave and murder those people, Cynthia. Just by getting themselves to believe that black people were their 'inferiors.' Just because they had darker skins than they had."

"Cynthia, Planned Parenthood compares a human fetus to another part of the woman's (mother's) body. But, they never compare it to a part of her body, that is necessary for survival, like the heart or the liver. They compare it to something that can be removed without resulting death. They call the agents that sit down with an abortion- minded mother 'counselors', because it makes them sound so much more professional. In truth, they have no training whatsoever. except on-the-job training and they are more like salespeople than counselors. They have a personal, financial interest in the woman 'choosing' abortion. In fact, they get bonuses and fulfill quotas to sell more abortions."

Cynthia inquired, "Bahd, how do-ah we-ah nah thahd lahf bah-genz aht cahn-sep-shun, Dahk-tah? Thahd thah bay-bay ehz-n't jehz' ah-nah-thah paht ahv mah bah- day, lahk mah tahn-cellz 'r' mah ah-pahn-ducks?" *"But, how do we know that life begins at conception, Doctor? That the baby isn't just another part of my body; like my tonsils or my appendix?"*

"Because, Cynthia, the baby has her own blood supply, even her own blood- type. Which can be, probably is, different from yours. There is also a structure inside your uterus called the placenta, which separates your blood from the blood of your unborn child. It keeps the child from getting sick from your waste products and nourishes the child with the good things that are in your blood. All the while, it keeps the toxic things away from your baby. There is also the briefest period of time in between the time that your uterus is too small for a surgeon to gets his instruments into you, in order to cut and scrape away the contents of your uterus: your baby and your placenta into the garbage and the time when there is too much ossified bone to safely dislodge the little one. The abortionist, I am loathed to say the word, "doctor", doesn't want to leave a little arm or a little leg behind in your womb to rot, because that would bring on an infection known as "septicemia".

We've come a long way as far as the study of this thing, Cynthia. When I gave you that pelvic examination in my office, I looked inside and felt your abdomen to see how far along you were. You are at the moment, seven maybe eight weeks along. This is the optimum time for you have the suction-curettage abortion. But, I don't do them because even though it's a-hundred-dollar-a-minute business. I swore an oath to: **"FIRST, DO NO HARM"**. And, that is why I had your blood sent to a lab for testing, to see what germs might be in it. We had only a small window of opportunity to keep those germs from making you and the baby sick. So, time was of the essence. Now that, we know that your blood is alright and that the baby's blood is also alright.

Antibiotic especially Tetracycline, at this stage of your pregnancy, would be bad for your baby, Cynthia. But, Chlamydia, Gonorrhea and Syphilis would be worse. Now I know that I won't have to prescribe Tetracycline for you. Which could turn your baby's teeth green when the baby teeth start coming in; but that would only be for your child's baby teeth. I think that the child's adult teeth would be white. You're going to have to decide whether you're going to continue this pregnancy or not Cynthia. I wanted the baby to have the best start in life and get you and the baby on antibiotics before things 'went south'. But, now we don't have to do that, because you and the baby won't have to battle any disease!" Then, Dr. Bonjour did something he had never done before. He offered to give Cynthia free prenatal care, free prenatal vitamins for the duration of her pregnancy and a free delivery at the Mercy Hospital in Portland, Maine. This pro- bono medical care was something new for both of them. And, she thanked him exuberantly.

Chapter Forty-Seven
LET GO AND LET GOD

The Cadillac Coupe de Ville was now securely nestled in the garage behind Melissa and Sara's mansion. And it was relieved of its "Merch" and that "Merch" was in the hands of the FBI and the DEA. The two older women pick Susan and Cynthia up, in the Caddy, with the Caddy. Melissa was driving and Susan was sitting in back with Melissa. This trip was taking them on an adventure and to Lewiston-Auburn; the four of them traveling, the thirty-five miles up Interstate 95. They were determined to pick up Cynthia's camper and Cyn was looking in the glove compartment for her camper pink slip and bill of sale from Tim Sample. Walter was watching the baby, and all four ladies were soon flying down the highway in pursuit of both a sought-after camper and an adventure in Vacationland.

They found His Excellency, the Bishop, at the bishopric of the Most Holy Trinity Church of Christ, an ornate and imposing structure on the top of a hill overlooking Auburn, Maine. The church sported a magnificent steeple, stained-glass windows that were over one hundred and fifty years old and a rustic stone exterior. Besides all this ostentation, the church was spiritually dead as Susan discerned.

Parking the Caddy behind the bishopric, they spied the camper parked in the church parking lot. His Excellency, the bishop told them that Bill

Lane had sold the airstream to him, but he couldn't produce any paper-work. Melissa pressed her advantage, presenting the vehicle registration, which was a legal document and in Cynthia's name. This was obvious proof, that Bill Lane had no legal right to sell something that didn't belong to him. Then she told His Excellency, that if he didn't give it back, she would have to call the police to mediate the dispute.

The Bishop didn't want any trouble with the police. So, he gave the camper back to the women. Melissa, who His Excellency recognizes from the Maine Historical Society's, Registry of Historical Buildings and Fami-lies really had some clout in this situation and she played it for all it was worth. They hooked the camper to the back of the caddy and drove it back to Portland. Then the sisters dropped Susan and Cynthia off at their apartment and drove the Caddy with its attached airstream back to Cape Elizabeth, where they stashed it in the garage behind the goat barn.

A new life for Susan and Cynthia had begun. They acquired a Castro Convertible Sofa and put it in the forward bedroom of their apartment, turning that room into both a living room and a bedroom. Susan told Cynthia that she considered a couch that didn't turn into a bed at night, to be a total waste of money and Cynthia said she concurred. Then, they acquired another waist-high dresser to put in the hallway opposite the bath. This would become a resting place for the crib mattress, which Ruth Burrell had purchased for Susan so long ago, and on which both women would be changing their children. Susan never looked back at the things which she had lost to The Way Ministry. She knew God would replace them and He did.

Their "living-room/bedroom" also sported a rocking chair adorned with red velvet cushions. These two items of furniture in addition to a fold-up play pen completed their living room ensemble and were aug-mented by an insulated drapery at the window. The women began sharing the fold-out bed. It was much more comfortable than the one that Susan had shared with Mike. When Cynthia got comfortable sharing a bed with Susan, she began telling her the awful history of her long career as a prostitute. This is how Susan discovered the horrible truths about the Prince, the wealthy gentlemen in Bath and eventually Binny and his purchase of Cynthia for nineteen thousand dollars. Cyn's longed for prayer to have someone hold and console her as she cried was answered. Wishing it had been Charlene, then realizing that Susan was more than a mother, more than a sister to Cynthia. Susan was a true friend; someone to whom she could cry out her story.

Cyn was beginning to show, when they found the Park Avenue Church of God. They went to church together, sitting together in a pew and singing hymns. Cyn was an apt pupil, learning to follow the hymnal and tossing coins into the collection basket. The only trouble was that she had had sexual relations with the pastor and every deacon and elder in the church. Apart from other denominations that call themselves, "sinners saved by grace", the Church of God confessed to "never sinning any more". You just had to hang around with these people for a few minutes and you knew that they still sinned. While taking up the collection one of the elders looked down at Cyn's swollen abdomen and thought, "Could I be the father?"

A modicum of spiritual insight made their services, which consisted of: saints speaking with new tongues out loud and out of order, saints falling down on the floor "slain by the spirit" and saints prophesying without praying a prayer of thanksgiving to God an affront to Him. Susan observed that the speaking in tongues and prophecies were genuine; however, when the pastor called for more speaking in tongues with interpretation than the Biblically recommends: "three" **(I Corinthians 14:27).** Certain believers who were deemed "worthy" got up to "interpret".

When this happened, supernatural things began occurring all over the church. This demonstration of "the spirit" was not from God and the evidence of this ruthlessly presented itself. It was apparent to Susan that this pastor and these elders had begun channeling devil spirits, not manifesting holy spirit. Their voices became deep, harsh and raspy and their cadence became slowed. Their speech patterns didn't even sound human anymore and the bats which lived in the church's belfry began to fly around the church during the service landing in the worshipers' hair. Presumably, God had had enough and withdrew His Spirit to a safer more reverential atmosphere. And though, these believers hadn't lost anything that Christ had done for them; they were clearly not in the center of God's will and it showed.

Cyn said to Susan, "Thahs sehz crah-pah! Led'z gaht oud ahv hee-yah!" "*This is creepy!* (crappy, who knows) *Let's get out of here!*" So, they sought fellowship in yet another church, much to the relief of the clergy at the Park Avenue Church of God.

Susan and Cynthia kept questing for a church in the city of Portland, Maine, where an outspoken Susan would be received and where Cynthia had not had relations with the entire pastoral staff. Maybe her previous concentration on clergy, who were given to the pursuit of sexual escapades was the way in which God kept Cynthia from contracting an STD. This was something she surely would have done, if she had not had "reg-gul-lahz" that were so selectively chosen. What Cynthia did as a prostitute was mostly listening to men's troubles. Men who were supposed to help their congregants with their troubles. Men who would just talk to Cynthia, while she lay next to them naked and leaning up on her elbow the way she had done when she was with the Prince so long ago.

Susan endeavored to teach Cynthia the Bible at home and led her into tongues, which Cyn learned to pursue, silently, and in private between herself and God. Susan also attempted to teach Cynthia the practical application of the foundational principals of the Word of God to everyday life. But, these excursions to Portland's "Established Building", helped them cultivate a Godly trait much to be admired and which they could never have obtained through the Way Ministry: tolerance. **Tolerance** is referred to in the Bible as: **"endeavoring to keep the unity of the Spirit in the bond of peace." (Ephesians 4:3)** and usually involves tact. It is one of most important things we can ever learn as disciples of Jesus Christ.

As Cynthia's pregnancy progressed, she clung the more to Susan for emotional support and security. She confided more things about her life as a prostitute, how oral sex made her gage; but she did it anyway so that she could make the right amount of money that Binny required of her for the day. How most of her 'all night' clients, were 'men of the cloth'. She confided that their sickening pomposity made her gage worse than oral sex. How most of her clients just wanted to have a beautiful, blonde teen-ager lying next to them on a bed and look at her and tell her all their troubles. It was pathetic that Christian men especially ministers treated Cynthia that way, like a thing to be rented for the evening. Then, deliverance came! Susan met a couple through Walter Malien named Steven and Roberta Fearon of the Falmouth Baptist Church. This is a rural area, that has retained the City of Portland, Maine's former name which it had when long ago it was a hamlet named, Falmouth.

Going to this distant, rural church was of necessity, if they were going to get some much-needed fellowship. It was an arduous journey and Cynthia balked at traveling in Steve's dilapidated, rusty Ford station wagon. She balked also at the church's indoor, outhouse. This attachment to the church precluded the congregation having to invest its precious resources in plumbing and running water. In the state of Maine, pipes in unlived-in structures such as "summer people's" cottages, came right across the lawn so that in winter weather, they could be disconnected and filled with antifreeze much like a car or a camper. These saints never had to fool with "water lines", because of the outhouse and the electric space heaters along the walls in the sanctuary gave them all the heat they needed. A sanctuary is what Catholics call the part of the church where they have the Eucharist and where Protestants call the place where they worship; because wherever believers worship is a sanctuary. Neither Cynthia nor Susan minded helping Steve turn on the heaters and light the oil stove. They also helped the pastor shovel the parking lot in winter.

The money they saved from not having to shoulder these plumbing expenses was generously applied to the support of missionaries in the third world. An activity to which Susan gave nodding approval. She was after all an avid supporter of Franklin Graham's "Samaritan's Purse", World Vision, Wycliffe Bible Translators, The Navigators and Elizabeth Elliot's ministry in Ecuador. Cynthia was also approving of the absence on their Pastoral Staff of men with whom she had had sexual relations. The two friends used this Sunday excursion to visit the woods near the church and pick wild- growing edible plants. Harvesting them, became for them a unique joy of the Maine countryside and a weekly activity much to be anticipated. Susan realized that Steve Fearon was no Biblical scholar; but he had a pastor's heart and a genuine gift ministry. (**Ephesians 4:8-11**) "**...He led captivity captive and gave gifts unto men... and He gave some apostles and some prophets and some evangelists and some pastors and teachers.**"

They would stroll through the waist-high grasses and shrubs. Among the hard-wood forests and copious wild flowers of rural Maine there grow fiddlehead ferns. These are called ostrich ferns and have a tall, spiral-shaped stem. These wild plants are gathered mainly in early spring; boil and serve with lemon-butter sauce. Cattails, which have an edible, young, male flower are also gathered in spring. These are a delectable potherb; sauté in butter until golden brown. Dandelion greens, which must be picked before the flower emerges, steam or sauté them and serve with bacon and garlic. Lamb's quarters, wild leeks, purslane are eaten as a potherb or in salads. Orache is an herb of the goosefoot family and has leaves that are covered with a white mealy substance you can fix them as you would spinach. These wild-growing plants can be prepared as you do, dock, polk and collard greens. All of them can be used as salad greens or as a steamed vegetable and are brimming with nutrients. To identify these wild-growing plants; please consult an online reference such as: www.missouribotanicalgarden.org/plantfinder or "Eat the Weeds", by Green Deane, www.eattheweeds.com and "Green Fun" by Maryanne Gjersvik, subtitled, Instant Toys, Tricks and Amusements Anyone Can Make from Common Weeds.

Chapter Forty-Eight
FREE INDEED

Lots of Christians like to talk about being "free indeed"; but very few of them actually enjoy doing it. Or for that matter even watching other people do it. When not foraging for sustenance in the Maine wilderness, Susan made a diligent effort to prepare Cynthia to take the test for her GED. She also tackled her textbooks and assignments in the Paralegal Department at Casco Bay College going after both an Associate's Degree in Paralegal Science and another in Legal Secretarial Science. Susan was on the Dean's List all the time that she was at Casco Bay College. They both endeavored to help one another in preparing for these two academic challenges. When Cyn passed her GED, she sought out a career with which she could identify. She became a licensed massage therapist getting her LMT certification from the East-West Institute. **"Therefore, my brethren dearly beloved and longed for my joy and crown, so stand fast in the Lord, my dearly beloved." (Philippians 4:1)**

Now, Cynthia was qualified to do something other than be a prostitute and she could also support her little son or daughter when he or she arrives. Meanwhile, Susan took her Final Exams for her AA in Paralegal Science. Steven and Roberta Fearon went to both their graduations. Steven was the most supportive pastor that either of them had ever known. Cynthia had a new career and Susan was diligently probing the Portland job market adding both a Legal Secretarial Degree and a Paralegal Degree to her resume. She submitted this resume to Bernstein, Shur in the hopes that her association with Mr. Nelson would help her in securing employment at this law firm. [**The best time to look for employment is when you already have a job, however low-level or temporary it may be.**] The inclusion of Mr. Nelson with Susan's references didn't hurt either.

Cynthia and Susan's relationship became so intimate, so supportive and genuine that Cyn finally began to divulge the depths of her depraved and sordid former existence. She tearfully told Susan her life story, while they were lying on the Castro Convertible Sofa bed of their apartment's forward bedroom at night. A bedroom which Cynthia and Susan turned into a living room-bedroom by day and augmented with beautiful, insulated draperies at the windows. Cyn told Susan how her step-father, Marlin Thompson had started sexually abusing her when she was only seven years old and that this exploitation led to a progression of trips to Bath in the camper. It was many times that Cynthia would speak of this atrocity, which was perpetrated upon her in childhood and then Susan would hold her in her arms and let her cry before they both fell quietly to sleep. It was during one of these "pillow-talks" that Cyn recounted to Susan how her "two fathers" Thompson and Zyfler sold sexual encounter with her to older men for a hefty price. Men who wanted to deflower a virgin and how after she actually lost her virginity they used a small quantity of her blood which they extracted by lancing her forearm and placing a blood-soaked gauze compress in her vagina to simulate the long-ago perforated hymen. Susan became both mother and sister to Cynthia as the Apostle Paul told the Corinthians: "For though ye have had ten thousand instructors in Christ, ye have not many fathers: for in Christ Jesus I have begotten you through the gospel." (I Corinthians 4:15)

"You never really had a childhood, Cyn, why don't you have one right now?"

Susan took Cynthia to more than just church, she took her to an amusement park that had been set up in the Deering Woods across Park Avenue from their home. [**Pregnant women can still go out and have some fun, despite their condition.**] There is always the merry-go-round, a reasonably safe activity and the amusement park also had a giant slide which, with Susan standing at the bottom as a "catcher", caused the rider to have an exhilarating experience with a modicum of accompanying danger.

Susan, being an authority on all things related to "Cheap Thrills" went with Cynthia to visit the Rosa True Child Development Center. Behind their main building is a spectacular playground, which is free to the public. One of the attractions behind Rosa True is a pile of railroad ties which makes an obstacle course both challenging and safe to access. Portland, Maine also has a public access rose garden to rival the one on Pennsylvania Avenue. The two friends availed themselves of this magnificent floral display and its adjacent jogging path which snakes endlessly through the Deering Woods. This is a public accommodation, which is available at all times of the year and which is swept and shoveled of snow in winter by volunteers.

When Fall weather gave way to the Winter cold, they joined in the annual citizen's foot trek up Munjoy Hill to take part in the "Portland Winter Festival". This is a long anticipate event in which the community assembles privately-owned sheets of cardboard, inner tubes, sleds and heirloom toboggans. These become vehicles to take the revealers down the Payson Tobogganing Run which starts at the top of Payson Park and progresses southward to the Back Cove of Casco Bay. This tobogganing run takes up a large portion of the north-east section of Portland and is a yearly attraction.

Susan and Cynthia played in the snow and threw snowball at one another. Just as Susan and Mike had done when they first moved to Portland.

This was the first time in her life, that Cynthia had ever had a fur-lined winter coat with a hood. She also had several pairs of long underwear, cotton tube socks under another pair of wooly socks and a pair of rabbit-fur lined red-velvet mittens. Over her cotton socks and wooly socks, Cynthia wore a pair of knee-high rubber boots.

Cynthia's "Whore Clothes" were replaced with a much more serviceable wardrobe, complements of Melissa and Sara Jordan and many of their Cape Elizabeth friends. Melissa wasn't above visiting her friends and neighbors. And, they collecting asked-for garments and brought them to the Grant Street apartment. Melissa would pointedly ask her wealthy friends, "Will you give me your used Maternity clothes and baby clothing, please". And sometimes, these things would just arrive in large paper bags left at Susan and Cynthia's door. They were either worn immediately or saved in a large steamer trunk for later. Susan had spotted this treasure in a resale shop and dragged it all the way home in Paul's little red wagon. The apartment hallway was becoming crowded with tricycles, rocking horses, a wagon and dolls of all varieties. These were piled on makeshift shelves and in banana boxes along the wall in the hallway.

Cynthia inherited maternity garments and winter apparel which were far finer than anything she had previously worn for warmth and stylishness. Her new wardrobe turned her into a much different woman and Binny wouldn't have recognized her on the street.

Cynthia now had her GED and an LMT (Licensed Massage Therapist) certification. Because of this, she now sought to establish a legitimate business even advertising her services in the Portland Press Herald. She also invested borrowed funds in the tools of her new trade: A portable massage table; massage oils; fragrant aloes and a motorized foot spa. She even became a practitioner of Aromatherapy. The smell of new-mown hay was Cyn's favorite; but she also liked Persian Lilac and Sandalwood. She also practiced the Science of Reflexology.

Reflexology requires the professional to first soak the client's feet in a hot foot bath and then massage them with fragrant oils. Cynthia wasn't averse to getting on her knees in front of a client, who occupied their rocking chair. Every professional has to invest in certain tools of their trade and Cynthia took what she did very seriously. She massaged and manipulated the different parts of the client's foot, which is said to relieve more than just foot pain. Reflexologists believe that this activity imparts healing to the whole body. Susan didn't want to disabuse Cynthia of these ideas as they were harmless and besides this just wasn't Susan's area of expertise. Susan and Melissa had taken Cyn to the dentist and for her first Christmas present ever; she got an electric toothbrush, floss, toothpaste, mouth-wash and a set of surgeon's gloves, masks, hair net restraints and paper booties to help her care for her clients who were "germophobic". Susan and Cynthia both believed that love is something you do not something you feel.

There were still customers that assumed that what Cynthia did was a front for a call girl ring and an occasional policeman from the Department of Vice came to her Grant Street apartment. He would always be disappointed to find that all he received from Cynthia was an actual massage and several police officers left the apartment with their constant back and foot pain much relieved. Police Officers returned again and again, becoming Cynthia's "reg-gul-lahs". Word of mouth advertising gained Cynthia many Police Officer "reg-gul-lahs" and other people that spent long hours standing and walking, also heard about her and benefitted from her professional care. Now the police and other people who stood for long hours on their feet sought Cyn out; paying for her services with soldierly good will.

A greatly-pregnant woman, who gave therapeutic massage, became the talk of Portland. That is except in the circles in which Binny had sequestered himself. He was still "hiding out" after his near miss with the

FBI and the DEA and never suspecting Susan and Cynthia, when "his car" was stolen and his "merch" locker looted.

One evening while Susan and Cynthia were getting ready for bed; they had taken to sharing the Castro Convertible sofa in the living room. Cyn's water broke. Susan immediately called Melissa Jordan, who came running; she then called Dr. Bonjour's pager and he met them at the hospital. Cynthia and Susan got into the back seat of Melissa's Buick Station Wagon and hurried to the Mercy Hospital, all the while doing the Lamaze Breathing Exercises that they had learned in the class they took together. Susan was an old hand at this as she had already had a baby. Melissa held little Paul as the two friends travailed together in the Labor Room. When the baby was crowning, Susan started snapping the same photographs that Wendy Theriault had taken several months earlier.

Cynthia was clutching the home-made swaddling clothes to her bosom as she gave the last push. The baby was born at the respectable hour of 11:23 p.m. Cyn wished that her precious little girl could have been born at home and as she held the baby in her arms; she was suddenly moved to great heaving sobs of joy and sadness. She had joy in her heart over the birth of her daughter and overwhelming sorrow, because she had no "real family" with whom to share this experience. "Mah-mah, Eeyah fah-gahv you-ah, Eeyah dohn-n't eev-vahn cahr ehf you-ah nev-vah ahskd fahr mah fah-gahv-nes'; Eeyah fah-gahv you-ah ehn-nay-wahy." *"Mama, I forgive you, I don't even care if you never asked for my forgiveness; I forgive you anyway."* Cyn declared out loud, deciding to name her daughter "Charlene", after her mother, who was now deceased.

Chapter Forty-Nine
CHARLENE

Cynthia began to wrap the swaddling clothes as per Susan's instructions, starting at the sole of her daughter's foot and binding her legs until the wrappings came up to the little one's arms which she bound down at the baby's sides. Then the wrappings, continued to her shoulders and neck extending under the little girl's chin and around her head. The nurses became alarmed at this, especially when Charlene began crying loudly. Susan was there to ward them off and when Walter came into the delivery room, tossing a dozen roses onto the bed. They took him for "the father".

Susan said, "Walter, she doesn't need those; she has a nice baby and anyway where did you get them? You're a wonder!"

She remembered the roses Mike had given her every time she had a miscarriage. Susan's eyes welled up with tears, when she remembered how much pain she had felt in losing those little ones. She went into the waiting room with Melissa and just hugged Paul. His life was the great purpose that gave Susan's life shape and meaning. Now on this important evening, Cynthia also had purpose and meaning in her life as Susan did. When her little girl was sent to the new-born nursery and Cyn was taken to a hospital room, she hugged Susan, Walter and Melissa thanking them for what they had given to her life.

About a year and a half later, the apartment on Grant Street became "too small" for the four of them and they moved to a much larger place with two smaller bedrooms for the parents and a master bedroom for the children. The apartment also had a very modern kitchen and dining room. They acquired more furniture at an estate sale to which David Cross had taken them in his new 1984 Oldsmobile 98. Susan was now living within walking distance of Bernstein, Shur and Sawyer, where she was working full-time as a Paralegal.

The money was good and so was life. At this point, the Way Ministry would have welcomed Susan back, because she was "believing for a bountiful increase"; but it was too late. She was still attending the Falmouth Baptist Church and Steve Fearon was still picking Susan and Cynthia up at their new apartment. Steve was the pastor that had seen Susan and Cynthia go from poverty to relative wealth and he was "The Man of God" as far as both of them were concerned. Cynthia expanded her businesses to include massage parlors in several locations. And a network of subcontractor, who were licensed massage therapists, now worked for her and several neon signs proudly advertising, "East-West Therapeutic Massage" were located all around the city. Cynthia decides to take over her old apartment on Congress and High Street. Binny had moved away and no one knew where he was. She considered the place "safe" now, even if Walter didn't approve.

He would come over to this downtown office, use the bathroom, get some water and consume any refreshments he found in Cynthia's refrigerator. Walter stacked his surplus tracts in a cabinet which Cynthia specifically provided for them. She considered herself one of his benefactors and supported him like other people support missionaries. He used the cabinet she had provided for him to store his bulk supply of tracts, his Bible and any outwear which he might need. Next to it was a very posh leather sofa and beside this sofa on an end table was a telephone. Cyn kept the little girl with her at "the office" and as the child grew; she began to walk. Cyn decided it was time to have the "Merch Pit" closed up and the Great Room's floor resurfaced. She hired carpenters to come in and build a perfectly fitting cover for this gaping wound in her parlor floor, sand, stain and dress it with polyurethane. When they were done it was a beautiful red oak floor.

Instead of the previous wretched, brown, woolen curtains at the windows, there were now sheer draperies and a neon sign advertising her business, "East-West Therapeutic Massage". This was just one of the three therapeutic massage parlors Cynthia had started. The police, at least the ones that hadn't yet availed themselves of Cyn's professional massage and foot care services, were convinced that what she offered was a massage of a different sort. However, the vice cops couldn't prove it and since she wasn't actually committing a crime, they had to allow her to continue. Every Thursday evening, John Mann, Richard Cook, Ralph Magwood, Cynthia, Susan, Melissa, Walter, Sara and a homeless saint with which Walter was sharing food and principles from the Word would fellowship in the great room that Cyn's ministration had taken from darkness to light. When Cynthia stood up to speak in tongues and interpret, Susan broke down crying. It was such an encouraging, comforting and imposing message that God gave the church through her that everyone was enthralled.

Paul was now in preschool at St. Elizabeth's and Cynthia had Charlene at Rosa True. The kitchen and formal dining room of their new apartment had modern appliances, granite counter tops and an Oster Kitchen Center, which Susan had retrieved from the Way Ministry. She had gotten it back through an act of God, after it had made the rounds of the entire Portland Way Branch, loosing several of it's attachments along the way, which Susan had to re-order from the manufacturer. Susan thought about sending Jim Simmon an invoice from a law firm with the order, bill of lading and the other documents she had saved from Oster; but she decided against it. He didn't know anything about this anyway; he never knew what was going on in the Portland Branch. After all, this was all Al Theriault's department.

Because of this questing after her Oster Kitchen Center, Susan had become on better terms with Anne Simmons. Anne visited Susan in her new, posh digs on the corner of Congress and Chestnut Streets, above the Persian rug store and nodded approvingly at the beautiful decor. After confiding the story about losing all of her wedding presents, Anne said, "And now Susan, you have gotten **exceedingly, abundantly above all you could ask or think." (Ephesians 3:20)** (Could you imagine reading this verse in Ephesians, and equating it with getting more stuff.)

"That is true Anne", Susan replied; "but, I've also learned something more important than that, I've learned: **"having food and raiment.. therewith to be content." (I Timothy 6:8)** Susan had only gotten two of her sterling silver forks back.

Susan went back into the kitchen and confronted the wait-staff, especially Jill Ireland. Imagine taking a poor widow's flatware worth approximately fifteen hundred dollars while you knew she was homeless with a new born, just because the pattern reminded you that Jesus is the vine and we are the branches. In response to all the shouting coming from the kitchen, Al Terriault came out there and immediately kicked Jill's little dog "Haifa" and Susan scolded, "Al Theriault, that was not your dog to kick and I don't care if you are the Branch Leader." Still it was Jill's place to defend her dog which she never would have done. In this kitchen, Susan prudently confined herself to recovering Larry Jaines' Bible with his name in gold on the leather cover. "How do we know this Bible is yours? A new believer queried, "How is this your Bible, if it says, 'Larry Jaines' on the cover. They called Larry on the phone, who had the branch of a tree fall on his car and blamed this on them or God or something. Larry admitted he had given this Bible to Mike Asta as collateral against a fifty-dollar loan which he had never repaid. Amazingly, Larry still hadn't amassed this small sum of money and let Susan keep the Bible. These people never had any money when being pressed to repay a loan or pay a bill and then they brazenly assured you that God would cover for them.

Anne shyly divulged the story about how her wedding gifts, which had been stored in a steamer trunk at the Way International had been broken into, stolen from and the gifts rewrapped and then presented to other believers also as wedding presents. Susan listened attentively, pouring her tea and made an occasional reference to her new career and improved lifestyle. But, though Susan longed to hear the Word of God taught rightly divided once again, the Falmouth Baptist Church was her church-home now and she swore she would never leave it, unless she moved out of The State of Maine. [**Concerning the subject of getting your needs met or living in poverty; some believers actually pray that God will not give them so much that they forget Him and begin to believe that they have acquired their bounty by the power of their own hands. These believers also pray that they should never have so little that they would be driven, out of want, to forsake the LORD's moral cannons and fall to stealing. You see, God isn't concerned about helping you get more stuff. He's concerned about having you learn more about a life dependent upon Him.**]

Even though Cynthia and Susan were the only believers at the Falmouth Baptist Church who spoke in tongues, the Baptists had the salvation thing down pat and they had figured out eternal life as well. These saints had also acquired right believing about the return of Christ and what Christ's Return portends. Besides this, they were a generous, nonjudgmental and supportive church to which Susan was glad to belong, even if she had to tip-toe around their faith statement. Cynthia also enjoyed their company, specifically because they never reminded her of her past sins. It's true that Susan had had a disagreement with an elderly saint that made the mistake of calling Catholics "AntiChrists", especially the Pope and Susan immediately reminded him that Catholics were Christians and part of the body of Christ. Steve Fearon wouldn't allow this to become a shouting match or a Bible bash as he called it and took a stand for **"Endeavoring to keep the unity of the Spirit in the bond of peace." (Ephesians 4:3)**

Susan showed the Children's Church how to make, a whistle from an acorn cup; a basket from the dried seeds of the burdock flower and crowns of flowers, that had six-inch stems and which had been gathered from the church's adjacent field of wild flowers. The children learned to twist the flowers together to form wreathes and crowns wearing them in their hair during services. And, they were blowing their acorn whistles all the way home from church. The kids wore Geranium fingernails as they sang their hymns. [**Geraniums can be brought to the church in flower pots and used in Sunday school in inclement weather.**] Susan also taught them how to make, Dolls from Hollyhocks and Red Maple Leaf Crowns. Please see: "Green Fun, Plants as Play" by Marianne Haug Gjersvik.

Susan and Cynthia's dark oak dining room table had a double-pedestal base surrounded by four matching chairs. But, the end chairs were captain's chairs, that featured ornately-carved arms and all six chairs had padded seats. Their chair backs were resplendent in the style of the French lyre-back splat. The China Cabinet was brimming with Havilland and augmenting their dining room table was a buffet table and a dry sink. This room comfortably seated six and the silver service consisted of: A sterling-silver serving spoon, a sterling-silver carving knife, sterling-silver serving dishes, a pair of sterling-silver candelabra and a large, sterling-silver charger. Cynthia and Susan found all of these treasures at an estate-sale auction to which David Cross had taken them driving his moving van. David Cross was renting these posh digs to them and he also owned thirty other building around town. He was an everyday millionaire, who though he had a generous heart was still a pretty shrewd businessman. Just like Donald J. Trump, but with millions of dollars not with billions of dollars. Susan had him over to the place many times, where he was always seated at the head of their table, opposite Susan and Cynthia, Walter and Samantha, Melissa and Sara and where Susan would serve a family-style, Italian dinner with several courses and fine wines. Susan and Cynthia also had Mr. Trusiani over with his little son, Paul.

These were magnificent accommodations, when compared to the Myrtle Street apartment where Susan had begun and Cynthia never ceased to thank God for His Beneficent Hand. Moving Susan and Cynthia to this new, luxurious apartment was David Cross's greatest pleasure and receiving the inflated rent, which these tenants could now afford, was also very enjoyable. He took them to auctions and taught them how to bid on merchandise, a skill which Cynthia picked up with alacrity.

The new apartment allows pets. So, Susan and Cynthia got a German shepherd named, "Heidi". The dog was trained to walk "off leash" and would travel with Cynthia as she pushed her daughter's stroller to work or to the day-care program at Rosa True. Pre-school was something which Cyn found of necessity for her daughter's cognitive development. She especially favored Rosa True's "Gross Motor Room" which features a truck tire suspended on a log chain. The swing that was created by this unique design made this room the focal point of an uncommon, developmentally-formative, athletic experience for preschoolers. Charlene's teachers diligently supervised this type of play and remarked thoughtfully about how intelligent and polite Charlene was for a girl of almost two. Charlene wore a starched and ironed dress to school every day and she and her mother took great pride in her appearance.

Chapter Fifty
BROTHER AND SISTER

Three-year-old Paul could almost walk home from St. Elizabeth's. He was becoming so tall, so fearless and so athletically inclined that Susan couldn't keep up with him. The teachers at St. Elizabeth's said that Paul had developed a unique game in which the other kids participated. He would sit at the front table behind his personal "drive a car" toy, which was brought from home and behind which he pretended to be a school bus driver. All the other kids in the nursery would sit on chairs behind Paul pretending that they were his passengers. He called this game, "Mr. Bus Driver" with every kid in his play group taking part in his fantasy. This proved much to Susan's delight and she was proud that Paul was beginning to form social alliances with other kids and developing some communicational skills. He had also taken an interest in what other kids wanted to play, think and do.

Charlene was becoming a proper little lady, wearing a dress to preschool every day, sitting in her stroller as Mom pushed it to Portland's West End and the Rosa True Child Development Center. Cynthia enjoyed this daily excursion with her daughter, as it helped them bond. Cynthia also found breastfeeding her daughter conducive to bonding. [**Cyn still nursed Charlene from time to time, even though the child had graduated to table food and had quite a few of her baby teeth. It is a real exercise**

in faith to put your breast into the mouth of a teething child.]

The two children had slept in one another's arms since the time that Charlene outgrew the bureau drawer and began to join Paul in the single bed in front of it. This single bed, which was Cyn's first bed in the apartment on Grant Street was given back to Cyn, as she assumed the role of co-parent of these two energetic youngsters. Susan had reclaimed her brass bed from the Myrtle Street place, when David Cross just brought it over one evening after Susan got home from work saying, "Eeyah tahr dahwn thah Mah-tahl Straight tahn-nah-mahn' tah-dahy, Sue-zahn, ahnd Eeyah thah-awet Eeyah'd brang thah brahss bahd, zo thad you-ah coahd uhz eht ah-gahn. Eeyah've gauhd you-ah post-tah tah." *"I tore down the Myrtle Street tenement, today, Susan and I thought I'd bring by the brass bed, so that you could use it again. I've got your poster too."*

After thanking Mr. Cross, Susan ran out to Porteous, Mitchell and Braun to purchase the most luxurious bedding she could find. Before Mr. Cross made this beneficent and unexpected delivery, Susan had been sleeping in the living room. Now she had a bedroom of her own and so did Cynthia. The children slept together in the "Master Bedroom" and Heidi slept in the children's room, where there was plenty of floor space and a braided rug on which she could lie and the children could play. A utility shelf served as their toy box and displayed a plethora of books, blocks and toys. Paul and Charlene's dresser drawers sported pictures of the kinds of clothing concealed therein and they both took great pride in the fact that they could dress themselves almost without assistance. Their chores consisted of routinely tidying up their room, feeding the dog and dressing or being dressed in the morning before "school". Charlene had a closet full of dresses purchased from Porteous, Mitchell and Braun and both children enjoyed rocking in their rocking chair and on their rocking horse.

The Castro Convertible Sofa was still good enough for their luxurious parlor and they had also purchased numerous book shelves, end tables and lamps. Walter would frequently stay over on the fold-out couch and their dining room became the destination location of frequent dinner parties. Susan entertained her office mates at "cocktail parties" where she served White Zinfandel and Beaujolais wines and home- made Italian cookies instead of the standard mixed drinks and canapés.

Heidi had become extremely protective of the children and followed Cyn to the office and preschool, off-leash and under voice command. Whenever Cyn left the apartment, the dog was right by her side. Heidi was like a third parent to Paul and Charlene. Paul called his little sister "Chary". They were beyond close!

Once Susan was a full-time paralegal, cocktail and dinner parties became a necessary business expense. Budgeting for these parties and saving all her receipts in a special file for a yearly income tax deduction, became automatic. Cynthia also had several business expenses, that she learned to deduct and she thought, "Hahw nahs eht ehz fahr meh tah hahv ah rahm-maht, who-ah wurkz aht ah lah fahm ahnd who-ah hahz ah tahx ah-tahrn-nah dahwn thah hahll." *"How nice it is for me to have a roommate, who works at a law firm and who has a tax attorney down the hall."* Cyn filed as a DBA; taking the depreciation on all her business component; her neon signs, her foot spas, her massage tables, the rental expense on her various massage parlors, her massage oils and her aromatherapy supplies. Cynthia was now an entrepreneur like David Cross and she had found a way of deducting even the cost of their dog's food and veterinary expenses from her taxes. These two women had becoming business savvy and it thrilled Melissa Jordan and David Cross, that Susan and Cynthia had benefited so much from their mentoring.

Chapter Fifty-One

"THE SNAKE"

(See Donald J. Trump reading this poem)

Like a snake slithering through the tall grass, Binny approached the stairway leading up to the third floor of the tenement in which he had once resided with Cynthia. A massage parlor now existed at the intersection of High and Congress Streets and though he expected to see Cynthia standing there in the center of the room, there was instead a very elegant leather couch. Against the wall at the top of the stairs was the cabinet where Walter Malien kept his tracts. Across the room and next to the kitchen wall was perched a wide professional, massage table. This was the only thing between him and the kitchen. The table graced an immaculate and glossy, fine-grained, warm, golden-colored, red-oak floor. Next to this table was a doorway leading into a wide kitchen, the kitchen where Cynthia and Walter had hung the last of the yellow wallpaper so long ago. The tea kettle was whistling.

There was also a very large neon sign in the window facing the intersection. It was visible to all but one lane of traffic and could clearly be seen by the people in the park across the street. It said: "East-West Therapeutic Massage". No neon sign could ever have proclaimed more assertively that this was a legal, tax-paying establishment, except perhaps for Cynthia's full-page advertisement in the Cumberland County Yellow Pages, which was listed under the section: "Spas, Rehabilitation and Massage Services".

The woman, who was seated in Cyn's kitchen awaiting a customer, was Samantha Gibbons. She was an employee of Cynthia's new business: East-West Therapeutic Massage Services of Cumberland County and an LMT, who had several years of experience. Samantha was taking a break, having some herbal tea and relaxing before her impending appointment with a client.

On the kitchen floor, next to Samantha lay a huge German shepherd, who was also obviously waiting for someone. It was four minutes after three, the slow period of the day and Samantha's client was late. When she heard the door chime sound, (Cynthia had installed a door chime that was activated whenever anyone mounted the stairway.) Samantha arose to greet her 3 o'clock appointment finding instead an unfamiliar man.

Not at all apprehensive, because of the presence of this large, loyal and protective dog; Sam strode confidently forward to greet the visitor extending her right hand. Binny shook her hand warmly exhibiting a smile and gentlemanly grace. He had a way of making strangers at ease around him. No one could say where he had acquired this trait; it was new to him. His appearance was also new. A clean-shaven, well-dressed, black man passed thirty; but not yet middle-aged was looking back at Sam over the tops of his aviator sun glasses. He was wearing athletic shoes, laced up and matching his black leather apparel. His swagger and his winning closed-mouth smile both concealed his bad teeth and gave him a disarming, cavalier demeanor.

Sam asked him who he was and he answered with his name and that he was a friend of Cynthia Hickey. She smiled broadly and asked him if he wanted to wait on the couch as she had a client due any minute. The client was an emergency-room nurse, who had just had a bunion removed and was there for a Reflexology treatment. These were always done in the kitchen and Sam already had the motorized foot spa in there filled with water and Epsom salts. She got right to work as her client's time was extremely valuable. Binny waited an hour to talk to Samantha again. As he sat on the couch and stared nervously out the window at the park across the street; he spied Walter Malien, that detestable, insignificant insect of a man; who had taken his Cyn away from him.

As the minutes passed by, the sunlight coming through the window dimmed and other clients began to pour into the waiting area. Cynthia, he discovered, was at an alternate location. She apparently had two offices and was about to open a third, this time in South Portland. Business was good and Cyn was making money. He was impressed; but still didn't understand what it was that she was selling. He couldn't believe that Cynthia had become a business woman; that she was now a highly-paid professional and that she had several employees!

He wanted to go across the street and punch Walter Malien out; but it was the middle of rush hour and there were people crowding the sidewalks. People were pouring in and out of Paul's Market, and they were also milling around in the adjacent park. There was no way he could assault Walter and get away with it. Binny bit his lip, his arms and legs throbbed with excruciating pain. This was because they had been pierced through so frequently with a hypodermic syringe.

He sought to cover the evidence of this; as well as he could with his long-sleeved, button-down, black, Salvation Army Store dress shirt. He wore this garment tucked into his black-leather pants and then he covered the whole ensemble with his long black-leather coat which was fur-lined and had a hood. All of this layered clothing was geared to disguise the fact that Binny was an addict. He thought about going downstairs and walking back down Congress Street to the homeless shelter where he lived. He pondered whether he should head over to Saint Luke's Cathedral not to worship but to eat at their soup kitchen. He also liked to go to the

McLellan-Sweat Mansion not to enjoy the museum; but to shoot horse out on the benches in front. He also liked, the Portland Public Library, where there was an outdoor grotto surrounded by stone benches. These locations were Binny's haunts. They were the places where Portland, Maine's addicted population of street dwellers would rest themselves and then surreptitiously inject the drug upon which they relied. Whatever drug that might be cocaine, heroin or speed.

Now that Binny was shooting up every day; he never strayed far from these four locations. He frequently shot his beloved heroin in one of these open-air; municipal locations; undisturbed by an indifferent and preoccupied Portland Police Department. He secretly injected the drug in between his toes; into the veins on his legs and even into the vein under his tongue. Whenever he spied Cynthia pushing the stroller up to the West Side of Portland accompanied by that big, scary, dog; he would slink around the corner and hide, shivering and cowering.

Binny was afraid of dogs, from his childhood he had been terrified of dogs: big, slobbering beasts; protective of their owners and domains. New York City where Binny originated had tried to outlaw the private ownership of dogs; not the yappy, little dogs that snooty women carried around in their purses; but the large, hazardous dogs like Pit Bulls and Rottweilers, that people walked on titanium chains. Mayor Ed Koch was convinced that these breeds of dogs were capable of attacking strangers on the street, while being walked. His honor the mayor had campaigned adamantly for a "safe" city; by "safe" Koch meant to make New York City devoid of large, vicious dogs and personal fire arms owned by law-abiding citizens. What his honor got instead was a city dominated by home invasions; gang-land slayings and open-air drug markets.

Like a predator stalking his prey, Binny stalked Cynthia now that he recognized her. Behind her new personae, Cyn was to Binny like a gazelle or a wildebeest. Some kind of tasty animal that he hoped could not protect herself; but Cyn could protect herself. That was because while taking classes at the East-West Institute, Cyn had also taken a course in Taekwondo Karate, along with the mandatory courses which she took to get her LMT. Now, with Heidi by her side, she had become a formidable opponent. Like the Wicked Witch of the West, Binny thought to himself: "Theze thengz mahs' beh dahn dell-ah-cot-lay, vary-rah dell-ah-cot-lay". *"These things must be done delicately, very delicately"*.

Binny began his planned assault on Cyn by acquiring an oversized T-shirt and carrying it around with him in his coat pocket. He first envisioned himself assaulting Cyn, then Walter but when his personal investigation revealed that Cyn had a daughter, who was a toddler, he had found the object of his interest.

His present situation seemed strange to him. He couldn't relate to it. He had always had a parasitic relationship, with his addicted customers, but now he was the addict, he was the host. Binny was feeling like a frightened animal, but only until he got his next fix. Then he felt fine. And when he didn't feel fine, he blamed his situation on Cyn, someone else and of course on Walter.

Without remorse and without respect of persons, the product he had conveyed to Portland's least fortunate citizens was now his master. This had begun a downward spiral occurring so gradually, so progressively that he barely noticing it. It came upon him as does a fever or a rash. He didn't do psychedelics any more. He hadn't done them in years. Now, even cocaine had lost its charm for him. Only heroin remained. There was only heroin and occasionally, some reds and wine. Binny was living on the edge of the real world. He was asking his body to give him more and more. Heroin was consuming more and more of his income and his strength. Like a teather that connected him to a hot-air balloon, this substance kept him attached to an aerial performance in which he merely mimicked the pursuits of normal human beings. He had become the puppet of a life which was more of a stage performance in which he engaged.

In the living room of their posh apartment, above the swanky Persian rug store, Susan and Cynthia had a heart to heart talk. They hadn't had one of these for months. Both of them were so busy with their careers and children, that they could hardly find the time to clean their unit. Walter had become a temporary domestic helper and so did Samantha. Cyn's employee from the High and Congress Street location was doing double duty as a domestic. Cynthia and Susan both occupied the same apartment and parented the same two children, but because of their busy lives, they were passing like ships in the night.

"Are you opening a new massage location, Cyn?" Susan began the conversation with an air of inquiry.

"Eeyah-'em thahnk-kehn au-boughd ehd", *"I'm thinking about it."* , Cyn's replied. "Eeyah hahv plahnz ehn mahnd tah ex-pahnd ehn-tah Sahth Pautlan'." *"I have plans in mind to expand into South Portland."* She said: "You-ah hahv tah gaht thah jah-ump uhn thah cam-pah-ti-shun, wahn you-ah'r ehn ah behz-nahz lahk thahs, 'cahz Eahs'-Wahs' ehz grahd-Jew-ate-tehn nuer pea-bahl awel thah tahm, ahnd they-ah cauhn't awel wurk fahr meh." *"You have to get the jump on the competition, when you're in a business like this, because East-West is graduating new people all the time, and they can't all work for me."* She disclosed this to Susan in hushed tones as she didn't want Samantha to over-hear. Samantha had more experience as a Licensed Massage Therapist than did Cynthia, but she lacked the ambition and the fortitude to start her own business. Some people don't want the responsibilities and headaches of entrepreneurship. These people fearful retreat instead to the security of a bi-weekly paycheck, preferring not to shoulder the trials and cares of managing a business.

Susan talked about some things that were going on at her office. One of the law clerks was taking the Bar Exam and Susan was encouraging him and helping him study and prepare. Heidi came into the room. She had been playing with the children, and getting them ready for bed. She now turned her attentions to the adults that were also in her care. Heidi was looking into the situation of the two mothers. She lay down next to Susan on the floor near the couch.

"You know, Cyn, I think you should keep Heidi with you all the time now and especially when you have Charlene with you and especially at the High and Congress Street location, because you just never know!" Susan said while gently stroking Heidi's head and long nose. Susan began the conversation with this animated advice. Walter had told Cyn the same thing. [**When you receive unasked-for advice from two different Christians, relatively at the same time, take this as an oracle from God, especially if these two Christians are not even members of the same denomination!**] "I'm glad that you got that old "merch" pit covered", she continued. "Bringing in carpenters to build a new floor in that area and having the whole floor resurfaced was such a good idea. You have really become an entrepreneur."

"Ayuh! Eht gauhd meh ah rah-dahk-shun ehn thah rahnt tah, ehtz mahd thahd lah-kay-shun ah moe-ah kohn-jean-yahl plahz fahr thah cly-on-tell, ahnd eht hahz ehm- prahvd behz-nahz fahr meh trah-mehn-jus'-lay. Eeyah-'em gaht-tehn nuer pea-bahl ehn awel thah tahm nah, ahnd Eeyah-'em thahnk-kehn ahv hi-rah-rehn sumb nuer stahf tah healp wid thah ov-vah-flow." *"Yeah! It got me a reduction in the rent too, it's made that location a more congenial place for the clientele, and it has improved business for me, tremendously. I'm getting new people in all the time now, and I'm thinking of hiring some new staff to help with the overflow."*

Cynthia had become the statuesque personification of feminine beauty

Susan knew her to be from the moment they laid eyes on one another. Cyn had always been a head-turner, but now she was like an object of art, like the paintings in the McLellan- Sweat Mansion, where heirs of the mansion were fighting for the right to relieve it of some of its multi-million-dollar paintings as the art connoisseurs had assessed them. Cynthia was Portland, Maine's most beautiful work of art and of course, she was God's. She had never abandoned the wearing of exquisite underwear, but her whore ensembles were definitely gone in favor of more serviceable clothing and Cynthia definitely believed in sensible shoes, which Susan had forgone in favor of high heels, but only for the office. Cyn had chided her telling her that her experience as a Reflexologist had acquainted her with many women who had ruined their feet with stylish shoes. Cyn always dressed comfortably, but modestly. Modesty was a shockingly-new trait in which she abounded, but her clothing made known to one and all that she was fit, muscular and had the confident bearing of an athlete.

Susan stroked her dog lovingly and began brushing her luxurious coat using a dog brush with steel pins on one side and bristle on the other. Heidi was from a long line of brave and intelligent working dogs. Heidi's father, Darth Vader, had gone into a convenience store with his master, walking off leash and on voice command, when they confronted an armed robbery in progress. The dog acted on instinct, subduing and disarming the robber, but when the proprietor of the store called the Portland Police Department they arrived and finding Darth standing over the robber with his teeth bared and to the alleged criminal's throat, instantly shot Darth to death. Then they applied direct-pressure to the robber's wounded trachea, which had received a minor injury more than an hour previously, an injury which was not life-threatening. Their ministrations to his windpipe cut off his airway, and gave him the brain damage her so-justly deserved, making him unable to pursue his chosen course of life, which was to rob and beat other people. Darth Vader, Heidi's father, had at least twenty puppies around Portland, Maine. Heidi's brothers and sisters served as: Seeing Eye Dogs, Police Dogs and Guard Dogs throughout the city. Darth Vader had been a grand champion of the Saccarappa Obedience Club of Portland, Maine and three times the winner of their working and herding dog division. Dogs from all over New England would sojourn to Westmont, Maine to compete for these top prizes. Darth who was from the Vom Wildweg Kennel was also awarded a Schutzhund-III title, in tracking, obedience and protection. This training is done all over America not just in Germany and it sets dogs apart as sought- after, breeding stock. The loss of Darth was a stunning blow to the entire German- shepherd owning family including the police. His killing was what Melissa Jordan would have called: silly, contemptible and speciesist.

The next morning Heidi went with Cynthia and Charlene to the massage parlor at the intersection of High and Congress Streets. Cynthia was pushing the stroller, with the pull-behind shopping cart suspended from one shoulder, she also brought Zip- lock bags from home and an empty coffee can. When they arrived at the "office", Samantha was already there, and had started brewing tea in the kitchen. Samantha was a wonderful employee. She had watched Charlene many times, while Cynthia was out food shopping or visiting her other massage location in the People's Building on Brackett Street. Samantha was also filling in at Cynthia and Susan's apartment, until the two women could get regular maid service. Cynthia wanted to get someone to clean her offices and make that person a regular part of her staff. Cyn and Samantha both provided sisterly care for the apartment, and the two children. And, Sam had become just like a second sister to Susan.

Sometimes, things don't always work out the way you planned. Cyn left her friend and employee Samantha in charge of her daughter, but just to be on the safe side, she left Heidi with her as well. What could go wrong? Before she left the office, Cynthia gave Susan a call at Bernstein, Shur, to tell her that she had to go out to "the Good Day Market". "Eehyah nehd tah pahk ahp ah few thengz." *I need to pick up a few things.* Cyn said.

Susan had arrived at work early, it was 7:00 a.m. and she had immediately begun working on the impending court appearance that Mr. Nelson had concerning an Insurance Defense case. Insurance Defense and Litigation was Mr. Lenard Nelson's area of expertise. Susan always arrived at the office early and stayed late. She was on salary; so, nobody noticed. Nobody that is except the partners, who rewarded Susan with a bonus at Christmas time; they were grooming her for the position of Office Manager and she knew it. Cynthia's phone call brought Susan out from behind the filing cabinet, where she was assembling Mr. Nelson's court documents and the exhibits necessary to win his case. **[When a man is a paralegal, he has a secretary, when a woman is a paralegal, she is a secretary.]**

Susan picked up the phone, it was Cynthia. "Eeyah-'em hee-yah aht thah Kahn-grahss ahnd Hayah Straight lah-kay-shun ahnd Sah-mah-thah ahnd Hah-dee 'r'wahch-ehn Chary. "Eeyah-'em jahs' gau-ehn oud fahr ah few min-ats tah pahk ahp sumb fah-ud. Do-ah you-ah nehd ehn-nay-theng frumb thah Gudd-Day Mah-cat ahnd Pahl'z?" *I'm here at the Congress and High Street location and Samantha and Heidi are watching Chary. I'm just going out for a few minutes to pick up some food. Do you need anything from the Good Day Market and Paul's?"*

"I'm thinking of making some Mango Chutney, we already have the Mango", Susan said. "Could you pick up some cumin, thyme and ground cardamom seed? I'll need some Acidophilus Milk from Paul's and we're out of olive oil. Good Day has some Morning Thunder Coffee, that I'd like to try at the office and could you pick up some Cremora at Paul's Market." They hung up and Susan got back to assembling her exhibits.

Chapter Fifty-Two
DEATH OF AN ANGEL

Samantha put the kettle on for tea. Charlene was fussing about being confined in the highchair. Samantha mixed up some all-natural, lukewarm, baby cereal in Charlene's bowl, the one with the blue elephant design on it. Her juice cup and her "blankie" were there with her in the highchair. Otherwise the child would fuss. She was twenty-three months old now and most of her baby teeth were in. Samantha felt the inside of Charlene's mouth with a finger and discerned that another baby tooth was about to erupt, perhaps a molar. Mom was going to be right back and the dog had curled herself up against the legs of the highchair. The door chimes sounded. A somewhat unfamiliar man appeared in the great room and approached the couch. He didn't have an appointment. Samantha remembered this man from two days earlier, he mentioned that he knew Cyn. She wondered how? It must have been through the natural food store on Bracket Street, she thought: "Pah-hapz, through-ah thah Gudd-Day Mah-cat Ah-sew- sea-A-shun." *"Perhaps, through the Good Day Market Association."* She neglected to inform Cyn of his previous visit, but since she couldn't remember his name, it didn't really matter. She thought it was Ben or something.

In his cold heart of hearts, Binny was contemplating how the death of her beloved daughter would affect Cynthia, how it would fill her with despair and send her collapsing in unbearable pain. He had never seen Charlene before and he didn't know her name. But, he knew Cynthia, and reasoned that if Cynthia had a daughter; she would love her. Cynthia loved everyone; she even loved Binny, even though he beat and used her. She still loved him. In fact, Cynthia was the only person, who had ever loved Binny. At the homeless shelter, where Binny lived, there was a large bin of donated clothing. Binny found a t-shirt in there; which was four sizes too large for him. He had it stuffed in the pocket of his coat and had been carrying it around with him for several days. As he approached the couch, Samantha smiled broadly and extended her right hand to him. He told her that he was waiting for Cynthia Hickey and then he sat down on the couch. He thought to himself: "Eeyah wahnt tah say thah fine-ahl ahct ahv Cyn'z nah plah- zahn' lahf plah oud." *"I want to see the final act of Cyn's now-pleasant life play out."*

Samantha said to him: "Eeyah-'ll beh ride bahk: Eeyah dohn' hahv ehn-nay Celestial Seasons Tay." *"I'll be right back; I don't have any Celestial Seasons Tea".* Paul's Market was just a few steps away and it was 9:30 in the morning, there was a man there and so was the dog. What could go wrong? As soon as she was gone, Binny picked up the phone on the end table next to the couch. Cynthia fussed over leaving this telephone in reach of the clientele, but since no one except her and her staff ever used it, having a wall phone installed in the kitchen was an unnecessary expense. "Hal-low, ehz thahs thah Aun-nah-mal 'troll? They-ah ehz ah lahj, vah-cious daug ehn mah au- paht-mehn' ahnd Eeyah nehd tah gaht huhm oud." *"Hello, is this the Animal Control? There is a large, vicious dog in my apartment and I need to get him out."* He gave the police the address, he knew it well from having lived there once. Then he hung up the phone and looked over at Charlene. He didn't know her name, but her wide-eyed, innocent, trusting face made him salivate. He only wished that her death could be slow and painful like the death of Roz and Charlene, Cyn's parents, had been.

The Animal Control officers arrived with a dog noose, which is a lasso on a long wand. They were skilled at capturing large, vicious, dogs and though Heidi put up a terrible fight, snarling and trying to bite them, but she was no match for the officers, especially since they had the dog noose. Charlene was upset at seeing what was happening to her beloved pet, she couldn't understand it. But, she was in the high chair and couldn't run after the dog to save her. She couldn't help Heidi at all. She began crying and fussing.

"Suhr-rah wahz ah vah-cious daug", *"Sure was a vicious dog"*, the officers said to one another as they dragged Heidi out.

Binny hugged the couch in the great room and pulled his feet up onto it from the floor, as he told the police: "Mah wahf ahnd Eeyah hahv ben hahv-vehn prahb-blehmz wid thahd daug fahr sumb-tahm nah. Thahnk you-ah, ah-fah-sahz, fahr prah-tect-tehn mah lit-tahl boy-ah." *"My wife and I have been having problems with that dog for some time now. Thank you, officers, for protecting my little boy."* Then as soon as they had lassoed Heidi, Binny slid into the kitchen and began pretending to spoon cereal into Charlene's mouth. The Portland City Police weren't particularly bright, but compared to the Portland Animal Control Officers, they were geniuses. The ACOs couldn't tell a male dog from a female dog or a little boy from a little girl, even when the child was wearing a pink dress. Maybe they didn't want to judge people for having a child with a confused sex assignment. As soon as the officers left with the dog, Binny put the oversized t-shirt over his coat and other garments.

At this point, Cynthia was purchasing the Morning Thunder Coffee, that Susan had requested and Samantha was greeting a client which she met in the coffee, tea and soft drink aisle at Paul's, where they sold six-packs of Moxie and other beverages in glass bottles.

Binny looked over at Charlene, he was still salivating. He was eager to begin his assault on her. He first slapped her for crying, he slapped her as hard as he could and in the face. Then, he couldn't waste any more time on an activity that wouldn't result in Charlene's death. So, while wondering what her name might be, he picked up the high chair with one hand and feeling very important, very powerful, he swung the chair into the back wall of Cynthia's kitchen, against her lovely yellow wallpaper. Then, he picked up the chair again spattering Charlene's brains and blood against the corner walls. He determined to shatter the child's spine and head and coat the area behind the table and himself with her blood and brains. Because of this, his carefully prepared t-shirt would bear a stain on it that he would cherish for a long time as a memento of this experience of power and privilege. He had carried this shirt around with him in his coat pocket for days, waiting for an opportunity to complete this task, unseen.

As soon as Binny finished, he took the shirt off, balling it up with his hand and stuffing it into the pocket of his coat, then he ran out of the massage parlor, flying down the stairway and out onto the street, his black coat blowing behind him. He ran back down Congress Street in the direction of the homeless shelter just as he had done, when he beat and kicked Cynthia several years earlier. How did Binny get to his final destination? It may have been that he hitch-hiked all the way to Lewiston-Auburn, a bloody shirt concealed in his pocket. The people of the State of Maine are surprisingly charitable, some kind-hearted person may have picked him up and driven him the thirty- five miles to safety. No one would have suspected that they had a passenger in the front seat with them, who had a bloody shirt in his pocket.

The light of the midday sun penetrated the kitchen window and cast its pale aura over this scene of devastation. Behind the table, the highchair lay in ruins on the floor, the bowl with the blue elephant design lay next to it shattered and spilling its contents on the linoleum tiles. Samantha was still talking to someone on the street, as she was walking back from Paul's Market. Sam didn't have another appointment for several hours, and Cynthia overtook her ascending the stairway ahead of her, leaving the pull-behind where Sam could find it and pull it the rest of the way up the stairs.

The pull-behind was brimming with raw vegetables, plastic bottles re-filled with olive oil and red wine vinager, sacks of different kinds of flours, a sack of bulgur wheat and another of buckwheat grouts. Cyn had also taken several zip-lock bags along with her, to steward the herbs and spices which she purchased, as well as an empty coffee can to hold the Morning Thunder Coffee that Susan had requested. Cynthia and Susan both agreed that recycling and reusing plastic and aluminum vessels was the right thing to do. Even now that they were relatively rich, they continued this practice that they had begun in poverty, because, they thought, it was better for the environment. This is why Cyn continued to use Susan's pull-behind shopping cart and walking or taking the bus everywhere, even though they now had a Cadillac convertible parked behind Mellissa and Sara's mansion in Cape Elizabeth.

Chapter Fifty-Three
WHAT TO NEVER SAY AT A CRIME SCENE

Cynthia and Susan's pull-behind was full of purchases, Cyn left it at the bottom of the stairway and trudged up the three flights of stairs. She intended to collapse on the couch and let Samantha pull it the rest of the way up the stairway. When she didn't see Heidi or Charlene in the great room, she went into the kitchen to look for them. Cyn found her daughter in the kitchen, spattered against the walls. She came back to the couch sat down in shock and tearfully dialed 911. Then she called Susan's office. Mr. Lenard Nelson had just left for court and Susan was relaxing on the daybed in his office. She had really pushed herself this morning in order to get him ready for court. The receptionist said: "Your friend Cynthia is on Line One, Susan!" Susan picked up the telephone pushing the button that connected her to Line One, while sitting behind the desk in Mr. Nelson's office. When she heard Cynthia's voice on the telephone, she got up and shut the office door. This was a conversation that she didn't want the people down the hallway to overhear. Cyn was crying, frantic and hysterical.

When the police arrived, they found Cyn sitting on the couch and on the telephone with a law firm. They thought that this was suspicious. Even before surveying the kitchen, they began questioning Cynthia.

"Ehd ehz awel mah fahlt" *"It's all my fault!"* she cried, muffling the rest of her statement with her tears. "Eeyah shahd-n'ah ahv gun oud tah bah fah-ud." *"I shouldn't have gone out to buy food."*

"We-ah nah whahd you-ah deed yahng lay-day, we-ah cauhn say eht ehn thah kitch-ehn". *"We know what you did young lady, we can see it in the kitchen."* Blubbering and sobbing, Cynthia doubled over on the couch gripping her abdomen. She was inconsolable, unresponsive and forlorn. The police weren't interested in consoling Cynthia, they gruffly informed her of her rights, as they handcuffed her behind her back. Then they manhandled her down the stairway to the street. Finding the shopping cart on the landing, they pushed it out of their way and proceeding to the squad car, which they had parked on the street in front of the tenement. Cynthia was forced into the rear seat. She could hardly sit up straight the handcuffs were making her lean forward. She fell over on her side to recline her bowed body and closed her beautiful, blue eyes.

The Police Station was a very modern building, newly minted and ready for anything. They asked her if she had ever been arrested before. She answered not a word, because she didn't want them to know the answer. She was remaining silent, which was her Constitutional Right. The officer wondered if it was legal to beat the information out of her. At that moment, he just didn't know.

Susan figured out where Cynthia was and came running down the street as fast as her high-heel shoes permitted. There were police everywhere and a pull-behind shopping cart on the landing at the bottom of the stairway. Susan pushed it out of her way and ascended the stairway as fast as she could. Five police officers were in the studio apartment. But, there was as yet no crime scene tape, no little plastic evidence tags with numbers on them, no plain clothes detectives and no CSI investigators. The police had already taken Cynthia away and in the center of the room was an officer, who appeared to be in charge. He approached Susan and said: "Thahs ehz ah crahm seehn mahm, theahr'z behn ah murd-dah! Ah lit-tahl girl. You-ah caun't bah hee-yah!" *"This is a crime scene ma-am, there's been a murder! A little girl. You can't be here!"* She asked him: "Where is Cynthia? Where is Charlene? Where is Heidi?" He said: "Theahr'z behn ah murd-dah, Mahm, ah lit-tahl gurl." *"There's been a murder, Ma-am, a little girl!"* Then he forcefully guided her back down the stairs.

Susan fell down the stairway crying, she grabbed the pull-behind, and dragged it out onto the sidewalk, as she did so. Samantha presented herself on the sidewalk in front of the building. She had been talking to Walter. Susan pulled the shopping cart onto the sidewalk and then across the street to the Congress Street Park. Sam was following her, asking questions which Susan couldn't answer. Walter inquired: "Whahd'z gau-ehn uhn au-crahs thah straight?" *"What's going on across the street?"* Susan collapsed into Walter's arms.

"Wh-ah 'r' zo mehn-nay pah-lease au-crahs thah straight?" *"Why are so many police across the street?"* Walter asked: Then he said it again: "Wh-ah 'r' zo mehn-nay pah-lease au-crahs thah straight, ahnd Wha-ah ehz ahn ahm-bah-lenz they-yahr?" *"Why are so many police across the street, and an ambulance there?"* She fainted and almost fell down on the brick side walk. Walter caught her and brought her over to the park bench. When she revived, Susan answered his question: "The police say that there's been a murder! The policeman said it was a little girl!" Susan replied.

Samantha inquired frantically: "Wahz eht Chary? Wahz eht Charlene? Way-ehn Ee-yah lahft shay wahz ehn thah hay-ah chahr ehn thah kitch-ehn! Whahd coahd hahv hah-pend tah har?" *"Was it Chary? Was it Charlene? When I left, she was in the high chair in the kitchen! What could have happened to her?"* They could hear the sirens howling, they felt the press of humanity, as people crowded around, looking across the street. Astonishment spread across the crowd, and Susan lost sight of her pull behind.

Walter began pulling the shopping cart up the street, his arm lovingly placed around a crying Susan's shoulder. Samantha asked: "What can I do, Susan?" Susan said: "I don't know where Cynthia is, I don't know where Heidi is either." I should go over to St. Elizabeth's to pick up Paul, Sam!"

"Eeyah cauhn gau fahr you-ah", *"I can go for you",* Samantha said.

"Oh, would you Sam? I just can't go down there right now, we'll wait here in the park for you."

"Suhr-rah, hah'z code wahd ehz: 'pahr-rah-keet'. Ehz-n't eht?" *"Sure, his code word is 'parakeet'. Isn't it?"*

"Yes, it is!" Susan said. "Walter and I will take your bag and wait for you on this bench." As Susan and Walter waited for her to return, Walter got up from the park bench and began obsessive-compulsively passing out tracts, again. [**You probably haven't given anyone a tract today! This guy got up to pass out tracts, after learning that a child he loved had just been murdered.**]

A cold shock had fallen over Susan. And when Samantha returned with little Paul, all four of them quietly pulled the shopping cart up the street to Susan and Cynthia's apartment. After they arrived home, Sam sat on Cynthia's bed and read a book to Paul. Susan and Walter went into the kitchen and began brewing some tea and putting away the food. Susan thought it odd that an insane person could function better than she could. Walter was the most rational person there. "Get up Susan", she said to herself. "Get up and start fighting". These were the same words that she had said to herself, when she came back from the Maine Medical Center, leaving Mike's mangled body stretched out on a gurney. It was there in that little efficiency apartment on the corner Pine and Main Streets, that Susan learned to rely wholly on God.

It was there, that she learned to wordlessly pray about every uterine contraction, every setback, and every need. From the time that she went to the junk yard, where they had her Toyota, telling the attendant: "I'm pregnant, and my husband was killed yesterday." To the weeks of homelessness, that she endured until she found Mr. Cross, to the move to Grant Street, where she lived by candle-light for three weeks until the electricity was turned on, these were the ways in which God had taught her to trust only Him. This was the way, God had prepared her for this moment. **Blessed be God, even the Father of our Lord Jesus Christ, the Father of mercies, and the God of all comfort, who comforteth us in all our tribulation, that we may be able to comfort them which are in any trouble, by the comfort wherewith we ourselves are comforted of God. (II Corinthians 1: 3 & 4)**

Now, as Susan sat in her splendid kitchen and sipped her tea, she thanked God for His provision as easily as she thanked Walter for bringing in the groceries and as easily as she thanked Samantha for picking Paul up from preschool. There was no time right now for speculation. She got on the phone and called Melissa and Sara, praying that they would be home. They were! When Melissa wasn't in the house, she was out in the barn and her sister Sara was never there. But, now they were both living in the recently rebuilt and remodeled mansion. They had become friendly and warm like sisters again. This was answered prayer.

"Melissa, something terrible has happened! Charlene has been murdered! And Cynthia and Heidi are both missing!" Great heaving sighs of grief spilled out of Susan's nose and mouth and down her cheeks.

"Charlene is dead?" gasped Melissa, she was incredulous. "What happened?" "I don't know, Melissa", Susan sobbed: "That's why I need you here", Susan cleared her throat and continued sobbing: "I think they've arrested Cynthia, but why would they do that. I talked to her this morning and she said she was going food shopping. I have the food she purchased. None of this makes any sense. The police wouldn't let me into the High and Congress Street place. They said it was a crime scene".

"Sara and I will be right over Susan. Are you in your apartment?" "Yes of course" Susan replied, still sobbing. "Where else would I be. I'm calling you from my apartment." She went to her big, brass bed to lie down, still carrying the phone.

Melissa and Sara parked their car on lower Chestnut Street and walked up the street to Susan and Cynthia's apartment. They didn't like to do this, because lower Chestnut Street was a bad neighborhood, but they were very good friends, like family. So, they did it. It was on Oxford and Chestnut, beside the very corner store, where Darth Vader had been killed that Melissa and Sara parked their expensive car praying that it would be there and in one piece, when they came back for it. Darth and his master had walked in on an armed robbery, when all the guy wanted was a newspaper and a pack of cigarettes. Before it was over Darth had been shot to death by the police.

When Susan got off the phone, she turned to Samantha and said: "Sam, I want you and Walter to stay tonight, I don't want Paul and I to be alone! Walter can sleep on the fold-out couch in the living room, and you can stay in the kid's room. Paul can sleep with me." Melissa and Sara arrived, it was an arduous journey for them, all the way from Cape Elizabeth to a bad neighborhood, where they parked their beautiful, expensive car on a slummy street hoping it would be there when they came back. Then they walked more than a block through a crime-ridden section of Portland.

"Let's find Cynthia and Heidi", Melissa said, once she had removed her coat. Then, she got on the phone and called the Portland Police Department. It was simple, she just did what Binny had done, she dialed 911. The woman answering police dispatch was a conversant and sensible human being. She explained that Cynthia was in booking, being fingerprinted.

Chapter Fifty-Four
ARRESTED FOR THE SECOND TIME

They handcuffed Cynthia behind her back. They dragged her down the wooden stairway. They put their hands on her head and pushed her out onto the sidewalk. The pull-behind was gone from the landing at the bottom of the stairs. Susan had it with her across the street in the park where she and Susan had met. Susan had collapsed into Walter's outstretched arms, sobbing. Susan never saw when the police push Cynthia into the back of a squad car. And when the squad car whisked Cynthia away to the Police Station, she was too overwrought to look up and see that her friend was being taken away. Walter wasn't taking notice either, he was concentrating on comforting Susan. He escorted her back up the street to her apartment, pulling her shopping cart behind him. Susan was leaning on Walter. She was in shock. Samantha and Paul were following behind. When they got up to the apartment, they realize that Heidi was missing. Susan thought: "Where is Cynthia? Where is the dog?"

Cynthia was being booked at the Portland Police Station. She was being process before ever being interviewed. This was contrary to procedure. They always interrogated a prisoner before booking. Cynthia was being booked on charges of First Degree Murder with Special Circumstances. She could get the death penalty. She didn't have an attorney. They told her that she only had one phone call, and she didn't want to waste it.

Melissa was on the phone with the dispatcher: "We've found Cynthia", she announced.

Chapter Fifty-Five
KINDNESS TO ANIMALS

Melissa said: "Now that we know where Cynthia is. Let's find the dog!" She was still on the telephone with the police-dispatch lady, so Susan went back into the kitchen and put the kettle on for more tea. She also looked around for some bread and jam. She was starving.

Heidi was confused. The dog-noose chaffed her neck and choked her. She couldn't get to her little girl, her ward. She felt the pole attached to the noose wheel her around and point her toward the stairway. She fought with all her might not to go down those stairs. When the Animal Control Officers pushed her out onto the street, there was a squad car parked in the red zone. This was a no parking zone, where the buses stopped and where their passengers boarded and were discharged. In front of the squad car was a paddy wagon designed just for dogs and one dog was already waiting in its other cage. He was a severely-dehydrated mongrel, who was apprehended on a Portland street. Certain dogs didn't get a time of reprieve before they were destroyed. This kind of dog was of the homeless variety: no tags, no shots and no ties to the community. He was a mangy, flea-infested, vagrant and Heidi was glad not to be sharing a cell with him, especially because she was just about ready to go into season.

The two officers that escorted Heidi down the stairway stood on either side of the paddy wagon door and pushed the dog noose up against the door discharging their prisoner into another cage. This was the procedure for vicious dogs that bite. Heidi had never been in a cage before. She had never been in a kennel or a shipping box as an airline passenger. She barked and howled in her grief. She wondered where her people were, and where her little girl was. She had no one to guard, no one to care for. She felt useless! She lay down on the cage floor and panted until she arrived at the Animal Control Center. It was there that she discovered that she was a prisoner and it was there that she saw her captor. An attendant named Bill strolled over to Heidi's cage. She barked at him and showed him all her teeth.

The other dog was dragged to a holding pen, that he would be sharing with several other dogs, who were all scheduled for termination. This was the immediate procedure with dogs that didn't have any tags. Heidi had both a license, which was her proof of vaccination and a tag that displayed her name and phone number. Bill realized that she was somebody's dog. From the looks of her, she had just been brushed and she was also ready to go into heat. He wondered if she had escaped her owner and was out seeking a mate. The manager of the center said that she was a vicious dog that tried to attack a man in his apartment. He also told Bill that the police dispatcher had announced that the apartment was recently the scene of a murder. Bill wondered how this had all happened in so short a space of time and then he called the number on Heidi's tag. It was difficult for him to see the number clearly, because Heidi was jumping up and down barking, growling and gnashing at him with her teeth. The phone was busy; Melissa was on the telephone with the police dispatcher. Bill decided to call back again when the line became free.

They sent Cynthia to the jail attached to the police station. There was a lot of paperwork to do when you had one of these. The booking officer yawned; it was near the end of his shift. The dispatch officer was still on the phone with Melissa. She didn't want to seem rude; but this was a matter to leave for tomorrow. The second-shift was just walking into the station and she was going home. She got up from her chair and stretched: "Weahl mahm, you-ah nah way-ah Cynthia Hickey ehz, dohn' you-ah? Ahnd thahd shay'z beh-hehn bahkd fahr Fars' Dah-gree Murd-dah wid Spah-shall Sir-cahm- stahn-says! We-ah wahl kohn-tahct you-ah tah-mahr-rah. Way-ahr do-ah we-ah cahl?" *"Well ma-am, you know where Cynthia Hickey is, don't you? And that she's being booked for First Degree Murder with Special Circumstances! We will contact you tomorrow. Where do we call?"* Melissa gave her the number of the Jordan Farms in Cape Elizabeth and then hung up the phone. She had to find Heidi. Cynthia was going to be alright for now, there was work to be done, while Mellissa was here in Portland. Melissa needed to get Heidi home and she reasoned that the first organization to call was the Portland-area Humane Society.

Melissa was after all a major contributor to the Humane Society, as she was also a major contributor to the Audubon Society and the Sierra Club. Everyone who was anyone in the animal rights movement knew Melissa Jordan of Cape Elizabeth and Diane Lord of the Laudholms' Family Farm in Wells, Maine their names were household words especially since Diane Lord had made a federal grant donating the land for the Rachel Carson's Wildlife Refuge and Melissa and Sara were dueling with Fredrick and Diane Lord to see which family could give the most to these "animal-rights organizations". This circle of people talked about the Jordans and Fredrick and Diane Lord like we talk about the Founding Fathers, or like Christians talk about the people in Foxe's Book of Martyrs.

Melissa made the phone call, it was 4:30 in the afternoon and everyone was about to go home for the day, but when they heard it was Melissa Jordan on the phone, the Director was instant to take her call. "Yes,

Ms. Jordan, this is Anthony Bennett, the Director of the Portland-area Humane Society, what can I do for you?" He said without a hint of any Downeast accent. Bennett was trained in the skill of conversing with important people: "contributors" as people in the Society liked to call them. After he made a few phone calls Anthony Bennett got back to Mellissa. He said: "Heidi is in the Portland-area Animal Control Center, Ms. Jordan."

"I'll go down there personally!" Melissa said. "Tonight, or at the very latest by tomorrow morning."

Susan grabs her pooper scooper, put it inside a disposable plastic shopping bag and Walter walked Susan, Melissa and Sara down the street to the corner of Oxford and Chestnut Streets. She put it into the back seat of Melissa and Sara's car and then Walter went back to the apartment and all three women went barreling down the street to the Animal Control Center asking for Heidi.

"Three women, and two of them are important donors. Anthony Bennett will be really mad at me, if I don't get this dog out of a cage tonight", Bill thought.

When dogs have more rights and more clout than people do, it is a very sad day for America indeed. Remember, nobody was trying to get Cynthia out of her cage, that evening and neither was she allowed any visitors for nearly 24 hours.

They ignored the parking restrictions in the lot next to the Animal Control Center hurrying into the building. They confidently strolled up to the counter and Melissa asked for Bill. He came running out, and shook her hand, almost bowing as he did so. He didn't recognize the two women with her, but Anthony Bennett had called his boss and told him to receive Melissa Jordan with all courtesy and promptness. He went over to the cage, where the snarling dog from this afternoon was lying down and when he approached, she became aroused.

Heidi recognized Susan and became her friendly, obedient self again. Like any dog that has been waiting for his or her master. She was both relieved and excited at the same time. They put Heidi on the leash that they have brought with them and lead her out to the car. Melissa and Sara dropped Susan and Heidi off at their apartment and went back to Cape Elizabeth.

Susan took Heidi and the pooper scooper into the alley behind the building. It was illegal to allow your dog to relieve him or herself within the city limits and on a sidewalk or an asphalt driveway or parking lot. Even if you were carrying a pooper scooper or a bread bag with you and picked up after your dog. The Portland City Council had passed a special ordinance, that because they believed the ammonia in a dog's urine destroyed concrete and asphalt, dog walkers would be required to walk their dogs down to someplace where there was grass, before the dogs would be allowed to relieve themselves. Walking a dog alone, in the dark and in a rough neighborhood was a singularly dangerous practice and for a municipal ordinance to require it didn't make sense and was discriminatory against women. At least that was what the women in "Take Back the Night" had alleged.

City Hall and the area surround it was completely covered over with concrete and asphalt. Besides most dogs, even Heidi weren't able to hold it till they could get to grass, or even understand why that was required. It was hard enough to get them housebroken, expecting a dog to hold it until he or she got to grass was just an absurd goal. Susan and Cynthia's new posh apartment house was right next to City Hall. Susan let Heidi into the alley behind their building and prayed that the police wouldn't catch her. (This ordinance was overturned by a referendum in the next election.) When Susan and Heidi got back up to their apartment, there was a time of seasonal prayer, which Walter led, and after which all four of them went to bed and tried to get some sleep. It had been a stressful, exhausting day. Susan got up during the middle of the night and paced in her room. She saw her sleeping son lying in the bed. She prayed for him, thanking God for graciously preserving his life.

The next morning Melissa received a phone call from the Portland Police Dispatcher: "Cyn-tha-ah ehz hee-yah nah, Mahs. Jah-den, baht we-ah'r gau-ehn tah hahv tah trahns-fah har tah thah Khan-tah Jay-ill ehn ah few min-ats." *"Cynthia is here now, Ms. Jordan, but we're going to have to transfer her to the County Jail in a few minutes."*

"That's awful!" Melissa said: "Doesn't she have an attorney?"

"We-ah'r ah lit-tahl bahkd-ahb ride nah, Mahm!" *"We're a little backed-up right now, Ma-am!"*

"Can't you keep her in your jail, until the lawyer gets there? What do I have to do?" Melissa pleaded.

"We-ah cauhn' do-ah en-nay-thehn tahll thah Pahb-blick Dah-fen-dah gahtz hee-yah mahm!" *"We can't do anything until The Public Defender gets here, Ma-am!"* The dispatcher said.

"We can pay for a private attorney", Melissa said. "Please keep my daughter where you are."

"Weahl, shay dah-zehn' hahv ahn ah-tahrn-nah nah Mahm ahnd we-ah dohn' hahv ehn-nay moe-ah rahm ehn thah pah-lease jay-ill." *"Well, she doesn't have an attorney now Ma-am and we don't have any more room in the police jail."*

"I'll pay extra, for my daughter to stay in the police jail", Melissa pleaded: "Please don't transfer her to the Cumberland County Jail, Please!" The police dispatcher acted as though Melissa had just tried to bribe her, and abruptly ended the conversation.

Chapter Fifty-Six
A BAILEY WIG

Susan went to work the next morning, it was a Tuesday. Samantha took Paul to daycare and Walter was staying in the apartment with Heidi. Susan immediately asks one of the associates at work, if he knew someone with criminal experience. This was a law firm that specialized in Insurance Defense and Litigation. They were singularly unhelpful in finding a lawyer with criminal experience. Mr. Lenard Nelson had apparently gone on vacation and was in St. Croix, where he had some property, so he couldn't be reached. Susan called Melissa and Sara from work. She gave Melissa her work number and told her: "I'll be right here, and available all-day long. If you know anything or find out anything, call me." Cynthia's bail was set at half a million dollars. It was late October of 1984 and the Portland Press Herald was buzzing around the Police Station, trying to sniff out a story.

Melissa and Sara went to see an attorney in Portland. They told him, that they would put their estate in Cape Elizabeth up as collateral for Cyn's bond. As soon as it became evident that the family could raise the bail money. Bail was withdrawn. Cyn wasn't getting out; that was final. The attorney they visited was in the phone book; his's name was Seth Bernstein. He wasn't related to Marvin Bernstein, who was the directing attorney and a partner at Bernstein, Shur. Attorney Seth Bernstein was in private practice and did some criminal law, but mostly he did divorce, orders of protection, repossessions and bank-collection law suits. He was frequently a Court-Appointed Lawyer and he wasn't used to dealing with people who had money. He always wore a sports coat with patches on the sleeves and twill pants to court and his hair hung down over his collar.

Susan made an appointment to meet with Bernstein on Exeter Street. She prayed for it to be at lunchtime, so that she wouldn't miss work and so, she wouldn't have to tell anyone at work what was going on. Seth's secretary, Linda was also the person who answered the telephone and the one who filed his papers at the courthouse. She received Susan into the only other room in Bernstein's office suite. They didn't even have a bathroom of their own. They had to go down the hall and share with two other law firms. Linda's desk was piled high with unfiled pleadings and the phone kept ringing off the hook. "At least", Susan thought: "he had a lot of clients". Unfortunately, though, most of them were trying to get free legal services. Bernstein had a general practice of law and no partner. He had clients who were suing people, who had injured them or they were being sued by people who said that they had been injured by them, but in those cases, Bernstein was usually suing a big insurance company, rather than suing on behalf of a big insurance company. In that case they were situations in which, he couldn't possibly win.

Insurance Defense which is what Bernstein, Shur did, was big business. And it netted Bernstein, Shur millions of dollars every year. Seth Bernstein's clients were involved in petty crime, real estate ventures that had gone south and bankruptcies. His office had boxes piled on the floor and papers piled on every chair. He was badly in need of another filing cabinet. There was a layer of dust on everything. Susan offered to do his filing after she got off work, if that would help him. He looked up at her over the tops of his glass, incredulously. This was the same way in which he had looked at Melissa and Sara when they offered up their estate in Cape Elizabeth as surety for Cynthia's bond.

Lawyers like Seth Bernstein didn't have monied clients and they didn't work full time, they worked all the time, coming in on weekends to close cases that were open too long, but they never got caught up. If he had been a law clerk at Bernstein Shur, they would have fired him long ago for not attracting the right clientele. The law is a cut- throat business at times. Seth said he had never done a murder before, while swallowing hard and shuffling some papers on his desk.

"There's a first time for everything, Seth. Item one is to bail Cyn out, right?" During the arraignment, the bailiff heard the words: "estate in Cape Elizabeth" and then took steps to rescind the bond offer of half a million dollars. Seth wasn't the only legal mind, who was unfamiliar dealing with people of means. Cyn's bail offer was declined, apparently, she was a flight risk.

Samantha on the other hand, had moved into Cynthia's bedroom at the apartment and was trying to get ahold of all her clients. At least those that had appointments at the High and Congress Street location, and found that they couldn't get into the building because of the police. Sam was setting up new appointments for them at the Brackett Street, "People's Building" office. She was not just trying to save Cynthia's business, she was trying to save her job, and then maybe take over Cynthia's business or at least, Cyn's client list, if she could. She was sitting in Cyn's apartment: working her appointment book, Cyn's appointment book, her own address book and the phone all day long, apparently for no pay at all. Susan didn't want to question a gift horse, but she thought that this behavior was suspicious.

Defending Cynthia had become a full-time job for Susan. She was thinking about giving notice at work, she had some savings after all. This, and the hours she spent on her knees were taking a toll on her professional life: "not enough prayer", she thought. Susan had just finished, Jerry Bridges' book: "The Pursuit of Holiness" and she had begun "The Kneeling Christian", by an anonymous nineteenth century Englishman. God seemed to be busy elsewhere lately, maybe it was just Susan being too busy. Seth Bernstein was the only person on the "Save Cynthia Team", who could get in to visit Cyn at the Cumberland County Jail. And, he never went!

It wouldn't have made a difference if Susan had quit Bernstein, Shur. She still wasn't an officer of the court or a family member. Cynthia's only legal family had been Charlene. The Portland Press Herald's investigative reporters were congratulating themselves on finding out about Cynthia's previous arrest in Bath. They got ahold of her mug shot and published in the evening edition of the paper and then erroneously reported that there had been "arrests", there weren't multiple arrests there had only been one. Cynthia had been a non-criminal professional for almost three years now. But when the paper reported again erroneously, that Cynthia had been at work, at the time of the murder they insinuated that "her work" was prostitution.

There was a quiet, solemn, monotony about this case. Everyone on "The Team" felt it. Susan met with Bernstein on her lunch hour as often as she could. She said: "Someone other than Cynthia did this thing Seth, someone who the police aren't even looking for. If we don't identify and find this person, and drag him or her into court. We're going to lose!" Seth Bernstein pondered her words.

"Well, I used to have a private investigator working for me." He said: "But he hasn't got much experience with actual investigation, he mainly just a process server. I can give him a call. He has a PI's license, after all. But, I wish we had someone else!" Susan thought about Agent Scott Rodgers of the FBI. She wondered if she could call in that favor from three years ago. He after all had offered her "something" for the contents of that "merch" locker. The police had settled on Cynthia and they weren't willing to muddy the waters by bringing in another suspect. It might engender "reasonable doubt", in the minds of the jurors! There weren't any jurors as yet, only a magistrate and he had ruled that Cynthia and her "aunts" and "sister" couldn't make her bail-bond. As soon as the bailiff heard the words "estate in Cape Elizabeth", the death knell on Cyn's half-a-million-dollar bail was sounded. She would not be able to get a bail-bond at all.

A defense attorney's worst nightmare had come to Seth Bernstein's doorstep, an innocent client.

Chapter Fifty-Seven
INNOCENT UNTIL PROVEN GUILTY

Susan hurried to court and then waited outside for an hour. Samantha was late, but she didn't miss anything. Mr. Seth Bernstein hoped that he would get both women to testify that day. The Bailiff said: "Awel Rahz", *"All Rise"* and everyone stood up. Cynthia was in the courtroom at the Defense Table, this was the first-time Susan had seen her since the Sunday night, before the murder. They locked eyes across the courtroom and then both looked away, as they each began to cry. His Honor, the Judge was sitting behind a raised platform, which performed the function of both a seat and a desk, making the occupant seem larger and more imposing than anyone else in the courtroom. Next to the bench was the witness box or stand. A place both confining and imposing, which caused everyone's attention to be focused on its occupant. Each of these structures included a microphone, that amplified the words spoken by these two imposing characters.

In front of the bench were two tables one for the Defense, and the other for the Prosecution. Seated behind these two tables were Cynthia Hickey and Seth Bernstein for the Defense, and two Assistant District Attorneys for the Prosecution. They were Frederick C. Moore and Charles K. Leadbetter. District Attorney Paul Aranson came in and out checking on the progress of the case. This was a very important case and he wanted to win as it was his first case as DA. Since both ADAs were new to their posts and since the DA was newly elected, they were all nervous and averting their eyes. Leadbetter had continuous halitosis, perhaps it was his dental carries. District Attorney Aranson was nervous, because he was newly elected and this was a capital murder case, Susan said hello to him on the street every day for years and had worked as a volunteer in his campaign. The gallery was full, as many people as could fit into the gallery were seated and there were more out in the ante-chamber. The bailiff wouldn't allow for standing room so many Portlanders waited outside the courtroom for a chance to sit down. They wanted to observe these proceeding as this was a sensational case and the object of much gossip. There were also several court reporters buzzing around the tightly-packed room, drawing sketches of all the participants including Susan, who thought the sketch of her which appeared in the paper the next morning was not at all flattering.

Attorney Leadbetter called his first witness, a police officer name Sargent Kenneth Maxwell, who was sworn in, took the stand and began telling the court what he had seen in the kitchen at The High and Congress Street, East-West Therapeutic Massage Parlor. When he said the words "massage parlor", people in the gallery snickered and chuckled to themselves. He told how he observed a high chair broken and lying on the floor and a stain of blood, which besmeared the walls and table in the kitchen. Then, the body of a tiny girl maybe two years old, lying on the floor, her head turn almost all the way around. The little girl was wearing a pink dress, white tights and black patent leather Mary Jane shoes. At least the Portland Police could tell a girl who was wearing a pink dress from a boy.

It was a shocking scene he said and that he would never forget it as long as he lived. He told the court that he was still having nightmares about it. Susan glared at Seth Bernstein; but it didn't provoke him to object to this statement, which was extremely subjective and prejudicial. Then he said that when he came back out into the great room of the establishment; the mother of the little girl was sitting on a leather couch with her legs apart and showing her underwear and talking on the phone with a law firm. He and his partner, Sgt. William Kenneth arrested her at once; because she admitted to the crime, saying: "Ehtz awel mah fahlt", *its all my fault*. Then the officer said: "thahn we-ah tahk har oud-dah thah bahd-dehn. Thehn, we-ah tahk har tah thah pah-lease stay-shun, ahnd bahkd har uhn char-jehz ahv Fars' Dah-gree Murd-dah, wid Spah-shall **Ser**-cahm-stah-says, puhd-dehn har ehn-tah thah Paut-lan' Pah-lease Jay-ill". *"then we took her out of the building and took her to the police station. Then we booked her on charges of First Degree Murder, with Special Circumstances, puting her into the Portland Police Jail"*. He said a few more things about the shocking scene in the kitchen, and how he had never seen anything like that before or since. He said that Charlene had blood all down the front of her dress. Her head almost completely turned around and pooled blood was inside of her shoes.

Next, the other officer, who was first on the scene, Officer William Kenneth got up and told the same tale as his colleague, the shocking scene, the shattered high chair, the mother on the phone with a law firm. The time had progressed toward 11:00a.m. They had been at this since 9:00a.m. and everyone including His Honor was tired, nervous, and a little hungry. Even Cynthia was hungry for the terrible jail chow, which didn't offer much variety for a vegetarian, much less a vegan. Mostly Cynthia was eating stale white bread from Fraunhofer's Bakery Outlet. She couldn't even get their bread in a can, because being in a can, it wasn't going to spoil so the jail didn't buy it. The warden of the Cumberland County Jail, where they had moved Cynthia, wouldn't buy that bread. This was because he only bought day-old bread, pretending that it was fresh and pocketing the monetary difference. They were all on the take.

When Susan testified, she said that she was the person that Cynthia was talking to on the telephone. She said that her law firm did Insurance Defense and Litigation and that Bernstein, Shur wasn't connected with the case in any way. She said that when Cynthia talked to her friend. Her friend was crying and hysterical. That they had been friends for a number of years now and that they shared an apartment. Attorney Leadbetter cross-examined Susan. He asked: "Aren't you living with the defendant?" He emphasized the words: "Living With", as though there was something wrong with two women living together.

Susan replied: "Yes, Yes I am."

And then he asked: "Doesn't the defendant give massages?" He tried to make the word "Massages" sound as dirty as possible.

And Susan replied: "Yes, Cynthia gives Therapeutic Massage and she is a Licensed Massage Therapist."

Attorney Leadbetter rolled his eyes and said: "No more questions for this witness at this time, but I retain the right to recall her, whenever it becomes necessary." And then he said to Susan: "You may step down, now, Mahs. Ah-stah." The whole thing was as confrontational as he could make it.

Susan said: "Shouldn't Attorney Bernstein dismiss me. He called me as a witness, not you." Attorney Bernstein shuffled some papers on the Defense table and looked away sheepishly.

After the recess, in which Susan saw another member of her law firm in the courthouse and hid. She hoped he hadn't seen her, because she had called in sick that day and said she would stay at home and try to sleep. It had already been since Sunday, that she had not yet slept. This was a Tuesday and she was exhausted. Walter was staying at her apartment with the dog. Paul was in daycare at St. Elizabeth's, where Samantha had dropped him off that morning. Maybe that was why she was late.

Paul was beginning to ask: "Where, Chary? Where ehz Chary?" Susan would break down and cry whenever he asked this question.

They had taken to sleeping together in the big brass bed for mutual support. Susan asked Walter to break down the single bed in Cynthia's room and lean it up against the wall. And, because she didn't know what to do with either Cynthia's few clothes or Charlene's numerous dresses, she left them where they were. She couldn't sleep. She ate sparingly and she consumed great quantities of tea. She paced back and forth from the kitchen to the parlor. The dog following behind her everywhere in the apartment. Walter was like a nurse to both Susan and Heidi. They both seemed to be in shock. Neither of them ate very much. Walter walked the dog every two or three hours. Heidi pulled on the leash, when they went out and he was afraid that she would pull it out of his hand and run off.

After the recess, the trial resumed, Samantha testified next, she said emphatically: "I didn't leave Chary alone! No! Not for a minute". This was at once, a lie, and besides it screwed up the time line. So, that it appeared that what Cynthia said at the arraignment was false.

Susan wondered aloud: "Could I speak again?" His honor banged his gavel and glared at Susan. Mr. Bernstein didn't call her anyway.

Samantha's testimony continued: "Eeyah sah har uhn thah straight, ahnd shay wahz pahl-lehn ah shap-pehn cahrt, Eeyah waht-tehd ehn thah pahk au-crahss thah straight ahnd thahn, shay ehn-tahd thah Hay-ah ahnd Cahn-grahss Straight plahz, thahn Eeyah jehz' dohn' rah-memb-bah". *"I saw her on the street, and she was pulling a shopping cart, I waited in the park across the street and then, she entered the High and Congress Street place and then, I just don't remember".* She seemed to be going in circles.

"Good, Susan thought: She's done! She just can't remember what lies she's already told. What a rat! She'd rather Cyn go down for First Degree Murder than admit that she wasn't a very good babysitter? Excuse me!"

Susan was dumb struck. She could barely get up from her seat and go back to her apartment. If any of her co-workers from Bernstein, Shur saw her on the street, Susan wasn't aware of it. She wasn't aware of very much. She believed that she had walked in front of the paths of several cars on the way home.

Somehow, she got home safely and then just collapsed on the brass bed. The room was spinning around! Susan got up and vomited into a waste basket. Then, she went back to bed and cried herself to sleep. Sometime after Susan passed out on the bed, Samantha came into the apartment. Susan wasn't sure whether she used a key. Susan couldn't remember whether Samantha was given a key or not. Maybe Walter rang her in. Paul woke Susan up; joyously greeting her and the dog. The dog was joyous to see him too. Susan wondered if she should ask Samantha for the key back. If there was a key?

The phone rang, it was Mr. Bernstein, he said he had gotten a continuance. He said the trial would be adjourned for at least two weeks. Susan fell asleep. She slept for 19 hours.

Chapter Fifty-Eight

"A FRIEND LOVETH AT ALL TIMES"

The highest form of friendship is a mixture of phileo love, such as David and Johnathan had for one another and the agape love all Christians are to share. David and Johnathan began their relationship with David becoming the hero of the Israelite people and Johnathan being the son of the reigning king and heir to the throne. But, both were believers and as Samuel prophesied, David was the true heir to Israel's throne, which was Saul, Johnathan's father's throne. In God's mind, Saul had already been deposed. Johnathan would never inherit his father's throne unless he turned to betrayal of a friend. Believing God's Word goes beyond having a document that indicates how, "God's plan for your life" can make your own plans for your life come true. It exemplifies laying down your personal interests and pursuing the leading of the Holy Spirit to fulfill God's interests no matter how arduous or how contrary to personal interest, they may be.

Samuel anointed David king while he was assembled with his father, Jesse's other seven sons. They were awaiting Samuel's statement from God. Samuel took a horn of olive oil and poured it on David's head, **"and the Spirit of the Lord came mightily upon David from that day forward." (I Samuel 16:13).** Johnathan as a standing believer wanted to serve God with all of his heart. Tragically, he would have made an outstanding king and it may have gone better for Israel if they had had him for their king rather than David, who failed in His mission several times during His reign. None the less, God had chosen David, a man after God's own heart and as such a loyal and pious Johnathan went about protecting and helping him to succeed in his appointed quest to fight for Israel. **"Now it came about when he (David) had finished speaking to Saul that the soul of Johnathan was knit to the soul of David and Johnathan loved him as himself." (I Samuel 18:1)**

Johnathan discovered that his father, Saul wanted to kill David. He could have merely stepped back and let that happen and the kingdom would have been his. But, he did the brave and selfless thing! He helped David escape. **"Johnathan, greatly delighted in David sayings and told him 'be on guard in the morning and stay hidden. I will stand by my father in the field, where you are and speak with my father about you if I find out anything I will let you know.'" (I Sam. 19: 1-3).** Saul hunted for David and sent servants to kill him, but they all began prophesying as did Saul when He went out to kill David, who was lying all night on the ground in Naioth, Hamah. During the time that Saul hunted David, Saul fell asleep in a cave. David could have availed himself of the opportunity to kill Saul, but he would not slay the Lord's anointed. Instead David cut a piece of Saul's clothing and then showed it to Johnathan to show him that he could have killed his father, if he had wanted to; but he didn't because he would not kill the LORD's anointed and betray his friend Johnathan.

Johnathan warned David about Saul's intentions; telling David by a sign of a shot arrow not to come back to the palace, but to stay in the wilderness and hide from Saul. All this help made Johnathan's life more dangerous, while preserving David's life. This is what friends do for one another. Phileo love is a powerful motivator, when coupled with agape love it is something that demonstrates visibly the tie that bind Christ's disciples together in an alliance that the pagan Romans commented on when they said, "see how they love one another!" The reason believers are supposed to go out witnessing in pairs is so that the world can see this love that we have one for another.

Susan and Cynthia had a bond which made them closer than sisters, so when Susan initiated her journey on a quest to save Cynthia, she took a backpack full of provisions, her son and her dog and went off to Cape Elizabeth to retrieve Cyn's Cadillac. When she got to Melissa and Sara's, Melissa was out in the barn. Susan shouted to her: "I'm taking the car, Melissa" and Melissa acknowledged her from the barn while tending one of her billy goats.

Susan raised the convertible top of Cyn's 1961 Candy-Apple Red Cadillac, Coupe de Ville and put the backpack in the trunk where Binny's "merch" had been three years earlier. Susan had with her, a hand-written note of directions to a compound in New Jersey, where Mike's father had lived before he came out to Illinois decades before. Mike had copied down what his dying father had said and placed the note in the sleeve of his bomber jacket. That jacket had been passed on to Walter Malien that morning after Susan had a prophetic dream about New Jersey. As Susan embarked on a trip to pursue Mike's quest to find the Italian side of his family, she acknowledged that God had a plan for her and Paul's lives. There was a new child seat on the back seat of the car, buckled down with one of the seat belts that Melissa and Sara's good foster- grandparenting had led them to install. Seat belts and child seats were virtually unknown at this time. Older vehicles had to be retrofitted in order to pass Maine's strict safety and air-quality standards. Elizabeth Dole, who was the Secretary of Transportation under Ronald Reagan from 1983 to 1987, had instituted Child Seats for every car that had a "baby on board". Before this, people would let their toddlers sit anywhere in the car, even on the driver's lap. Children sustained terrible injuries in car accidents with no Child Seats, seat belts or head protection required. Sometimes people would have to take an older, pre-1968 car to a mechanic and have him drill holes in the back-seat floor boards to permanently attach the seat belts.

"I need to thank her", Susan said to herself, as she approached the goat barn one last time, getting down on one knee, as the UPI Photojournalist, had done so many years ago she took Melissa picture with one of her he-goat's, there was a breathtaking seascape behind them. Susan put Paul in the child seat and with Heidi beside her on the front seat, she buckled her seat belt lamenting that there was as yet no such device for a dog. They left Cape Elizabeth and continued down Route One until they came to New Hampshire where Route One merged with Interstate 295. Following the coast, she saw many gorgeous seascapes along New Hampshire's craggy bluffs. When she came to a rest stop in North Hampton, she took her three-year-old for a bathroom break and the dog for a walk. Then they continued on to Marlborough, Massachusetts where she found a restaurant and ordered the blue-plate special, which was beef stew with peas and carrots, salad and bread. Susan fed Paul from her plate and afterward they continued on to Hartford, Connecticut where there was a rest stop on Highway 91. When Susan walked the dog again, she noticed blood coming down the dog's hind leg. Heidi was at last, "in season". Susan was convinced that her "heat" had been delayed or interrupted because of the stressful experience, Heidi had the afternoon that Charlene had been killed. she was after all a very sensitive dog. But Praise God, she had bounced back now. Susan decided not to walk her, off-leash, until after her "heat" was over.

If this had been earlier in the season, the Connecticut foliage would have attracted a following of leaf-peeper. But, now that the fall leaves had fallen and there were no other people crowding the highway. This dearth of other motorist on the Connecticut roadway signaled the end of Indian summer and the beginning of dead fall, early winter. After walking Heidi, Susan got on the road again for the hundred-mile journey to New Rochelle, New York, which is famous because of the musical, "Forty- Five Minutes from Broadway" and also as the fictional home of the character, Robert Petrie that Dick Van Dyke portrayed in the television series named for him. When they got to New Rochelle, they were one hundred miles from the Pine Barrens and Susan decided to drive through non-stop until she reached her destination. She looked on the map again.

The piece of notebook paper containing instructions Mike had penned while sitting at the bedside of his dying father. They told how to get to the Apponi-Carbone Compound in the Pine Barrens. Mike scrawled these directions on a piece of notebook paper balanced on his lap so many years before. He had pushed this note paper down inside the sleeve of his bomber jacket. Susan was loath to give a cold and homeless this jacket and kept it by her bedside until that morning. She just couldn't part with it until God had inspired her to withdraw the note from its sleeve and start off on this quest. Now she knew why God wanted her to keep it and why He wanted her to give it to Walter after that dream. The note would lead her to Paul Asta's former home. Her son's grandfather was once a made man in the Apponi-Carbon Olive Oil Company. He met Jean Miller at a church picknick, a mixer with the Trenton Meeting of Friends. He was smitten with her and also with the Society of Friends. She had parents in Illinois and she took him to meet them. He remembered that her father wore overalls with a white shirt and tie underneath. Jean's parents were just heading out to Meeting when he drove up to their farm house with Jean in his car.

This is the epitome of the witness protection program, instituted under

Assistant Attorney General, Gerald Shur for the Special Services Unit of the Organized Crime and Racketeering Division of the Department of Justice. Except, Paul Asta wasn't testifying against anyone! He just wanted to get away. Mike's father said he was shocked and in love with how they never locked their doors and how everything on the farm was so open and inviting. He was intrigued also with Quakerism and wished for a simpler, quieter life. Mike's plan to seek out his dad's family, began when Susan became pregnant and they made plans to visit New Jersey to find Paul Asta's roots. However, Mike had been killed and Susan and little Paul became homeless, carless and destitute. Now all of that had change and according to the leading of God going to the Apponi- Carbon Compound was of necessity. They entered the Pine Barrens area of New Jersey and an icy, cold dread came over Susan, like she and Mike had experienced traversing the Scarborough Marsh. Susan determined in her mind never to see her apartment, her job or her furniture again. She was going to sacrifice all of these worldly goods to God in order to save Cynthia.

In the center of the Pine Barrens there was an old bridge that led onto a desolate dirt road. Then a beautiful, old, abandoned house which was surrounded by sparse trees with a creek running behind it. She turned onto the dirt road as per the instructions on the note. A beautiful church appeared, it also seemed abandoned and then an entire town was visible through the trees appearing to be abandoned as well. She drove down the main street in between two lines of store fronts. At one time, this had been a bustling thoroughfare. But now, it was a scene of wonderous desolation. When they had gone to the end of the street, in between two towering oak trees, she found an insignificant dirt road winding through the overgrowth of stunted pines. On the outskirts of this town, directly in the middle of "the Pines", "the Barrens", "the Pine Barrens", "the Piney Woods", a walled compound became visible through the trees with a small foot bridge separating it from the road. Susan had traveled as far as she could down this road. She could go no further in the car! She was going to have to abandon the Cadillac as well and go the rest of the way to the compound on foot, balancing Paul on her hip. Every part of her formerly affluent life was slipping away. She had nothing left to abandon.

Chapter Fifty-Nine

"THE ITALIAN FAMILY AS A COMMUNE"

Based on an article in the New York Times Magazine.

She comforted herself by remembering the trek that Elizabeth Elliot had made into the Equadorian jungle, with her three-year-old daughter, Valerie, balanced on her hip. Susan went into the trunk of the car one last time. She pulled the clothing and food out of it taking only the dried fruit and one can do dog food, a P38, a jar of baby food, several pull-up Pampers for night-time use with children who were being potty trained and wet the bed. Susan figured that if these people extended their hospitality to her over night, she didn't want Paul to wet their bed. She walked about a mile up the road in the direction of the compound dreading its inevitable approach.

After taking the dog off her leash, which only three hours earlier, she had sworn not to do, she walked the rest of the way on foot to the forbidding, gray, stone enclosure. This edifice gave her the chills. It was a depressing sight. An icey chill engulfed her as she forced herself to approach the compound. God was inspiring her to continue on. As she moved toward the structure, Franco Scallifini saw her and walked out to meet her, his weapon in hand, his dog at his side. His dog, Zig, was a big-boned and well-proportioned German Shepard.

Zig and Heidi met each other like long lost friends. Siegfried Wolven had been arrested the previous year, when he had bitten thirty-five people within the space of two hours. He was scheduled for termination, when Franco arrived at the police station. The police had placed Zig in a human jail cell awaiting transfer to Animal Control. Zig's human being was a childhood friend of Scallifini and a highly-decorated Viet Nam combat veteran. Carl Fugate was at work when two teenaged home invaders broke in. Zig was lying on the kitchen floor and after mauling them severely, he chased them out onto the street where a number of pedestrians tried to save them from him. Zig bit all of them too!

Franco brought Zig to the compound to save his life and Carl was so grateful that he barely noticed the location or the sad fact that he wouldn't see Zig again. Scallifini thought that if Zig ever had a son, he would give the pup to Carl. Susan who was balancing her son on her hip, thanked God for the dog's exceptional confirmation and that he was not a Rottweiler. Zig first sniffed then mounted Heidi, who was definitely in estrus. This turned out to be a very good breeding indeed as they both had several dogs in their lineages that were grand champions.

Susan extended her right hand and said to the man approaching her, "Salutare", which means *"to greet"* in Italian. How did she know to greet him in Italian?

"Ciao, Lo Sono, Susan Asta, la' madre di Paul Asta, il nipote di Paul Asta." *"Hello, I'm Susan Asta the mother of Paul Asta, the grandson of Paul Asta."* The great mansion of Carlo and Pearl Apponi in the center of the Pine Barrens was thrown open to Susan and her son Paul. Italian hospitality is legendary, especially to those who are "la 'bangue" *their blood*. Paul's feet never touched the floor and Paul's great aunt Pearl Apponi made the best Cannolis in New Jersey. They served a big Italian dinner with heaping platters of spaghetti, lasagna, rigatoni, insalata, ravioli, a roasted chicken, and all in Paul's honor. The table conversation was in Italian, which was Susan's mother tongue. A solid slice of the chocolate cake, which had "PAUL" written in white butter cream topped off wonderful dinner. Mike Asta's father was her brother. The meal was rounded off with candies and liqueurs. In a really united, large Italian family, diner lasts for at least five hours with ecstatic hugs and kissing on both cheeks and even kisses on the lips. The family being Catholic, had the photographs of each loved one hanging on the walls in the dinning room with exuberant celebrations participated in by all.

Susan said: "Scusa, Voglio plarare con." "Excuse me, I want to talk to Mr. or Sir (the main man of the place). "Signor Carlo, in privato", *Carlo in private"*, Don Carlo was an older person and extremely quirkish and garrulous. Over a bottle of wine and while they were at the table, she asked him: "Se vuoi per favore?" *"If you would please?"* And when they retreated into his chambers, Susan showed him the photograph of a beautiful, little, two-year-old girl with blond curls and blue eyes. Susan tearfully divulged: "Questa bambina era come mia figlio, Carlo, qualcuno l'ha ucciso; il suo nome era, Charlene, ed e ci hanno fatto pagarila madre, Cynthia, il mio migliore amico con il crimine anache se lei non-era neli appartamento al momento quando e' successo." *"This little girl was like my own daughter, Carlo, someone murdered her; her name was "Charlene" and they charged her mother, Cynthia, my best friend, with the crime even though she wasn't even in the apartment at the time that it happened."*

"Suo dipendente, Samantha, mi ha detto fuori dal Tribuanle", "Her employee, Samantha, told me out of court", (She didn't want to say, "God told me this", because she didn't want Carlo to think she was insane, having just met him.) "al processo che c'era un nome e che ha detto che sapeva di Cynthia e poi esso appena ciccato per me era Binny. Samantha bentito il suo nome e mi ha detto che era 'Ben o qualcosa del genere' che li quando whe ha lasciato per ottenere tazzadi te Celestial Seasons Tea. Era una cosa stupida da fore, ma Samantha e' una persona fiduciosa." *At the trial, that a man was there and that he said he knew Cynthia and then it just clicked for me that it was Binny. Samantha heard his name and told me that it was 'Ben or something' he was there when she left to get some Celestial Seasons Tea. It was a stupid thing to do, but Samantha is a trusting person."*

"Charlene era solo ventitre mesi vecchio quando aveva ucciso, Carlo, e sua madre non avrevve, potuto fare di perche' amava quella bambina. Entrambi abbiamo fatto! Oltre, a lei era fuori l' acquoisto di cibo, Ho il cibo! Controllo degi animali ha detto che un uomo ha evuto asportare Heidi. Heidi e' il cane che ho portato qui con meh." *"Charlene was only twenty-three months old when she was killed, Carlo! Her mother couldn't have done it, because she loved that little girl. We both did! Besides, she was out buying food, I have the food! Animal Control said that a man had them take Heidi away. Heidi is the dog that I brought here with me."*

The bitch, Heidi was lying down in the outer compound exhausted from mating with the dog, Zig. Carlo went back to the table "Rintham-bito" *I have become a baby again!* and then he made an impassioned argument to the family: "L'assassino di un innocente dovrebbe ottenere Gius-tizia!" *"The killer of an innocent baby should get Justice!"* The following day, Susan called Bernstein Shur and said she was lying down with a headache, which was true. She just didn't tell them that she was lying down with a headache in New Jersey. Back then, they didn't have caller I.D. So, Susan went back to Portland to resume her career and have another meeting with Seth Bernstein. They went over the case again and she told him, that he needed to introduce the idea at trial that there may have been another person at the crime scene and that Cynthia wasn't there, that she was out grocery shopping. "Seth, this would give us reasonable doubt, the police aren't even looking for Binny, they never looked for him. We need to find him and drag him into court. Otherwise, we're going to lose! I have a friend who is a detective, perhaps he can find Binny, before this continuance is over?"

Bernstein said that his discovery had turned up an intent on the part of Attorney Charles K. Leadbetter to introduce the child's bloody clothes and the little shoes that had blood pooled in them at trial; as exhibits for the prosecution. Susan said: "That's good Seth, Cynthia didn't have any blood on her when she was arrested and the killer would have been covered with it. Seth said he wanted to suppress this evidence anyway, because it was "prejudicial". The man had let an hour of prejudicial testimony in court stand and now he wanted to suppress physical evidence as prejudicial, which could clear his client. Seth was incompetent in the extreme, Susan stormed out of his office, her Italian temper getting the better of her. She went back to the Apponi-Carbon Compound again and this time Franco follows the Caddy back to Maine. He was driving his late model Lincoln Continental Limousine. He was a soldier for the Apponi-Carbon Olive Oil business and a made-man. Franco knew how to find people who the police could not find. Pearl Apponi took Paul on her lap and kissed him; and he being an affectionate child her returned her kiss. Carlo and Pearl Apponi owned fourteen legitimate businesses throughout New Engl and. "Ora" *"Now"*, she said to her husband, "nipote." This means *"grandson"* "Abbiamo un nipottino, per che possimo lasciare il nostro businesses." *"We have a little grandson, we can leave our businesses to."*

"One must not exaggerate." There will be no need of communes in Italy for a long, long time; but the traditional Italian family is a commune plain and simple. Franco and Susan stopped at the Scarborough Marsh on the way back to Portland. They got out of their respective vehicles and Susan told Franco: "Mike, e motto propno qui, Franco. E l'autista ubria, Arthur

Bickford, che lo ha ucciso e' ancorra guidando antorno probabilmente ubriaco mentre parliamo adesso." *"Mike, died right here, Franco. And the drunk driver, Arthur Bickford, is still driving around; probably drunk right now."* Susan said angrily and Scallifini pledged to her: "Sara' esgtta per Mike pure." *"I will exact vengeance for Mike as well".*

Chapter Sixty

PUPPIES

Sixty-one days after her adventure in New Jersey, Heidi gave birth to six puppies and Franco came back to Portland, going at first to the crime scene and nonchalantly acting the part of a police detective or an FBI special agent. His expensive, Italian silk suit didn't define him as a plain clothesman; but the PPD never noticed. And, Franco pretended not to notice that they did no policework, while hanging out at Cynthia's Congress and High Street massage location. The police sat all day at Cyn's kitchen table. They smoked; they ate pastries and they dropped their cigarette butts on the blood-spattered floor. Franco continued to speak to the police like he belonged, like he was one of them, even though he wanted to kill all three of them for their ineptitude and laziness. The PPD often hung out at crime scenes, compromising the evidence and making it impossible for the landlord to rent the unit, because it was still "under investigation". This was their cynical alternative to going out onto the street and perhaps having to observe a crime in progress, then being confronted by the inevitable paperwork that that would entail.

Susan took Heidi for her morning walk and discovered that her dog was in labor. She had blood coming down the back of one leg and she was whining while she peed on the asphalt behind the building. Susan called the office and told the office manager that she was having woman troubles and would have to take one of her sick days. She didn't tell them that her woman troubles were actually her dog's woman troubles. Susan was in the "puppy room" kneeling on the Portland Press Herald's as Seth Bernstein made the phone ring. Susan was annoyed to answer; but then he may have had some news about Cynthia. He didn't. Only that he couldn't get her out on bond and that he would be seeking another continuance.

"Oh hello, Susan. How are you this morning?" "My dog is giving birth, Seth, snap it up!" "We're getting another continuance."

"Oh, no we're not", she said, "your job is to get Cynthia bail and then an acquittal in that order. Is that clear?" She was on her last frayed nerve; Seth's arrogance and pomposity were getting the better of her, while Heidi began pushing."

"Get her out, Seth, I can't be on the phone any longer; Heidi is giving birth right in front of me. Wrap it up, Seth! You've stalled long enough!" People didn't usually talk to lawyers like this.

"I'm paying you for one reason, Seth. I can't do this myself; I'm only a paralegal and the guys in my law firm are Insurance Defense and Litigation and Corporate Taxes. Capisci? (Italian) *Do you understand?* Now, get it done, or I'll find someone who will." They hung up simultaneously.

Then, she dialed Mellissa, "Mellissa please come and bring Sara. Heidi is giving birth!" Heidi was giving the last push for the first puppy and was stressed and exhausted.

"We'll be right there Susan", Mellissa hung up.

Susan petted her dog and spoke sweetly to her, encouragingly. How much do dogs really understand of the English language? It's your tone of voice, right? Susan was nervous; she wasn't even this nervous when Paul and Charlene were being born. Well, at least in the hospital you have doctors and nurses; this was all on Susan and the dog. She wished Cynthia was there. Cynthia would know what to do. Walter had broken Cynthia's bed down and tilted it on its side against the wall several weeks earlier. Walter had been such a help and Mike's jacket looked so good on him. The bureau with Cyn's clothes in it was against the bed, so that it wouldn't fall on the dog and her puppies. Cyn's closet was still full of clothes, Susan looked at them and wondered if Cyn would ever wear them again; she knew Charlene would never wear hers. It was time to give Charlene's dresses and hair bows away. She kept thinking, "Cyn will be getting out pretty soon now and she will know how to dispose of them, I should just leave everything as it is."

Susan had tried to bring clothing to the jail for Cyn to wear, that's when she discovered that the inmates had their own uniforms and that the jail staff wouldn't allow Cyn to wear regular clothes. They wouldn't let Susan see Cyn anyway. Susan wasn't family! Well, why weren't they "family"? They were as good as married, the parents of the same two children. Tears welled in Susan's eyes when she thought, "only one child, now!"; but she had to remain serious. The dog needed her. Only Seth Bernstein could get in to see Cyn and he never visited her. He was too busy. He after all, had other clients and he had to stay in touch with the reporters from the Portland Press Herald.

The only reporters from the Press Herald that came to the apartment were the one's who wanted to do a little personal interest story. So, how's this for personal interest, Cyn's dog was giving birth. Cyn was on bread and water, because everything the jail served had some kind of meat in it. It was canned meat that was going bad and day-old bread. Susan wanted to bring her some rice with fresh vegetables in it. Steven and Roberta Fearon could get in there, he was after all Cyn's pastor. Seth Bernstein was no help whatsoever.

As Susan was kneeling in front of the dog, she decided to pray. What's the harm? As she began to pray, Heidi gave another push and a second puppy came out. Susan praised God for her dog and for her puppies. While her praises reached God's throne, the doorbell rang; it was Franco. He seated himself on the couch. The next time that the bell rang, Franco answered it, letting Melissa and Sara into the apartment. Sara had done this hundreds of times with the nannies on Jordan Road. Heidi had been a maiden dog before Zig and she needed someone like Sara. Sara was familiar with how to sooth a four-footed mother and brought with her a surgical gown, a hair net, gloves and booties. This outfit would protect the puppies from Parvovirus. Sara was in the puppy room and continued kneeling down in front of Heidi, soothing her and encouraging her as Susan had done. Finally, allowed to go sit on the couch, an exhausted Susan put her head in Franco's lap and began to breath a sigh of relief. It's always the little things that get to us: It's the piles of laundry and the everyday crises of life that get to us; but when a real tragedy comes along people suddenly pull together.

The phone rang again and this time it was Pastor Steve; Susan answered and said, "Heidi's giving birth; I can't go to the prayer meeting tonight. Give my regards to the saints. They had long ago stopped resisting this word, "Saints" just let her speak the Word of God to them and left her alone. They no longer objected, because they realized that it did no good. And, Susan didn't try to convince them of anything anymore, just let them be themselves and loved them as they were, wrong believing and all. Maybe Joyce Meyers would teach on this subject, about the followers of Christ being saints and not sinners, or maybe a little of both. This was knowledge they just couldn't receive from Susan. Steve didn't know enough of God's Word to teach on this. Steve concluded the phone call and Susan took up a position by the door of the puppy room. Heidi gave another push and let out an audible sigh as she gave birth once again to a third puppy. Melissa went into the kitchen and began brewing tea.

"I know you're suffering right now, Heidi; but in a few minutes, it will all be over." The puppies, who were already born, fought to get to Heidi's teats, they whined and cried and Sara's expert care made her leave them and their mother alone as much as was humanly possible. Some people make it a policy to let their dogs give birth outside and never visit until the next day. There are also "pipe dogs", a tragic situation existing in puppy mills, especially those that are out in the countryside on farms, where they also grow marijuana. Heidi would never become a "pipe dog", because she was loved and protected. Melissa escorted Susan back to the kitchen. They sat together like expectant fathers while the kettle whistled and the doorbell rang once again. This is perhaps how men bond with one another, awaiting the conclusion of their duties in life. Fatherhood and the comradery of war make men share some kind of personal male-bonding that Susan and Melissa now shared. This time, Franco let Walter into the apartment and directed him to the kitchen. Heidi gave birth to three more puppies that evening. Sara said that six was an acceptable number for a first litter and was thrilled to find out that the father was a well-bred German with great conformation.

She told Susan that her neighbors in Cape Elizabeth would be interested in some fine, guard-dog stock; but Susan replied that the police, search and rescue and Guiding Eyes had to come first. Sara presented Heidi with a dish of delicious goat's milk, brought in from the kitchen by Melissa who had poured it into Heidi's stainless- steel dish. Stainless steel makes the best dog dishes, mainly because you can put it in the dishwasher; but stainless steel can be placed directly on the burners of a stove and brought to a boil to reduce and microbes that might be growing in the dish. Sterilizing your dog's dish is an important part of keeping them healthy. Melissa poured Joran Farms goats milk from a bottle into Heidi's dish and Franco said good night to Walter and the ladies going to a hotel for the night. He had spent the day pretending to be a cop or at least not getting in the officers' way as he did their police work for them. That wasn't hard to do. The one good thing about the Portland Police Force was that they never interfered with a person who wanted to do police work in their vicinity as long as it didn't cause them to get up from a seated position.

It goes without saying that the PPD didn't do a proper job of investigating this crime. They said "Ehtz cahse clahzed", *"It's case closed"*, as soon as they had arrested Cynthia, never puzzling over the question of why a person unbesmirched by the stain of blood could have committed so bloody a crime. After all, she did say, "It's all my fault" and that was enough for them. It made Franco angry to think about how lazy and stupid they were. Thinking that the taxpayers were financing their languor made him sick. But, it wasn't any of his business and he was determined to remain on his mission and not let himself become distracted. Doing some more digging around, he endeavored to discover the source of the traces of cocaine and heroin on the plastic bags he had found in the metal locker at the bottom of the deep well under the floor boards. He wouldn't have noticed this well, if he hadn't observed the minute difference in the colors of the two kinds of wood above it. The new wood, that was expertly installed over the well, was a lighter red than the rest of the floor. There was also a subtle outline of black which defined the newer floor in that area. The plastic bags of cocaine had distribution numbers on them. Franco knew that these numbers would lead him to the perpetrator of this crime against the innocent. In his pursuit of the truth, Franco returned to Portland several more times intent on solving this case and saving Cynthia's life. Susan perceived that he was both relentless and faithful and it endeared him to her.

On October 27th 1984, John Lane (36) and Cynthia Palmer (29) shared an attic apartment together in the Lane House. They live with her two daughters: Five-year-old Sara and four-year-old Angela. So, when John Lane put little Angela Palmer into the oven of their electric stove and propped a chair against the door the little girl kicked with her feet and screamed, "Daddy, please let me out!"

Eventually, the neighbors began to hear and smell what was going on in the apartment, and when the police came it was too late to save her. John Lane and Cynthia Palmer were sitting on the sofa in the living room listening to her screams and playing Christian "praise" music on their stereo. John Lane appeared to be insane, when he claimed that Angela had a devil and that he was forced to burn it out of her. Lane got life in prison; but Palmer took a plea deal, because she agreed to testify against Lane and so had the charges against her reduced from second-degree murder to manslaughter in exchange for her cooperation. The Judge banged his gavel and acquitted Palmer of the manslaughter rap. So, even though Palmer was in the apartment when Angela's murder occurred, she was acquitted; while Hickey whose lawyer, Seth Bernstein insisted was out of the apartment shopping at the time of her daughter's murder was charged for first-degree murder, with special circumstances which carried the death penalty.

These two riveting cases captured the attention of everyone in all three cities and people were talking about them for weeks; but seldom did anyone compare them to one another. The murders of Angela Palmer and Charlene Hickey had become front page news in the Portland Press Herald. However, no reporter every said anything about the case of the "Two Cynthia's". The paper erroneously reported that Cyn was "at work" not at the grocery store; because one of her massage locations and the Good Day Market were in the same building, the People's Building. This left a lot of people confused, especially when the paper printed her mug shot from being arrested for prostitution in Bath, nearly five years earlier. This became an issue and obscured the fact that she was currently pursuing a reformed and professional life.

Even when a reporter interviewed her pastor, Steve Fearon, he couldn't keep it straight and when Pastor Fearon said that she had gotten her GED and was now an LMT most people didn't know what that meant or that it was a perfectly legitimate business. Franco returned to Portland, Maine for several more months, pretending to be an FBI agent. He went into the crime scene; where three Portland Police officers were having coffee and dropping their cigarette butts on the bloody brain-spattered floor. When Franco saw it, he wanted to kill all three of them; but instead he went back to his limo and returned with a crowbar. He wanted to smash the officers' heads in with it; but seeing what the police had not; he broke up the floor covering the old "Merch Pit" determining that the floor had been rebuilt in that area and that new wood had been installed. He descended the stairway and found the "Merch" locker at the bottom of the stairs. It was covered with the sweepings of the floor which Cyn had showered down on it so many years ago. There were needles and filth covering it.

The glassine bags Franco discovered down in the "Merch Pit" were filled with a residue of cocaine and they had distribution numbers on them that matched the numbers in the ledger Franco had gotten from New York. They had been there all the time and the police never found them. they wouldn't have found the numbers significant anyway, because the didn't understand them. He called upon Susan at her apartment explaining the incident at the crime scene. She was intrigued. They were sitting together in her parlor holding hands, when they heard on the News that Cynthia Hickey had been killed in the Cumberland County Jail. Someone had come into Cynthia's cell, the reporter said and stabbed her in the abdomen with a homemade knife composed of paper mache called a shiv. It didn't make any sense to Susan; she buried her head in Franco's chest and began to cry. Franco got right up and told her that he had to make a phone call. He went to the nearest payphone and called Carlo telling him: "La Madre e' morta!" *"The mother is dead!"* and that the guy who perpetrated this crime, Susan said she thought it was Binny, would no longer be useful to bring into court. "Come vuoi procedure?" *"How do you want me to proceed?"* he asked. He explained to Carlo that he was going up to Lewiston-Auburn to look for Binny, because he had found distribution numbers on a glassine bag he had found at the crime scene. Franco remembered that while Susan was showing the photograph of little Charlene to Carlo and the rest of the Family at the Apponi-Carbon Compound; Carlo Apponi had made an impassioned plea for *"Justice for the Murdered Children"*.

When Franco asked him, what should be done, now that Binny was no longer useful in getting Cynthia Hickey an acquittal. Carlo said: "Dovrebbe essere morte per tutti coloro che a livello internazionale avrebbe ucciso un bambino. Ora che la madre e morta, la prova e terminate e non c'e niente da guadagnare portando Binny tora a Portland, e lui trascinando in tribunale come Susan ha richiesto." *"It should be death for anyone who would intentionally kill a baby. Now that the mother is dead, the trial is over and there is nothing to be gained by bringing Binny back to Portland and dragging him into court as Susan requested."* Carlo said emphatically, over the phone: "Non c'e nessuna utilita piu di questo Binny, ucciderlo Franco. Egli e non piu possibile cancellare la donna. Solo ucciderlo in qualunque modo sembra buono con te!" *"There is no more usefulness for this Binny, Franco, just kill him. He can no longer clear the woman. Just kill him in whatever way that seems good to you!"* Franco told Carlo: "A quanto pare, che: 'Se uccidi, ti trovero' cosa (dichiarazione) alcuni agenti di polizia vogliono dire, non si applica nel caso la polizia della citta di Portland." *"Apparently, that: 'if you kill, I will find you', thing (statement) some police officers like to say, doesn't apply in the case of the Portland City Police."* They never wanted to find another perpetrator (Binny) anyway. They always intended for Cynthia to go down for this. So, after they arrested her, they stopped looking for other suspects.

Chapter Sixty-One
"RETRIBUTION"

On the way to Auburn, right outside of Lewiston, Franco saw two fellows selling drugs on the street corner. The younger of them had a balloon filled with cocaine in his mouth; he was a lad of maybe 14. The other one had just put a large roll of tens and twenties in his jacket pocket; he looked like he was about 19. They always separated the drugs from the money in this way; so that if they encountered the police, one of them could toss the money away, while his companion could swallow the drugs they were carrying. Forcing both of them into the back of his limousine, Franco questioned them at gunpoint.

Franco said to the younger one: "Swallow your balloon."

His companion handed over the roll of currency without an argument. Franco asked them: "Who is your wholesaler?" Thinking he was a DEA agent, they refuse to tell him; but the vehicle wasn't right. He should have been driving a Ford Crown Vic and this was a Lincoln Continental Limo. So, they were puzzled, confused.

Franco trained his automatic weapon with the silencer on the younger one's Adam's apple, he said: "Swallow your balloon or you're a dead man."

The kid said: "Eeyah'dah beh ah dahd mahn en-nay way; thahs sehz ah lee- thal dose ahv cahk. He-eh'z naught pie-ehn meh ee-nuf tah swahl-lah thahs mahch cahk- kayn." *I'd be a dead man anyway; this is a lethal dose of coke. He's not paying me enough to swallow this much cocaine."*

"He, who?" Franco inquired. The kids immediately gave up Bill Lane.

"Where"? Franco asked. They told him about the Lane House and after he got the information, Franco threw the roll of bills out the window. The drug dealers exited his vehicle as rapidly as they could and Franco got behind the wheel.

Finding Binny in the basement, Franco approached him. He was led by the glow of a single scented candle, a candle that illuminated that entire corner of the basement which had once been Cynthia's private bordello. Binny had been lying on the mattress and box spring in the corner; he was wearing his beloved T-shirt with the blood stain. He enjoyed seeing himself in it; he knew about Cynthia's death because it had been all over the news. The radio reporter said that Cynthia was stabbed in the Cumberland County Jail and was dead. Binny smiled and thought: "They-ah wahl stahp thah ehn-vahst-tah-gay-shun nah. Eeyah-'em ehn thah clare. They-ah ehz n**ay wahy** they-ah cauhn lahnk meh tah thahs murd-dah. They-'ahr naught gau-ehn tah prah-sah- cute nah." *"They will stop the investigation now. I'm in the clear. There is no way they can link me to this murder. They're not going to prosecute now."* He gleefully thought.

"Bahd, ayur, they-ah ehz ah gahy ehn thah bahs-mend wid meh, ah gahy Eeyah-'ve nev-vah seehn bah-fahr. Eeyah wun-dah ehf thahs ehz Bahl Lahn'z dah-strahb-bu-tah?" *"But, oh there is a guy in the basement with me, a guy I've never seen before. I wonder if this is Bill Lane's 'distributor'?"*

Franco caught him by his shirt collar using his neck to turn his whole body around in one motion; this is what Walter Malien had done several years earlier, saying: "Get your coat, your going for a ride". In horror, Binny realizes that he must be talking to an FBI or a DEA agent or maybe a Police Detective. He recovered his sensibilities and demanded his phone call, a lawyer, something.

Franco placed a piece of duck-tape over Binny's mouth. He took Binny's coat from him and put it on himself, then he used more duck tape to secure Binny's hands behind his back. He led him out to the driveway putting him into the trunk of the limo. Franco attached a leg shackle to Binny's ankle and taped his feet together. Binny was paralyzed with fear; he didn't even kick much. Not that it would have mattered if he had. The leg shackle had a cinder-block for an anchor and concealed within it was a glow stick. Beside Binny in the trunk of the limo, Franco had placed a cattle prod and a pair of fisherman's chest waders. Binny had the entire trip from Lewiston-Auburn to the Scarborough Marsh to think about that cattle prod and the chest waders (forty-one and a half miles) and how could the authorities possibly use these two devices? The cattle prod wasn't turned on, neither had Franco activated the glow stick.

Arriving at the Scarborough Marsh, Franco was wearing Binny's coat over his Italian silk suit. Quickly he donned the pair of fisherman's chest-waders that he had next to Binny in the trunk. Binny had time to think about these too. It was finally time for Binny to become the key-player in his own private, little drama. Franco activated the glow stick and took out the cattle prod. When they were deep in the Great Salt Marsh, which is like a cone of silence at night, Franco removed the duck tape on Binny's mouth so that he could hear him scream. Franco's first word was a word Binny would never recognize. A word that Franco remembered hearing from his earliest childhood memories. The word: "Ma-fia" "My daughter". Franco said it in English too, so that Binny could hear it and know what was on Franco's mind. What Franco intended for him. "Ma-fia", *"My daughter"*, he said again as he touched the cattle prod to Binny's genitals. Both their hearts were racing.

The cinder block attached to Binny's leg was like an anchor he had to drag along behind him, inside of it a child's toy; a little, green "glow stick" designed to light up Binny's trail through the Marsh. Franco thought how the glow stick would have delighted little Charlene; how she would have played with it in the evening twilight of the room where she and Paul played with their dog. Wearing his chest-waders over his Italian silk suit and Binny's black leather coat over the whole ensemble, Franco quickly turned up the setting on the cattle prod. Franco touched the cattle prod to Binny's genitals as he began his hunt. A hobbled Binny dragged his pain-wracked and addicted body through the Marsh, his tortured limbs crying out for the drugs that he craved. Franco touched the cattle prod to Binny's hind portions again and again. The instrument rested against Binny's buttocks and just below them on his testicles. Franco wished that Binny's hindmost portions were not covered by his black leather pants. "It's a shame to waste all this electrical current on black leather; but it was a mistake that Franco could not rectify now.

"Nah!" "Eeyah-'em" "Naught!", "Eeyah did-n'ah doh-eht!" "Nah!" "You-ah cauhn't do-ah thahs tah meh!" "Eeyah hahv mah ridez!" "Eeyah did-n'ah do-ah eht!" *"No! I'm not!" "I didn't do it." "No!" "You can't do this to me!" "I didn't do it!" "I have my rights!" "I didn't do it!"* And with that, Binny fell back into the Marsh behind him. He descended into the muck on the way to the snowy egret rookery dragging his cinder block and glow stick.

A green, phosphorescent trail followed Binny through the Marsh; it led Franco to the Egret rookery, half a mile from the road. Franco followed Binny wearing the fisherman's waders over his clothes, cattle prod in hand. Franco touched the cattle prod to Binny's genitals and buttock again and again. He waited while the birds pecked out Binny's eyes bringing them to their chicks. "Nay!" "Eeyah-'em sah-rah!" "Eeyah, deed eht!" "Baht, Eeyah-'em sah-ray!" "Eeyah-'ll do-ah en-nay-thehn!" (Binny was contributing to the sustenance of an endangered species.) "Eeyah-'ll gahv yah en-nay- thehn." "Nay!" "Eeyah-'em sah-rah!" "Eeyah, deed eht!" "Baht, Eeyah-'em sah-ray!" "Eeyah-'ll do-ah en-nay-thehn!" "Eeyah-'ll gahv yah en-nay-thehn." *"No!" "I'm* s*orry!" "I did it!" "But, I'm sorry!" "I'll do anything!" "I'll give you anything!" "No!" "I'm sorry!" "I did it!" "But, I'm sorry!" "I'll do anything!" "I'll give you anything!"* Binny's flesh would serve a useful and valueable purpose. It would sustain numerous new baby birds. How Diana Lord and Melissa Jordan would have been delighted to know that the rookery of this endangered species would soon be thriving. Thriving because of this night feeding of their young.

Franco followed after Binny to see the egrets carry off little bits of his clothing with which to line their nests. Casually feeding his flesh to their young, while he was yet alive; leaving Binny's bones to sink into the bottom of the deepest part of the Marsh. Franco left the head lights on in his limousine; the high-beams guided him back to the car. He emerges from the Scarborough Marsh wearing the rubber waders with his Italian silk suit and Binny's beloved coat untouched by the mire. He went directly to the Limo's trunk, after all he was a professional; removing the waders he put them away along with the cattle prod. Then Franco returned to the front seat of the car and retrieved his weapon.

Driving back to Portland, Franco observed a drunken man vomiting by the side of the road. He pulled over and walked to a black, 1968 Chevy C10 and asked the driver for his license as though he was a cop. It was Arthur Bickford. Bickford was too drunk to remember to ask for a blood-alcohol test, where a drunk driver's blood is drawn by an emergency-room nurse. This is a practice in the State of Maine and lowers the drunk's blood alcohol level significantly, as he or she waits by the side of the road usually for an hour sometimes more. It also takes the nurse away from the ER where lives could be saved. When Franco saw the name Arthur Bickford on the license, he remembered what Susan had told him about the man who killed Mike

Asta in the head- on collision and was always driving drunk thereafter. She said that Arthur Bickford was a menace to society. He realized that this was the same truck and the same man. He took out his gun with the silencer, firing two shots into Bickford's head. Then with Binny's fur-lined, leather coat flowing behind him; he walks back to the limo.

When Franco got back to Portland, he went directly to Susan Asta's apartment. She led him into her splendid dining room and seated him at the head of her extravagant oak dining table. He told her in Italian and only in the most general terms, respectful of her feminine sensibilities, how he had taken care of Binny and Arthur Bickford in the Scarborough Marsh and on its adjacent roadway. He politely informing her that: "Binny will mai uccidere piu' bambini e Arthur Bickford non guidera mai ubriaco ancora." *"Binny will never kill any more children and Arthur Bickford will never drive drunk again."* Franco pledged to Susan on his honor as a gentleman, that the fire that consumed Angela Palmer in the oven of the Lane House in Auburn, Maine was awaiting John Lane, when he got to prison and then again after death. "Ho ottenuto giustizia per te Susan, e per Charlene." "I have gotten Justice for you Susan, and for Charlene."

Susan didn't sit and eat with Franco instead she brought him course after course from the kitchen, serving him on the Havilland China taking away one plate from the right, while providing him another from the left. Susan continued in this manner serving him a seven-course classic Italian dinner. Killing killers is always hungry work. Susan thought about Jesus hanging a millstone around Binny's neck and plunging him into the midst of the sea. **Matthew 18:6. "But, whoever causes one of these little ones who believe in me to stumble, it is better for him that a heavy millstone be hung around his neck and that he be drowned in the depth of the sea."**

The first course was Antipasto served with a Shiraz. She accompanied the antipasto course with an assortment of cheeses, olives, crusty bread and a silver dish of garlic-balsamic vinegar and olive oil for dipping. The second course was Insalata (Italian for salad) consisting of a Caesar salad with anchovies on the side. She served this to him with a glass of Chardonnay leaving the bottle on the table. For the third course, she presents him with a Minestrone Soup: which is a thick vegetable soup including coarsely chopped green onions, basil leaves and garlic all of which were sautéed in virgin olive oil, these vegetables were then diluted with beef stock, into which diced tomatoes, zucchini, green beans and great northern beans were added. Susan had learned this recipe from her mother and she prepared it the previous night; storing it in the refrigerator so that the flavors of the ingredients could marry, then she served it piping hot and sprinkled with freshly-grated Parmesan Cheese. This was a treasured recipe that had been in her family for generations.

Susan only served one glass of wine per course as she didn't want to make Franco drunk before his drive back to New Jersey. For the fourth course, he had Spaghetti with Portabella Mushroom Marinara, served with a glass of Merlot. Fifth was the Entrée: a delectable pork loin with roasted potatoes, onions and the rest of the portabella mushrooms. She slow cooked this roast that afternoon and served it to him with the Mango Chutney she had made soon after Charlene's murder. Susan prepared the Chutney months in advance and served it to him in a silver dish. With this he drank a glass of Valpolicella. The sixth course was a fruit and cheese platter which he just picked at and finally Franco had lemon gelato.

After dinner, Susan put her arm around Franco's shoulder almost protectively, walking him down the hallway to the parlor and as they passed Cynthia's bedroom. Franco observed that it had been converted into a room for Heidi to have her puppies. The small bed had been dismantled and was leaning up against the wall and a piece of plywood was propped sideways against the doorway. The floor in Cynthia's room was covered deeply with copies of the Portland Press Herald and the smell of new life was wafting into the parlor. Susan donned a surgical gown, paper booties and gloves as she went into the room and began holding up puppy after puppy for Franco's inspection. There were six of them, their ears were all up now and they were ready to be sold or given away. Susan held up the pick puppy, a male that closely resembled Darth Vader. Susan bestowed the puppy and a new pet carrier upon Franco. He thought about giving the puppy to his friend Carl, who he would drop in on as he returned home to New Jersey. As Susan walked him to the door and kissed him goodbye passionately on the mouth.

The End